Sweet Awakening

by

Marjorie Farrell

A TOPAZ BOOK

TOPAZ
Published by the Penguin Group
Penguin Books USA Inc., 375 Hudson Street,
New York, New York 10014, U.S.A.
Penguin Books Ltd, 27 Wrights Lane,
London W8 5TZ, England
Penguin Books Australia Ltd, Ringwood,
Victoria, Australia
Penguin Books Canada Ltd, 10 Alcorn Avenue,
Toronto, Ontario, Canada M4V 3B2
Penguin Books (N.Z.) Ltd, 182–190 Wairau Road,
Auckland 10, New Zealand

Penguin Books Ltd, Registered Offices:
Harmondsworth, Middlesex, England

First published by Topaz, an imprint of Dutton Signet,
a division of Penguin Books USA Inc.

First Printing, May, 1995
10 9 8 7 6 5 4 3 2

Printed in Canada

For my daughter, Caledonia Kearns,
"my girl that I'm proud of "

ACKNOWLEDGMENTS

Many thanks to my agent, Ruth Cohen, for her efforts on behalf of this book, and her moral support. I am also grateful to Hilary Ross, my editor, for letting me take this subject on.

Lenore Walker's work on battered women who kill was a great resource.

Susan Amussen gave me historical perspective on domestic violence.

Mary Jo Putney gave me generous support and help in the revision of the manuscript.

In *The Fatal effects of Gambling exemplified in the Murder of Mr. Weare and the Trial and Fate of John Thurtell* I found the historical incident of the suit against Oldfield et al.

And to all battered women, I salute your courage. A percentage of the royalties from this book will be donated to the Jane Doe Fund.

Prologue

"What do you think she will be like, Giles?"

"Hmmm?"

Lady Sabrina Whitton poked her twin in the ribs. They were both stretched out on the grass on their favorite spot: Camden Hill, where one could see for miles over Somerset. It was a hot day, and Giles, who had dozed off in the sun, was rudely awakened by his sister's not so gentle nudge.

"Quit that, Sabrina," he growled.

"But what do you think she's like?"

"Who?" muttered Giles.

"Who? Who else would I be talking about but Lady Clare Dysart? I wish Mama and Papa had never invited her. This was to be a wonderful summer, and now we will have a baby tagging along after us."

"Hardly a baby, Brina. She's only three years younger than we are. And you know why she is spending the summer with us. She has no one her age at home, and her parents are worried about her."

"She's had no one for ten years. Why are they all of a sudden worried! Why spoil our summer?"

Giles raised himself on one elbow. "I hardly think one small ten-year-old girl can spoil things, Brina. She'll tag along, and there is Lucy Kirkman. She's only eleven, and we can invite her over to keep Lady Clare company."

Sabrina brightened. Lucy had shown the definite signs

of a first attack of calf-love this summer. She would probably jump at the chance to come to Whitton and see Giles. "You are right. I don't know why I am being so awful about this. It is only that since you started school, we only have summers and holidays together."

Like most twins, Giles and Sabrina were close. Although they were both physically and temperamentally very different, they had an almost uncanny ability to sense what the other was feeling. And until Giles had left for school two years ago, they had been inseparable.

On the surface, Sabrina appeared the stronger personality. She was the one who rushed headlong into things. Enthusiastic, impatient, impetuous, and very bright, she was the despair and delight of their governess. She loved her studies in mathematics and French and was bored to tears by the classics. Giles, on the other hand, loved literature and history and could read classical Greek as though he had been born to it. His French accent, however, was laughable. His intelligence ran quieter, deeper, and of the two, he was the better scholar.

Sabrina, with her dark brown curls and dark brown, almost black eyes, and sparkling personality, had the air of a gypsy, and in fact, her father would often tease their mother, saying that had she not had twins, he would have wondered what handsome young Romany had stolen her heart.

Giles had straight brown hair, which was always falling over his eyes, which looked brown or green, depending upon his mood. He looked just like his father, his mother would joke back to her husband.

But they were well matched, for all their differences. Sabrina had the tendency to run headlong into mischief, and Giles, with the steadiness that balanced his equally adventurous spirit, would pull them out of various scrapes his sister had involved them in. They shared a sense of the ridiculous. Most important of all, they were devoted to each other.

* * *

Giles glanced at the sky. "Damn. We are going to be late if we don't hurry. I'll race you home, Sabrina." He jumped up and was mounted before his sister had taken in his words.

"Blast you, little brother." Sabrina had been born seventeen minutes before Giles and never let him forget it. She mounted quickly and sent her horse after him.

They pulled up, hot and sweaty, just minutes after the Dysart coach. The servants were carrying in Lady Clare's luggage, and a small figure was being helped down. She stood in the drive, looking lost and bewildered, and Giles's heart immediately went out to her. She was a sprite-like child, smaller than most ten-year-olds and with a halo of pale gold curls around her face. Giles dismounted first and handed the reins of his horse to Sabrina, who looked at him with annoyance. He wiped his sweaty palms on his buckskins and extending his hand to the child, introduced himself.

"Giles Whitton, Lady Clare. My sister and I were out riding and lost track of the time, so excuse our dirt. But we welcome you to Whitton."

Clare looked up shyly and whispered her thanks. Her eyes were dark blue, almost purple, and her lashes black, despite her fair complexion.

"Come," said Giles, holding out his hand. "Let me bring you in and introduce you to Mama." He didn't even throw a glance at Sabrina, who was still mounted, still holding the reins of Giles's mare. She had never seen Giles respond that way to any female. Certainly not Lucy Kirkman. Somehow she knew that what appeared to be a small thing, Giles's instant response to their small guest, signaled that everything was about to change.

Clare Dysart was the youngest child of the Marquess and Marchioness of Howland. They had had two children, a boy and a girl, almost immediately after their marriage. Fifteen years had passed before Clare's birth, and her parents always jokingly referred to her as their midlife "surprise," making it clear that they had thought their child-rearing days were over.

When Clare arrived, her brother was away at school and her sister was almost grown. By the time Clare turned four, her brother had started university and her sister, having had a brilliant first Season, had made a very successful marriage and was living in Kent. The marquess and marchioness, having settled their elder offspring, were quite taken up with one another, and although they genuinely loved their youngest, were too used to dealing with grown-up children and too dedicated to their own lives to pay her the attention she needed. As a result, Clare came to think of herself as an afterthought.

She was a very loving child and adored her mother and father. She hero-worshiped her older brother, who tousled her hair and brought her little treats on his visits down from Oxford, and she despaired of ever being quite as beautiful as her older sister. All her affection remained unexpressed, however. She kept it hidden, and no one guessed how much she wanted to feel a part of a family whose ways of being together had been set years before she arrived.

Her parents thought of her as quiet and reserved, never guessing at the depth of her need to love and be loved in return. They were not unaware of her isolation, however, for there were no children her age and rank in the neighborhood. And so, when she seemed old enough to travel from home alone, they wrote to their old friends, the Whittons, asking if their daughter could spend the summer in Somerset.

Clare had been terrified at the thought of leaving home. She might feel like an outsider, but it *was* home and she dreaded meeting the Whitton twins. Up until now her playmates had been her dog and her white mice, upon whom she lavished all her affection. She was also a great reader and moved easily in the realm of fancy. The thought of being forced to talk to and be with a brother and sister who no doubt would regard her as a burden, made the journey to Whitton a misery.

She had stepped down from the carriage, frozen by her fear and shyness and looked up into the friendly, warm eyes of Giles. She immediately recognized that in him she had protector and a champion, and some of her terror disappeared. She had found a Sir Galahad, she thought, as he took her hand and led her to the door.

Sabrina, who at first thought she would hate Clare for taking some of Giles's attention, found this impossible. It was clear that Clare did not have a guileful or mean bone in her body, and that she looked up to both the Whitton twins. Sabrina discovered she liked being admired for her adventurous spirit. Too often she was criticized for being hoydenish, but clearly Clare thought she was wonderful.

When they discovered that Clare was an excellent, albeit cautious rider, they began to include her on their favorite rides. At first she was quiet, listening to their continuous chatter and giving only one- or two-word answers to their efforts to include her. By the end of the first week, however, she was opening up more, and her innocent, but revealing replies to their questions about her family made both Giles and Sabrina realize how lucky they were to have their parents and each other.

"I feel beastly now, that I didn't want her here," said Sabrina one afternoon when she and Giles were waiting for Clare to join them for a ride. "She sounds so alone and . . . well, not precisely unloved. But imagine one's parents referring to one as a 'surprise'! Of course, Mama and Papa are always joking about how *you* were unexpected, Giles," teased his sister. "They were thrilled with their firstborn, and then, just as they were both admiring her, along came the son and heir."

"Now you know the midwife had told them Mama was big enough for twins. It must have been difficult, those first few months, dealing with such a demanding infant as yourself, especially since Mama declined a wet nurse."

They both smiled at the thought of their unfashionable mother, who, as she had often told them, couldn't bear the thought of sending them to someone else or separating them so early on. They had always known they were lucky in their parents, but had rather taken it for granted until Clare came along.

That first summer was almost perfect. Almost, because of Lucy Kirkman.

Lucy, who was the daughter of the local squire, rode over on Clare's third day. Miss Kirkman was a rather precocious eleven and a half, physically as well as temperamentally, and as Sabrina had guessed, had developed a tendre for Giles. Giles was oblivious to Lucy's condition and treated her as he treated all their neighborhood companions.

He had certainly never treated her as solicitously as he did the Lady Clare Dysart, and Lucy resented it immediately. She was introduced to a shy, elfin creature, who seemed to be attached to Giles's coat sleeve. It was obvious that Giles assumed that Lucy would be pleased to have an additional playmate, and so she acted delighted. But underneath the mask of friendliness was an angry jealousy. She had hoped to capture Giles's attention with her new riding habit, which attractively outlined her developing figure, and he hardly gave her a second glance.

If there was anything that brought out the worst in Lucy, it was vulnerability. She got along well with Sabrina because she knew Sabrina wouldn't let her get away with any bullying. But Clare's shy passivity made her want to torment her, and so she did.

Not openly at first. Lucy could be very subtly mean, and so on various occasions that they all were together, she would make comments about how kind Giles was, how self-sacrificing, all in a way that made Clare feel that she was only a sort of charity case. She began to worry that Giles was spending time being nice to her when he would rather be off exploring with his sister and Lucy.

Lucy had uncannily gone right to her greatest weakness: the feeling that she was someone who had come along at the wrong time, who needed more attention than people had the desire to give.

Gradually, as Clare became more at home with the twins, Lucy's attacks began to be less subtle. She would invite the twins over in front of Clare and make half-hearted apologies to her for leaving her out, always putting it down to Clare's age.

Sabrina saw what was going on almost immediately and would turn Lucy's comments off with a smile, managing to get Clare included after all. Giles didn't notice a thing. Since Lucy Kirkman didn't interest him in the least, the thought never crossed his mind that she might be seeing him as anything more than an old playmate.

In fact, he had never yet felt anything more than a friendly interest in a female. His feelings for Clare were uncomplicated: she called forth all his chivalrous impulses. He had felt sorry for her at first. Lucy had been right about that. But he also genuinely came to like her as he got to know her better. She was younger, smaller, and far more fragile than his sister, and she gave him the opportunity to feel protective for the first time. It made him feel strong and manly, and he enjoyed the feeling, as well as the flatteringly grateful glances Clare gave him with those purple-blue eyes.

Along the course of the summer, Lucy progressed to outright teasing, which she made seem good-natured. When they all went fishing one afternoon, Clare disgraced herself by crying over the task of baiting her own hook. After Giles patted her shoulder and did the distasteful job for her, Lucy lost control and spilled the small basket of wriggling worms into Clare's lap.

No one had seen her do it, and when Clare jumped up with a horrified shriek, Lucy laughed and immediately apologized sweetly for the "accident." She had tripped over a tree root and would not have upset little Clare for anything. As Giles rushed over to comfort his small guest, Lucy dared Clare with her eyes to tell the truth.

Clare could only look back at her, wide-eyed with hurt and utterly incapable of defending herself. It wasn't that she hadn't sensed Lucy's hostility, but at first, she thought it justified. After all, she was a nuisance, a tagalong, an afterthought, even here. At the same time, she couldn't understand it at all, for she had nothing in her own range of emotion with which to compare it. She had never had any desire to tease or hurt anyone, and so she was paralyzed by Lucy's attacks. She would never have wanted to hurt Lucy. Why would Lucy want to hurt her? Why would anyone want to torment anyone, for that matter? And so she stood mute and passive as Giles brushed the mud off her dress. And it was that very muteness and lack of reaction that made Lucy want to dump another basket of worms on her. How could she just stand there and not fight back? Not say something? Not reveal what a witch, she, Lucy, had been these past weeks? Clare stood there, with that pathetic wounded look in her eyes, as Giles comforted her. Why, it was just as though she were asking for it!

And so, when Giles led Clare over to the stream to clean off her hands, Lucy couldn't help herself. She pushed Clare in, saying: "There, you great baby, that will clean you off!"

The stream was shallow, and there was no real danger, as both Giles and Lucy knew. In fact, Clare was already scrambling to her feet by the time Giles recovered from his surprise and waded in to "save" her. But the look of distaste on his face when he turned back to Lucy overwhelmed her, and she choked back a sob of anger and grief, grabbed her pole and basket, and walked off without a backward glance.

Sabrina watched her go, glad that Giles had at last seen the real Lucy. She liked their old playmate but had been rather worried that once she set her heart on Giles, she would somehow finally get him. After all, many a match was made in the country before a girl even got to London for a Season. She turned back to her brother, who had stripped off his shirt and was wrapping it around a bedraggled and dripping Clare. Sabrina wondered as she walked over to comfort their new friend, if perhaps Lucy had a reason to be jealous after all.

That first summer set the pattern for the next four. Clare would arrive at the beginning of July and stay for six weeks. Clare became more sure of herself after the obvious warmth of her welcome back the second year. She became more of an equal as the years went by and the difference in their ages meant less, but she never lost her admiration for Sabrina's spirit or her affection for Giles as her "Galahad." Giles was her hero, ever since that first summer when he had finally seen Lucy Kirkman for what she was. He had saved Clare from her tormentor, threatening Lucy with immersion in the manure pile if she ever hurt Clare again, leaving Lucy cowed and distantly friendly to Clare ever since.

Giles was also her friend. He and she could talk about books for hours. And, she eventually realized, Giles was becoming something more.

It happened the last summer they were all together, the summer before Giles was to go up to university. It was the end of August, and the three of them had planned to go berrying on Clare's next to last day. But that morning Sabrina sent word through her abigail that the summer cold she had been fighting had finally won, and she was going to spend the day in bed. So Giles and Clare went alone, after an early breakfast.

It was a glorious day. The heat of the past week had been broken by an evening thunderstorm, and everything was made fresh and green and sparkling again, as though it were June, not August. As they walked to the raspberry thicket, Clare and Giles chatted easily, and perhaps nothing would have changed, were it not for the fox.

Giles saw her first, a quivering flame weaving herself in and out of the raspberry brambles. He stopped and put his hand on Clare's arm. "Look, Clare," he whispered.

Giles had touched her before, she was sure. He must have over the years. Then why did it feel as though this was the first time? They stood very still, and Giles kept his hand on her arm the whole time they watched the vixen make her way so close to them. Then, at the same moment it seemed, Giles became aware of where his hand was, and the fox became aware of them and was gone in a moment, leaving them each flustered by the physical intimacy.

"Well, that is something that Sabrina will be sorry she missed," said Giles nervously, bringing his sister into the conversation as though that would make her physically present.

"It was wonderful, Giles," said Clare, and she was not sure whether she meant the sight of the fox or the sensation of his touch.

It was a black raspberry bramble, and the fruit sparkled garnet and onyx. Every leaf, every tiny hair on every berry leaped out at Clare in detail, so awake and aware was she. As she picked, she put a few ripe berries in her mouth and tasted rain and sun and sweetness.

"Now, Clare, save some for Mrs. Pleck, or we will have no raspberry crumble for tea," teased Giles as he popped a berry into his own mouth.

Clare watched his arm reach out. She had never noticed before how brown his arms were in the summer and how the hair on them was bleached gold by the sun. He was wearing a light cotton shirt with the sleeves rolled up, and as he reached again, she could see his arm muscles ripple. She was so flustered by the languorous feeling that was stealing over her that she thrust her arm in to reach for a cluster of ripe berries and jerked it back with a low cry.

Giles was at her side immediately. "You have to go slowly and carefully, Clare," he said sympathetically as she looked at her arm. One scratch was deep, and the beads of blood welling up looked like tiny berries. Giles patted her arm gently with the tail of his shirt while Clare protested.

"Close your eyes, Clare, and open your mouth," he chanted the old childhood charm, "and I will give you something to make you feel better."

Clare tilted her face toward him. Giles placed a few ripe berries on her tongue, and just as she closed her mouth over them and began to open her eyes, he leaned over and kissed her.

Although it was a soft and gentle kiss, the intensity of their feelings surprised them both. Giles drew back immediately, embarrassed and ashamed. Clare was only fourteen, hardly out of childhood, although her body was beginning to look like a woman's, he realized, as for the first time he took in the soft curves of her.

When she opened her eyes, he stammered something about how his mother would always tells him as a child that a kiss would make it better, trying to put the moment in a safe and familiar context.

"But I am sorry, Clare, I should not have done that."

Clare wondered at his apology. She supposed he was right; he should not have kissed her. Giles had surprised her, but she had also surprised herself. She would have had the kiss go on longer, with the sun beating down upon them and the sweet berry juice running down her throat and the soft pressure of Giles's lips making her feel as wet and juicy as a berry itself.

They filled their pails quickly, and by the time they reached Whitton, their everyday camaraderie had reasserted itself. But when Clare returned home to Howland, she was very happy to think about her parents' comments over the past two years. "It would be an ideal match," her father had told her mother.

And so, although the regular visits came to an end that summer, she kept up a correspondence with Sabrina and the two families sometimes got together for a holiday. There was no formal agreement, but it was assumed by both the Whittons and the Dysarts that by the time Giles was down from Oxford and Clare came up for her first Season, their children would see what an ideal couple they would make.

Chapter One

London, 1816

Lady Straiton's ball always took place on Thursday evening of the third week of the Season. It was her way of ensuring that hers would be the first real crush, for she purposely waited until everyone had arrived in London, even the Whittons, who invariably came up to town late.

"It gets worse every year," complained the earl, as he peered out the coach windows trying to see if the carriages in front of them were moving at all. "I always swear we will decline the invitation, and damned if you don't always talk me into it, Helena."

"Now, William, you know one cannot refuse the countess. Why when the Allandales did one year, she made sure they were hardly seen anywhere else." Lady Sabrina stole a glance at her brother, who, as often happened, was turning to her at the same time to share his amusement. Although Giles had not been a witness to this little contretemps for four years as Sabrina had, he was familiar enough with similar scenes, both in London and the country, with his father protesting a social obligation and his mother gently but firmly persuading him into it.

"I have to confess I sympathize with Father," said Giles. "I am not looking forward to being squeezed and trampled on the dance floor. But I bow to your greater social wisdom, Mama," he added with a teasing grin.

His mother rapped him with her fan. "Don't encourage your father, Giles. And I thought you would be looking forward to this evening. The Dysarts will be there, and you have not seen Clare for over a year."

"We are finally moving," interrupted the earl, not wanting his wife to go further. He was hoping, nay, planning on this match, which he considered ideal for both families, but knew that the quickest way to put up a young man's back was to push him at some eligible young lady. And this would be the first occasion that Giles would be meeting Clare as an eligible match. Whatever the unspoken understanding up until now, Clare had been too young and Giles too busy taking his first in Classics to see each other as anything but old friends. While the earl trusted to the deep and long friendship between them, many things could happen in a girl's first Season. And a young man's, for that matter. For although Giles had come to London off and on, this would be the first spring that his attention would be free and undivided. And there would be many new and attractive young ladies present beside Clare.

The earl need not have worried. By that last summer, Giles had known that he loved her. It had grown slowly, this love, developed naturally and organically out of their old friendship. He had never spoken of it, however, even to Sabrina. And especially not to Clare, although he was sure she must know how he felt. On one hand, he was absolutely certain that she felt the same way and at the end of her first Season would announce their betrothal. On the other, he was still protective of her. What if, by some small chance, he were wrong? What if she met someone during this spring? He knew Clare very well: if he spoke to her, if he revealed his feelings too soon, then she would feel under an obligation, both to him and their two families. So he had decided to leave her free for the rest of the spring before declaring himself.

After what seemed a week, their coach pulled up to the Straiton's front steps. There was another wait before they were announced. Although, as Giles muttered to Sabrina, he couldn't see the point of announcing their arrival, since no one could hear anything over all the noise.

They pushed their way slowly through the crowd toward the ballroom, where Giles began searching for Clare. He hadn't thought he was being obvious, but Sabrina tugged his sleeve and said, "There she is, Giles, over there. I am so eager to see her. And doesn't she look delightful?" She took her brother's arm and let him make a path along the edge of the ballroom until they came to the small group of which Clare was a part.

Clare looked more than delightful, thought Giles as he greeted her. She was dressed in a pale lavender silk gown with a silver gauze overskirt. A dark purple ribbon was threaded through her blond curls, which made her eyes look violet.

Giles realized anew how pretty she was. He had never seen her dressed for a ball before. And he had put their summer kiss out of his mind. But he felt desire stir as he gazed down into her eyes. She was fully a woman, he realized, as he glanced down, appreciating the way the silk clung to her under the near transparent overdress. His eyes went to her sweetly rounded breasts which were exposed enough to make her gown fashionable but not immodest. Giles wondered how it would feel to brush his hand against one. When he had resolved to keep his feelings to himself for awhile, he had not reckoned on the intensity of his desire, only the strength of his love. It was going to be much more difficult than he thought to delay his proposal.

He found himself stammering out some ridiculously obvious comment about the crowd while Sabrina moved forward and gave Clare a hug.

"It is so good to see you again at last," his sister said, while Giles stood tongue-tied. "How are you liking your come out? I am sure your card has been full from your first evening."

Clare smiled. "Not always full, Sabrina, but I haven't

had to hold up the wall for longer than a dance or two on any one evening."

"I should hope not," declared her friend.

Giles finally found his voice. "I hope you will be able to find one for me tonight?"

Clare looked over her card carefully. "I am not sure but that I can squeeze you in, why in an hour or two," she replied. As she saw Giles frown, she immediately reached out her hand to touch his arm in reassurance. "Of course, I am only funning, Giles. In fact, after this next country-dance, I am free for a cotillion if you wish?"

"Clare, Clare, you must play harder to get," said a familiar voice. Both Giles and Sabrina looked over in surprise as they realized that Lucy Kirkman was a member of Clare's group. "*I* cannot fit you in until the end of the evening, Giles," she said with a teasing smile.

"Well, the last dance it will be, Lucy," he replied, moving over to her side.

"Whatever are you doing, hanging around with that cat," Sabrina whispered to Clare.

"Why, she has been very kind to me. I knew so few people, and she has introduced me around and made me feel comfortable, Sabrina."

"I am sure it is only because it makes her look kinder than she is and enables her to feel superior, Clare." And if she is close to you, it is insurance that she will be close to Giles, thought Sabrina. Lucy had never again shown what Sabrina thought of as her real self to her brother after that first summer, and Giles and Clare seemed to have forgotten her behavior. But Sabrina didn't trust her an inch and began to worry that Lucy might manage to snag her brother after all. And what defense would Clare have against her?

If Sabrina was correct about Lucy, then Miss Kirkman must have been very unhappy during the next few weeks. Indeed, more than a few young ladies looked forward to the Viscount Whitton's appearance, for he was not only the heir to the Earl of Amesford, but most attractive in his own right, with his changeable hazel eyes and athletic physique. But after that first dance, there was never any doubt in anyone's mind that Giles was presenting himself as Clare's suitor.

Giles did his best not to monopolize Clare, for he really did want her to have a chance to meet a wide range of young men. When she finally accepted him, which he fully expected she would, he wanted it to be out of choice, not familiarity.

But it was hard to keep away. The stirring of desire he had felt on that first night had quickened into something much stronger, and Giles found himself looking for opportunities to brush Clare's arm or keep a hand on her waist a little longer than was necessary in a dance. He went gently and slowly, however. She never pulled away from physical contact, but he was never sure whether she felt a matching desire. But her seeming innocence regarding his growing attraction only made him feel more protective, and he enjoyed fantasizing how he would be her teacher in the art of making love.

Clare was delighted by Giles's attentions. She had wondered all year about this Season. She knew that both families assumed an eventual engagement. It was certainly what she wanted. What could be more ideal than to have her good friend Giles as her husband? And her first few weeks in London did nothing to change her mind. Despite the fact that she was meeting handsomer young men and more sophisticated older ones, there was no one to compare with her memories of Giles. She had worried that he might have changed. After all, she was not anything so very special. What if he arrived in town and immediately fell in love with someone like Lucy Kirkman? She could hardly blame him, for Lucy and the other young women were much more attractive and confident than she.

But Giles made it clear that nothing had changed, and within a week, their relationship was as easy and close as it had ever been. And perhaps a little more interesting, for Clare *was* aware of Giles's touch when they brushed hands over a glass of punch, or when he pulled her a little closer than was necessary during a dance. She found it very pleasant, this new dimension to their friendship.

Clare was sure that Giles would propose before the end of the Season, and she would, of course, accept. She began to let herself indulge in daydreams of their life together as husband and wife. They would read to each other at night in front of a cozy fire and then retire early. Giles would kiss her gently and hold her close. Eventually they would have children. Perhaps twins, for didn't that run in families? And grow old together. Clare would have tears in her eyes when she pictured them gray-haired, walking slowly around the garden at Whitton, and hearing the sounds from the lawn where their grandchildren would be playing.

"When *are* you going to offer for Clare?" asked Sabrina. She and Giles usually breakfasted early, before their parents got up, and so they were alone.

Giles groaned. "Is it that obvious? I have been trying not to be, or to crowd her too much."

"Perhaps it would not be to anyone who didn't know you well. Or the situation. But we've all taken it for granted for years, haven't we?"

"That's exactly why I haven't wanted to presume too much. I wanted to make sure that Clare feels free when she says 'yes.' " he answered.

"Aha! So you do assume success!"

"I am reasonably confident, Brina," said her brother, with a smile. "After all, we have loved each other as friends for a long time. That is a very strong foundation for a marriage."

"What of passion, Giles? Do you feel that for Clare?"

Giles felt his face grow warm. "Really, Sabrina, *you* should be the one blushing after asking such a question," he answered.

"But it is an important one, don't you agree?"

Giles cleared his throat. "Speaking for myself, I can say that I feel a growing, mm, physical attraction to Clare."

"And Clare?"

Really, his sister was incorrigible, thought Giles. "She is clearly not repelled by physical contact."

"But has she responded?"

"Sabrina, this is really none of your business."

"Oh, Giles, don't get prim and proper on me. Of course it is. I love you and want you to be happy. Mama and Papa have always had a strong response to one another. We have both had that as a model, and speaking for myself, I will not settle for anything less."

"And is that why you are still looking?"

"Don't try to change the subject, Giles."

"I have been proceeding slowly because of Clare's innocence, Sabrina."

"Then she hasn't maneuvered you outside for a kiss?"

"Of course not."

Sabrina laughed. "Well, Lucy Kirkman would have by now."

"Lucy Kirkman? Whatever has she got to do with this?" Giles responded, completely baffled.

"Oh, just that I have thought she's had her eye on you for years. I wondered whether you might finally have noticed it. In fact, I worried a little about Clare ..."

"There is not, nor ever could be anyone but Clare for me, Sabrina," her brother replied seriously. "I think I probably started to love her the day she arrived at Whitton, looking so lost and lonely."

Sabrina sighed.

"I have just declared my passion, and you are still not satisfied?" teased Giles.

"Oh, don't mock me, Giles. I am sure my fantasy of the perfect marriage is just that, a fantasy. It is only that I would not want a man to be too much my protector. I have always believed that true passion can only exist

when a man and a woman feel that they give to each
other equally. And I am being very stupid, you are right,"
she confessed. "It was clear from the first that you and
Clare were made for each other. I am sure that passion
needn't spring up overnight, but may also grow slowly.
Indeed, I'll probably be warming my cold, spinsterly
hands in front of your fire for years to come."

Giles reassured his sister that there was no possible
chance of her remaining a spinster. After she left, he sat
by himself a few minutes, over a cold cup of coffee. He
adored his sister, and in some ways was closer to her than
he was to Clare. And yet he knew he would never have
chosen to marry a woman like Sabrina. He disagreed with
her. He believed that passion between a man and a
woman was sparked partially, if not wholly, by the fact
that a woman depended on a man. Clare was the perfect
wife for him. However, he thought it would do no harm
to maneuver Clare onto a balcony for a kiss, just to test
his theory.

Accordingly, after a vigorous country-dance with her at
Lady Bellingham's rout the next night, Giles asked Clare
if she would like to step out into the garden. When she
smiled shyly and agreed, Giles led her out and they spent
five minutes walking up and down the path admiring the
flowers and chatting comfortably about nothing in particular. There were a few other couples outside also, but
Giles purposely guided them down a path that led to a
small garden bench.

"Come, sit down next to me, Clare," he said.

Clare sat gingerly near the edge of the bench. She
might be inexperienced, but she was not stupid. She knew
she was about to receive a kiss, and although she was nervous, she would not act coyly reluctant, not when she had
been wondering about the possibility of another kiss for
the last four years. When he put both hands on her shoulders to turn her toward him, she closed her eyes and lifted
her face. Giles smiled down at the sight: she was all ex-

pectant naïveté, and he leaned down and brushed her lips lightly at first. Clare's eyes flew open, and as he gazed down into them, he slipped his hands around her waist and neck and bringing her up to him, close enough to feel her breasts brush his chest, leaned down to kiss her again, this time less gently and more insistently. He could feel her shiver and slowly tried to tease her mouth open. She didn't resist him. Indeed, she tentatively began to kiss him back. But she was afraid of the strength of her own feelings, and so her lips never parted. Giles pulled away after a moment, and assuming that Clare was overcome with shyness, grasped her hand and led her back down the path, chatting about this and that until she began to relax. When they reached the ballroom, she looked up at him and said softly: "Thank you, Giles," and then hurried off to join Sabrina and a group of her friends.

Giles watched her go and thought that all in all, even though it was not quite the kiss he had wanted, it had been a successful attempt. Clare was obviously one of those women who would be slow to discover the passionate side of her nature, but he felt they had made a good beginning tonight, and he intended to get her alone again soon.

When Clare crawled under the covers that night, she replayed the scene in the garden. She had never forgotten that first kiss. And this second had not been disappointing. She had felt the same rush of longing, the same shakiness in her legs, the same desire for the kiss to go on forever.

Yet she had been a little frightened of her feelings. Had Giles also wished that the garden, the flowers, the people inside the ballroom would fall away so that all that existed was the two of them? Did he even remember their first kiss? He had no doubt kissed many women since then. What made her special? Perhaps he had only kissed her because it was expected of two people whose betrothal was practically assured?

The intensity of her response and her inability to communicate it to him thrust her back into the childish insecurity she had never quite left behind. Her love and affection felt locked inside her. She needed Giles to open the door, to show that he loved and needed her, to meet her newly awakening passion with his own.

But they would have another opportunity, she reassured herself. Perhaps even tomorrow night at the Carstairs's ball.

Chapter Two

An invitation to the Carstairs's ball was a sign that one was part of the crème de la crème, and so there was quite a ripple of conversation when Lord Justin Rainsborough was announced. At first, no one recognized his name, but then one old dowager remembered that he was a distant cousin of Lady Carstairs who had spent the last five years in the West Indies and had just returned upon inheriting the title from the recently deceased Earl Rainsborough.

Miss Lucy Kirkman, who had caught this last tidbit, hurried over to the edge of the ballroom where Clare and Sabrina were standing with a few other young ladies.

"That is the new Earl Rainsborough," she announced. "Isn't he the most devastatingly handsome man you have ever seen?" she whispered. Sabrina smiled to herself as she watched Lucy subtly adjust her gown so that the bodice was lower by a half an inch.

Clare looked across the floor to where Lord Rainsborough stood surveying the crowd. His gaze met hers in that instant, and she turned away, embarrassed to be caught staring. But Lucy was right. He was the most striking man she had ever seen. He was tall, well built, and dressed all in black, which together with his black hair and tanned face made his gray eyes quite startling. What would it be like, she wondered, as she listened to the conversation around her, to be held in his arms. She was immediately horrified to be fantasizing about him, for wasn't she almost a betrothed woman? Not to mention the fact that she was hardly the sort of young lady who would attract such a man's attention. Lucy Kirkman was much more his type.

It was therefore no surprise when Lord Rainsborough, accompanied by his hostess, was introduced to Lucy and the cluster of young men and women around her. The young men included him in their discussion of the current derby favorites, but since Lord Rainsborough was but newly arrived in England, he could hardly contribute his opinion.

Clare had never before been so awake to a man's presence, even Giles. She could feel him with every cell in her body, and every cell seemed to be quivering like blancmange. When he turned toward the ladies, she found herself fussing with her bracelet, snapping and unsnapping the clasp. In a moment, he would ask Lucy to dance and she could relax.

When she heard him address her instead, she was so flustered that she left her bracelet undone and it slipped off her wrist and fell right at the earl's feet. Without thinking, Clare reached down to pick it up at the same time as Rainsborough and their hands met. His touch made all the hairs on her arm stand up.

"Here is your bracelet, Lady Clare," said the earl, smiling down at her.

Clare was crimson with embarrassment. "Thank you, my lord."

"Here, let me fasten it for you," he added as she fumbled with the clasp. Clare extended her arm and shivered as he gently closed it over her wrist.

"This is a lovely piece. I see it matches your eyes perfectly."

It was a pretty compliment, though hardly original. But somehow, Lord Rainsborough's tone made Clare feel that no one had ever really seen her eyes before. A thrill went through her, but she recovered enough presence of mind to thank him for his help.

"I was wondering . . . although I hardly think it would

be likely . . . would you have a dance free this evening?"
Rainsborough asked.

In fact, Clare did not have a dance free. But she
couldn't bear the thought of letting Rainsborough go, for
he would never ask her again. She glanced over her card.
Captain Barton was down for the next cotillion. Did she
have the courage to lie? To insult a perfectly nice young
man? She looked up and saw Lord Rainsborough's plead-
ing look and threw caution and courtesy to the winds.

"Why, as a matter of fact, it seems like my next dance
is free."

Clare was very grateful that the dance was struck almost immediately and that Captain Barton was across the
room. She and the earl moved off before her promised
partner could reach her.

It was as thrilling to have Rainsborough lead her
through the dance as she thought it would be. He never
drew her too close, but just the feel of his hand around
her waist as they came together in the figures of the
dance was enough to make her feel as though she had no
bones.

They did not speak, but let themselves be lost in the
music. It was surprising, but despite the differences in
their heights and the fact that it was his first time partner-
ing her, it felt to Clare that they had been dancing together for years, so easily did they move together.

When Rainsborough returned her to her companions
and bowed his thanks and walked away, she watched him
go with her heart in her heels. That was that: the first and
last time Clare Dysart would dance with the most handsome, charming man in London. But he *had* danced with
her and not Lucy Kirkman or the Honorable Susan Maxwell, so that was something.

Later in the evening, when Giles came to claim one of
his dances and take her into supper, she was unusually
quiet. Her body was still in the arms of Lord Rainsborough, however ridiculous the feeling. It was certainly
not with Giles. She moved through the rest of the evening

like a sleepwalker, hardly noticing Giles's hand when it brushed hers at supper. And later, when Giles asked if she wished to step outside for some fresh air, she took his arm and allowed him to lead her out without even thinking about his intentions. When he leaned down to kiss her, she experienced only a fleetingly pleasant sensation and Giles pulled away, puzzled by her lack of response.

"Are you feeling well, Clare? You seem a bit distracted. Or are my kisses too respectful," he added with a smile. "I promise you, they need not be."

Clare felt terrible. This was Giles, her dearest friend and here she was, distracted by the memory of a light touch from a complete stranger.

"I apologize, Giles. Of course it is not your kisses. I am just rather tired tonight. I danced every dance, you know."

"I hear you even jilted Barton for a dance with the mysterious Lord Rainsborough. He seems to be quite a charmer. He managed to get Lady Allendale on the floor, and she rarely dances with anyone but her husband and her sons," he teased.

Clare could understand Lord Rainsborough's success very well. She thought she would have the same response to him at fifty or seventy as she had tonight. She was immediately horrified by her thoughts. Here she was imagining herself with someone else other than Giles, as though Lord Rainsborough had asked her to marry him and she had agreed and was fantasizing about their long life together. She resolved to wipe all such unrealistic dreams out of her mind and concentrate on Giles. He had not declared himself yet, but she was confident he would. And it was to him she would promise her love and loyalty.

Clare would have kept to her resolve had Rainsborough ignored her. But he didn't. The day after the Carstairs's ball, she received a small corsage of violets with a sweet note from him thanking her for their dance and making a comparison between the flowers and her eyes. That night at a musicale, he made an obvious beeline for her, and Clare was very much aware of the whispers around her. And later in the week, when Lord Rainsborough called and asked if he could have her company for a short stroll in the park that afternoon, Clare did not know what to say. She had no other commitments, but Giles did tend to drop by in the afternoon and so she often kept them free. But they had no formal plans, after all, she thought, suppressing a pang of guilt. Giles *did* rather take it for granted that she would be available for his company. Stirring up a little self-righteous annoyance helped her push Giles's disappointed face out of her mind. She smiled at Lord Rainsborough, thanked him for his lovely flowers, and agreed to walk with him.

Of course, her abigail accompanied them. And since it was almost the fashionable hour, they were hardly alone. Yet it felt as though the earl had drawn a protective circle around them. He was attentive, charming, and amusing as he told her tales of the West Indies. Clare was fascinated by his descriptions of exotic flowers and birds.

"But I have been monopolizing this conversation," he said apologetically. "Tell me something about yourself, Lady Clare."

"Indeed, there is very little to tell," replied Clare with a nervous laugh. "I'm afraid I have never traveled farther than to Glastonbury with the Whittons."

"Ah, yes. Viscount Whitton and Lady Sabrina. They seem like a delightful pair."

Clare's face lit up. "Yes, they are my dearest friends, almost like family." She went on to explain how much younger she was than her own brother and sister.

"I am happy to hear you describe them as family, Lady Clare," said Rainsborough. "I had heard rumors that you and Whitton were promised to one another."

Clare flushed. "There is no official betrothal, my lord. That is, Giles has not asked me yet, although I am sure he will . . . oh, dear, that sounds quite bold of me, doesn't it?" Why, she thought, was she downplaying what was a very real, albeit unspoken understanding? And why was Lord Rainsborough happy to have her describe Giles in brotherly terms?

"Then there is no real reason for you to turn away another suitor, my lady?" Lord Rainsborough asked in such a tone that Clare felt he was actually caressing her with his voice. But before she could even think of a response, he turned them around and in normal accents said, "I think I see an old acquaintance over there. Come, let me introduce you."

The next day, when Clare had received a small box of candied violets from the earl and a note thanking her for her kindness to a stranger returned home after many years, she decided that, really, there was nothing to be concerned about. She *was* a sympathetic listener. She too knew what it was to feel a kind of outsider. And the earl had somehow sensed that. He had only wanted an afternoon's companionship after all.

She picked out one of the sweets he had sent her, and licked at the crystallized sugar. The question was, what did she want? Why did her mouth want to be nibbling at Lord Rainsborough's lips, those full and sensuous lips that could curl up in the most charming smile? Why was it Rainsborough's arms around her that she imagined and not Giles's? Giles was her beloved friend, her champion, her childhood Galahad. Why did Sir Galahad no longer hold the same appeal? How could she find anyone as good as Giles? As familiar?

She loved Giles. She had no doubts about that. She had quietly given him all the affection she had stored up. All the love her family didn't seem to need from her. Not that she had ever spoken of it. But it was there, waiting for him.

She knew that Giles loved her. But *why* did he love her? Because they were old friends? Because it was easy to let affection carry one along into a marriage that both sets of parents wanted? Because he was used to the idea?

Clare wished she had someone to talk to. Her usual confidant was Sabrina. But she could hardly say to Giles's sister, "I love your brother dearly. But I am beginning to wonder if I *love* him, if you understand what I mean?" But Clare herself wasn't sure she knew what she meant.

The earl's attentions, which had started quietly, became much more noticeable over the following days. He always made sure to have two dances with Clare, one of them the supper dance when at all possible. On the few occasions that Sabrina and Giles were not present, Lucy Kirkman made sure that they knew the latest. At first Sabrina was merely amused and pleased for Clare. After all, it was quite a compliment to be sought after by one of the handsomest men in London. After a while, however, she began to worry. Giles continued his quiet attendance on Clare, but there were no more visits to the gardens, and several times when he called in the afternoon, Clare was already out with Rainsborough. Really, it was time both of them woke up, thought Sabrina. Giles needed to woo Clare more energetically, and Clare needed to see that Rainsborough was all charm and no substance. Not that Sabrina had any real evidence of that. Not much was known about him, but what was seemed perfectly respectable. He was handsome, intelligent, very charming, well-to-do, and the inheritor of a respected title. Yet for Sabrina, he seemed too good to be true. She was disappointed in Clare, for she knew, with her twin's sixth sense, that Giles was hurt, although he gave no outward sign of it.

One afternoon, while she and her brother were finishing a light nuncheon, she finally expressed her concern.

"Are you at all worried about Lord Rainsborough and Clare, Giles?" she asked bluntly.

"Rainsborough and Clare?" he responded coolly. "I wasn't aware there was anything to worry about."

"Oh, Giles, don't take that tone with me. You know what I mean. He may not exactly be 'mad in pursuit,' but his attentions have become more noticeable these past few evenings."

"I wanted Clare to enjoy her first Season, Sabrina, which is why I have not declared myself formally. I am happy if she is enjoying her flirtation. I'd far rather she make a real choice rather than accept me because it has been understood by our families that we will wed. We have always had a deep affection for each other and that is a far better foundation for marriage than a brief infatuation."

"Then you do at least admit the possibility that she is infatuated by Rainsborough?"

"I am not blind, my dear sister. Nor stupid. But I am quite sure that when the Season ends, I will be announcing our betrothal."

"I hope you are right, Giles. I myself think you need to make a stronger push for yourself. After all, Clare is young and inexperienced. I would hate to think of her being overwhelmed by Rainsborough's sophistication." Sabrina felt a bit devious, but she knew that an appeal to Giles's sense of responsibility for Clare would rouse him to action better than an appeal for his own best interest.

"You don't think he is any real danger to her reputation, Sabrina? Or her virtue?"

"What does anyone know of Rainsborough, Giles? He has been away for the past six years, after all."

"Perhaps you are right, and it is time I declared myself."

Sabrina smiled across at her brother. "I think you should, Giles. And soon!"

Chapter Three

Giles had not been as indifferent to the situation as he had led his sister to believe. He had become increasingly concerned over the past two weeks as it became clear that the earl was pursuing Clare, but what he had told Sabrina was what he had told himself: that Clare needed to enjoy a flirtation before she committed herself to marriage. Except that this was beginning to look like something more than a light flirtation. The earl was very handsome and very charming and quite single-minded in his attention. Giles had to admit to himself that he did feel more than a twinge of jealousy each time Rainsborough approached Clare and he saw the expression of surprised delight on her face. She had never looked up at him like that. Oh, she was always pleased to see him, pleased to dance with him, but they were old friends, so how could his attentions surprise her? And while he had no insecurity about his attractiveness to women, he had to admit he looked fairly unprepossessing next to the darkly handsome earl. What he had said to Sabrina was true: he trusted Clare. He trusted her loyalty to their friendship. But perhaps it was time that he stepped in, before Rainsborough caused too much gossip or demanded a passionate response from Clare that Giles knew she was not ready to give. Tonight he would make it clear that Clare was spoken for.

It was unfortunate for Giles that as he and Sabrina were about to set off for the Allendale rout, it was discovered that one of his grays was favoring his hind leg and

had to be replaced. It made them late, and by the time
they arrived, Rainsborough had claimed Clare as a supper
partner, her waltzes were all taken, and Giles had to settle
for one country-dance. Giles ended up squiring Lucy
Kirkman into supper and had to listen to her pseudo-
sympathetic observation on Clare's obvious preference
for new faces.

"I had thought that you and she would have announced
your betrothal by now, Giles," she said.

"Oh, I wish to give Clare every opportunity to enjoy
her first Season," he answered. "I am quite pleased to see
my future wife such a success." It was perhaps unwise to
have been that open, but Lucy had quite driven him to it.

He was not pleased to watch Clare and Rainsborough
out of the corner of one eye. The earl was sitting very
close to her and seemed to be whispering compliments
into her ear, if her blushes were anything to go by. And
after supper, Giles was never able to get Clare alone.
Then, after a waltz, Rainsborough and she slipped out
into the garden.

The last week had been as disturbing for Clare as it had
been for Giles and Sabrina. She knew she was falling in
love with Rainsborough. Nay, she *had* fallen in love with
him almost at first sight, she now realized. For what else
but love was that strong sensation of being drawn inevi-
tably to him. And of him being drawn to her.

For he *was* drawn to her, like a magnet. The attraction
between them was almost palpable, and she was amazed
that there wasn't some visible sign, like a shower of
sparks when his hand brushed hers.

The earl had been very respectful, of course, merely
holding on to her a little longer than necessary after a
dance, and once very lightly brushing her cheek while re-
placing a flower that had fallen out of her hair. On that
occasion, she had been surprised that her hair didn't catch
fire.

How could she feel this way about someone other than

Giles? Why didn't Giles, who was so dear to her, not create such passionate longing? How could she be so foolish as to fall in love with someone so handsome and so sophisticated. She was surprised, over and over again, when Rainsborough continued to call, continued to send little gifts, and continued to send her violets once a week. When he approached her, she felt so special and valued that it was hard to keep only a polite response on her face. She knew that her eyes gave her away. But she couldn't help it.

She began to wonder if she and Giles were too close. Maybe a long friendship was *not* as good a foundation for marriage as she had always thought. Maybe they had both taken their parents' wishes too seriously. After all, passion was a most important ingredient in a marriage, wasn't it? When Rainsborough invited her for a stroll in the garden, she went without even a backward glance.

It was a warm night, and the scent of roses perfumed the air. They seemed to be the only couple outside, and when Rainsborough took her hand and led her away from the center of the garden, Clare almost stopped breathing. When they reached the garden wall, the earl released her and they stood there for a moment before being drawn inexorably toward one another.

Rainsborough did not need to reach down and tilt her face toward his, for Clare's face was already lifted, her lips parted and ready for his kiss. As soon as he touched her mouth, she was lost. Never had she felt such desire. Never had she felt so desired by someone else. Not even Giles. For one moment, she could see her old friend's face, and then the kiss wiped everything else from her mind. And when he finally released her, Clare thought she would die from the disappointment.

"Lady Clare ... I don't know what came over me." She had never seen the sophisticated earl at a loss for words before. "I admit I brought you here to steal a kiss or two, but didn't intend this." He gazed down into her eyes and took a deep breath. "Perhaps I did," he admitted. "From the first moment I saw you, you have had an effect on me that no other woman has ever had."

Their kiss had gone far beyond what was allowable, and Clare knew she should feel outraged. But instead she only felt so wanted. And she wanted him in return. She wanted his mouth on hers again, she wanted to run her fingers through his thick black hair, and she wanted to be in his arms.

Rainsborough reached out his hand and stroked her hair lightly. "I had intended a far lengthier courtship, my dear. Indeed, I feared I could not win you. I know you are almost promised to Lord Whitton." He traced her cheek gently with his finger. "Would you consider marrying me, Clare? I do not ask because I should after a kiss like that, but because I am not sure I can live without you," he added in a hoarse whisper.

She had thought herself the only vulnerable one. He was wanted by every woman in London, and for weeks she had expected one or another of them would take him away. That such a current of attraction flowed between them continually surprised her. She was always expecting it to disappear as quickly as it had come.

She had expected his kiss. She had even halfway known how strong would be her response. What she had not expected was the expression of insecurity on his face. He wanted her to say yes, and from the look in his eyes and the tone of his voice, he *needed* her. Nothing could have moved her more.

"I would do more than consider, my lord," she answered, lowering her eyes shyly.

He was very still, his finger still on her cheek. "Do you mean that, Clare? I couldn't bear it if you changed your mind. What of Whitton?"

Clare lifted her eyes to his. "Giles is an old and dear friend, Justin, and I love him as such. I always will. But I have never felt with him what I feel with you. I never knew it could be like this."

Clare could think of nothing but the sweetness of candied violets as she was lost in the sweetness of their second kiss. It wasn't deep, but they nibbled and teased each other with lips and tongues until Justin pulled away again. She moaned her disappointment.

"Whitton has never kissed you like this?"

Clare was so dazed she could only shake her head, wondering why she must be made to think of Giles when all she wanted was Justin.

"I am glad." Rainsborough took her left hand and stroked it with his thumb. "I want you to be wearing a sign of our betrothal, Clare. I will speak with your parents tomorrow."

Clare lifted her face for one last, quick kiss, and they walked slowly back to the center of the garden. She took a deep breath and thought it was no wonder roses were considered the flower of love. Surely she was breathing in not air, but love and roses.

The next morning, Clare lay in bed reliving every moment in the garden. For the first time in her life, she felt the center of someone's attention. It was hard to believe, but the handsome and sophisticated Justin Rainsborough had pursued her single-mindedly, had kissed her into oblivion, and had shown her a side of himself she would never have guessed existed: his vulnerability. He truly had not been confident that she would accept him. And once she had, he was determined to secure her. Giles had never made her feel like his life depended upon her. But she refused to think of Giles today.

Her parents always breakfasted early, and so Clare had the breakfast room to herself as usual. On this morning, she was thankful, for she could not have faced her mother and father and kept her secret. After breakfast, she wandered restlessly through their conservatory and out into the town house garden before she made her way to the music room. Once there, she was still unable to settle into anything more than a short, distracted practice. Finally she summoned her abigail and set off for the Pantheon Bazaar, where she purchased several pairs of gloves and stockings, which she had no need for at all.

When she returned home, she saw Justin's carriage outside their door, and once she was inside, saw that the library door was closed. He *had* come, she thought. Not that she had really doubted him, but it still felt a little like she was living in a dream. She had sent her maid for her embroidery basket, brought it into the morning room, and attempted unsuccessfully to keep her hands steady and her threads untangled, while she awaited her parents.

Only her mother came in.

"Your father is closeted in the library with Lord Rainsborough, Clare. I am sure you know why."

Clare blushed. "Yes, Mama."

"There seems to be nothing objectionable about the young man. The title is an old one, the estate is in excellent condition, and his income more than adequate."

Clare nodded, keeping her eyes on her work.

"And he is sinfully handsome. And devilishly charming. I wonder why just those adjectives came to mind," Lady Howland added. "He has been away for over five years and before that, was raised up north, so that we don't know much about him," she mused. But he is most certainly head over heels for you, my dear."

"And I with him, Mama," Clare said boldly.

"What of Giles? There has never been any formal agreement, mind you, but our understanding and the Whittons was that you and Giles would make a match by the end of the Season. Either of these young men would make you a fine husband, I am sure, but you have known Giles for so long, Clare, and I thought there was a deep affection there."

"There is, Mama," Clare replied quietly. "Giles and I are good friends, and I hope will remain so. Had I never met Justin, I am sure I would have lived very happily as Giles's wife. But now that I have, I cannot imagine marrying anyone else. I am aware now that I could not give Giles the same kind of love that I bring Justin."

"You know your own heart best, Clare," said her mother. "Your father and I see no real reason to refuse Lord Rainsborough. I will tell Maurice to send the earl in."

Shortly after her mother left, the butler admitted Justin and closed the door behind him.

The earl ran his hand through his hair and looking over at Clare, gave her a charmingly boyish grin. "I think I survived the ordeal. I hope you still want me, Clare."

The thread of insecurity in his voice was genuine, and again, his vulnerability touched Clare deeply. As she rose to go to him, he approached her quickly and said, "No, I should do this properly," and bending over her hand, lifted it to his lips and kissed it.

"Lady Clare Dysart, I love you with all my heart. Will you do me the great honor of becoming my wife?"

No one, not even Giles, had ever declared his love for her. Clare was so moved that she couldn't speak, but only nod her consent.

"You *do* love me, Clare?"

"Oh, Justin, yes, yes. More than anyone in the world."

He pulled her up by the hand and enfolded her in a tender embrace. After a few minutes he released her, and bending down, teased her lips with his. Their response to one another was as immediate as the first time. The kiss might well have gone on for hours, but they both finally heard Lord Howland's not so subtle cough at the door and broke apart from one another.

"Well, I can see we had better schedule a wedding date soon," said the marquess with a smile.

"The sooner the better, sir," said Justin, recovering his dignity. "I hope the betrothal notice can go in immediately. I want everyone to know that Lady Clare is mine," he added, gazing down at her with such loving possessiveness that Clare could have melted at his feet.

"I will send the notice to the *Times* tomorrow, my

lord," agreed her father. "And we will see you tonight at the Farnham ball?" he added, subtly dismissing Justin.

"Yes. Of course."

"It will be difficult, I am sure, but you will not make yourselves obvious or a subject for gossip, I trust." Lord Sefton made it as a simple statement, but both Clare and Justin heard it as the command it was.

"No, sir. I will treat Clare no differently than I have been."

"Humph. That has caused comment enough," said the marquess with a smile. "Good day to you, Rainsborough."

"Good day, my lord. And thank you." Justin gave Clare a humorous longing look from behind her father's back as he left.

"Sit down, Clare." Her father put his hands behind his back and looked down at his daughter. "I know that your mother has talked to you and she says you are absolutely sure that Rainsborough is the one."

"Yes, Father. I love him very much."

"And what of Giles? The boy has loved you for years, and your betrothal has been taken for granted by our two families?"

"But it was never formal, Papa," Clare protested. "Oh, I know, you and the Whittons expected it. *I* expected it," she continued with some wonder in her voice at how her life had taken a direction she never could have foreseen. "But Giles and I only love each other as good friends, after all."

"That is an excellent basis for marriage, Clare."

Clare could not imagine speaking openly about passion, especially to her father. "I know, Papa. And as I told Mama, had I never met Justin, I am sure Giles and I would have had a good marriage. But surely, Giles would never be happy with a wife whose heart was given elsewhere."

"And Rainsborough has your heart?"

"Oh, yes, Papa."

Lord Howland cleared his throat nervously and looked around the room as though searching for something. Finally he found it: a celadon vase on the mantel. He fixed his gaze upon it as though he had never seen it before as he haltingly addressed his daughter.

"You know, Clare, your mother and I were completely unprepared for you. We were older than the usual parents when we had you, and are positively ancient now," he said with a rueful smile, as he ran his hand over his thinning white hair. "I always worried that you might feel . . . I don't know . . . anyway, that is why we sent you to Whitton. So you could experience a more normal family life."

"Yes, I know that, Papa, and I am grateful."

"I would not like to think you are throwing away the steady warmth of affection for the fireworks of . . . uh . . . passion, Clare. Especially if you might have felt your parents lacking . . . in . . . Oh, damn it," said the marquess, turning toward his daughter at last. "Your mother and I love you, child, even though we have probably done a poor job of showing it. We were out of practice, you see," he added, with a sad smile.

Clare's eyes shone with unshed tears. "Oh, Papa, of course I know you loved me."

"Of course, but you were a lonely, quiet little thing."

Clare laughed shakily.

"And look how you have grown into a very beautiful young woman. It is no wonder Rainsborough is in love with you." Lord Howland cleared his throat. "If you are happy, then your mother and I are."

"I am, Papa," said Clare softly.

"But there are Giles's feelings to consider. He cannot find out about your betrothal through the *Times*. You must tell him yourself."

"Yes, Papa."

"And I hope you are right that it is only the affection of old friends that both of you feel."

Chapter Four

"Won't you be joining me in the park this morning?" Sabrina asked her brother as he came down for breakfast. Giles was not dressed for riding and he looked tired, as though he had not slept well at all.

He smiled at her apologetically. "Not today, Sabrina. I have an errand and a visit to make. You will be pleased with me, I think," he added with a mischievous smile. "The errand is to Rundell and Bridge's and the call to the Dysarts.

Sabrina sighed with relief. "I am glad that you are at last taking some action, Giles. I noticed when Rainsborough and Clare went out to the garden last night. *And* when they came back."

Giles's face became serious. "As did I. That is when I decided I couldn't wait any longer. Rainsborough is a thoroughly charming man. I would like to say villain, but he seems to be above reproach, both in background and behavior. But he is so damnably handsome and so attentive."

"But what is between you and Clare is deep and long-standing, Giles."

"I notice you didn't say, 'But you are ever so much more good-looking, Giles.' "

"You are quite a handsome man, my dear brother," said Sabrina. "But even a loyal sister must admit that any woman might be affected by Rainsborough's appearance."

Giles groaned.

"Clare is not the superficial sort, Giles. I am sure she is just enjoying her triumph. After all, it has quite made her Season. Nevertheless, I am glad you are going to speak at last."

Giles had long ago picked out a betrothal gift. It was a simple pendant set with a deep purple amethyst to bring out the violet in Clare's eyes, and just the right length to nestle in the hollow of her throat. He had had it set aside for him at the beginning of the Season when he first saw it. It felt good to be standing there, watching the jeweler wrap it for him, knowing that Clare would soon be wearing it.

He had thought to do the correct thing and speak to the marquess first, but his lordship and his wife were out, he was informed. He had himself announced to Clare, for after all, both families had been planning the match for years. He was sure that Lord Howland would forgive him.

Giles was shown into the morning room where he found Clare paging through *La Belle Assemblee*. She colored when Giles was announced and unable to sit still, rose to meet him.

"Good morning, Giles," she said in a low voice.

"Good morning, Clare." Giles was more nervous than he thought he would be and found himself fingering the jeweler's box that he had thrust into his coat pocket. "It is a lovely day today. I was hoping to convince you to drive with me this afternoon?"

Clare looked up and then down again in confusion. "Thank you, Giles. I am committed elsewhere this afternoon, but I am glad you called, for I have something I wish to speak with you about."

Clare finally perched herself on the edge of a chair, and Giles was able to sit down.

"I did not come only to ask you for your company this afternoon, Clare."

Clare could not look him in the face. His tone was serious. Surely he could not have been planning to offer for her today of all days. The day she must tell him of her betrothal to Rainsborough.

"We have been friends for a long time, Clare."

"Yes, Giles." Oh, God, he was.

"You know I have a very deep affection for you."

"And I for you, Giles."

"And that our parents have expected . . : although of course, it has never been formalized . . . that we might make a match of it."

He was making his offer. But he was not, Clare realized with relief, declaring an undying passion for her. He was making his offer rather matter-of-factly. He did not need her like Justin did. Not Giles. Not her friend and protector. Thank God, she didn't have to worry about him. He would be disappointed, she was sure. But his very being did not depend upon her. It made it much easier for her to say what she had to say.

"There is something I must tell you, Giles," she said, finally lifting her eyes to his face.

From her tone, Giles could tell it was important. And it was clear she was not rushing in to accept his proposal before he had even finished making it. He kept his face carefully expressionless.

"You know that I have been in the company of Lord Rainsborough almost as much as I have been in yours for these past weeks. At first, I was only surprised and flattered that he sought me out."

Giles wanted to protest: "But why would you be surprised, Clare? You are a lovely woman. You should just have accepted his attentions as your due." But he kept quiet, waiting for her to finish.

"Then, as I got to know him better, I realized that I had very strong feelings for him and he for me. We are very much in love, Giles," Clare said in a rush, as though to keep him from any protest. "It happened so quickly, so unexpectedly. He spoke to Father yesterday. The betrothal will be in the paper tomorrow," she finished in almost a whisper.

"I see. Then, may I be the first to wish you happy, Clare?" What the hell else could he say? He had been the worst kind of fool, taking for granted that her feelings for him were as strong as his for her. Never imagining that someone like Rainsborough could sweep her off her feet. Thank God he had made no declaration of love.

Clare reached out her hands to his. "Oh, Giles, I never meant this to happen. I never dreamed it *could* happen," she added tremulously. "I hope you can wish me happy wholeheartedly."

Giles lifted her hand to his lips and gave them a gentle kiss.

"Of course, my lady."

"And it is not as if we ever fell in love," added Clare, as he let her hands go. "We have been the best of friends, and I hope we will always remain so."

"I hope so, too, Clare."

"I expected us to build a long and happy life together based on that friendship, Giles. Had I not met Justin, I think we might have done that. But Giles . . ."

"Yes, Clare?"

"I now know what would have been missing. I want you, as my dearest friend, to find what I have found. Someone who is everything to you."

Oh, but I have found her, Clare, *vie de ma vie*. I found her many years ago. I expected to cherish and protect her for all of my life. But I have been such a *good* friend, Giles thought bitterly.

"Perhaps I will, Clare, he replied with a fleeting smile. "But I must go now." As they stood up, he felt the lump in his pocket. Well, it *had* been purchased as a betrothal gift, he thought, as he pulled it out.

"I would like you to have this, Clare."

"Oh, no, Giles, I couldn't," she protested, embarrassed all over again that he had come with every expectation of being accepted.

"It is a small gift, Clare. Just something I saw that made me think of you."

She took the box and opened it with trembling fingers. It was only a simple pendant, but the stone was such a deep purple and the filigree setting so exquisite that she almost handed it back. "It is *too* beautiful, Giles! And you meant it as a betrothal gift."

"And so it still is," he said lightly. "You are betrothed. Surely a gift from an old and dear friend is quite in order?"

She looked quickly up into his face. There was nothing there to disturb her. No sign of a broken heart. Just Giles, with his shock of brown hair falling over his forehead, his hazel eyes warm with affection.

"Thank you, Giles. For this. And for being so understanding about Justin."

He was gone quickly, and Clare fingered the pendant, knowing that despite their protestations of continuing friendship, things had changed between them forever.

There were more than a few "I told you so's" traded at the Eliot's supper dance after the betrothal announcement appeared in the papers. And a handful of gentlemen pocketed substantial sums, having bet that Lord Rainsborough would carry the day. Lucy Kirkman was one of the most vocal commentators. After offering her very sincere congratulations to Clare, she made sure to tell as many people as possible of her concern for Giles. "It must have been such a shock," she intoned. "He has loved her since we were all children, you know."

Sabrina, who had heard Lucy's comments thirdhand, was furious. It was bad enough that Giles was suffering. It would be outrageous for people to know about it. And so she merely laughed when people would come up to commiserate with her. "Of course there had been an unspoken family arrangement. Everyone knew *that*. But it was based upon friendship. Giles was the first person Clare told and the first to wish her happy, you know," she announced to all and sundry. When she got to Lucy, she invited her to take a stroll around the edge of the ball-room and informed her, keeping the sweetest of smiles on her face, that if she heard one more bit of gossip about her brother, she would personally push Lucy's face into the nearest punch bowl.

"Sabrina, I was not trying to spread gossip! I just felt such sympathy for Giles. But of course I will say nothing more, if you think it best."

"Thank you, Lucy. And neither of us would wish Giles to hear of this conversation, I am sure."

"Of course not."

Sabrina was satisfied that Lucy would keep her mouth shut. Unfortunately, she would not be able to stop her from going after Giles. Well, let her make a fool of her-self, Sabrina thought. He has never seen anyone but Clare, and he never will.

Clare had dressed very carefully for the supper dance. It would be the first time she and Justin would appear in public officially betrothed, and she wanted him to be proud of her. She put on her newest gown, a lilac silk that was covered by a delicate gauze overslip of an even lighter lilac. Giles's gift was on her dressing table, and she fingered it thoughtfully. He had been so sweet and so understanding. Wearing his gift tonight seemed a pledge of her continuing friendship, she decided, and so she had her maid fasten it around her throat. It was the perfect length and the very simplicity of the setting made one fo-cus on the deep purple depths of the stone and then the violet of Clare's eyes.

She was very glad she had worn it when she saw the look in Giles's eyes as he greeted her warmly and pub-licly congratulated her on her betrothal.

Clare had never thought of herself as competitive with other women. Indeed, she saw herself as having very little to offer in contrast to some of this year's beauties. But she had to confess to a certain satisfaction as she saw the

look of envy in several women's eyes. She had captured
the heart of the handsomest man in London, she thought,
as she and Justin whirled around the room, in their first
waltz of the evening, and she let herself enjoy her moment of triumph.

Several people had complimented her on her appearance, particularly mentioning her pendant. She thanked
them and said to a few that it was a gift from an old
friend. After their dance, when Justin had invited her out
onto one of the balconies for some fresh air, she assumed
he was taking the opportunity to steal a kiss or two, and
after he closed the French doors behind them, she lifted
her face. He only stood there, arms crossed, looking
down at her.

"What is wrong, Justin," she asked, puzzled by his reaction.

He reached out his hand and lifting the pendant with
his finger, pulled it gently and then a little harder, so that
Clare had to move closer to him.

"It *is* a lovely piece, my dear. And it certainly does
match your eyes." He was only repeating the compliments she had already received but in a tone she had
never heard from him before. "Who *did* give you this,
Clare?"

What had seemed like a simple gesture of friendship
earlier in the evening now seemed rather foolish and naive. "Giles gave it to me, Justin. He *is* an old friend, and
one who had ... certain expectations that were disappointed." Clare had not told Justin of Giles's proposal,
only that she had personally informed him of her own. "I
only wore it," she continued, "to show my appreciation of
his understanding and friendship. He really does wish me
happy, Justin, as I am, my dear," she added, putting her
hand on his arm.

Justin closed his eyes for a minute, and when he
opened them, Clare saw such a look of insecurity that it
quite tore at her heart.

"I am sorry, Clare," he stammered, releasing her. "It is

only that I cannot quite believe that you really love me. After all, you and Whitton have had a long history between you."

"Only of friendship, Justin," said Clare quietly. "I see now that I was very naive and insensitive to wear the necklace this evening. I think I did so partly because I feel so guilty about my treatment of Giles. Because I feel sorry that he has not found the love that I have." She reached her hands up and struggled with the clasp. "Here," she said, grasping his wrist and turning his hand over. "I won't wear it again if it disturbs you."

Justin's fingers closed over the pool of gold, and his thumb fingered the facets of the amethyst. "I can almost summon up some sympathy for Whitton myself, for I can't imagine what it would feel like to lose you to another man," he said, as he slipped the necklace into his pocket.

"You do not have to imagine it, Justin, for it will never, ever happen. You have all of my heart, forever."

They did not kiss then, or later that evening, but Clare felt closer to Justin than she ever had. It was something she would never have expected: that the most heartbreakingly handsome man in London was only another insecure human being like herself. The fact that their need was mutual, as well as their passion, convinced her that their marriage would be a long and happy one.

Giles had had very mixed feelings about Clare's decision to wear his pendant. His first and last reaction was a surge of simple affection. He knew Clare very well, and knew she had worn the amethyst as a message of friendship. The sweetness of her nature was one of the things he loved her for. But for much of the evening, he had to admit, he was angry and heartsick. There was the necklace, fitting as perfectly as he had envisioned it, drawing compliments about Clare's eyes, but he was not the man beside her basking in the glow of those compliments. He was on the sidelines watching her wear what he had meant to be his own betrothal gift with Justin Rainsborough as her betrothed.

He was aware of the gossip. Who could not be? He had known about the wagers weeks ago and had ignored them. In fact, had he not been one of the objects of speculation, he would have bet on Giles Whitton himself over a flashy newcomer like Rainsborough. Which only showed what a fool he was. He responded to the veiled sympathy that was offered him by smiling and saying how pleased he was that Clare had found someone who could make her happy.

It was a long evening, however, and his mouth was stiff from all the smiling. He was very aware of the betrothed couple, and when they disappeared onto one of the balconies, he had a hard time concentrating on his conversation with his companions. When Clare and Justin emerged, Giles noticed immediately that Clare's neck was now empty and overheard her explanation to a curious acquaintance: "No, no, the pendant was not lost, although it may well have been. The clasp is defective, and luckily I discovered this before I did lose it."

The clasp defective, my eye and Betty Martin, thought Giles. Justin Rainsborough did not want his wife-to-be wearing anything that was a gift from a former suitor, even if that suitor was an old family friend. Well, I am not sure I blame him, Giles admitted to himself. It was sweet of you, Clare, but naive to think that you could carry some symbol of loyalty to our friendship into this marriage. Rainsborough expects all your loyalty to be with him, as well it should be. And he has begun as he means to go on.

Giles slipped away early, eager to get away from the gossip and the looks of pity and the sight of Clare and Rainsborough waltzing together as though they were one person already and not still two.

The next morning as Giles was finishing the morning paper in the library, his butler knocked at the door.

"Come in," he called.

"I beg pardon, my lord, but a footman from the Rainsborough household just delivered this." The butler held out a small brown paper parcel.

Giles reached out and closed his hand over it, a puzzled frown on his face. "Thank you, Henley." Whatever would Rainsborough be sending him? he wondered, as Henley closed the door behind him. And then, as he turned the parcel over, he knew. He opened the paper, and out slipped the amethyst necklace he had given Clare. It lay there on his desk, the jeweled pendant resting on a pool of gold chain, but all he could see was the way it had nestled in the soft hollow of Clare's throat. He threaded his fingers through it and spread them apart, letting the pendant dangle and catch the sunlight.

"God damn his small soul to hell," he whispered fiercely.

It was a fragile piece, which is what had drawn him to it in the first place, and the filigree broke easily as his fury took him over. The stone fell out and onto the floor and Giles ground it under his heel, wishing he could reduce it to powder and with it all the passionate longing which he had tried so hard to subdue. But it remained whole.

How *could* she love Rainsborough, someone capable of such a gesture? How could she have turned her back on our friendship? Giles didn't know what was worse, his desire for Clare, which could never be satisfied, or his sudden anger at her. She had betrayed her own affection and awakening passion for him. For desire *had* been between them, he was sure of it. He had just been so bloody careful with her. Instead, he should have swept her off her feet, the way Rainsborough had.

He picked the small jewel off the floor. It was scratched from the heel of his boot, but its purple depths still reminded him of Clare's eyes. He scooped up the chain and walked out of the library and downstairs to the main hall. He thrust the broken chain and pendant at the footman stationed there, saying, "Here, get rid of this. I never want to see it again," and walked straight out the door, leaving the servant gaping at the gold in his hand, wondering whether taking such a valuable piece to a pawnshop might constitute a technical obedience to his master's order.

Chapter Five

Clare sent a note to Sabrina the morning after the supper dance, asking her to call that afternoon. She did not have the courage to visit the Whittons yet and chance encountering Giles. But she knew she and Sabrina must talk, or she risked losing a treasured friendship.

When Sabrina arrived, Clare joined her in the drawing room and asked the butler to send in some lemonade and biscuits.

"Please sit down, Sabrina."

"I can't stay for very long, Clare, so don't bother with refreshments," her friend answered rather coolly.

"I am glad of them myself, Sabrina. You may do what you wish."

Sabrina sat opposite Clare and without preamble said: "How could you do this to Giles, Clare? And after all you have been to one another these many years."

Clare colored, but answered with a calmness that amazed her. But she was so sure of her heart, that it seemed easy to speak from it at last.

"Giles and I have been dear friends, Sabrina, just as you and I have been."

"The friendships can hardly be compared, Clare! You know Giles has always loved you."

"As I him. I think the two of us know our relationship at least as well as you do, Sabrina. Giles has never spoken or acted in any way other than a dear friend might. Of course, we both knew what our families expected. And I expected, for that matter. I told Giles that had I never met Justin, I am sure we would have settled down very happily together. But I *did* meet Justin, Sabrina."

You really did make a muddle of things, Giles, thought Sabrina. "But you hardly know him, Clare. Surely to choose infatuation over a long-lasting friendship is foolish . . ."

"It is love that is between us, not infatuation, Sabrina. I have never had anyone love me like this. Justin loves me, Clare Dysart, for myself. He may appear quite alarmingly handsome and sure of himself, but I know him. He not only loves me, he needs me. No one has ever needed me before," said Clare, her voice shaking.

"Oh, Clare, I am sorry for going at you," said Sabrina, getting up and sitting beside her friend on the sofa. "It is just that . . ." She was going to say: I hate to see Giles heartbroken. But it wouldn't be fair to expose her brother's pain or make Clare feel worse than she already did. So she just continued: ". . . That I am very disappointed. I so wanted you for a sister."

"Thank you for trying to understand, Sabrina. I have always felt that we were like sisters already. I hope my marriage won't change that?"

Sabrina gave Clare a fierce hug. "Of course not, my dear."

Just then, the butler knocked and entered with his tray. Sabrina went back to her chair, while he placed her lemonade on the table between them. His entrance gave both young women the opportunity to collect themselves. When he left, Sabrina lifted her glass and said: "Here is to your happiness, Clare. You deserve to be loved."

"Thank you, Sabrina." Clare was blushing as she accepted the toast.

"Now, when are you planning the wedding?"

"Very soon," admitted Clare. "We are hoping to marry in late June or early July so that we will have most of the summer in Devon." Clare hesitated. "I was hoping . . ."

"Yes?"

"I was hoping that you would stand up with me, Sabrina."

"I would be honored, Clare."

They chatted then about wedding gowns, and what flowers would be available, and by the time Sabrina left, she was almost resigned to Clare's choice. It had surprised her to hear the depth of Clare's need to be loved and needed. And yet it shouldn't have. After all, she knew what Clare's childhood had been like: not desperately unhappy, of course, but lacking in those essential ingredients. The way Clare had described Rainsborough made Sabrina begin to understand what had drawn her to him and away from Giles. Clare had always needed Giles. From the beginning he had acted as her protector and champion. But how would Clare ever have known how much Giles loved and needed her? The pattern in their relationship had been set early on, and both had become used to it. Clearly, they all, particularly Giles, had taken too much about Clare for granted. She could only hope that Giles would someday find someone else. And before Lucy Kirkman got her claws into him!

At a cost known only to himself, Giles was successful in presenting himself as an old friend and not a heartbroken suitor, and the gossip died down after a short time. But the effort was occasionally almost too much for him, especially the evenings like tonight when Rainsborough and Clare, having danced every waltz together, disappeared onto a balcony for what seemed like hours. He was very glad, therefore, to hear the honorable Andrew More announced as a late arrival.

"Andrew!" he exclaimed when his old friend approached him, "Why have we not had the pleasure of seeing you earlier this Season?"

"The law is a demanding mistress, Giles," responded Andrew. "Although perhaps a demanding one is easier than an unfaithful one?" he added with sympathetic irony.

Had it been anyone else, Giles would have been furious

at the insult to Clare. But he had known Andrew since their first year away at school, and he knew that it was only affection that was behind the animosity.

"Hardly unfaithful and most certainly not to be categorized as a mistress, Andrew," warning him by his serious tone that Andrew had gone almost too far.

"I apologize, Giles. I shouldn't have said that. But my God, man, your betrothal has been expected for years. And I know you have loved Clare for that long."

"And you've never understood it."

Andrew flushed with embarrassment. "I have never said anything of the sort, Giles."

Giles grinned. "No, you haven't had to. It is only that I have never glimpsed anything beyond polite friendliness between you and Clare whenever you've visited us at Whitton."

"I am drawn to a more spirited sort of woman, Giles." He hesitated. "I must confess that I am surprised that Clare chose Rainsborough over you. She always seemed so shy and insecure to me. Your steadiness seemed just what she needed."

"Evidently he sparked something in her that I did not," Giles said bitterly.

"Setting your feelings aside, do you like him?" asked Andrew curiously as he watched Rainsborough lead Clare back onto the dance floor.

"I have tried to be objective, Andrew. I want Clare to be happy and to all appearances, Rainsborough seems to be the man who makes her so. But he always hovers over her so protectively. And does not like it one bit when I ask for the occasional dance. Though why he thinks it is a pleasure rather than a torment for me, I am sure I don't know. But I have to continue the 'good friend' to keep the gossips quiet."

"You are a very attractive man, Giles, in your own right, and before he came along, Clare seemed to be yours. I can understand his insecurity."

Giles sighed. "I suppose you are right, Andrew. And there is no way I can be rational about this anyway."

There was a moment of silence, and then Andrew asked very casually: "Is Sabrina here tonight?"

"Yes, she is in the garden with young Bewley."

Andrew raised his eyebrows. "Bewley? Are we to wish your sister happy this year?"

Giles laughed. "Not at all, Andrew. Bewley is suffering from an intense case of calf-love for the Honorable Susan Maxwell, and sought Sabrina's aid in arousing the young lady's jealousy. As far as I know, Sabrina's heart is still free."

Andrew laughed and immediately changed the subject. But when Sabrina returned, he unobtrusively joined the group of friends who surrounded her and obtained a waltz for later in the evening.

When Andrew came to claim his dance, Sabrina felt the familiar thrill of attraction that had plagued her ever since he had spent a fortnight one summer at Whitton five years ago. He was the first man, and indeed, he seemed the last who affected her so. But he had never shown the least sign of interest, and so she had kept her feelings to herself, hoping they were only temporary and that someone else would eventually come along and claim her heart.

"I was happy that you had a dance free for me, Sabrina," said Andrew. She felt herself grow warm with pleasure and wondered if Andrew did feel an attraction to her after all. But she only answered calmly that she, too, was glad of the opportunity to be his partner. "For you are too absent during the Season, Andrew."

Andrew continued almost as though she hadn't spoken. "I know how close you and Giles are, Sabrina. How is he holding up under the strain of having to act the family friend with Clare?"

Sabrina mentally scolded herself for having been so foolish, even if for only a moment, to think that Andrew

More had any special interest in her. "He does not talk about it, even to me, but I can sense his heartbreak."

"How did this ever come about? The friendship between Giles and Clare goes back so far. And she never seemed the sort to be swept off her feet by charm and flattery."

"I can only guess at the reason," said Sabrina. "I believe that what she and Giles felt for each other went beyond friendship, but my chivalrous brother did not wish to hurry her. I don't think he ever revealed his need for her or his passion. Evidently Rainsborough did, and that meant everything."

"I see." And Andrew did. Granted, given his status as a younger son, he couldn't let himself indulge in any fantasies about Lady Sabrina Whitton. But if he had been free to, he would have acted very differently from Giles and not held back for anyone.

He smiled down at Sabrina sympathetically, and they shared a wordless minute of understanding. It was one of Giles's most endearing qualities, this ability to separate his own need from the need of those he loved. And it was his greatest strength that had become his greatest weakness. In protecting Clare from his own desire, he had lost her.

The rest of the Season went by very quickly for Clare as she was caught up in the whirlwind preparations for her wedding. On her wedding day itself, she felt as though she were standing and looking through a kaleidoscope. All was a blur as she dressed and drove to the church. And then there were the moments that stood out perfectly, as things shifted and fell into place: Giles's face looking set and serious as she moved past him down the aisle, a glimpse of her mother from the altar, looking so much older than she had remembered her, and Justin, gazing into her eyes as he said his vows with such loving intensity she thought she might faint.

During the wedding breakfast, Giles came over to congratulate them. It was the first time he and Justin had said more than a few words to one another, and Clare was hoping that one day they could all be comfortable. It was obvious, from the way Justin's hand tightened over hers, that this was not the day. He and Giles smiled smiles that came nowhere near their eyes and uttered the usual formalities.

"I wish you both happy."

"Thank you, Whitton."

It was only when Giles was turning to leave that any real emotion was expressed. He turned back quickly and said fiercely: "Clare is very dear to me, Rainsborough. I know that you will treat her as the treasure she is."

"She is even dearer to me, Whitton. You need not concern yourself further with her happiness."

Given the coldness of Justin's tone, his answer was like a slap in the face. Giles colored, nodded, and bowed his farewell to both of them.

Chapter Six

They set off on the first stage of their journey early in the afternoon, planning to stop in Farnborough. One of Justin's cousins owned a small house there and had placed it at his disposal.

"Do you mind if I close my eyes for a while, Justin," Clare asked as they left London behind. "I find I am exhausted from this past week." She slipped her hand in his and leaned her head against his shoulder.

"Not at all, my dear."

Clare was asleep almost immediately and did not wake up until they were only an hour from Farnborough. She could tell from the light that it was late afternoon and was horrified that she had slept so long.

"I am so sorry, Justin."

Her husband looked at her with affectionate amusement as she sat up and smoothed her hair.

"No need to apologize, Clare. Actually, I am very pleased that you feel so comfortable with me."

Clare blushed. It *had* felt very natural to be that close. And tonight they would be even closer.

Justin's cousin had made sure that his housekeeper had everything ready and had left a light supper for them.

"This is so much nicer than an inn, Justin. I am grateful to your cousin," Clare said as they sat down to eat after washing up.

"I wanted our first evening to be ours alone, Clare. No friends, no relatives, no servants. I wanted you to myself," he added, putting his hand over hers. Clare would

have been very ready to push her chair back and go upstairs right that minute. It amazed her that although she
certainly had some natural fears about the night ahead of
her, for the most part she was eager to become Justin's
wife. His slightest touch made her feel such desire that
she was left breathless.

It seemed a long time until dinner was over. "The
housekeeper will be here tomorrow, so we can just leave
the dishes," said Justin with a smile. "Perhaps you would
like to go up first, my dear?"

"Oh, yes, of course," stammered Clare. She had not
known how to make the move herself and was grateful to
her husband for initiating things. She could feel his eyes
watch her as she went up the stairs, and she hoped he
would not be long in following.

He wasn't. She had just finished turning down the covers on the bed and was sitting in front of the pier glass,
brushing her hair when Justin appeared at the door.

"Let me, my dear," he said and coming close, he took
the brush, and leaned down and kissed the nape of her
neck. Then he drew the brush through her curls gently.
She could have sat there forever, in a trance of pleasure, but he put the brush down and whispered into her
ear: "Your hair is very thoroughly brushed, my dear. And
I am hoping that all my good work will be in vain. Come,
let us to bed."

Clare crawled under the covers and watched as Justin
began to undress. Although he had been back in England
for months now, his skin was still bronze from his years
in the West Indies, and instead of modestly lowering her
eyes, Clare looked at him admiringly as he took his shirt
off, exposing his well-muscled arms and chest. When he
started to unfasten his trousers, she did look down and
heard him give a soft laugh.

In a moment, he was sliding in next to her. "I am sure
that you and your mother spent hours picking out this exquisitely frothy night rail, Clare, and, unfortunately, I am
going to slip it right off you."

Justin leaned down to give her a light kiss and sliding his hand down her leg, began to push her gown back as he traced the shape of her leg with his fingers. He rested his hand on her belly for a moment and then in one quick movement, grasped the gown with both hands and pulled it over her head. Clare lay there under the covers, very still, wondering when he would touch her. She wasn't sure what part of her body wanted to feel him most: her lips, her breasts, or that unexplored territory between her legs.

Her lips must have wanted him first, for that was where he began, gently at first, and then more insistently. She lay still for his first kiss, but when he teased her mouth open, she found she quite naturally put his arms around him and drew him closer.

One of his hands was now on her breast, cupping it, circling the nipple with his thumb. And then, wonderfully, he slid down and took it into his mouth, teasing the nipple with his tongue, the same way he had with her mouth. She moaned with delight as he leaned over her.

The bedcovers were hampering him, so he threw them off and crouched down above her, looking down into her eyes with such passion and tenderness that she had to close her own or be overwhelmed.

She slid her hands down along his back and traced the line of his waist and hips. She could feel his manhood brushing her belly, but only had the courage to lightly touch it with her fingers, marveling at the combination of satin softness and hardness. Then he was kissing her belly and using his gentle fingers to part her thighs. She was embarrassed that he would feel how wet she was down there; she seemed to be turning into liquid.

"Please, Justin," she moaned.

"Not yet, Clare. I want this to be as comfortable for you as possible." And so he first brought her to an exquisite climax with his fingers before finally pushing himself very gently at first, and then harder, into her innermost self.

It hurt for a few minutes, but then she was caught up in the rhythm. Her own pleasure had been so great that she was amazed at how wonderful it felt to have him come in great shudders inside her.

They slept with Clare cuddled in front of him and made love again almost before they were fully awake the next morning. This time it was even better, if that were possible, and Clare lay there afterward, her body still, but feeling as though the ocean was moving through her, pushing her gently, flowing and ebbing as the rhythms of his loving had.

They reached Rainsborough late in the afternoon, and Clare first saw her new home just as the sun began to strike the upper windows, lighting them up and making the faded red brick look pink and warm.

"It is lovely," she said, after Justin helped her down from the carriage.

"I am glad you like it, Clare. I was worried you would feel a bit isolated here in Devon."

"But how could I feel that way when I have you, Justin."

He leaned down and gave her a quick kiss before he led her over to be introduced to the servants lining the drive.

And indeed, for their first six weeks, Clare felt as though she and Justin were living in a world as golden, warm, and sweet as a globe of honey.

"This *is* our honeymoon," Justin had said one night as he scandalized and delighted her by drizzling the sticky sweetness on her breasts and in her navel and then licked it off. She blushed and giggled, saying: "Turnabout's fair play," and did the same to him. They were sticky with honey and sweat as they finally made love and then took turns washing the other, which led to another hour of lovemaking, this time on the carpet, since the sheets were too sticky.

"Whatever will the maids think?" Clare whispered as she lay in his arms.

"Do you care?"

"Perhaps not. You are turning me into a wanton, Justin."

"Good, so long as you only play the wanton with me." It was an odd thing to say, thought Clare, but she forgot it immediately, as Justin kissed her into oblivion.

They spent most of their time together, exploring the countryside on horseback or on foot, for it was almost as new to Justin as to Clare. He ignored estate matters, turning everything over to his manager, and when Clare protested that she should be learning her way around the house, he merely said, "Leave that to Mrs. Clarke. I pay her enough."

Justin turned down all invitations and turned away all visitors for the first few weeks. Every bit of his attention was concentrated on his wife, and Clare felt loved and cared for in the way she had longed to be all her life.

One morning she had arisen early, and dressing quietly so as not to awake her husband, had gone for a short walk before breakfast. It was lovely to be out while the grass was still wet with dew and heavy with gossamer webs that would be invisible later in the day. It was the first time she had had to be alone in months it seemed, and she reveled in the hour.

When she turned back and came in sight of the house, she was surprised and touched to see her husband, his shirt unbuttoned, his hair still tousled from sleep, setting out to look for her. She waved to him gaily and as he ran over to her, she saw that look of vulnerability in his eyes that had so touched her.

"Where *were* you, Clare?" he asked, his voice almost harsh with worry.

"Why, Justin, I only went out for an early morning stroll," she answered. "You were sleeping so soundly, I didn't want to wake you."

"Don't ever leave without telling me again, Clare," he said fiercely.

"Of course, not, my dear. Not if it worries you so," she answered, puzzled by his vehemence but very touched by his concern.

After their time of solitude, however, it became clear that they would have to let the world in. Justin began riding the estate and going over tenant concerns with his manager, while Clare finally got Mrs. Clarke to show her through the house and introduce her to her responsibilities. And early in August, instead of tossing all the invitations back in the tray, Justin lifted one up and said: "The Lyntons have invited us to a supper dance. Do you wish to go, Clare?"

"That would be lovely, Justin. I am looking forward to meeting the people who will be our neighbors and friends."

The baronet and his wife were an older couple with two children, a daughter, and their oldest, a son who had been serving in India for two years. Lieutenant Lynton was home on leave, and the supper dance was in his honor.

Justin and Clare arrived late, just before the move into supper. Clare had been placed next to the young lieutenant, who was a delightful young man only a year older than she. He had merry brown eyes, a quick smile, and kept her laughing through most of he meal with amusing tales about his time in the East.

"You are giving me a very unrealistic view of war, I am sure, Lieutenant," she said as they got up from the table.

His face became serious for a moment. "Indeed, I have. But I have found looking for any humorous possibilities enables me to survive, Lady Rainsborough." His eyes were bleak, but only for a moment, and without thinking, she laid her hand on his arm in silent sympathy. She felt

Justin behind her, and withdrawing her hand, slipped it through her husband's arm.

"Lieutenant Lynton was keeping me well amused all through dinner, Justin."

"So I noticed, Lynton."

Clare was surprised at her husband's tone, which was cold and dismissive. "I will see both of you later," she said quickly. "I am looking forward to my waltzes," she added, smiling up at each of them.

But later, she was surprised to have Justin approach her for the dance which was to have been young Lynton's.

"Oh, Justin, I would love to dance with you again, but I am promised to the lieutenant."

"Not anymore. I convinced him that a newlywed couple wanted all their waltzes together, unfashionable though that may seem," he answered lightly, lifting her chin with his fingertip and looking down into her eyes with that passionate concentration that always undid her.

"As long as he doesn't feel I slighted him, Justin, I am happy," she replied after they moved off.

On the ride home, however, Justin started to question her.

"Whatever were you and Lynton laughing at over dinner, my dear?"

"Oh, he kept me entertained from beginning to end with one foolish story after another about the army," she answered.

"I see. And your hand on his arm? Was that in response to his good humor?"

"Why, Justin! I do believe you are jealous." Clare laughed.

"Why was your hand resting so long on his arm, Clare?" Justin demanded in a hard voice that Clare had never heard before.

"You are not teasing me, are you, Justin? You are quite serious," she said, wonderingly.

"I assure you, I am."

"I hardly remember why. I think it was that I accused him of glossing over the reality of a campaign, and for a moment or two, I could sense the pain beneath his laughter. And he is so young to be in the middle of a war. It was a natural gesture of sympathy, I assure you." Clare could still not quite believe that her husband was upset.

Justin took a deep, ragged breath and then said, in his own familiar voice: "Forgive me, Clare. You are so warmhearted, of course you would be touched by his situation. Who would not be."

"Justin, you could not really think that the lieutenant held any attraction for me?"

"Why not? He is young and handsome in that uniform."

"He is a boy, Justin. And you are a man. The only man for me," she added quietly. "The man I love with all my heart."

"Forgive me, darling, for my moment of madness?" her husband said, putting his arm around her and pulling her to his side.

"There is nothing to forgive, Justin. I know you only said it because you love me," she answered, all her tension drained away as she cuddled against him.

That night, her husband's lovemaking was more gentle and at the same time, more passionate than ever, and Clare marveled that even after six weeks of marriage and a minor disagreement, their love, which had seemed perfect that first night, was only becoming stronger.

Giles had known that Clare's wedding would be torture, but he had hoped that if he could take the pain of seeing her as Rainsborough's bride, then he would have faced the worst and could begin to recover. As he drove down to Whitton, however, seated next to Sabrina, he realized how often he had fantasized Clare beside him. How he had dreamed about this summer. She would have accepted his proposal and come down to Whitton for her first visit as his fiancée. They would have walked and fished and ridden and accepted the congratulations of their neighbors and friends. They would have ... Giles clenched his fists as he replayed the scene. They would have kissed again. He had gone so slowly with Clare, this Season, and then, suddenly, there was Rainsborough.

Giles spent much of the journey looking out the coach window, and Sabrina could get no more than one-word answers from him, no matter what topic she raised. She was very aware of his pain. All their lives they had shared a special wordless communication, sensing each other's slightest change of mood. Had it been any other than Clare who had hurt him, Sabrina would have pushed and prodded Giles until she got him to open up to her. But this pain was so deep and so private, that she couldn't speak, but just sat in silent agony herself, hoping that time, the great healer, would work its way with her brother.

The first weeks home were the worst of Giles's life. He was up early in the morning, either riding or tramping the hills for hours. In the afternoon, he closeted himself in the library, losing himself in his study of Persian. He had become quite an Orientalist at Oxford, and had translated several poets. His reputation had followed him down from university, and the Home Office often called upon him for translation of various messages, official and otherwise. He thanked God for his interest now, for trying to find the right phrase in English to fully express a poet's intention was the only thing that kept his mind off Clare.

After a while, however, he had been everywhere alone that he had visited in fantasy with Clare. Having faced down the worst, he realized he would survive her loss. Perhaps he would even come to think of her as she did him: an old and dear friend. Perhaps by the fall, he would be able to see her and simply enjoy her presence in his life. He hoped so.

Early one morning of his third week home, the groom brought both his gelding and Sabrina's mare to the front of the house. When Giles looked at him inquiringly, the man said that Lady Sabrina had informed him last night that she had planned to ride with her brother.

"Well, if she does, she had better get herself down here, then," said Giles as he heard his sister coming down the steps behind him. He sounded annoyed, but was secretly glad that she had taken the initiative to join him.

"I am right behind you, little brother."

Giles turned and gave her the first real smile she had seen on his face in weeks.

"Good morning, Sabrina. I hope you are willing to forego breakfast, for I intend to be out for a few hours."

"I had Cook pack us a picnic," she answered, pointing to the saddlebags on her mare. I thought we could ride up to Camden Hill and breakfast there?"

"I would like that."

The fields were shrouded in mist, and the two rode silently through the early morning fog. Their silence was a comfortable one, however, and Sabrina, who had been worried about breaking into Giles's lonely routine, knew that she had been right to do so. When the sun finally started to burn the mist away, their horses perked up, and they had an exhilarating gallop before winding their way up to the top of the hill.

"I could never have lived in Kent," said Sabrina, waving her hand at the scene below them. "It is too flat. Too much of a sameness."

"I love our west country, too," said Giles, really seeing his surroundings for the first time in days, other than just as a backdrop to a ruined dream. The hills and the hedges were a shifting canvas of greens as the clouds covered and uncovered the sun, and his heart lifted at the sight of it.

Sabrina pulled the saddlebags down and spread out the old cloth Cook had provided.

"Ham and cheese and fresh bread and apples, Giles."

"I am ravenous." And he was, to his surprise.

The apples were a bit mealy, for they were the last

from the cellar, and as Sabrina bit into hers, she shrieked and sprayed apple all over her riding habit.

"Found a worm, have you, Brina?" teased Giles. "Well, save it for fishing."

"It is not *funny,* Giles," complained his sister in the same tone she had used as a child when he teased her. "I might have swallowed it."

"Here, have some cider," said her brother. "That will wash everything down. The worm might have had a twin for all we know," he added, with a wicked grin.

Sabrina choked on the cider, and then, looking over at her brother, she had to laugh. "You are as awful to me as ever, Giles."

Giles lay back and watched the clouds scudding over the sun.

"Do you remember the day Clare came to Whitton for the first time? We were lying right here on Camden Hill, wondering what she would be like."

"I remember," Sabrina said softly.

"I didn't fall in love with her that summer. I think it was two years later. But I knew very early that it was Clare, Sabrina. I've loved her for a long time."

Sabrina reached out and grasped her brother's hand. "I have been worried about you, Giles."

"Oh, I will be all right. I admit I have been in hell since the betrothal announcement, but I seem to be coming back. Although, I must agree with Virgil, that the road from Avernus is not easy."

"I know all the right words to say, Giles, but I don't think they would mean anything to you."

"Like: 'You will get over it. You will find someone else.' Or 'time heals all wounds?' I've been saying them to myself. I just wish . . ."

"What, Giles?"

"I just wish I liked Rainsborough better."

"You could hardly expect to like your rival, Giles!"

"No, I don't mean I need to become his friend. It is

just that he seems . . . I don't know . . . too charming . . .
too handsome."

"He also seems to love Clare very much, Giles," said
Sabrina hesitantly. "She told me that for the first time in
her life, she felt someone really needed her."

"*I* need her, damn it," said Giles bitterly, as he sat up
and took a drink from the bottle of cider. "But she never
knew that, did she? She thought I only loved her as a
friend and was going to offer for her because it was the
expected and comfortable thing to do. *That* is what hurts
the most, Sabrina. That I have only myself to blame for
all this."

"You can't blame yourself for Rainsborough's existence, Giles. They fell in love. It happens all the time."

"I know, I know."

"At least you will speak of it now. I was worried about
you, Giles."

"You don't need to. I will survive this. Coming home
without her was very hard. But I am used to it now. By
the time I see her in London this fall, I am sure I will be
able to look at her as an old and dear friend. My love
started as friendship, so I am trusting that it can be that
again."

"I am sure it can, Giles," said his sister reassuringly.
But she was not sure at all, and she knew that he wasn't
either.

Chapter Seven

September, 1816

"You look exquisite, my dear."

"Thank you, Justin," Clare smiled at her husband's image in the pier glass.

"Here, let me fasten that for you. You can go, Martha."

Clare shivered as his hands brushed her neck. The sapphire and diamond choker he had given her as his wedding gift fit snugly around her throat and matched the blue of her silk gown perfectly.

"What *is* exquisite is this necklace, Justin," said Clare. "I am almost afraid to wear it."

"Nonsense, my dear." Justin leaned closer and kissed her right where her shoulder met her neck, and then turned her face to his for a long kiss.

"I suppose we *have* to go to the ball," he groaned, pulling away at last.

Clare laughed. "Of course we do. It would look very odd, indeed, if we avoided Lady Bellingham."

"Well, I warn you, Clare, I am going to be a very unfashionable husband and claim as many dances as I can. I hate sharing you with anyone." He leaned down and kissed her again, and Clare gave herself over to the delight of being so cherished. Of course, by the time their kiss was over, her hair was no longer perfect, and Martha had to be summoned back. And, as had been their pattern this Little Season, they arrived late to the Bellingham ball.

"How many minutes tonight, Bertie?"

"Twenty-seven and a half. It looks like Crewe is closest again."

"Lady Rainsborough looks delightfully flushed tonight, don't you know," said Crewe, pocketing his money.

"Damn. You would think that after a few months of marriage, they wouldn't still be in one another's pockets."

"I know his sort," said Marlow, looking over to where Justin was hovering over his wife as she greeted their host and hostess. "Won't let her out of his sight. Wants her all to himself."

"Even I admit it is quite romantic," said Crewe with a mock sigh.

"I suppose you could call it that," said Marlow, with a shuttered look. "My father was like that with my mother," he added and left abruptly, leaving his companions nonplussed.

"Tomorrow, I am betting on a half hour."

"Ah, but look at the way he is leading her out onto the floor, Crewe. Forty minutes, at least."

Clare loved dancing with her husband almost as much as making love with him. Although she was unaware of the more vulgar comments, she knew that people were amused at the Rainsboroughs' devotion to one another. Let them laugh. She didn't care, for she and Justin had something that most couples could only dream about.

She had seen the Whittons out of the corner of her eye when she and Justin had moved onto the dance floor. She and Sabrina had exchanged a few short notes during the summer, and she was looking forward to catching up on the local gossip. She had spent so much time at Whitton that it had almost become a second home, and she enjoyed hearing all the news, from the midwife's latest delivery to the absentminded vicar's newest gaffe. After her waltz with Justin and a cotillion with Sir Maximillian Ongar, she made her way over to where Sabrina was talking with a group of friends.

"Clare! You look positively blooming," said Lucy Kirkman, sliding her eyes down to Clare's waist.

Clare blushed. She was not increasing yet, but one of the embarrassing things about being an obviously besotted couple was that everyone, at one time or another, took the opportunity to subtly or not so subtly inspect her waistline.

She had learned to ignore them, and just said, "Thank you, Lucy."

Sabrina rescued her by enveloping her in a warm hug. "You do look wonderful, Clare. As does Justin."

"I would say that marriage agrees with both of you," said a voice behind Clare. It was Giles, and Clare held her breath as she offered him her hand. He merely held it gently for a moment and smiled down at her affectionately. It was her old familiar friend Giles who stood there, as relaxed and comfortable as he had ever been. She let her breath out in a soft sigh. The Whittons had come up to town late, and this was their first sight of each other since the wedding breakfast. And thank God, it was as she had hoped: they were still friends.

"Do you have a dance free for me, Clare?"

"The next two are spoken for, Giles, but I do have the first waltz free."

"Good. Then put me down for it. And Lucy, I believe this cotillion is ours?"

"Indeed it is, Giles," replied Lucy, smiling like the cat who had gotten the cream as they moved off.

"I swear I have become reconciled to your marriage, Clare," said Sabrina. "But I am not sure I will ever forgive you if I end up with Lucy Kirkman as a sister-in-law."

Clare laughed with relief and amusement. She was grateful that both Sabrina and Giles seemed able to admit her back into their easy companionship.

Clare was with Justin when Giles came to claim his waltz.

"Good evening, Whitton," her husband said politely, his eyebrows lifted inquiringly.

"I believe this is our waltz, Clare," said Giles lightly. "I was lucky to get one," he added, as he sensed rather than saw Rainsborough stiffen. "Your wife is one of the most sought after ladies at the ball."

Rainsborough gave him a cold, fleeting smile, and Giles was sure he could feel the earl's eyes boring into his back as they walked away. Earlier in the evening he had made up his mind to act the old friend as much as possible. Maybe if he acted long enough it would become true. God knows, it is not easy, he thought, as Clare placed her hand in his and he clasped her around the waist. All the perspective and peace he had gained over the summer disappeared as she looked up at him and smiled.

They danced well together; they always had. And after the first few minutes of tension, they both relaxed and began to give themselves over to the music and the movement. Giles was even able to get Clare laughing with the latest story about Reverend Brill.

"He didn't really start to read the wedding service at a baptism!"

"He did. Only a few lines, but enough to frighten the godmother and godfather out of their wits."

Since the godparents were the most dedicated bachelor and spinster in the village, Clare could only laugh.

"Come, let me return you to Justin." Giles walked her back to where Rainsborough was standing. Standing out like a sore thumb, thought Giles, for he was right on the edge of the dance floor where they had left him.

"May I get you a glass of punch, Clare?" he asked after he handed her over to her husband.

"Thank you, Giles," Clare replied with a smile. "I am thirsty."

Giles bowed and as he moved away, Justin grabbed Clare's arm.

"I think we will be going, my dear."

Clare looked up at him in surprise. His face was set and hard, and his thumb and forefinger dug into her arm. "Going? Where, Justin. Giles is getting me some punch," she added, completely puzzled by his reaction. A look of pain and surprise passed over her face as his grip got even tighter.

"Ah, yes, Giles. Your old friend Giles."

Justin's voice was so cutting that Clare felt he had flicked her with a whip.

"I don't understand what you mean, Justin. Are you feeling ill?" she stammered. "Is that why you wish to go home?"

"The sight of you smiling up into his face does make me feel sick, my dear. And I do not intend to stand for any more of it." Keeping his hold on her arm, her husband guided her across the room, nodding and smiling all the while, as though all were well. He made their apologies to their hostess, claiming that his wife was not feeling quite the thing. Lady Bellingham smiled knowingly, and Clare was handed into their carriage before she realized what was happening. Justin, who had finally released her, sat across from her, his face an unreadable mask. She winced as she rubbed her upper arm. She would have bruises in the morning, she was sure. She was feeling quite disoriented. Surely Justin, her loving, tender Justin, had not hurt her like that? It felt like an ugly, dark stranger was sitting opposite her. One who resembled her husband, but had somehow taken his place by some sort of wizardry. She was afraid to say anything, afraid to arouse his anger, and so she just sat silently, hoping that when they walked through their door, Justin would have been returned to her.

But when they reached St. James Street, instead of following her up the stairs as was his wont, Justin merely dismissed the footmen and asked their butler to bring him brandy in the library. Clare was left standing on the stairs, hoping for a glance from Justin, a kind word, anything to indicate that this was all a dreadful misunderstanding of some sort.

She dismissed Martha as soon as her abigail had undone the tapes of her gown. She didn't want her to see the marks of Justin's fingers on her arm. Her hands were shaking as she undid the clasp of the sapphire choker, and she looked down at it as it lay glittering on her dressing table. She had danced and laughed with a number of partners these past few nights. There had been no difference in her behavior with Giles, had there? Surely she had not given Justin any reason for distrusting her? Had she let Giles hold her too close? Had she looked up at him differently? She couldn't help caring about him, for he was her oldest and dearest friend. What *had* she done to make Justin behave like this?

She slipped her dress off and pulled her night rail over her head and looked over at their bed. This was the first night in their marriage that Justin had not helped her undress. The first night, in fact, she thought with a blush, that she even had her night rail on getting into bed.

Suddenly she remembered Lieutenant Lynton and her husband's insecurity. Of course, she thought with relief. If he was jealous of someone I didn't even know, then he would naturally feel vulnerable the first time I danced with Giles. When he comes up, I will tell him I understand.

But he didn't come up, and after what felt like hours, but was, in truth, only one, Clare decided that she would go down to him.

All the servants had been sent to bed, and the only light downstairs was coming from under the library door. Clare knocked gently and when she didn't receive any reply, took her courage in both hands and opened the door.

Justin was standing by his desk, back to the door. He had a glass of brandy in his hand, and the decanter next to him was already half-empty. Clare was surprised and concerned, for she had never seen him drink much more than a glass of wine since she'd met him. He must really be upset with her if he had drunk so much brandy in such a short time.

"Aren't you coming up to bed, my dear?" she asked timidly.

He turned around then, and she saw that his face was flushed and his eyes expressionless.

"I am surprised that you desire my company, Clare," he said in the same cutting tone he had been using since her waltz with Giles. "I am sure you would prefer to have Whitton next to you."

"Justin, you must know that is not true," responded Clare, trying to answer calmly and patiently, now that she understood that his behavior was coming from his sense of insecurity. "I danced with Giles because he is an old friend. If there was anything I did to give you another impression, I am sorry. But you are my beloved husband, and Giles only a friend, nothing more."

"Don't act the innocent with me, Clare. I saw the way you lingered on the dance floor, looking up at him, leading him on, and right in front of me. I am sure that gossips will have a field day." Justin gulped down the rest of his brandy, and as he turned to pour another, Clare moved next to him, putting her hand gently on his arm, saying softly: "Please don't drink any more brandy, my dear."

Without even turning to look at her, Justin backhanded her across the face, sending her stumbling against the sofa. She pulled herself up and stood there, hand to her reddening and swelling cheek, mouth open, gasping for breath. She was afraid her legs wouldn't hold her, but she managed to support herself against the sofa arm. Surely she was in the middle of a nightmare. Surely she would wake up in a moment, next to Justin in their bed. He would kiss away the fear and then make love to her in that wonderful way he had of combining tenderness and passion. But her fingers could feel the cold leather of the sofa arm, and her cheek was throbbing. Her tongue gently probed her teeth, and she was horrified to realize it was automatically checking to see if any were loose. She gave an hysterical sobbing laugh to think that she, Lady Clare Rainsborough, was standing there wondering if her husband had loosened any of her teeth. She had seen women of the lower classes missing teeth and sporting black eyes, and she had pitied them for marrying bullies. But this could not be happening to her. She was the daughter of a marquess, the wife of an earl.

Justin had turned at her laugh, and Clare backed as far as she could into the sofa. It was as though he were truly seeing her for the first time that night: hand to her swollen cheek, shrinking from him, and he let out a deep groan. His eyes were alive again and the cold mask gone, and he reached out his hand slowly and gently, to pull her hand away from her face.

"Oh, my God, Clare. What have I done?"

She looked up at him, pain and fear in her eyes. It hurt for her to talk, but she managed to say slowly: "I swear, Justin, Giles is nothing but an old friend."

"Don't, Clare. Don't even say it. I know he is. Truly I do. I . . . I don't know what came over me. I think it is just that I love you so much and can't stand to see you with anyone else."

"But I am not with anyone else, Justin. I am with you."

He reached out and gently touched her livid cheek. "Did I do this, Clare?"

She only looked the truth at him.

"I know you can never forgive me, Clare, but I swear I didn't even know what I was doing. It must have been the brandy. I don't usually drink, you know," he babbled. "Oh, God, you can't believe I would ever knowingly hurt you like this?" He looked down at the empty glass in his hand and hurled it into the hearth. Then he poured the contents of the decanter onto the fire, and the flames leapt blue and high. Both Clare and Justin watched them as though mesmerized until they died down.

"I will sleep in my dressing room tonight, Clare," he said without looking at her. "I am sure you don't want me to touch you. I swear I will not drink like that again. But, oh, my dear, don't look at Whitton the way you did tonight. It cuts to the quick."

Clare couldn't stand it. It had been a nightmare after all, albeit a waking one. A short, brandy-induced madness that had overtaken her husband. And only caused by his love and need for her. Of course, he would be jealous of Giles. It was understandable. After all, she had almost married him. Would have married him, had not Justin come along.

She couldn't stand the sight of her husband's back any longer. She slowly walked over to him and slipped her hand in his. "I don't wish to sleep alone tonight, Justin," she whispered.

He lifted her hand to his mouth and brushed it gently. "Are you sure, Clare? I would not blame you."

She leaned into him and felt him shudder as he softened against her. "Come, Justin, let us go upstairs."

They walked hand in hand as though they were two children finding their way in the dark. When they reached Clare's room, Justin gave her one more chance to send him away, but she just shook her head, smiled, and led him in.

He had never been so gentle. There was a basin of water on the nightstand, and he made a cool compress for her cheek, holding her in his arms as if she were a baby. Then he slipped her night rail over her head and laid her back on the bed.

"I am afraid to kiss you, Clare," he whispered, and she saw that he had tears in his eyes. "I don't want to hurt you more."

"There are other places to kiss besides my mouth, Justin."

He began with her neck and shoulders, and moved down to her breast. His tongue caressed each nipple, and then suddenly he took one breast into his mouth and sucked on it like a child sucking on a sugar teat.

Clare guided his hand in between her legs. Soon they were rocking together, slowly at first, and then faster. He came first with broken cries that were echoed by her own a few moments later. And then tears from both of them.

"Clare, you are the most precious thing in my life," he whispered. She reached out to caress his face and felt it as wet as her own.

"As you are for me, Justin," she responded, pulling his head close to her breasts and kissing the top of his head softly.

The next morning Clare looked dispassionately at herself in her glass. Her upper arm was indeed marked by purple bruises, but those could be concealed quite easily by several of her morning gowns. It was her face that was the problem. Luckily her eye was not affected, but her cheek was still swollen and red, and she expected it would be a day or two before she was back to normal. She would have to cancel all her engagements for the next two days, for she could not imagine any excuses that would explain her appearance.

When Martha came in to help her dress, Clare saw the maid's eyes widen at her mistress's appearance.

"Oh, Martha," Clare said with mock despair, "I was looking for a book to put me to sleep last night and was foolish enough to think I could make my way without a candle. I bumped right into the doorjamb. I vow, I am almost happy, for it gives me a day or two to myself to rest."

Clare chattered gaily about this and that as Martha helped her dress and arranged her hair. Usually it was Martha who gossiped away, but this morning the maid seemed to have little to say and Clare couldn't bear her silent scrutiny. But it was no one's business, after all, thought Clare defensively. Certainly not her abigail's.

"Please direct Peters to turn down all my invitation for today and tomorrow, Martha. And I will breakfast up here," she added, gesturing at the small table by the window.

"Yes, my lady."

Martha was devoted to her mistress, as were all the servants, and she went down the stairs muttering to herself, "Walked into the doorjamb, my arse. That handsome husband of hers did that to her, I wager." After she gave Clare's orders to the butler and the cook, she went looking for the housekeeper, Mrs. Clarke.

"You will not be seeing the mistress downstairs today, Mrs. Clarke."

The housekeeper looked up from her accounting in surprise. "Is my lady not feeling well? Can she be increasing," she asked expectantly, after a moment.

"No, no. Her stomach is fine," said Martha, pulling up a chair opposite. "It is her face."

"Her face?"

"All red and swollen. And her arm all purple with his fingerprints."

"Whose fingerprints, Martha? Whatever are you saying?"

"I seen my ma's face like that often enough," responded Martha bitterly. "I can tell when a man has hit a woman."

"Lord Rainsborough? Strike Lady Rainsborough? I am sure you are mistaken, Martha." Mrs. Clarke's tone had become quite cool. "Why they are absolutely devoted to one another. He has never been anything but loving when I see them together."

"Aye, well my stepfather was like that, too. Could charm the birds out of their nests, when he was in the mood to do it. And then in an instant, if my ma did one little thing wrong, like scorch his shirt collar, he was on her."

"I am certain you must be wrong. Did Lady Rainsborough say anything to explain her appearance?"

"Oh, she had a good story. My ma could have written books, *she* had so many stories, too. My lady said she went down to get a book from the library and ran into the doorjamb. And pigs can fly," added Martha.

"Then I am sure that that is what happened, Martha,"

replied Mrs. Clarke. "You can hardly compare your mother's situation with that of the quality," she said repressively. "And you are not to go spreading this story of yours around, do you hear? Lord Rainsborough is a kind man. Why, I have hardly heard him raise his voice to a servant, much less his wife."

Martha got up with a dramatic sigh. "Oh, I will keep quiet, Mrs. Clarke. But for my lady's sake and no one else's. But mark me, the first time is never the last."

Justin had been up early that morning, and Clare did not see him until early afternoon. She had spent the day quietly reading and embroidering and was so enjoying the peace of a day without social obligation that she was almost grateful to her husband for providing the opportunity. She did feel a pang of guilt when Martha brought up Sabrina's card. "Peters wasn't sure if you wanted to turn Lady Sabrina away with all the other ladies."

"I would welcome her company, Martha. But not today," said Clare, her hand automatically feeling her cheek, as she had off and on all day to see whether the swelling had gone down at all. "Tell her I am not feeling well."

"Yes, my lady."

A short time later, Martha was back. "Lord Rainsborough wishes to know if you will see him," she announced in absolutely neutral tones.

"Why, of course," said Clare, laughing nervously. Justin had never asked for permission before this. Theirs had been a delightfully informal marriage, with both feeling quite free to walk in on the other at any time.

Martha admitted Justin and closed the door behind him. She stood for a minute outside, glaring at the door as though he could feel her through the solid wood. "You had better not touch her again while I am around, my lord," she muttered, before she moved off.

Justin looked almost as bad as she did, thought Clare with some genuine amusement. His face was pale, and his eyes a little swollen from the drinking and from his tears of the night before.

"Good day, my dear," she said, in tones as close to normal as possible.

"I am sorry I ran off this morning, Clare. I confess, I couldn't bear to look at what I'd done to you."

"Well, Justin, neither of us is a pretty picture today," she said lightly. "But we must put this behind us and move on," she continued more seriously.

Justin reached into his pocket and pulled out a small oblong box. "This is a sort of pledge, Clare," he said quietly. "I saw it and thought of you immediately."

"Justin, you did not need to do anything like this," she protested.

He came over to her and put his finger gently on her lips. "Hush, my darling. Close your eyes and let me fasten this." Clare felt his fingers brush the nape of her neck as he fastened a small necklace around her throat. She was relieved it was nothing as big as the sapphire choker, for he had been far too generous with jewelry during their short marriage.

"Stay there," he whispered into her ear, "and keep your eyes closed." He went and got her hand mirror from the dressing table and coming back, held it in front of her. "Now you can open them, Clare."

Clare opened them and caught her breath in surprise, gratitude, and strangely enough, dismay. Around her throat was a delicate gold chain and suspended from it a heart-shaped amethyst. It was so similar to Giles's gift and so different from Justin's usual taste that there was something disturbing about it. Clare fingered it gently, completely at a loss for words.

"I don't know what to say, Justin."

"You don't have to, Clare. It looks just how I imagined it: a perfect length and a deep enough purple to bring out the violet in your eyes. I have always regretted making you remove Whitton's gift, Clare, for it *was* flattering. Now you have something as lovely that I gave you."

"It is very beautiful Justin. I will treasure it." Clare was touched and grateful, and she wished she felt only that. But her gratitude was somehow marred by a feeling of . . . well, she couldn't quite put her finger on it. It just seemed strange that Justin would want to remind her of Giles, after his jealousy. It was as though he were giving her and Giles a sort of message. Almost marking her as his own. Normally she loved his slightly possessive shows of affection. They made her feel essential to him. But although the necklace was an exquisite piece and she would wear it to honor Justin's gesture, she was sure she would never feel quite comfortable in it.

It was three days before Clare's face was back to normal and when the Rainsborough's finally reappeared at the next rout, the glances down at her waistline and the inquiries after her health were not subtle at all.

Sabrina was at Clare's side almost immediately, solicitous and concerned. "I was getting really worried, Clare, when Peters sent me away again yesterday."

"I hated to do it, Sabrina, but I was still not feeling quite myself," apologized Clare.

"I don't mean to pry, but I hope it wasn't anything serious?"

"No, just fatigue and a cold. And *no,* I am *not* increasing," added Clare, with a twinkle in her eyes, answering Sabrina's unspoken question. "And don't you start inspecting my waist. I promise you will be one of the first to know, after Justin, of course," she added.

Giles had seen their arrival from across the room. Clare was dressed in lavender sarcenet and had violets threaded through her hair. There was a flash of purple at her throat as she walked by a candelabra and he realized it was something new, obviously a gift from her husband. When he saw her with Sabrina, he made his way over.

"Clare, I am very happy to see you here," he said after they greeted one another. "When I came back with your punch the other night and you had gone, I was afraid you had been taken ill. And then Sabrina told me I was right. You are recovered, I hope?"

"Lady Rainsborough is completely recovered, Whitton," said a voice behind Giles as Justin joined them. "Thank you for your concern."

"Clare is an old friend, and I will always be concerned for her welfare," Giles said easily.

"Ah, but that is not at all necessary, Whitton, for she now has a loving husband to care for her. Come, my dear, I wish to introduce you to someone who has just returned from the West Indies. I want him to meet my beautiful wife." He took Clare's arm and they were gone very quickly, leaving Giles and his sister looking at one another in consternation.

"Well, Rainsborough certainly is making his feelings clear, Sabrina."

"Oh, Giles, I am sorry. I am sure it is none of Clare's doing. She still has all the old affection for you. And though I am loathe to say it, were I Rainsborough, I would be tempted to keep my wife away from old friends and suitors."

"Oh, I can understand it," said Giles. "Although what he thinks he has to worry about, I don't know. Clare was clearly besotted from the first time they met. He has no rival in me," he added bitterly. "Did you see her necklace?"

"Yes. Isn't it the one you gave her, Giles? I thought it was a pretty gesture on her part to wear it again."

"No. It is enough like mine to remind you of it and different enough to give the clear message that if anyone is going to bring out the purple lights in my wife's eyes, it will be me, thank you very much. It is an odd gift, don't you think, Brina?"

"Perhaps you are just overly sensitive because it is Clare, Giles."

"I suppose so. Well, message received, but I'll be goddamned if I do not claim a dance with her tonight and whenever I will."

* * *

Although Clare had told herself that Justin's jealousy was a thing of the past, that the incident was closed, that she had convinced him she felt nothing for Giles, she had made sure to fill her dance card quickly and only had a country-dance available for her old friend. She had been relaxed for their fateful waltz, but for this dance she was still and unresponsive, always wondering whether Justin was somewhere on the sidelines watching. Her smile was forced, and after the music stopped and Giles led her off the floor, she thanked him breathlessly and asked him to take her over to where Lucy Kirkman and a few friends were chatting. It was clear to Giles that she was dismissing him, but he only smiled a polite good-bye, as though nothing had changed between them.

Clare was relieved that her husband had not been hovering a the edge of the dance floor, but engrossed in conversation with a group of acquaintances. Since she had no more dances with Giles, she was able to relax and enjoy the rest of the evening. Her waltzes with her husband were delightful, and they left early, each eager for the passionate lovemaking they knew was to come.

And when Clare awoke the next morning and looked over at her sleeping husband, she knew that difficult as it was to pull back from Giles, it was well worth it if it kept her husband happy and their marriage as solid as it had every indication of being. There was only one thing that would make her happier, she decided, running her hands across her belly. That was to satisfy all the gossips and give Justin the son he and she wanted.

Chapter Eight

The rest of the Little Season passed by quickly and uneventfully. Clare felt she did a subtle balancing act between avoiding Giles whenever she decently could and at the same time, not making it noticeable, either to the gossips, or she hoped, to him. It had been worth the effort, however, for Justin had been true to his word and not only avoided strong drink, but went out of his way to prove he trusted her. In fact, one evening, he even commented that he wouldn't like to think she was slighting Whitton on his account, nor would he want any gossip to that effect, and hadn't she better save at least one dance for him this week?

They left for Devon before most of the ton in order to avoid the worst of the early winter weather. Clare was delighted to be home again and threw herself into holiday preparations with the enthusiasm of a child. And, indeed, she felt like one and intended to have the Christmas she always wanted. When she missed her monthly course in the beginning of December, she hugged her secret to herself, not wanting to tell Justin until she was absolutely sure she was increasing. But what a lovely secret to carry during the Christmas season.

Invitations came to the house as thick and fast as snowflakes. It seemed to Clare that all their neighbors, both those that had gone up to London and those who had remained in Devon, were planning something in the two weeks before Christmas. They accepted most of them, but not all, for Justin put his foot down when he saw the shadows under Clare's eyes after a particularly busy few days. But the Viscount Ware's St. Lucy's Day ball was one that no one in the neighborhood would miss. Ware Hall was always hung with decorations early, and redolent of evergreens. The viscount and his wife were excellent hosts, and the food was always better from one year to the next, or so everyone always exclaimed.

Clare was surprised and felt a moment of concern when she thought she caught a whiff of spirits as Justin handed her into their carriage. She told herself she was being foolish. If Justin had had a drink, surely he had a right to celebrate the holidays with a taste of brandy.

"Lady Rainsborough. It is delightful to have you with us your first Christmas in Devon." The viscount, who was a hearty man with a great booming voice, looked over at his wife. "Aren't we, my dear?" His viscountess, who was comfortable with her husband's enthusiastic personality and lack of self-consequence, merely took Clare by the hand and said: "Come, my dear, let me introduce you around. You have met most of the neighbors, but there are a few you have missed."

One of those she had missed was Sir Percival Blake, who had been in Canada and the United States and had only returned in November. He was a handsome gentleman, quite different from Justin, with pale blond hair and equally pale blue eyes and a prominent nose, who looked to be five years older than her husband. He obtained both a cotillion and the privilege of taking Clare into supper, and she had to admit that she found herself looking forward to supper, for she had always wanted to travel and was particularly interested in America.

Sir Percival was as delightful a supper companion as she had expected, and had her laughing and shivering in turn at his stories, which went from humorous to dramatic in minutes. She was enjoying herself so much that she actually forgot Justin's presence, which was the first time that had happened since they met. When they finally left the Wares', Clare was bubbling over in the carriage: "Can you imagine, Justin, the city of Boston was actually constructed around cow paths? And Sir Percival told me he spent many weeks living with a native tribe and learning their ways."

Justin was silent while Clare chattered, and it wasn't until he requested a footman to see Lady Rainsborough into the house, that she smelled the liquor on his breath.

"Go on, Clare, go in," he waved impatiently. "I am just going to take a turn around the drive to clear my head."

It was all right then, she thought. Well, why shouldn't it be all right? It was the holiday season, her husband was in the mood to celebrate with his neighbors, and he intended to clear his head by a short walk on a clear, cold evening.

She was in her night rail and wrapper with Martha brushing her hair out when Justin came to her room. He took the brush from the maid and dismissed her, saying, "I will finish getting Lady Rainsborough ready for bed, my girl." Martha glanced over and met Clare's eyes in the mirror. "Yes." Clare nodded. "You must be tired from waiting up for us. Go to bed, and I will see you in the morning."

"Yes, my lady." Martha had smelled the liquor on Lord Rainsborough's breath and wasn't sure she wanted to leave her mistress alone with him, but she didn't have a choice. And his tone had been calm enough. He didn't seem overset. As far as she knew, he had been nothing but gentle and loving with his wife after that first incident.

After Martha shut the door behind her, Justin began drawing the brush through Clare's curls, gently at first, which lulled her into a state of relaxation, and then suddenly harder.

"Justin, that hurt, my dear. I think my hair has been brushed enough anyway," she said with a laugh, and reached up her hand to take the brush.

Rainsborough put the brush in her hand, and closing his over it, twisted her wrist until she winced with pain. "There, there is your brush, my dear. And there you sit, admiring yourself in your glass like the whore you are."

Clare sat speechless. It came out of nowhere, this attack, and all she could do was look aghast at her husband's face in the glass. His eyes were icy and opaque, his face flushed with drink.

"Justin, I think you have had too much brandy again," she said as calmly as she could.

"Don't talk to me about what I have or haven't been drinking. Who wouldn't drink if he had to watch his wife fawning over a blowhard like Percy Blake."

Oh, God, it is the same thing all over again, thought Clare. Lynton, Giles, and now Sir Percival. "I wasn't fawning, my dearest," she replied sweetly and evenly, as though he wasn't accusing her of almost-adultery. "It was only that Sir Percival is a good storyteller. Why, I even told you one of his most amusing tales on the way home." Clare was sure if she was quiet, if she didn't raise her voice, if she inhaled and exhaled slowly, imperceptibly, if she didn't move, didn't disturb anything further, Justin would surely stop.

"You should know a good storyteller, my dear, for you are one, too, so meek and mild and sweetly humoring your drunken husband." Rainsborough ran his hand up her back and then her head, and grasping a handful of hair he suddenly stood up and dragged her with him.

Clare gave a low whimper. "It hurts, does it, my so treacherous wife?" Rainsborough wrapped his hand even more tightly and pulling her face back, began slapping it, at first softly and then harder.

Martha always knocked twice in the morning, for Lord Rainsborough always spent the night and sometimes sent her away, saying his wife was not ready to get up yet. She knew what *that* meant. Most likely that he was up again and at her. Although she had to admit, her mistress always looked like a contented cat in the morning.

Today, however, there was no answer at all. She was about to go in, but hesitated. If they were right in the middle of it, *she* wouldn't want to be the one who walked in on them. And so she sought out Lord Rainsborough's valet.

"Is his lordship up yet, Price?"

"No, and not likely to be for a while, Martha," said the valet, making a repeated tippling motion with his hand.

"Did he spend the night in his own room, then?"

"Yes, although it is the rare night that he does that, Martha," said Price with a wink.

Martha hurried back to Lady Rainsborough's room. She knocked once more, but this time didn't wait for an answer.

Her mistress lay curled up like a child, still asleep. Martha was smiling as she watched her until she saw the bowl of dirty water and bloodstained cloth. She was very aware of when Lady Rainsborough's monthly course was due. She knew it was three weeks overdue and had been secretly happy for Clare. Perhaps her mistress had had a sudden onset last night? She could have been increasing and lost the child in this early stage. She leaned over Clare and shook her gently, worried that Clare's deep sleep was perhaps a sort of faint from loss of blood.

Clare groaned at Martha's touch and turned over to see who was pulling her up out of oblivion. She could only see out of one eye, and it was hard to say Martha's name with her swollen lip.

"My God, what happened to your face, my lady?" Martha whispered and then answering herself said: "Never mind, I know just what happened to your face. That bastard. That stinking bullying bastard," she muttered.

"No, no, Martha," Clare protested.

"Don't you try to tell me no more stories about doorjambs, Lady Rainsborough. I didn't believe the first one, and I won't believe it now. Come now, sit up and let me see what he's done to your pretty face."

Clare let herself be supported by Martha's arm, while the maid gently probed her nose and eye.

"Your nose is not broken, no thanks to him. And the eye looks to be all right. Why ever didn't you call out for me, my lady?"

Because I had no voice, Martha, thought Clare. Because I wasn't really there. Because it was only a dream. No, an eternal nightmare.

"Oh, I know it is none of my business and what could I have done anyway against him? Well, you are certainly not getting out of bed today or anytime this week." Martha hesitated and then decided she had to ask. "The blood on the cloth, my lady. That was only from your nose? You don't need any cloths do you?"

Clare blushed crimson and instinctively put her hand on her belly. "No, Martha, if I am right, I will not need any for the next eight months. I don't think last night will have an effect, do you," she asked anxiously.

"Not if you stay in bed and let yourself sleep and heal. I will bring you some porridge and tea, and get some witch hazel from the stillroom."

"Thank you, Martha. Can you tell Mrs. Clarke that I am not feeling well. That I can't help her today with the holiday preparations."

"Of course."

"And Martha?"

"Can you keep Lord Rainsborough away for a few hours? I don't want to see him like this."

"I will do what I can, my lady."

But Lord Rainsborough did not try to see his wife that morning. He slept late and then after a light breakfast in his room, called for his horse and rode away "as though demons were after him," said his valet to Martha.

"And I hope they are," she answered. "Well, at least he will be away from my mistress."

Clare stayed in her room, eating very little and dozing off for most of the day. She slept so much, she was afraid she would be awake all night, but sleep was evidently what her body and spirit needed, and she slept through the night with no problem.

She awoke early the next day and got herself out of bed and over to her glass. Her face looked even worse today, if that were possible, as the bruises began to show.

She was standing by her window watching the early morning mist lift and blow away when she heard the door open and shut behind her.

"I am feeling much better this morning, Martha," she announced, but when she turned, she saw her husband standing by the door and quickly moved back behind the armchair that sat in front of her window. Her eyes were wide with fear, and her hands gripped the back of the chair convulsively.

Justin stood there silently, gazing at the damage he had done.

"It is far worse this time, isn't it, Clare?" he said in a tone that held both disbelief and despair.

Clare nodded.

"I don't know what to say? What is there to say? I . . . I don't know what happens to me, Clare. I think it is because I love you so much. The drink brings out the dark side of that love."

Clare stood silent, still wide-eyed and fearful.

"I went for a long ride yesterday, Clare. I know what I have to do. I know I promised this before, but this time, I mean it. I will not touch a drop of wine or brandy again; I swear it on my life. I know you will not want me near you for a while, but I hope you will regain your trust in time. I hope . . ." Justin's voice broke on the words. "I only hope I haven't killed your love for me."

The face was her beloved Justin's face. The eyes were his, no longer the hard, shuttered eyes of a violent stranger. And the gray eyes were full of tears, as were hers all of a sudden. Healing tears.

"I have loved you from the first time I saw you, Justin, and I have never stopped. I just don't know how to convince you of it. To make you see that no other man could ever replace you in my heart. Not Giles, certainly not Lynton or Sir Percival," added Clare with a watery smile.

"I know that now, Clare," said her husband fervently. "It is the alcohol that takes over, and I become . . . I don't even know who I become . . . someone who is terrified that he might lose the most precious thing he owns."

Justin took a step closer, and without thinking, Clare came from behind the chair and walked slowly over to him.

"I must be sure that you mean it, Justin. You *swear* that you will not drink again?"

"I swear it on my immortal soul, Clare."

She shuddered as she stepped closer and his arms gently enfolded her. "I hope so, Justin, for I am not only thinking of myself. I am also thinking of the safety of our child."

Justin put his hands on her shoulders and stepped back. "Child, Clare? You are increasing?" The look of happiness on his face was everything she had hoped for.

"I wasn't going to tell you until after the new year. Until I was quite sure. But yes, although it is early yet, I am quite certain."

"This is a new beginning for us, Clare. I will let you rest now . . . I will not . . . bother you with my presence at night. Until you want me."

"Oh, Justin . . . I will rest today. And I fear I won't be fit for any public appearances all week. But please don't leave me alone at night, my dear."

When Martha brought her breakfast up, Clare was seated in the armchair by the window.

"I see you are feeling better this morning, my lady."

"Yes, Martha, much, much better."

Martha looked at her inquiringly. "No one must know what happened, Martha. In or out of the household."

"I am sure no gossip would ever escape my lips, my lady."

"Let the servants know that I believe I am increasing and am suffering from fatigue and morning sickness."

"Yes, my lady."

"And Martha . . . Lord Rainsborough will be joining me here for supper this evening."

"I see, my lady." Martha's tone was noncommittal, but Clare was sure that she disapproved.

"It is only that he cannot deal with strong spirits that this happened, Martha. He has given me his word that this will never happen again."

"Of course not, my lady."

"And Martha?"

"Yes, my lady?"

"Thank you very much for taking care of me last night," said Clare, reaching her hands out to her maid's and clasping them. "I very much appreciate your loyalty and affection."

"Thank you, my lady." And you will always have it, my poor, innocent young lamb. Martha was only a few years older than Clare, but she felt almost ancient in experience as she left her mistress happily drinking her tea and dreaming, no doubt, of her husband's visit that night. He must be an expert at making love, this Lord Rainsborough, to make a woman so easily forget the blows those same hands could deal out.

Chapter Nine

"I see you are dressed for Aston's riding party, Sabrina. He seems to be becoming more marked in his attentions. Are you taking them seriously?" Giles's tone was light, but the intent behind the question was serious.

Sabrina sat down at the breakfast table and motioned the footman to make her up a plate.

"If you mean to ask do I intend to encourage him, why, no, Giles, I don't."

"You have been out for . . ."

"Four years. I know I am almost on the shelf," she said humorously.

"Hardly. But you have never lacked for eligible suitors. Has not one touched your heart?"

"Not one, Giles," she answered with a rueful smile. It was the truth, as far as it went. Not one of her admirers had ever made her heart skip a beat. It was only Andrew More who had that effect on her. And he had certainly never presented himself as anything but an old friend of her brother's.

She had hoped that Aston, who was not only a very eligible suitor but a good-looking man, would have sparked something in her. But she had to accept the fact that for now at least, an attraction to another man did not seem to be in the cards.

"I have always thought that you and Andrew would be well matched," said her brother thoughtfully, with that uncanny ability that they shared to pick up on the other's thoughts. "But he is so sporadic in his attendance during the Season," observed Giles, his voice trailing off.

"Andrew More has never given any indication of a special interest in any woman," Sabrina replied lightly, and then changed the subject. "Have Mother and Father gone through the mail already?"

Giles looked down at the small pile next to him. "Why, yes, I believe so."

"Is there anything there for me?"

Giles put his newspaper down with a sigh and with exaggerated patience, sorted through the mail. "You are always so *patient,* my dear sister. An invitation to the Blunts for Wednesday next. An invitation for me from Franklin to spend a week in Lincolnshire."

"Will you go?"

"Perhaps. I enjoy his company, and I would be glad of a change of scene."

"But you would leave Lucy behind to waste away, would you, Giles?" teased his sister.

"The day Lucy Kirkman wastes away for love . . . She hasn't let me alone for an instant since Christmas."

"You haven't looked particularly bored in her company, though, Giles."

"No," he grinned. "I have to admit she is good company. I prefer a woman who knows what she wants and goes after it to one of those docile misses in London."

"Such humility, Giles."

"Well, you were the one warning me against her, Sabrina! It is quite clear that she wants me. I do not think it takes being too full of myself to acknowledge that!"

"And will she get what she wants, Giles?"

"*She* clearly thinks so," he answered with a maddening smile, and went back to his newspaper after passing the rest of the mail over to his sister.

At least he could joke about it, Sabrina thought. Seeing Clare and Rainsborough together during the Little Season had been hard for Giles, she knew. But it had also put some distance between him and his lost dreams. Sabrina certainly hoped Lucy would *not* get what she wanted in the long run. But if her pursuit amused her brother and kept him from dwelling on Clare, then God bless the little hellcat!

"A letter from Clare! Oh, I am so glad. I haven't heard from her in weeks." Sabrina exclaimed aloud without thinking and then regretted it. But Giles merely looked over at her and smiled blandly, asking, "I hope she is well?"

"She sounds happy . . ." Sabrina scanned the note quickly. "As a matter of fact, she is increasing." She hated to say it, but he would find out sooner or later.

"Why, that is wonderful. I am sure she will make an excellent mother."

Sabrina knew her brother well enough to know that the news must have felt like a deathblow to another one of his dreams about Clare. But if the easiest way for him to deal with the news was not at all, then she wasn't about to force him.

Giles had thought the wedding was the worst, until he came home to Whitton without Clare. Then, seeing her in London with Rainsborough. But surely this was it: the knowledge that she bore another man's child. Surely it should have been over when his dream died. He'd suffered, as was only to be expected, but each time he was quite sure he'd moved on, something would take him by surprise and he would realize that what he thought was one dream was really many interconnected ones. Well, thank God, if she was increasing, Clare would not be available for much this Season. And maybe by spring, he would have discovered an interest in Lucy Kirkman that was equal to hers for him.

"Do you know whether Lord and Lady Rainsborough are in town yet, Sabrina?" asked Lucy over tea and pastries at Gunther's.

"I am not sure," said Sabrina with a worried frown. "The knocker is on the door, but I have received no answer to either of my notes. Perhaps Clare is not feeling well. Although she might have written a few lines . . ." Sabrina's voice trailed off.

"Ah, yes, I heard she is increasing. I am very happy for her," said Lucy, licking a bit of cream from one of her pastries.

"For Clare, Lucy?" asked Sabrina with a wry smile.

"Of course. But mostly for me. Giles can hardly spend his time daydreaming about a woman whose waist is expanding and ankles are swelling!"

Sabrina laughed. "Oh, Lucy, you are outrageous."

"I know you would not be thrilled with me as a sister-in-law, Sabrina. You think that Giles deserves someone sweet and loving like Clare. But she treated him worse than I ever would, you must admit. I am just honest about what I want."

"I find myself admiring that in you, Lucy, much to my surprise! But I believe Giles needs someone different." Someone who *loves* him, thought Sabrina, not just *wants* him, as though he were a prize to be won.

"I promise you, Sabrina, Giles does *not* need someone like Clare. Oh, she brings out the knight on the white charger in him. As would Lady Helena or the Honorable Susan Maxwell, whose mothers are always pushing their daughters at him, I might add. I, who am motherless, must do my own pushing," she added humorously.

Perhaps if your mother had not died when you were three, you would have had someone to check your determination to get your own way, thought Sabrina. And you are right, Giles does not need a girl like Lady Helena. But neither does he need a woman like you. He needs someone a little softer and more loving than you and stronger than Clare. Sabrina surprised herself by that last thought, which felt like disloyalty to an old and dear friend. But if Clare hadn't really loved Giles, then her brother was indeed better off without her.

That evening was one of the first crushes of the Season. Given the fact that the Duchess of Winston liked to have every inch of floor space taken up with either people or exotic plants, neither Giles nor Sabrina would have expected to see Lord and Lady Rainsborough immediately. They were attempting to make their way through the crowd when they heard the Rainsboroughs being announced behind them. Sabrina felt Giles stiffen, and she automatically put her hand on his arm in sympathy.

When they reached their destination, a cluster of friends and acquaintances, Sabrina allowed herself to search through the crowd, looking for Justin, who was tall enough to stand out even in this crush. But when she found him, with Clare by his side, she audibly drew in her breath, for Clare was as slim as ever. In fact, Clare, who had sometimes been referred to as a Pocket Venus, was almost unattractively thin.

"She must have been ill, Giles," Sabrina said without thinking.

Her brother looked down at her in surprise. "What are you talking about, Brina?"

As the conversation continued to flow around them, she pulled him closer to her side and gestured to where Rainsborough and Clare were standing. "Clare told me she was increasing, Giles. She must have lost the baby," Sabrina whispered.

Giles blanched. "She looks awful."

"Yes. Take me over to her, will you Giles?"

"Of course." Giles made their excuses and leading the way, cleared a path in front of them while holding onto his sister's arm. When they reached the Rainsboroughs, Sabrina pushed past her brother to greet Clare with a hug. Clare felt brittle and unresponsive in her arms, and Sabrina released her quickly.

Justin Rainsborough greeted them politely enough, but both brother and sister could tell that he wished them back on the other side of the room.

Giles kept Rainsborough busy with questions about his estate while Sabrina moved Clare over to one of the nearby pillars.

"I am so surprised to see you looking so, my dear," she said without preamble.

Clare looked at her blankly and then blushed. "Oh. The baby. I lost it shortly after I wrote to you, Sabrina. I should have told you, I know. But I am still very tired. Not quite recovered, I guess."

"You are so thin, Clare."

Clare looked down as though to see for herself. "Why, yes, I did lose weight. But I am beginning to gain it back." She tugged nervously at the sleeves of her dress, as though she wanted to be sure they covered her thin arms.

"May I call on you tomorrow, Clare?"

Clare hesitated, and her eyes darted over to where her husband was talking to Giles. "Why, yes, of course, Sabrina. I will be at home to visitors after one."

Sabrina chatted with her for a few minutes and then returned her to her husband. She pulled at her brother's arm. "Come, Giles, I think the first country-dance is ours, if we can make our way over to the dance floor! The duchess has outdone herself this year, don't you think, Lord Rainsborough?" Sabrina smiled brightly up at him, almost daring him to respond.

"Yes, indeed," he answered, putting his arm protectively around his wife. "In fact, it is so crowded, I think I will get Clare home early tonight.

He was true to his word, for when Sabrina looked for her friend later, she was already gone.

Sabrina made her promised visit the next day, only to find Clare entertaining two women who were mere acquaintances. There was no time for any intimate conversation, and she left early, but not before she made Clare promise to come for a ride in the park with her later in the week.

Their ride, however, was hardly more satisfactory, for

Clare was subdued and not at all forthcoming about her life in Devon or the loss of the baby. Sabrina did not want to pry, and so they had, what was for her, a disappointing time together. When nothing improved over the next few weeks, she decided to consult with her brother.

She interrupted him one rainy morning in the library.

"Giles, I am very worried about Clare."

Giles looked up from his book. "Why is that, Sabrina? When I saw her at a musicale last week, she had more color and seemed to have put back a little of the weight she lost," he replied noncommittally.

Sabrina hesitated. "I know it may still be painful for you to talk about her, Giles, so I was reluctant even to bring this up, but it is not just the physical I am concerned about. She doesn't seem quite herself."

Giles closed his book and took a deep breath. Sabrina was right. He didn't want to think about Clare. It was much easier that way. He sat quietly for a few moments, listening to the steady fall of the rain outside the window. If he opened himself up to Clare again, it would be painful. But how could he ignore her if she was really in trouble?

"Tell me about it, Sabrina," he said quietly.

"It is hard to describe. It feels to me that she is not really . . . present at times."

Giles looked up with concern in his eyes. "Women can sometimes be so affected after childbirth, I understand. Perhaps a miscarriage would also leave its mark?"

"Oh, no, Giles. I don't think Clare is seriously melancholy in the way you mean. I remember Mrs. Crane in the village and her melancholia after her second child. It is nothing like that. It is more that Clare seems only to be going through the motions of being polite and dancing and making calls. She does not feel available to me in the same way. Well, perhaps that is all it is: the fading away of a close friendship. After all, her husband should come first, shouldn't he?"

"And how do they seem together?" Giles had tried to avoid them as much as possible this Season.

"Oh, not as much in each other's pockets as they were before, Giles. At least all that dreadful wagering has stopped," she added with a smile. "But they appear very happy together."

"Perhaps it *is* as you say, then, Sabrina. Clare has grown beyond her old friends. She has her own husband, her own life in Devon."

"I know, I know. But it still bothers me."

"I have been ... not avoiding her precisely, but only asking her for an occasional dance. Maybe I should try to act more the old friend than a disappointed lover, and see if I can offer her some comfort if she needs it."

Sabrina was right. Clare was not herself. The trouble was she wasn't quite sure who that self *was*. Clare Dysart had certainly not been a vibrant, self-assured young woman like Sabrina. But Clare Rainsborough, in the early days at least, had felt cherished and loved and alive, finally not anyone's afterthought. She had discovered passion; she had learned what it was to be an elemental part of someone else's happiness. She had experienced Justin as a sensitive and expert lover. He had made her believe ... no, not made her believe, she had experienced herself as the center of his existence. Until that first blow. Which of course had been an aberration. Until the next one. But it was so clear that brandy brought out his insecurity and distorted his personality, and when he was not drinking, he was her loving husband again.

But she was beginning to feel that she was living in almost parallel lives. Which was, of course, not possible. Surely there was only one: either one's husband was generous, kind, tender, and passionate (which was her life most of the time). Or he was a jealous, bullying tormentor. Which was her life for such a small portion of the time that she surely *must* be imagining it. Or somehow causing it.

What was her marriage? A blissfully happy one, for months at a time? Or the living hell that occurred occasionally and for only a day or two? Clare sometimes thought it would have been easier to have Justin beat her regularly. To know that he despised her. To be sure that he was a brute with no redeeming qualities. Then she could have hated him back. Or maybe even left. But how could she hate him when he so clearly *did* love her? So desperately needed her. Was so sorry after the brandy got the better of him. Gave her more pleasure in their lovemaking than she had ever thought possible.

There was no one she could talk to about it. Her parents would never understand, and, in fact, had wanted her to marry Giles. She missed her intimate conversations with Sabrina, but how could she tell her anything? It was too shameful to talk about. And how could Sabrina understand what a good husband Justin was most of the time. A piece of her heart longed for Giles. He had understood her and protected her when Lucy Kirkman had bullied her. But it would be even more impossible to talk to him.

Perhaps it was all over anyway. They had been in London almost a month, and Justin had not touched any spirits. They both were recovering from the loss of the baby. Justin had been slow to return to her bed, but Clare had finally convinced him that she was ready, and so the last few weeks had felt almost like a second honeymoon. So surely she was the happily married Lady Rainsborough after all.

Giles wasted no time in seeking Clare's company. The evening of Lady Petersham's rout he made sure to secure a supper dance with her. Rainsborough was very polite about it—but then Rainsborough was always coolly polite with him.

He watched her closely as the patterns of the dance brought them together. She had more color than she had at the beginning of the Season, and she seemed fairly relaxed with him.

When it was time to go in for supper, he made sure to choose seats on the edge of the crowd so they had a bit of privacy.

"I have not had a chance to really express my sympathy, Clare," said Giles. "I imagine it takes awhile to recover from such a loss."

Clare felt tears spring to her eyes. She felt she was back in the presence of her old friend, and all the constraints of the last year were gone.

"Thank you, Giles. It has been difficult. But Justin has been very supportive," she added.

"I am sure. Sabrina has been rather worried about you, though," he added, trying to keep his tone light.

"Oh, she need not, Giles. I know I have been a little distracted, but I had hoped to be spending the spring with my feet up on a hassock rather than doing the full round again. It is taking me awhile to shift my expectations."

"I hope that your loss does not mean . . . that is, I trust you will be able to . . ."

It was the first time Clare had ever seen Giles ill at ease, and she was touched and even a little amused. "If you mean will I be able to have other children, Giles, the answer is yes. The doctor assured me there were no lasting effects."

Giles saw a fleeting look of deep sadness in her eyes, even as she said what should have been good news, and wondered at it. It was gone so quickly, however, that he could almost believe he hadn't seen it.

"I did not mean to pry, Clare. I think Sabrina and I just wished to make sure that our old friend was happy," Giles said, reaching out and holding her hand affectionately.

It was so lovely to know who she was for that moment: the Clare whom Giles loved as a friend, the Clare Giles had always taken care of, that all the distress of the past few months had disappeared. Clare smiled up at Giles just at the moment Justin pulled up two chairs near them for himself and his supper partner.

Giles felt Clare stiffen and immediately let go of her

hand and began chatting about inconsequential things, making sure to include Rainsborough and his companion in the conversation. Rainsborough smiled and responded, but as usual, his smile didn't reach his eyes. Oh, well, thought Giles, there would always be this tension between them. It was only natural. And at least he had satisfied himself about Clare's state of mind. For the first time in months, he began to think that it would be possible to be with Clare in that old, relaxed way of friendship.

The next morning at breakfast, he reassured Sabrina and told her that he thought Clare was merely working her way through her sorrow at the loss of the baby. "She said she was finding it hard to adjust to a full Season when she had not expected to participate much at all."

"I *am* glad that you spoke with her, Giles. I am supposed to visit this afternoon, and perhaps now that I am less worried, our visit will be more relaxed."

But Sabrina was turned away that afternoon and for the next week, as were all others. "Lady Rainsborough has come down with a very bad cold," the butler told all her callers, "and would receive visitors when she recovered."

Sabrina made herself remain calm and did not even begin to look for Clare in the evenings until a week had passed. But it was fully ten days before Lady Rainsborough attended anything in the evening, and when she and her husband were announced at the Fraser's musicale, it was noted that she looked almost as pale as she had in the beginning of the Season. All agreed it was a shame that she should have recovered from a miscarriage only to succumb to another illness.

Rainsborough hovered protectively, and for her first few nights back, turned away any and all requests for dances and made sure she was home early. "It is wonderful, isn't it, that even after almost a year, he is such a loving husband," said more than one matron to another. "Yes, she is a very lucky woman."

Any of the times Sabrina managed to spend with Clare was short and unsatisfactory due to her husband's hovering. But she was torn between feeling happy that he was so good to his wife and experiencing his protectiveness as a vigilant control.

It wasn't until the third day Clare was back in circulation that Giles had the opportunity to obtain a waltz. As he clasped his hand around her waist and they moved off to the music, Clare kept herself distant, head and eyes down. After a few measures, Giles shifted his hand to pull her in a little bit closer, and although she responded to his signal, she did not relax for a moment of their dance. And when they were making one last whirl around the floor and his hand tightened under her ribs for an instant, he felt her wince and heard a little gasp of pain escape her lips.

"Are you all right, Clare?" he asked anxiously. "Do you want me to take you out for a breath of air?"

"No, no," she protested immediately. "I am fine, Giles, really I am. I um, pulled a muscle the other day when I was reaching up to get a book down from a high shelf. Very foolish of me." She felt as tense to him as an overstrung lute string, ready to break at the slightest twist. Something was wrong, but he couldn't imagine what. And he certainly couldn't ask again. He was not going to push anything on her in this state, not even his friendship.

"Clare does not seem fully recovered from her illness, Rainsborough. I hope she hasn't come back too soon."

Giles was intrigued by the expression on Rainsborough's face. At first he looked as worried and responsible, as any husband might. Then, it seemed for an instant—but only that—an expression of pain and guilt flitted over his face. Yet immediately his eyes hardened and he said, with an edge in his voice, although it was calm and polite enough:

"Thank you for your concern, Whitton. I realize you are an old friend and have Clare's best interest at heart, but I am her husband and therefore know what is best for her."

Giles bowed to both of them and moved off, feeling both furious at such an obvious dismissal, and concerned. But the man, much as Giles couldn't like him, was right. *He* was Clare's husband, and whether Giles liked him or not, certainly seemed to have Clare's best interest at heart.

Chapter Ten

"Are you and Lucy joining us at the theatre tonight, Giles?"

Her brother, who had just taken a bite of toast and was washing it down with his coffee, mumbled and nodded his head.

"Was that a yes, dear?" his sister asked with exaggerated sweetness, in exactly the same tone their mother would have used, were she with them in London, rather than with their father in Paris, on what they considered a "second honeymoon."

Giles swallowed. "Yes, it was a yes, Sabrina. Do you mind if we do?"

"Of course not. In fact, I have become quite resigned to your . . . friendship with Lucy."

Her brother grinned. "My . . . friendship? Are you trying to oh so subtly ask something, Brina?"

"*Are* you going to make her an offer, Giles?"

"The wagers are three to one in favor, Sabrina. What do you think?"

"I think that you are being most annoying, Giles. Surely your twin sister should be kept informed of the state of your heart."

"I have given very serious thought to it. Lucy and I have spent a great deal of time together, and she is very good company. I need a wife, and the Kirkman land runs with ours."

"You have spent a great deal of time together because Lucy makes sure that you do, Giles."

"Sabrina, I m not obtuse. Of course I know Lucy sought me out. But perhaps that is what I need: a woman who wants *me*."

"But do you love her?"

"I have a great deal of affection for Lucy. And we know each other's foibles very well by now. I think we would get along quite comfortably."

"Well, then?"

"I haven't quite made up my mind. But if I were going to wager . . . ?"

"Yes?"

"Odds on, Sabrina," he said, pushing away from the table. "Will you join me for a ride this afternoon?"

"Of course."

"Then I will see you later. I am off to the Home Office."

"Another diplomatic bungle to straighten out?"

"It seems that I am the only one they can find who can translate Persian and interpret a report's deeper meaning."

After her brother left, Sabrina sat staring into space. Lucy Kirkman as a sister-in-law. She had seen it coming, certainly, so she was almost prepared. But not entirely. She so wanted Giles to have love. He deserved it after losing Clare. Lucy wanted him, Lucy liked him. Lucy even had affection for him. But Lucy, as far as Sabrina could see, was incapable of any deeper feelings.

Of course, he wasn't the only one who had lost Clare, she thought. Before Clare had arrived in London for the Season last spring, there had been talk of Sabrina coming for a summer visit. But during the Season, the visit had never even been mentioned, and Sabrina had received no answer to the two short notes she had sent Clare in August. Lord and Lady Rainsborough had come up for the Little Season, but their attendance at social events had been sporadic. Sabrina had had one or two very short and unsatisfactory visits with Clare. It was as though her friend had retreated behind some wall. Yet she and Rainsborough seemed as close as ever and even left for Devon early, well before the holidays, and without even a good-bye to her old friend.

Although Sabrina had very much wanted her brother's comfort and counsel, she had avoided talking about Clare. Giles seemed to be over her, at least from all outward appearance, and Sabrina did not want to reopen the old wound. As to whether the wound had ever truly healed, she was not sure. She suspected not, for if it had, she was sure her brother would have been looking for love again, and not settling for Lucy Kirkman.

Lucy would certainly make an attractive wife, if nothing else, thought Sabrina that night, when Giles and Sabrina arrived at the theatre. She was dressed in primrose muslin, which was a wonderful color for someone with her dark brown hair. Her eyes were full of life and enjoyment. I have to give her that, thought Sabrina. She has energy enough for the two of them. When she is getting what she wants!

"Oh, look, there are the Rainsboroughs," said Lucy. "I wondered whether they would come up for the whole Season. Or whether Lady Rainsborough was increasing yet. He is the most handsome man and so devoted, don't you think, Sabrina?"

Sabrina looked across to the Rainsborough box. Justin's tan had never faded completely, and his black hair and dark skin and cool gray eyes were still a powerful combination, even after all this time. She watched as he turned solicitously to Clare, pulling out her chair for her and getting her settled. Sabrina leaned forward and waved. She thought she saw a slight frown crease Rainsborough's brow, but it was gone by the time he alerted Clare, and they both gave discreet waves over to the Whitton box.

"She looks as pale and thin as she did last spring after losing the baby. Do you think it has happened again,

Sabrina?" remarked Lucy, who had no qualms about speaking what was on her mind. Sabrina answered casually: "I don't know, Lucy. I haven't heard from Clare for an age." Sabrina was very glad to see the curtain going up and the pantomime begin.

Clare stayed in the Rainsborough box during the interval, but Sabrina saw Rainsborough in the lobby procuring a glass of punch. Dragging Lucy with her, she approached him.

"Ah, good evening, Lady Sabrina, how lovely it is to see you here," he said with a smile that held no real pleasure.

"Good evening. May I come back with you and say hello to Clare?"

"Of course."

Sabrina dismissed Lucy, saying she would be safe in Lord Rainsborough's company and that she would return shortly, and then followed him back to his box, chatting about the play.

"Here is Sabrina to see you, my dear," Rainsborough announced.

Clare, who had seemingly not moved since the curtain came down, started and turned around. She blushed slightly when she saw Sabrina and gave her a hesitant smile.

Clare was as thin and as lacking in color as she had been at the beginning of last spring. And there was something about the way she held herself that worried Sabrina. There was both a tension and a fragility in her bearing that made Sabrina feel that if she should but touch her, Clare would shatter. So she did not give her a warm hug of welcome, but merely took her hand and squeezed it affectionately.

"I hope your holidays were as festive as ours, Clare. Did you have much snow in Devon?"

"We had some snow, Lady Sabrina, but we are so near the coast, you know, that it melts almost immediately."

Sabrina wanted to say rudely: "I didn't ask you,

Rainsborough." Instead she smiled down at her friend and said: "Will you be home tomorrow? I would love to catch up on the last few months, Clare."

Clare's eyes automatically glanced over at her husband, and Rainsborough smoothly answered Sabrina for her.

"We have only just arrived, Lady Sabrina. Perhaps you could give us a few days to get settled before you call?"

"Of course. Well, I had best get back to my seat, Clare. It is good to see you both."

She was looking to him for *permission*, fumed Sabrina, as she walked back to their box. Permission to see her oldest friend! Well, I will make sure I call the beginning of next week whether Lord Rainsborough approves or not. Being solicitous about his wife's health is one thing; keeping her friends away from her was quite another.

Four days later, Clare watched her husband going through their cards and invitations. She had almost become resigned to the fact that he made all the decisions about their social life, even to the extent of telling her whom to see and whom to turn away on afternoon calls. She caught her breath when he lifted up a piece of vellum with Sabrina's handwriting on it.

"Sabrina Whitton will never give up, will she," said Rainsborough. "I should think it would have been obvious to her by now that you do not wish to continue an intimate friendship with either her or her brother."

"I won't see her if you don't want me to, Justin," said Clare, trying to keep her voice free of anything that may have been construed as desire to see her old friend.

"I appreciate your willingness to go along with my wishes, Clare," said her husband, smiling his approval. "But you had better see her. If you completely ignore the Whittons, no doubt the gossips will seize upon it."

"All right, Justin."

"What were your plans for the day, Clare?"

"I need a new pair of gloves, Justin. I thought I would go to the Pantheon Bazaar and do a little shopping this morning. I will take Liza with me, of course. If that is all right with you," she added timidly.

"Of course, my dear. And just make sure this afternoon, when Lady Sabrina calls, you see her on her way quickly."

Clare lowered her eyes to hide her disappointment and nodded. After all Clare's neglect of their friendship, Sabrina would hardly expect a long, cozy afternoon. But, oh how she missed her old friend's company and counsel.

"Do we have plans for this evening, Justin?"

Rainsborough fanned out the invitations. "I think the Winstons' ball, don't you?"

Clare nodded. "Of course, my dear."

"Wear your new gown for me, Clare."

"I will, Justin." It was a lovely gown, with an underslip of ivory and the palest gray gauze overslip lightly sprinkled with tiny rhinestones. Clare had felt she was dressed in gossamer thread spun by faeries when she had tried it on. "Are you riding this morning, Justin?"

"No, I am merely dressed in my buckskins for show," he answered sarcastically. "I will see you later, Clare."

"Yes, Justin." She had never gotten used to the sarcasm that he employed more and more with her. But she tried to dismiss it from her mind, and getting up from the breakfast table, summoned Liza.

Everytime she saw her abigail's bland face she felt a surge of loneliness. Liza had been with her for a year now, but she still missed Martha. Martha had cared about her. Martha had defended Clare, better than Clare defended herself. Of course, Justin couldn't tolerate her and had dismissed her, choosing the new maid himself. But Clare never felt so alone as when Liza was with her.

She saw several women that she knew at the bazaar, and smiled and nodded and chatted away about the price of silk scarves. She knew, as she walked away from them that they were gossiping about her appearance. Had she

been increasing again and lost another baby? Was she capable of giving Rainsborough an heir? No, she could have
told them, she had not been with child this winter, for
which she was profoundly grateful. Not that she could
ever share her relief with anyone. And not that anyone really *cared* why she looked unwell. She was alone and
friendless in a bed of her own making, and she must lie
in it until she died. At times over this past year, she had
actually prayed for death, but most of the time, she just
hoped there would be no more beatings, that this time,
Justin would keep his promises never to drink again,
never to touch her again except in love. Or at least, that
his next beating would not be any harder than the last.

"How was your visit with Clare this afternoon?" Giles
asked as he helped his sister on with her cloak. Sabrina
looked up in surprise. She had not mentioned her decision
to visit Clare, as far as she recalled.

"No need to look surprised, Brina. I was looking for
you this afternoon and a footman told me where you had
gone. You don't need to be so protective, although I appreciate it. I have long been resigned to the situation."

"I know, Giles. But there doesn't seem much point in
talking about my worry when neither of us can do anything about it."

Giles was silent until they reached the carriage and
then asked quietly: "And what worries you, Sabrina?"

"It is not just that Clare looks unwell. I feel that there
is an inner fragility that goes beyond any of her old dif-
fidence. She initially seemed . . ." Sabrina hesitated.

"Yes? Go ahead, say it, Sabrina."

"So happy in her marriage. But now . . . well,
Rainsborough is always hovering over her and certainly
seems affectionate enough . . ."

"Has she said anything to lead you to believe their
marriage has changed?"

"Nothing. She didn't say much at all. We chatted about
this and that. Anytime I approached anything personal, I

could almost see a wall drop between us. And yet, at the same time, I have this strange feeling that our Clare is trapped behind that wall, waiting to ask for help. But help for what, I don't know."

"If she doesn't ask, we certainly can't give it to her. And neither of us has the right to interfere with what is, ultimately a private affair," said Giles with such finality that Sabrina wondered if she had been wrong all along. Maybe Giles was completely heart-free where Clare was concerned.

However he had sounded to Sabrina, Giles was unable to ignore what she had told him. He watched Clare carefully that evening, as unobtrusively as possible. She danced with her husband several times, and throughout the night they rarely had their eyes off each other, or so it seemed. But he could not make up his mind whether Clare's glances over to Rainsborough were loving or something else ... something closer to watchfulness or fear.

Giles did not ask Clare to dance, but he noticed that the young Earl of Bewley was hovering around her and danced with her twice. Bewley was an amusing fellow, and Giles felt a pang when he saw Clare laughing up at him once or twice during their waltz. It was the happiest he had seen her look in a long time. Shortly thereafter, however, he noticed that Clare was gone and Rainsborough also. He was relieved to see that her husband was making sure she didn't exhaust herself. He and Sabrina were likely worried for nothing. Even the oldest and closest of friends drifted away from one another. He just needed to accept that that was what was happening with Clare.

Clare sat very still as the carriage carried them home. It was never a good sign when Justin gave their excuses to their hostess and took her home early. She was trying to review the evening: she had been with Justin for most of it, however unfashionable that appeared. She had not spoken with Sabrina and had barely acknowledged Giles when he bowed to her. She had not danced with Giles the past few nights, nor had he asked her. She *had* allowed young Bewley to get her a glass of punch after their second dance. Could that have been it? But surely Bewley would not threaten Justin? He was three years younger than she was, after all.

When they got home, Justin handed her down with exaggerated politeness and told her he would be up soon. She started up the stairs slowly and watched him go down the hall to the library. He had had Madeira to drink at supper and several glasses of champagne at the ball. And there was always a decanter of brandy in the library. When he went there before coming upstairs . . .

Liza helped her out of her gown and into her night rail.

"Do you want me to brush your hair, my lady?"

"Please, Liza." Clare said yes not because she liked the abigail's company or the brisk way she brushed her mistress's hair. She wanted to keep Liza there as long as possible. Sometimes it made a difference if her abigail was with her when Justin first came up.

Justin opened her door just as Liza was finishing.

"You can go, Liza," he said. He was talking slowly, so as not to slur his words, and Clare trembled as he closed the door and came up behind her. He put a hand on each of her shoulders and dug into her flesh with his fingers.

"Who are you thinking of tonight, Clare? Whitton seems to have been avoiding you."

"I am not thinking of anyone, Justin," said Clare. It was hopeless to think she could get through to him, but she always quietly denied his charges.

"Perhaps it is the young Earl of Bewley? He is a very handsome young man, if you go for that sort of pretty face, isn't he, Clare?"

If she said "no," he would call her a liar. So she said: "Yes, Justin, he is very good-looking."

"And you enjoyed your waltz with him, I could tell."

His hands had moved so that they were resting on her throat, and as she swallowed, she could feel them tightening.

"It was a waltz like any other, Justin," she whispered. She was looking down at her dressing table, staring at her brush and comb and hand mirror. She noticed a few grains of powder that had spilled, and thought, inconsequentially, that she would have to make sure that Liza cleaned it up. She could not lift her eyes and look in the pier glass. If she did, she would meet the hard, bloodshot eyes of her husband. She saw the face of the loving Justin less and less these days. This past year it was not months that went by, or weeks, but days before his transformation into the man who despised her and took pleasure in hurting her. He had to be too drunk to do much tonight, please, please God.

Of course, she didn't really believe in God anymore. How could she? She had promised before Him to love, honor, and obey her husband. Under the laws of God and man, she was helpless. Once, last summer, she had tried to talk with their vicar. She had thought that maybe if he talked to Justin, it might help. But as soon as he realized what she was telling him, he only said in his Sunday-sermon voice that her husband knew far better what was best for their marriage than an outsider, all the while looking at her with distaste, as though she had dropped a squashed, but still wriggling snake on his desk.

But it helped to calm her fear to say, "Please God, please God," even though she now expected no answer. If his representative on earth wouldn't help her, was disgusted by her, then why should God help?

"You smiled up at him the way you used to smile at me, Clare. You are leading him on, just like you led me on. *He* thinks you love him, just like I did."

It did no good to protest or to get angry. To cry. It only made him worse. So she just said, in the even, calm voice she had worked so hard to master: "No, Justin. I have only loved you. I still only love you." Although she was not sure that was still true. But she would make it true, by constant repetition, or else what did her marriage or her life mean?

She felt his hands tighten again, and there was pressure against her windpipe.

"I could kill you very easily, right here, right now, Clare. And unlike Othello, I would have all the right in the world on my side if I choked the life out of my Desdemona."

He had begun threatening her life in the last six months. At first she had thought he was only pushed by the brandy and his insane jealousy into making insane threats. But after he had choked her into unconsciousness twice, she began to fear not only for her sanity, but her life.

She couldn't say anything now, because his hands were pressing so hard against her throat that her vision was beginning to cloud. Then the pressure released. She was alive. He had not choked her to death tonight. She would not be able to go out for a few nights because of her face. He would calm down. He would come in and apologize tomorrow or the next day and she would have a little time to feel safe.

It took Justin three days this time. Clare had kept to her room, with Liza helping her climb stiffly into her bath and bringing her meals up on a tray. The maid's face remained passive and expressionless on these occasions, and she never commented on Clare's bruises. She never expressed any sympathy or anger, the way Martha had. And whenever she saw Justin, she greeted him as if he were exactly what everyone else thought him: an attentive husband. After watching her abigail during the first months of her employment, Clare had decided that Justin, who had dismissed Martha, was most likely paying Liza very well to ignore what was going on.

When her husband finally knocked on her door, Clare was sitting up in bed working on her embroidery. She wasn't very good at needlework, but found the concentration it demanded of her kept her mind off everything else.

Justin's face looked as it always did on these occasions: open, caring, grief-stricken at her appearance. And there was still a part of her that responded to him, who believed him. In fact, Clare knew he meant every word of his abject apology. He *was* sincere, he *did* intend never to drink again, he *did* need and depend upon her. She was certainly, in every way, the center of his life. That was what had been so difficult throughout their marriage: that she believed him. That he was the man she had married. The trouble was, he was not only that man, but someone else. Both were real, she had come to understand. She had married a man who was two different men: one the tender lover, the other, an insanely jealous, abusive tyrant. And the more the latter showed his face, the more Clare wondered if soon the two Justin's would become one, one who would keep his often-stated promise, and choke the life out of her one night.

"Your father called on you today, Clare," her husband announced after the familiar ritual of a tearful apology.

Clare was surprised. Her parents rarely came up for the Season now, and when they did, it was later in the spring. "I wonder why they are here," she said. "In Mama's last letter, she wasn't sure they were coming at all, much less this early."

"Evidently your father has some business to take care of." Justin hesitated. "I told him you were feeling ill, but would call on him in a few days."

Without thinking, Clare felt her nose. The swelling had gone down, and her eye, which was also discolored, was almost back to normal. Justin flinched when she did this, and she reached out for his hand. "I think I will be fine by Wednesday."

"Clare."

"Yes, Justin?"

"I think I am going to make an appointment to see Dr. Shipton. I have heard he has had great success in helping people reduce their dependence on laudanum. Perhaps he can help me with brandy."

This was the first time that Justin had ever admitted that his problem was beyond his own strength or resolve. Clare felt a stirring of hope. Maybe there was a God after all.

"Oh, Justin, I'm sure that he could help you. And I would do anything that you needed me to do to help."

"I know that, Clare," he said quietly.

That night, when he returned to her bed, Justin slowly and tenderly caressed and kissed her. At first, she could not help from shrinking back, and when he felt this, he groaned, and she stiffened in fear.

"I don't blame you for being frightened, Clare. I won't ask you for anything that you don't want to give."

And his restraint had the effect it always had: her fear subsided, and the old feeling of love and passionate response took over. This time, she thought, as they lay there in each other's arms, this time he *means* it.

Chapter Eleven

The Marquess of Howland *had* come up to London on business. But he had also come up because he and his wife were worried about his younger daughter. Although her marriage had disappointed them, it had started off well, and he and the marchioness, after seeing their daughter's happiness, decided perhaps they had been wrong to push Giles Whitton. Justin Rainsborough seemed an excellent husband.

They had been concerned by her appearance last spring, but knew that recovery from a miscarriage could take time. The couple had visited them once and had seemed very happy together. But they had also been expected for the Christmas holidays and had canceled at the last minute in a note from Rainsborough, citing Clare's need to recover from the Little Season and their desire to celebrate the holidays at home.

Clare had never been sickly as a child, and her mother wondered whether she had suffered another miscarriage. "Or perhaps she is increasing again," she told her husband, "and doesn't want to raise our hopes until she is farther along."

But here it was April, and the gossip that had reached them about Clare's appearance indicated she was still in poor health.

After his failed visit to his daughter, the marquess decided it was time to visit the Whittons and see if Clare had confided anything to her old friends.

"The Marquess of Howland, my lord. He is calling for

Lady Sabrina, and when I told him she was out, he asked for you."

Giles looked up from his translation in surprise. Since the Dysarts were old friends of the family, naturally they had seen each other over the past two years. But since the wedding, it had not been often, and Clare's father had never called on Sabrina before.

"Show him in, Henley, and bring us some tea."

"Yes, my lord."

When the door opened to admit the marquess, Giles was surprised to see how he had aged. It was always easy to forget how much older Clare's parents were than his.

"Please sit down, sir."

"Thank you, Giles."

"Would you like some tea? Or perhaps sherry?"

"Tea will be fine, Giles. It is too early for spirits. At least for me. But you go ahead, if you wish."

"I never drink during the day," Giles answered with a smile as the butler handed the marquess his tea. "That will be all, Henley," said Giles, dismissing him.

"You must be wondering why I have come."

Giles smiled. "I confess to some curiosity. You were looking for Sabrina first, I understand."

"Yes. I was hoping that she might help me sort out my concerns about Clare." The marquess hesitated. "It seemed more appropriate to start with Clare's friend. Of course, you were also friends, but . . ."

"But I am also a rejected suitor. Don't worry, I understand, Edmund. I don't think either of us can tell you very much, however. Sabrina has not heard from Clare very often these past two years."

"Wasn't she to visit Devon last summer?"

"It never came off. Clare wrote a note saying she wished to postpone the visit, for she was feeling indisposed."

"I called on my daughter the beginning of this week and was told the same thing. Do you think Clare is seriously ill, and they are both keeping it from us, Giles?"

"To tell you the truth, Edmund, I don't know what to think. Clare never seemed to recover the weight she lost after losing the baby. I had even wondered if she had lost another?"

"If so, her mother and I have not been told. But there is the source of our worry: we have been told so little. There she is, in Devon, and we only get occasional short notes telling us how happy she is. And then we see her or hear from the gossips how unwell she looks. Rainsborough is a very solicitous husband, however, so it seems she is lucky there," he added, and then realizing to whom he was speaking, apologized immediately.

"It is water under the bridge, Edmund," Giles reassured him. "Rainsborough *is* very protective of Clare, and I have been hesitant to approach her too often. And she has made no effort to keep up her friendship with either me or Sabrina, although Sabrina has never quite given up on her."

"I see. Perhaps it is just as well Sabrina wasn't here, then. I shouldn't have bothered either of you," said the marquess, getting up from the sofa.

"Of course you should have," replied Giles. "Perhaps we have held back too much when we shouldn't have. Would you feel better, Edmund, if I sought Clare out and tried to determine whether your worries are groundless?"

The marquess turned toward Giles, his face brightening. "Would you, my boy? Her mother and I . . . we never had the same closeness with Clare as with our older children. She came so late, you see. And her visits to Whitton were so important to her. I have always been sorry . . ."

"So have I, Edmund. But it has been two years, and I have moved on."

"So I hear," said the older man with a smile. "Lucy Kirkman has been after you for years, you know," the marquess replied, happy to tease Giles and lighten the conversation.

"You sound just like my sister! Don't worry, though. I

am not the sort to let a woman catch me unless I want her to!"

Giles knew that Rainsborough usually visited his club every afternoon, and decided to call on Clare when her husband was out. He was admitted by the Rainsboroughs' butler the next afternoon and shown into the drawing room.

"I will send up your card, my lord, and see if Lady Rainsborough is able to see you."

"Thank you."

When the butler returned, however, he offered Giles an apology and explained that Lady Rainsborough was resting. "She has been unwell these past few days and needs her rest before attending Lady Petersham's gala tonight."

Giles frowned. He very much wanted to see Clare alone in her own home, for he felt that was the only way he would get her to open up to him. But he was hardly in a position to insist, so he took the butler's message with good grace and bade him tell his mistress that he hoped for a waltz that evening.

"I will tell her, my lord," said Peters as he showed Giles out.

Unfortunately, Rainsborough was just coming up the street as Giles was leaving.

"Good afternoon, Whitton," he said coldly.

"Good afternoon," said Giles , bowing politely and continuing on his way. With anyone else he would have stayed and chatted and admitted the reason for his visit, but for some reason, Rainsborough's coldness set up his back.

Justin questioned his butler as soon as the door opened.

"Was Lord Whitton here visiting Lady Rainsborough, Peters?"

"Yes, my lord. He called on my mistress, but she told me to tell him she was resting."

Justin's face lightened. "Good. If we are going out tonight, she needs her rest," he said solicitously.

"Yes, my lord." Peters's face may have remained blank as a good butler's should, but the conversation in his head with Rainsborough would hardly have amused his employer. *There he goes again, the kindest husband you would ever want to meet, making sure my lady gets her rest. Making sure no one can see how he treats her!*

Most of the household was of course aware of the situation between their master and mistress. Most of them didn't like Lord Rainsborough. But he had chosen his servants well: men and women who were older or had received a less than glowing reference from their previous employers. None of them was in any position to protest his treatment of Lady Rainsborough. And, after all, they would say to themselves, what a man does with his wife in the privacy of his home is his business, no matter what a rough business it was.

Justin entered Clare's room without knocking. She was sitting by her window reading, and she started when she heard him come in.

"Justin! I didn't expect you back from your club so early."

"Apparently not, since Whitton was here, calling on you."

Clare tried to gauge her husband's mood. She could not smell any liquor on his breath as he came closer, and that was a relief: He sounded angry, but not out of control, thank goodness.

"I was quite surprised when Peters sent up Giles's card," she answered matter-of-factly. "I told him to tell Giles I was resting."

Justin passed his hand over his forehead, and his expression cleared. "I know, Peters told me, Clare, but the thought of you meeting with Whitton privately . . ."

"Which I have never done, Justin," she quietly reassured him.

"I know, I know. Well, I should leave you to get your rest," he said, dropping a kiss on the top of her head.

"Justin? Did you have a chance to schedule an appointment with Dr. Shipton?" Clare asked hesitantly.

"Dr. Shipton? No, not yet, Clare. In fact, I am not even sure I really need to see him after all. I have had no trouble refraining from spirits these last few days."

"I am glad to hear that, Justin, but I would be very happy if you consulted with him anyway."

Her husband waved his hand at her and said impatiently: "I'll think about it, Clare, but don't put any pressure on me. I am competent to judge my own state of mind."

After he left, Clare sat there for a while, her book forgotten in her lap. Why had Giles come calling on her? She had had to turn him away, of course. And thank God, she had, for who knew what would have happened with Justin coming home early. Perhaps Sabrina needed her? But then wouldn't Sabrina have called? Giles had been spending so much of his time with Lucy Kirkman. Perhaps he wanted to tell her of his betrothal before announcing it publicly. Or perhaps he wanted to know why she was avoiding her old friends. That was the most likely reason, she supposed, and therefore she was glad to be able to send him away, for she could hardly give him the real reason.

She felt the knot of fear that was her constant companion tighten in her stomach. It had relaxed a little these past few days because of Justin's decision to seek out medical help. She had allowed hope to revive. Hope that at last the nightmare her marriage had become would be over and the Justin she fell in love with would return to her. Well, Justin had not said he wouldn't go, she reassured herself. He just didn't want to be badgered about it. She would not mention Dr. Shipton for a while. And she would continue to be hopeful.

The Rainsboroughs had become so erratic in their attendance at social functions that Clare's card was rarely full. Giles made sure he made his way over to where she

stood with a group of acquaintances early that evening
and confirmed his waltz. There was no way for Clare to
refuse him, and she tried to tell herself that all would be
well. Justin was not drinking, and she had reassured him
just this afternoon. She did her best to keep away from
the Whittons, but one could hardly turn down an old
friend in public. So she just smiled and let Giles write his
name on her card. She looked around for her husband,
hoping she could catch him and explain, but he was deep
in conversation on the other side of the room. And by the
time she had danced a few sets and looked for him again,
she was dismayed to see him accepting a glass of champagne. But one glass never set him off, she reassured herself, and when she saw him making his way into the card
room, she was relieved. He wasn't hovering over her tonight as much as usual, and if he stayed at the whist table
long enough, she would have already finished her waltz
with Giles.

When Giles came to claim her hand, she gave him a
nervous smile and let him lead her out.

When Giles put his hand around Clare's waist, he was
appalled at how he could feel every rib through her gown.
For a moment, a terrible fear seized him: perhaps she *was*
seriously ill. But when he looked down, he saw a pale
face, not the hectic flush that accompanied consumption,
and so he made himself relax and pay attention to the music.

After the music stopped, he kept Clare's arm through
his, and leaning down, asked if he could have a few minutes alone. Clare's eyes darted desperately around, but
Justin was nowhere in sight, and so she nodded her agreement. Clearly Giles was going to persist, no matter what,
so she might as well get it over with.

There were a few small rooms off each side of the ballroom, and Giles walked Clare over to one and let the door
close behind them.

He sat Clare down on a small sofa, but remained standing. She glanced nervously at the door, and her fingers began pleating the skirt of her gown.

"Giles, did you have something particular you wanted to say to me?" Her voice was tight with tension.

"You are not afraid to be alone with me, are you, Clare?" Giles asked, appalled at how far from the ease of their old friendship they were.

"No, Giles, of course not. I just don't want any gossip to start up." She could hardly tell him it was her husband she feared. Why didn't he get on with it, so she could be back in the ballroom before Justin noticed her absence?

"Sabrina and I have been worried about you, Clare. I know that time changes things, even old friendships, and perhaps it is only that your marriage takes up most of your attention. But you have not looked well this past year, and Sabrina has found it difficult to find enough time with you to ask why."

Clare attempted a casual, almost dismissive tone. "I am of course grateful for your concern, Giles. I must confess that my marriage to Justin has been unfashionably time-consuming, and perhaps I *have* neglected my other relationships. I assure you, though, that I am quite well."

"Your father and mother do not think so."

Clare looked startled. "My parents?"

"Your father called on me the other day to ask me if Sabrina and I knew if you had perhaps had . . . another . . ."

"No, Giles, I have not lost another baby," Clare answered quietly. "I am sorry my father dragged you into what is essentially a private matter."

"Your parents are worried about you, Clare. As are your old friends," he added.

"Their concern is touching, but a few years too late," she answered bitterly. "You may assure my father that I am quite well and very happy, Giles. And now we had best be getting back."

Giles felt utterly frustrated. He had done his best, but Clare was clearly unwilling to open her heart to him or to

anyone. He offered her his hand as she got up, and
brought her back to a small group of mutual acquaintances where he stayed and chatted for a few minutes before excusing himself to seek out his next dance partner.
Neither of them noticed Rainsborough, who had been
standing in the doorway of the card room and seen them
emerge.

Clare felt her husband's hot breath and smelled the
brandy fumes as he leaned over her from behind.

"I think I will get you home early tonight, my dear.
You don't want to tire yourself." His hand gripped her
arm like a vise, but she kept her face empty even though
she could feel the pain of old bruises.

"We ladies are always envious of your wife, Lord
Rainsborough," commented one of the group surrounding
Clare. "She is very fortunate to have such an attentive
and observant spouse. I hope she appreciates you as much
as you deserve," Lady Brett teased.

Rainsborough smiled his most charming smile as Clare
made her excuses to their hostess, but said nothing to his
wife as he led her to the door and hailed their carriage.
He took Clare's cloak from the footman and draped it
over her shoulders himself. When his hands brushed her
throat, she shuddered. He must have been drinking the
whole time he was in the card room, she thought. Had he
seen her come out of the anteroom with Giles? Oh, God,
she hoped not. But what other reason did he have to rush
her off so early in the evening?

Chapter Twelve

"Get up."

Clare uncurled herself slowly and then pulled herself again into a fetal position as she felt Justin's boot against her back.

"Get up, slut."

Clare bit down on her hand as Justin kicked her again. There was nothing she could do to protect her back, nothing she could do at all except keep herself from screaming in pain by biting her own fingers to distract herself.

Justin reached down and grasped her by the hair.

"I said, get up, bitch."

Clare allowed herself to be pulled into a sitting position, and as Justin let go of her hair, she pushed herself up with her hands and stood on shaky legs with her back to the mantel. She hoped her ordeal was almost over. Usually Justin's kicks meant that the beating was coming to an end. Although these past few weeks, he had started choking her. She shivered.

"What were you and Whitton doing in the anteroom, my lady whore?"

Clare said nothing. She had already given her usual calm explanation and denial in the carriage, which never convinced him anyway. He had pushed her into the library as soon as they arrived home and sent the butler up to bed.

Here she was, Lady Rainsborough, being beaten sense-less by her husband while their servants slept comfortably on the third floor. They all knew about it, of course, but it was none of their business after all.

She watched fearfully as Justin clenched and unclenched his hands against his side as though he were fighting to keep them from going around her throat. She backed up against the mantel, and his hand reached out and grabbed her neck. All of a sudden, he let her go and walked over to the desk. Was it over at last? She was afraid to hope so.

He was opening a polished wooden case, and she almost dropped where she stood when she saw it contained a pair of dueling pistols. Please God, he wasn't going to challenge Giles. Oh, God, if she were responsible for Giles's death, she would kill herself.

"Lovely, aren't they, Clare?" Justin lifted one of the pistols and sighted down the barrel. "I am an excellent shot, as you know."

She nodded.

"And Whitton? Well, I have seen him at Manton's. Would you like to have us fight over you, Clare. Is this what this is all about?"

"No, Justin, no," she answered in a low, shaking voice.

"I think you are telling the truth. Because you would not wish me to kill your lover, would you, Clare?"

"He is not my lover. You know that, Justin."

"What I know is that you are a sneaking, conniving woman, rank as a bitch in heat, Clare. But I will give you a chance. Admit that you have been Whitton's lover and promise never to see him again, and I will not challenge him."

It would be hard, but there was obviously no choice. And she hadn't really seen Giles much in the last year, so what would there be to miss?

"I promise I will never speak to him or see him again, Justin."

Justin drew next to her and slowly ran the barrel of the pistol down her cheek. "That is only part of what I asked, Clare."

"I swear I will never see him again, Justin. But how can I tell you we have been lovers when it is not the truth?"

Rainsborough pressed the pistol against her temple. "Tell the truth, Clare, and I will let you and Whitton live. Lie to me again, and I will shoot you now and take the other pistol and kill him in the middle of a waltz, if needs be."

She knew he meant it. He had almost choked her to death twice already. She didn't care about her own life anymore. In fact, she almost would have welcomed the release. But to let Giles die?

"All right, Justin. But you must swear to me that if I tell you the truth and keep my promise, you will let Giles alone."

Rainsborough lowered the pistol and said in a quiet, almost tender voice, "I swear it Clare. Once I am satisfied, this need never happen again."

Clare took a deep breath and said: "Yes, Justin, you are right. Giles and I have been lovers. But I swear, as God is my witness, that I will never see or speak to him again." Forgive me, Giles, she thought, for damaging your name and for the hurt this may cause you.

Rainsborough dropped the pistol on the rug. "So you *have* been lying to me all this time," he whispered fiercely.

"Yes, Justin."

He grabbed her by the neck, and her eyes widened in fear.

"Justin, I did what you asked," she said desperately. "You must keep your promise."

"I only promised this scene would never happen again, Clare. And it won't," he added as he tightened his hand around her throat.

Clare backed away, but it was foolish to even imagine she could get away. She felt she was leading him on and could feel the pressure on her windpipe and her breath being cut off. He was leaning into her, and her back was now bent over the desk. He was going to kill her at last, she thought. Why not let him? Her legs buckled, and she began to sink down, down, toward death. It would be so easy ... she couldn't fight him ... it was over ...

As her knees gave way under her, she instinctively reached back to keep her balance, and her hand brushed the corner of something heavy and cold. Everything in her had been saying, "Yes, yes, just let go, Clare. Just sink down and it will be quickly over, and you will be free." And then, from some place in her that she didn't know existed, came a "No." She couldn't scream it, because his hands were choking off her voice and breath. But it rose and rose until she thought it would burst through the top of her head. "No, no, no." Her hand closed around the neck of a brass candlestick and in the last moment before she lost consciousness, she raised it and brought it down on Justin's head as hard as she could.

He released her instantly and slumped to the floor. She stood there, gasping for breath, her whole being still silently shouting, "No!" Oh, my God, he was moving, he was getting up, he would come after her again, he would kill her this time. She didn't think, she just moved. The case was open, the pistol was lying in it, she lifted it, and as he began to rise, arms open, she walked toward him, as though into his embrace, pressed the pistol against his chest, and fired. He fell back, eyes wide open in surprise. His left arm twitched, and Clare, terrified that he was going to come after her again, scrambled over to where the other pistol lay on the floor. He groaned, and seemed to be trying to pull himself up. Clare approached him slowly, and pressing the other pistol against his temple, fired. He slumped down in front of her and lay still.

"Oh, God," she whispered. "Oh, God, I don't know how to reload them. What if he wakes up?" She looked around desperately and grabbed the poker from the fireplace. She stood over her husband, dress drenched in his blood, hands and body shaking, saying, "No, no," over and over again. And when Peters, who had been awakened by the shots, came into the library, he saw his mistress standing over her husband's body, brandishing the poker.

"Lady Rainsborough?"

Clare looked up for one minute and then back down, as though afraid her husband would attack her if she relaxed her vigilance even for one moment.

"Did you see him move, Peters? He is going to kill me. Don't let him get up again. I won't let him kill me," she added, gripping the poker more tightly.

The butler looked at his mistress and down at Rainsborough. The master was not moving. The master would obviously never move again. The master was well and truly dead.

He walked over to Clare and gently took the poker from her hand.

"You will not need this, my lady. Lord Rainsborough is dead."

"No, no, he can't be. I saw him move after I shot him."

"I think you must say nothing, my lady," said the butler as he led her over to the sofa. "Until I summon a Runner."

"Yes, a Runner could stop him," whispered Clare. Then her face crumpled. "But I can't tell him what happened."

Peters patted her hand reassuringly. "Of course you can, my lady. You can tell him it was a dreadful accident. Will you be all right if I leave you alone for a few minutes?"

Clare nodded, and the butler left to awaken a footman and send him off to Bow Street.

Clare pulled at her dress. It was wet and sticky and uncomfortable. And red. Surely she had been wearing her green silk this evening? She looked down at Justin and shuddered. He was lying very still, and his clothes were stained the same red as her own. How strange. She swallowed and winced. Why was her throat so sore? They had come home early from the ball. Justin had pulled her into the library ... Her head was pounding and all after that was a blank. All she knew was the terror. Justin was going to kill her. But Justin wasn't moving, so maybe she was safe until Peters returned.

She had no idea how long she sat there watching her husband closely for any movement at all. She heard voices in the hallway and then the butler was back, accompanied by a Bow Street Runner.

"I found her standing over him with the poker," Peters said in a low voice.

The Runner surveyed the scene. Lord Rainsborough lay on a red and blue Turkey carpet with a hole in his left temple and another through his chest. Lady Rainsborough sat on the leather sofa in a bloodstained silk gown, looking up at him in confusion and fear.

"You will not let him kill me, will you?" she asked fearfully.

She was either in a state of shock or she was a damned good actress, thought the Runner.

"No, no, of course not, Lady Rainsborough. Please watch your master for a moment, Peters," said the runner in order to reassure her. "May I ask you a few questions about tonight?"

Clare nodded.

"It appears from your evening dress that you and your husband were out tonight?"

Clare nodded again.

"May I ask where, my lady?"

"We attended the Petersham's ball."

"I see. And when did you leave the ball?"

Clare frowned. "I think it was about one. We left early, you see."

"And you came straight home?"

"Yes."

"And then what happened, Lady Rainsborough?"

Clare twisted her fingers together and plucked at the

blood-soaked bodice of her gown. "I . . . I can't remember."

"You are afraid your husband wants to kill you, my lady?" The Runner looked at her for a long moment. "You have bruises on your throat, and your face is swollen. Was it your husband who did that?"

Clare only looked at him blankly.

"Has he done this before, Lady Rainsborough?"

"Done what?" she whispered.

"Beaten you."

"Justin? Justin is a most loving and affectionate husband," she said in a calm, detached voice. "He would never hurt me."

The Runner rose and addressed the butler. "Clearly your mistress is in a state of shock, Peters. Wake her abigail so she can see her up to bed. I'll summon another Runner and make sure the house is guarded all night."

"Is my lady under arrest, then?" asked the butler, horrified to be employed in a household with such a scandal breaking around him.

"Of a sort. It certainly looks as though she killed Lord Rainsborough. But she is in no condition to be brought before anyone tonight. And I wouldn't want to see a lady like that in Newgate anyway. I will just make sure she stays here safe and sound, until a coroner's inquest. Does your mistress have family in London? Or a close friend? Someone who could be here when she awakes?"

"Her father and mother just arrived in town," said Peters, "but they are both quite old, and it would be a dreadful shock . . ."

"Surely she has some woman friend?"

"Lady Sabrina Whitton," the butler answered hesitantly. "But Lady Rainsborough has kept very much to herself this last year or so."

"But they were once close?"

"Oh, yes."

"Well, summon Lady Sabrina in the morning. Your mistress needs someone with her to help her out of the state

of shock she is in. I will get clearer answers out of her
when that happens."

"Yes, sir."

"Has Lord Rainsborough any relations who should be
notified?"

"Just a distant cousin in Lancashire, sir."

"Well, best let the family man of business take care of
notifying him. I will have the body removed in the morning."

Peters blanched. "Yes, sir."

Sabrina, who was an early riser, was just getting
dressed when their head footman knocked on her door.
She looked over at her abigail questioningly and motioned for her to answer it.

"Whatever is it, William," said the maid, opening the
door less than halfway. "My lady is just getting ready for
breakfast."

William cleared his throat nervously. "I have a note
from the Rainsborough household," he said. "Their butler
delivered it himself and said it is urgent."

The abigail put out her hand. "All right. I will give it
to her."

"The Rainsborough's butler delivered this?" asked
Sabrina, looking at the folded square of paper in her
hand. She was almost afraid to open it. Something must
have happened to Clare.

"Yes, my lady."

Sabrina sat down at her dressing table so that her maid
could do up the last tapes of her morning dress, and
opened the note. "Lady Sabrina, Lord Rainsborough has
been shot. Lady Rainsborough has need of a friend." Peters.

"Surely this must be some joke," muttered Sabrina.
"But you say Peters delivered it himself?"

"Yes, William said he was very insistent that you get it
right away."

Sabrina stood up suddenly, jerking the last tape out of her abigail's hands.

"Have a footman pour me some tea. I will be going to Lady Rainsborough's directly."

"Yes, my lady."

Sabrina was out the door and down the hall, knocking on her brother's door.

"Giles, Giles. Are you awake?" She could hear him groaning. He had come in late last night, and she had seen him drink more than was his wont after his tête-a-tête with Clare.

"Giles!"

"All right, Sabrina, all right. This had better be important." Giles opened the door and looked both annoyed and bleary-eyed as he tied his dressing gown together.

"The Rainsborough butler delivered this a few minutes ago," said Sabrina, thrusting the note at him.

Giles looked up from the paper with a puzzled look on his face that would have been almost comical under any other circumstances. "Rainsborough dead? Shot? Was it intruders?"

"I don't know, Giles, but clearly I must get over to Clare immediately."

"I will go with you," he said instantly.

"I think it would be better if you told her parents, Giles. No doubt the servants are already gossiping, and I wouldn't want the Dysarts to hear it thirdhand."

Giles frowned. "I suppose you are right. Please give Clare my sympathy."

"I will," said Sabrina.

Chapter Thirteen

As she turned onto St. James Street, Sabrina saw that there was a Runner standing in front of the Rainsborough town house. It must have been attempted robbery, she thought. Perhaps Justin had surprised a burglar in the act. The Runner moved in front of the door as Sabrina came up the stairs and asked her to identify herself.

"I am Lady Sabrina Whitton," she answered frostily. "I was summoned early this morning to be with Lady Rainsborough."

"All right, my lady. No need to get so high in the instep. I was told to keep everyone out except for my lady's friend. Which is you," he added with a smile as he opened the door for her.

Peters was almost effusive in his greetings when Sabrina entered the hallway. "Thank you so much for coming, Lady Sabrina, This has been a horrible ordeal, horrible. I will show you up."

As Sabrina mounted the stairs, she saw another Runner off to her left standing in front of what she thought was the library door, and she shivered. That must have been where the intruder broke in, she thought. That could have been where Justin was killed.

Peters knocked softly on his mistress's door, and Liza opened it.

"Lady Sabrina Whitton to see my lady," he announced in a solemn whisper.

"Come in, Lady Sabrina," said Liza with a relieved smile. "I am very worried about Lady Rainsborough."

Sabrina walked very quickly past Clare's abigail, eager to take Clare in her arms and hear the whole dreadful story, and then froze mid-way.

"I can't get her into bed, Lady Sabrina," whispered Liza behind her.

Clare was standing to the left of her bed, back to the window, holding a small iron fireplace shovel in her hands. She was still in her green silk ball gown, or what had been green silk. It was now stained so horribly that Sabrina gasped.

"I could not get her to take it off, my lady," whispered Liza.

"Clare," Sabrina said softly. "I am here, my dear. I am so sorry that Justin has been hurt."

Clare lifted the shovel in front of her. "I will *not* let him kill me," she said fiercely. "I will not."

"You are safe, Clare. There are two Runners here. The intruder will not come back."

"Justin?"

"I don't know yet, my dear, but I think he is dead," said Sabrina gently.

"But I saw him move," said Clare in a terrified whisper.

"Then, perhaps he is not dead," replied Sabrina, reassuringly.

Clare began to shake. "If he is not, then I am."

Sabrina looked over to Liza, bewildered by her friend's words.

"The master is dead, Lady Sabrina. I keep telling her that, but she doesn't seem to believe me."

"But why then . . .?"

"Oh, it was no robber, my lady. It was Lady Rainsborough who killed her husband."

Sabrina looked at Clare and really saw her for the first time, not just the bloodstained gown. Her friend's face was red and bruised, and her lips were swollen. There were livid marks around Clare's throat, she realized, just as though someone had been trying to strangle her. And if there had been no intruder, then Clare was terrified of Justin. Of her own husband.

Sabrina took a deep breath. "Liza, could you please bring some hot water for Lady Rainsborough's bath."

"I tried to get her to take that gown off, but she wouldn't, my lady," said the Liza, eager to explain that she, Lady Rainsborough's abigail, had not been negligent.

"Perhaps I can persuade her."

"Yes, my lady."

Sabrina walked over to her friend. "Clare, will you let me help you take off this gown?"

Clare backed away. "But I saw him move, Sabrina."

"Clare, if I went down and . . . saw Justin dead, would that reassure you?"

"Would you, Sabrina? Would you make sure he is dead?" Tears started running down Clare's cheeks. Sabrina was here. Sabrina would make sure Justin couldn't get up from where he lay and begin to choke her again.

"Yes, Clare. But you must sit down and rest while I am gone."

Clare shook her head.

"You will be all right alone for a few minutes?"

Clare nodded.

"I will be right back," Sabrina assured her.

Sabrina made her way down the stairs and approached Peters. "Lady Rainsborough is fearful that her husband is still alive."

"Lord Rainsborough is most certainly dead, Lady Sabrina."

"I promised her I would see for myself, Peters."

The butler frowned. "She won't sit, she won't bathe, she is in a state of shock, Peters."

"It is not a pleasant sight, Lady Sabrina," he warned her.

"Neither is Lady Rainsborough."

The butler approached the Runner guarding the library

and then summoned Sabrina. "You can go in for only a minute, my lady."

The Runner pushed open the library door. Justin Rainsborough lay on his back, eyes wide open as though searching the ceiling for an answer to his predicament. His shirt was as horribly stained as Clare's dress, and there was a dueling pistol on the carpet beside him.

"They will be by for the body shortly, my lady. Have you seen enough?" asked the Runner.

Sabrina, who was holding her hand to her mouth, nodded.

"Are you all right, my lady?"

"Yes, yes."

"Get the lady a chair," said the Runner sharply, after looking more closely at Sabrina's face.

Sabrina sank into it gratefully, and put her head between her legs for a few minutes.

"I am sorry, Officer. I am not usually this hen-hearted."

The Runner patted her awkwardly on the shoulder. "Now, now, my lady, it is a hard sight for anyone not used to it. And even for those of us who are. The lady did a fine job on her husband."

"Then it *was* Clare?"

"Found standing over him with a fireplace poker, worrying that he was going to get up and attack her!"

Sabrina shuddered. "Oh, God, and we never even suspected that anything was wrong."

"Happens all the time, my lady."

"This?" asked Sabrina, gesturing toward Justin's body.

"Well, usually it is the wife lying there dead," admitted the Runner. " 'But no one ever suspected, Officer,' or even more likely, 'But it were *his* wife.' "

Sabrina stood up and swayed.

"Are you sure you are all right?"

"Yes, yes. I must get back to Clare."

Clare was still standing vigilant, but her arms relaxed a little when Sabrina returned.

"Did you see him? Is he truly dead?"

"Yes, Clare, I saw him. He will never threaten you again."

Clare drew a deep, ragged breath and lowered her arm. "Threaten me? I wish it had only been threats," she added with an ironic smile.

The bath had been filled, and the water was steaming. "Come, my dear, let me help you off with your dress." Clare stood quietly while Sabrina undid her tapes and let the gown slip down around her feet. She lifted her arms like a child as her friend pulled the underslip over her head and then lowered them as Sabrina undid her stays.

Sabrina had been shocked to see Rainsborough's body, but almost more horrible was seeing Clare's. Her friend was thin to the point of emaciation, and both her belly and her back were discolored with bruises, old and new. As Sabrina helped Clare into the bath and began to sponge her down gently, she realized that the marks on her friend's body could only have been made by something harder than a fist: something like the toe of a boot. As she squeezed warm, soapy water down Clare's back and watched it run down, she could feel the tears slipping down her own cheeks.

"How long has this been going on, Clare?"

Clare was silent, and Sabrina looked into her eyes and repeated her question gently.

"I don't know. From the beginning, I guess," replied Clare in a sleepy, faraway voice.

"Why didn't you tell me, Clare?"

"Why, what could you have done, Brina?" Clare answered calmly, almost dreamily.

Killed Rainsborough myself, thought Sabrina.

The hot bath and a cup of hot chocolate laced with rum that Sabrina ordered made Clare relaxed and sleepy enough so that when Sabrina put her to bed, she fell asleep almost immediately. Sabrina sat by her side for almost an hour until Peters knocked softly and informed her that lords Whitton and Howland had arrived and were inquiring after Clare.

"I will be right down, Peters." Sabrina pulled the covers higher around Clare's shoulders and gently brushed her friend's hair back from her face as though she were a child. "Come, Liza, sit here and stay with her until she wakes."

The marquess was sitting in the morning room looking very old and very tired. Giles was pacing the carpet when Sabrina walked in and rushed over as soon as he saw her.

"Where is she, Sabrina? Is she all right? Was she injured also?"

"She is asleep now, Giles."

"And Rainsborough?" asked the marquess.

"Lord Rainsborough is indeed dead, my lord."

"Does Clare know yet?" Giles asked worriedly.

Sabrina's laugh was mirthless. "Yes, Giles, Clare knows. Now. Although at first she was terrified that he wasn't." Sabrina sank down into the nearest chair.

Giles stood in front of her, nonplussed. "I am not sure what you mean, Sabrina? Why would Clare want her husband dead?"

"Oh, Giles, sit down," Sabrina replied with a tired sigh. "We have all been so blind. Clare is responsible for her husband's death. There was no intruder, no burglar. There was only Clare."

"You are quite mad, Sabrina," said her brother angrily. "Clare is too gentle to hurt anyone, much less a beloved husband. A loving husband."

"A not so loving husband, Giles. A husband who beat her . . . and kicked her. And, from what I can see, must have been trying to choke her to death."

The marquess buried his face in his hands. "Oh, my poor child."

"I do not understand, Sabrina. Rainsborough doted on Clare. Everyone knew that. Why, he was overprotective, if anything."

"I am not sure I understand, either, Giles. But I have

seen the bruises on Clare's body and on her throat. And I saw her face this morning, Giles. She was terrified. She must have seen him move after she shot him, and she wouldn't even take her gown off until I promised to see for myself that Justin was dead and not going to come after her again." Sabrina shuddered.

"My God, Brina, you didn't see him, did you?"

"I had to, Giles. It was the only way to get her out of that bloody gown and into bed. And that, by the way, was not a profanity but the literal truth," she added with a bleak smile.

Giles put his arm around her and drew her close, and Sabrina let herself cry softly against his shoulder.

"Where is Clare now?" asked the marquess.

"In bed, asleep. I gave her a hot bath and some chocolate liberally laced with rum. But you should probably call a doctor for her, for I am sure she was in a deep state of shock."

"I will take her home with me," Clare's father declared, rising slowly from his chair. He came over to Sabrina and awkwardly patted her on the shoulder. "Thank you for being such a good friend, my dear."

Sabrina put her hand on his arm and replied: "I hardly deserve your thanks, my lord. Poor Clare has been absolutely alone in this ordeal for two years. I should have known something was wrong."

"No, no, my dear. Everything is much clearer now, isn't it, Giles? Her 'illnesses,' her pulling away, her husband wanting her all to himself." The marquess's face became hard. "I am glad she shot him. Had I known what he was doing to her, I would have done it myself."

Clare's father was back within minutes, shaking with indignation and fear. "They won't let me take her home, Giles. There are two Runners here to make sure she doesn't 'escape!' According to them, she is a suspected felon and we are lucky she is not in Newgate!"

"Sit down, Edmund, sit down. There is no sense in

your becoming overwrought," said Giles, leading the marquess over to a chair by the fireplace.

"We must do something, Giles," said Sabrina. "It is obvious that she was in fear for her life. No one could condemn her for defending herself."

"Rainsborough was her husband, Sabrina. He had every legal right to beat his wife."

Sabrina flushed with anger. "Giles!"

"I mean legally, Sabrina. And we all know that Lord Tarnas occasionally physically 'chastises' his wife and no one thinks twice about it. After all, it is considered a private matter."

"How can you be saying these things, Giles?"

"I am merely trying to point out that to some people a husband's absolute authority over his wife is acceptable. Indeed, society and the law take it for granted."

"Do they take bruises on the belly and back for granted? Bruises that could only come from vicious kicking for granted? I would take you both up to see her, except that I don't want her disturbed. Her throat has his finger marks imprinted on it, Giles!"

"And it is all my fault," said her brother quietly. "I insisted upon seeing her alone last night, even though she didn't want me to. She knew what he would do to her, her oh-so loving husband."

"There is no use for self-recrimination now, Giles," said the marquess. "I am her father, and I should have seen what was going on. But we must put all our energy into finding someone who can prove her innocence."

Giles was silent for a moment. "Do you have anyone in mind, sir?"

The marquess shook his head. "The family solicitor has no experience in preparing criminal cases, but perhaps he knows someone else who could do the job."

"I was thinking of an old school friend of mine," offered Giles. "Andrew More. He is the younger brother of Viscount Avery."

"Does he have any experience in . . . criminal cases," asked Clare's father. It was hard even to say the word.

Giles smiled his first real smile of the morning. "Yes. He is a sort of black sheep in the family as a matter of fact. They had hoped that he would become a solicitor to some Lord So and So instead of a barrister. I don't think his father ever knew Andrew intended to try cases. He does do enough work for the wealthy to earn a very good living. But he is fascinated by criminal work and takes on a number of charity cases. He likes defending the underdog. And I'm sure he knows a few experienced solicitors who can help prepare the case."

"Will he take Clare on, do you think?"

"I will see him this afternoon, sir, and do my best to convince him."

Chapter Fourteen

Andrew More looked around his office in despair. Unfortunately his new clerk was no more organized than his employer. The books that he had been using last week were still piled up on his desk, with slips of paper sticking out, marking the cases he was interested in. His desk was cluttered with briefs. And although his usual way of working was to create a small amount of chaos around him while focusing intently on the task at hand, even he had a hard time ignoring this mess.

He was very grateful, then, to have a visitor announced, and when he heard Giles's name, went directly into the front office to greet him.

"Giles! What an unexpected pleasure. Come in, come in. Bring us some coffee, Jepson, will you please?"

Giles, whose mood was far from light under the circumstances, looked around and laughed out loud. Andrew's office looked just like his rooms at Oxford years ago. It was obvious his friend could still ignore everything around him when he was intent upon his work.

"Don't laugh, Giles," said Andrew, throwing up his hands in despair and lifting Blackstone's journal off the most comfortable chair so that Giles could sit down. "It is too much, even for me today. And my new clerk is excellent in many ways, but organization is neither of our strong points. But enough of my disorder. It is good to see you."

Giles smiled. "And you." And it was, even under such circumstances. Andrew's presence had always lifted his spirits. His friend had the enviable capacity to throw himself, heart and soul, into his work, and at the same time, appreciate the absurdities of life. He was a very dedicated man, Andrew More, and with his dark hair and thick eyebrows, could appear intense and brooding when involved in untangling a legal intricacy. But then, when his problem was resolved and his frown smoothed away, he went from looking like a Gothic hero to a lighthearted gypsy. He had always been a wonderful foil to Giles's more evenly serious temperament.

"I have not seen you anywhere this Season, Andrew. In fact, your mother was remarking upon your absence only the other night."

Andrew groaned. "So my mother sent you over to drag me off to a ball or two? She and my older brother keep hoping that if they introduce me to every elderly earl in need of a family lawyer, I will become respectable. They should know better by now, Giles. And if they think any Society mama is going to let her daughter within ten feet of a youngest son, they are more foolish than I could have imagined."

"Actually, I was asking your mother about you, Andrew. I've missed your company. And no, your family didn't send me. I am here to ask your advice and perhaps help in a very serious matter."

At that moment the clerk knocked and came in with a tray of coffee and fresh rolls. "Put them down over . . . well, wherever you can find the room, Jepson. Thank you."

When the door closed again, Andrew poured a cup for Giles. "Here. Now that I look at you, I can see you need this. What is wrong, Giles?"

"Justin Rainsborough was shot to death last night. By his wife."

Andrew choked on his coffee. "You are bamming me, Giles.

Clare Dysart murdered her husband? Clare, who wouldn't say boo to a goose?"

Giles fingers tightened around his cup handle. "I know you were never overly fond of Clare, Andrew," he said stiffly.

"I never disliked her, Giles. I just always thought you needed a stronger woman. Someone more like your sister."

"One Sabrina is enough in anyone's life!"

"And she chose Rainsborough over you. That was another thing I confess I have held against her."

"Well, she has paid for it more than anyone should," said Giles, so grimly that Andrew put his coffee cup down and instantly responded.

"I apologize, Giles. Here I am being flippant and unsympathetic. What do you need of me?"

"I need you to defend Clare."

"Has she been charged? Arrested?"

Giles hesitated. "Not as far as I know. Not formally, anyway. There are two Runners at the house, and it is clear that she will not be allowed to leave. Not that she is in any condition to."

"That is good news. Did she confess to the murder?"

"She didn't have to. Evidently she was found standing over Rainsborough's body brandishing a poker, terrified that she *hadn't* killed him."

"But she had?"

"Clare shot him in the head and chest with his own dueling pistols."

Andrew lifted his eyebrows. "Then I guess there is no way to make the argument that she thought he was an intruder?"

"Hardly."

"And why are *you* coming to me, Giles, and not her father?" he asked quietly.

"Clare's father doesn't know anyone involved in criminal law." Giles hesitated. "And I feel responsible."

"How so?"

"It seems . . . evidently Rainsborough was not doting but insanely jealous and controlling. And violent, very violent. Sabrina and I had been worried about Clare. She has pulled away from everyone. I insisted on seeing her alone at the Petershams' ball, even though she didn't want to. I think that set the whole thing off."

And, of course, you still love her, thought Andrew, looking over at his friend's set, closed face.

"From what little Sabrina could gather, he has been"— Giles swallowed hard—"beating Clare for at least a year. Perhaps longer. We really don't know. She was beaten last night. Sabrina has seen her. Surely you could argue self-defense?"

"It is a very tricky case, Giles. After all, a man has the right to beat his wife."

"But surely not to kill his wife, Andrew."

"We would have to show that she was in real fear for her life, Giles. Not an easy thing to do."

"And if you can't?"

"If I can't . . ." Andrew let the words hang there between them.

Giles shuddered. "Surely she would not hang, Andrew. A woman? A countess?"

"I am afraid she would be lucky to hang, Giles. The punishment for a servant who kills his master or a wife who kills her husband is the same as for petty treason: being burned at the stake."

"What!"

"It is still the law. Of course, no one has been burned in the last fifty years or so. But the statute still exists."

"Oh, my God. Clare." Giles buried his face in his hands.

Andrew stood up and put his hand on Giles's shoulder. "I will do what I can, Giles. The sooner I talk to Clare, the better."

"She was in shock, according to Sabrina. She is sleeping now."

"I'll come by this afternoon, then."

Giles lifted his face. "Thank you, Andrew. If anyone can do this, you can."

"I will do my best." Giles stood up to go. "And Giles . . ."

"Yes?"

"Clare's father hired me. Sabrina can visit Clare and keep you in touch. I will do so also. But you must stay away."

Giles started to protest.

"I am not concerned about gossip, Giles. Or at least, only in so much as it impinges on the case. There can be no suspicion of collusion between you and Clare."

"I see," replied Giles stiffly.

"For God's sake, Giles, I know there was no reason for Rainsborough's jealousy, man. I am telling you this as a lawyer."

"Oh, God, Andrew, I hope you can help her."

And so do I, thought More as he watched Giles leave. So do I.

Giles sent a message to Sabrina telling her that he had spoken to Andrew and that the lawyer would visit Clare later that afternoon. He asked his sister to offer his sympathy to Clare and explained why he could not do so in person.

When Sabrina read his note, she frowned. Clare needed all the support she could get. Why was Andrew More treating Giles almost as though he was a guilty party.

Clare had slept the morning and noontime away. When she finally awoke, dull-eyed from the aftereffects of her evening and the rum, Sabrina was next to her.

"How are you feeling, my dear?"

Clare was puzzled for a moment by Sabrina's presence. Justin would not like to have Sabrina Whitton by her bedside. Justin would be angry, and she would have to placate him. Justin might start drinking and . . . Then she remembered. Justin was dead. Sabrina had promised her that. She sank back against the pillows.

"Would you like a cup of tea, Clare? Perhaps some toast?"

Clare nodded. She realized she was very thirsty, and when she swallowed, her throat hurt. She put her hand up to her neck, as though to hide the bruises when she remembered why.

"I know what he did, Clare," said Sabrina softly.

Clare let her hand drop back on the covers.

"I saw the bruises last night when I helped you bathe. Was this why you kept us all away?"

Clare flushed and turned her face away. After two years of hiding it, now everyone would know that Justin beat her. That she had been helpless to stop him. That somehow, she wasn't sure how, it was all her fault.

She winced as the back of her head touched the headboard, and suddenly she saw Justin's hands holding her and banging her head against the mantel. Then the scene, which had flashed suddenly into her mind, was gone. Surely that had happened last night? She could feel the pressure of other memories pushing like a river against a lock, but she was unable or unwilling, she wasn't sure which, to release them.

What was Sabrina asking her? Was this why she had kept her friends away? How could she answer that? How could she possibly explain to anyone what her life had been like?

Sabrina patted her hand. "It is all right, Clare. You don't have to say anything. Here is Liza with some tea."

Clare put all her attention on the familiar ritual. Would she like sugar? Yes. A piece of toast? Thank you. The first swallow hurt her throat, but as the tea began to work its magic, she savored each sip, as though it were her first time tasting it. Perhaps it was only the stimulating effect of the tea, but somewhere deep inside her, she was beginning to feel alive again in a way she hadn't for two years.

Sabrina had been silent, but after the cups had been cleared, she said hesitantly: "I received a note from Giles, Clare. He has called on an old school friend. Andrew More."

Clare was puzzled. Why was Sabrina telling her something so inconsequential?

"Do you remember his name?"

Clare shook her head.

"He is the youngest son of the Earl of Collinworth. Brother to Lord Avery. He is a barrister."

So Giles had called on an old friend, a barrister and sent a note to Sabrina who was sitting here by her bedside to tell her that? Clare knew there was some meaning in this, something to do with her, but she couldn't quite make the connection.

Sabrina had been hoping that mentioning Andrew would be self-explanatory. That Clare would understand why Giles was sending him. But she could see from the questioning look on her face that Clare was still at a loss.

"Clare," she said quietly but firmly, "you were found standing over Justin, terrified that he was still alive. There is a Runner downstairs who is here to make sure you don't leave the house. There will have to be some sort of . . . inquiry." Please God, it wouldn't go to trial, prayed Sabrina to herself. "You will need legal advice."

The river was pushing hard against the lock—so hard that Clare felt she would be swept away if any water were released. Terrible things had happened. But she couldn't look at them. Not now. Not yet.

"Please . . . no," she whispered.

Sabrina grasped her hand. "Oh, Clare, he must see you and find out what happened. But I will stay with you, dear, and send him away if it gets to be too much."

Andrew More was not looking forward to his meeting with Clare. He had met her twice on summer visits to the Whittons while Giles and he were on holiday from university, and despite his friend's obvious love for her, he had been unimpressed. Clare had seemed nice enough, and certainly pretty enough, but she lacked a certain something . . . energy, personality . . . Andrew couldn't quite put his finger on it. Of course, it could have been only that she was not Sabrina.

It had been a cool, cloudy morning when Giles had visited his chambers. It had turned into a clear, warm day, and Andrew, who had chosen to walk to the Rainsboroughs' town house, was hot and sweaty by the time he arrived.

The butler had obviously been expecting him, and it only took a few minutes with the Runners, whom Andrew knew quite well, to establish that he would likely be acting as Clare's counsel and needed to interview her privately.

"You may tell Lady Rainsborough her lawyer's here," said one of the Runners to an obviously annoyed Peters. It was galling to the butler to have his authority diminished, but he could hardly challenge an officer of the law.

A few minutes later, Peters admitted Sabrina into the drawing room, where Andrew was waiting.

"Sabrina, it is delightful to see you again," said Andrew, standing as she entered. "I did not realize you were still here."

"Thank you for coming so quickly, Andrew. Please sit down." Sabrina had only seen Andrew a few times this Season, and the flicker of attraction that was always activated by his presence made her notice, almost without her wanting to, the way his hair was damply curling at the ends, and the odd way his eyebrows drew together when he was intent upon something.

"Is Lady Rainsborough available?"

"She doesn't want to see you, Andrew. She is in a very vulnerable state. I am sorry for your trouble, but I think it best if you come back in a few days."

"A few days? In a few days they will be holding a coroner's inquest, Sabrina. Whether she wants to or not, your friend needs to talk to me. And she was not so fragile last night, was she?"

Sabrina looked at Andrew in amazement. "I beg your pardon, Andrew, did Giles not tell you of the situation?"

"He told me Lady Rainsborough shot her husband with his own dueling pistols." Andrew's tone softened. "He also told me that it seems possible it was in self-defense."

"Clare had been brutally beaten. And it is clear to me that it was not for the first time."

"The law allows a man to beat his wife, Sabrina."

"If you are only here to quote the law to me and Clare, then you might as well leave right now," Sabrina said, furious at his insensitivity.

"I am a lawyer, Sabrina, so it is natural for me to quote the law," said Andrew, with a devilish twinkle in his eye. "I am only trying to point out to you that Lady Rainsborough needs to convince the coroner's jury and the coroner that, despite his rights under law, she had reason enough to defend herself from her husband's attacks. Under law, a wife is essentially her husband's property, and he can do what he likes with his own, if I may take the part of the devil's advocate for a moment, and express society's view of things."

"Clare is the one who needs an advocate, not that devil of a husband of hers, Andrew."

"Well, yes, that is, after all, what I have been saying. I must question her immediately, no matter how painful that process is for her."

Sabrina sighed. "All right. But she is in no condition to come down. I will take you up."

Just outside of Clare's door, Sabrina turned and whispered, "I don't know if you will be able to get anything out of her, Andrew. She thought Justin was still alive and able to come after her again. I am not sure just what she remembers about last night."

Clare had put on her silk wrapper and made her way stiffly and painfully to the chair by her window. She nervously pulled the wrapper tighter when Sabrina entered, bringing Andrew More into the room. Giles had sent him to help her, so she supposed she must see him, but what she could tell him, she didn't know.

Chapter Fifteen

Andrew had seen Clare a few times this Season and had, like others, noticed how thin she had gotten. Now he was shocked at her appearance. She was so pale that the bruises on her face looked almost worse than they were, if that were possible. Her mouth looked lopsided because of her swollen lips, and when she greeted him almost inaudibly, he could tell it was physically painful for her to talk. He was so filled with pity that all his previous dislike of her fell away, and for the first time since Giles had approached him, he felt like he wanted to defend her.

Sabrina had called for a tray of lemonade, and it arrived almost immediately. After a few moments of commonplaces exchanged between Sabrina and himself, as they sipped and watched Clare ignore her glass, Andrew thanked Sabrina for her company, but asked if she would leave Lady Rainsborough alone with him for a few minutes.

Sabrina protested as Clare lifted her hand as though to grab her friend.

"Clare wishes me to stay."

"I understand that," said Andrew kindly. "But if I am to defend her, I must establish a relationship with her myself. I need you to leave," he repeated firmly.

"I do not wish to leave, Andrew. I cannot leave her to be interrogated without any support." Sabrina was furious that he would even suggest it.

"Then I can do nothing here," said Andrew, starting to get up.

Sabrina was just opening her mouth to deliver a cutting set-down when Clare spoke.

"No." She put out her hand to Andrew. "No, you can stay. I must do this. You can go, Sabrina."

Sabrina could see that it took all of Clare's courage to say this. How could Andrew More not see it. Clare needed her friend, not a possibly unsympathetic barrister.

"I don't want to leave you alone, Clare."

Clare was silent for a moment and then laughed softly. "Justin is dead, Sabrina. I can safely talk to a man alone or in company, without being afraid. I will be all right, I promise you."

After Sabrina had gone, Andrew handed Clare her glass of lemonade. "Here, drink this, Lady Rainsborough. You need your strength."

Clare sipped slowly, wincing a bit as the tart liquid hit her cut lip. But she was thirstier than she had realized.

"If I am to be able to defend you, I need to know exactly what happened last night, Lady Rainsborough."

Clare could feel the pressure again. "I don't think I can remember, Mr. More."

"Why don't we start earlier in the evening, then. You attended the Petersham ball?"

Clare nodded.

"With your husband?"

"Yes."

"Had you quarreled or had any disagreement earlier that day?"

"No . . . not really."

"Tell me about it."

"Well, Giles had called on me that afternoon. But I sent him away," Clare hastened to add. "Justin met him as he was leaving and was . . . upset."

"Upset?"

"Justin sometimes is . . . was jealous if I pay any attention to other men."

"And did you?"

"Did I what," asked Clare with a puzzled look on her face.

"Pay attention to other men. Or more specifically, to Giles?"

Clare was taken aback by More's tone. It sounded almost hostile and reminded her of Justin. "Sometimes I smiled and laughed-with someone. But that is all. And I purposely didn't see Giles that afternoon."

"But your husband was jealous. And you are saying there was no basis for it?" Andrew's voice was gentler. She was confessing to a smile or laugh as though it were adultery. Just what had Rainsborough done to her, he wondered.

"Justin was a doting husband. He didn't like it when anyone spent much time with me. Or if it looked like I was enjoying another man's company. He was especially sensitive about Giles. Because we were almost betrothed before I met Justin."

"Yes, I remember. So, you sent Giles away and then you and your husband quarreled."

"No," said Clare, shaking her head. "Justin apologized for his suspicions. And I reminded him"—Clare frowned as she began to remember—"I reminded him that he had been planning to visit with Dr. Shipton."

"Dr. Shipton?"

Clare lowered her eyes. "The doctor has had some success in helping people reduce their dependence on laudanum. Justin thought he would see if he could help him overcome a certain dependence on spirits."

"Lord Rainsborough drank too much?"

"Not all the time. He could abstain for weeks at a time. But when he did drink, then . . ." Clare folded her hands across her stomach.

"When he drank?"

"That was when he would get jealous. Accuse me of terrible things . . ." Her voice trailed off.

"Hit you?"

She nodded. "I was so hopeful when he first mentioned Dr. Shipton."

"I understand. You loved your husband, Lady Rainsborough?"

Clare's eyes filled with tears. "I loved him very much. Once." The last word was almost inaudible, and Andrew almost missed it.

"Once?"

"I don't know if I still loved him. You see, it was almost like living with two husbands: the Justin who loved me, and the Justin who beat me. At first it was the Justin who loved me that I lived with most of the time. But lately . . ."

"For how long?"

"For at least a year I have wondered if I have been going mad. If I could trust my own perceptions. Because the time he was not drinking became shorter and shorter. I was having a hard time remembering the Justin whom I had loved." Clare paused and then continued slowly and painfully. "But then he would be there again, for a short time, and of course, I still loved him."

"Let us go back to yesterday, Lady Rainsborough," said Andrew as he watched Clare twisting her hands together harder and harder. "You were in harmony with one another by the time you left?"

Clare nodded.

"Did anything happen at the ball?"

"Justin and I danced. Then he went into the card room. I saw him with a glass of champagne, but I was hoping he would have only one. It was all my fault," she said in an agonized whisper.

"What was?" Andrew asked gently. What could she possibly have done to merit such a beating?

"Giles asked if he could see me alone. I let him convince me to be private with him. I thought Justin was playing cards. I thought we would be out of there . . . that he wouldn't see us."

"And what did Giles have to say to you?"

"That my father had asked him to speak with me. That my family and friends were concerned about my health."

"And did you tell him about your . . . troubles?"

"Oh, God, of course not," said Clare vehemently. "I have told no one. What could anyone do, especially Giles."

"Perhaps someone could have challenged Lord Rainsborough with his behavior?"

At the word challenge, Clare put her hand to her forehead.

"Are you in pain, Lady Rainsborough?"

"No. Yes. It is just that I can't let it through . . ."

Andrew reached out for her other hand and held it loosely in his own. "How do you know that your husband saw the two of you?"

"He made me leave early. He made his usual accusations."

"Which you denied?"

Clare pulled her hand from Andrew's and laughed mirthlessly. "I have always denied them. As quietly and calmly as I could. I never let myself be drawn into a quarrel. The few times in the beginning when I did, it only made things worse." She continued in a level, voice that sounded to Andrew as though she were somewhere else. "Sometimes, if you are quiet enough, he will stop."

"Stop what, Lady Rainsborough," Andrew asked very quietly.

"Stop hitting you. Or kicking you."

"Did he hit you last night?"

The river was swelling, swirling, pushing against her brain. The lock wouldn't, couldn't possibly hold it. Clare moaned. Oh, God, the water was rushing over, and she was being carried along with it.

"Did he hit you last night, Lady Rainsborough?" Andrew kept his voice as soft and even and expressionless as possible.

"Yes, yes. I kept *telling* him nothing had happened. I

promised him I would never see Giles again. He said if I promised, he wouldn't challenge him."

"How did he hit you?"

"Oh, as usual," Clare said with a tired smile. "My face. He banged my head against the mantel."

"Did he kick you?"

"Oh, yes," Clare said, almost matter-of-factly. "That usually ended it. But something had changed these past few weeks. He . . ."

"Yes?"

"He had started choking me. I thought he was going to kill me this time. And he took out his pistols. I did what he asked: I admitted we were lovers, I said I would never see Giles again. I would have said anything to keep him from challenging Giles. But then, he said he was going to kill me anyway."

"But you said there was nothing between you and Giles?" Andrew kept his voice innocently puzzled.

"Don't you understand?" said Clare, suddenly standing up. "Don't you understand? He said he would challenge Giles. He would have killed him. Giles, who had never done anything but try to help me. Who loved me. Who was my dearest friend. I would have said anything. I would have admitted to anything to prevent that. Justin promised that if I admitted to it, that this would never happen again."

"What?"

"The beating. But he tricked me. He put his pistol to my head . . . and I . . ." Clare was backing away from Andrew, not seeing him, seeing Justin. "I hit him with the candlestick from the desk."

"Didn't that stop him?"

"He started to get up," said Clare, looking down as though she again saw her husband. "He was getting up, and I remembered the pistol, and I walked right into his arms, and I shot him."

Clare was shaking violently from head to foot, and Andrew started to approach her slowly.

"Don't you come near me," she said. He stopped. "He moved. His arm moved, so I picked up the other pistol and put it to his head. But then I was so afraid he wasn't dead, that he would kill me and then Giles after all . . ." She took a long, deep, shuddering breath and then said calmly, almost like a child who has been comforted after a nightmare: "But Sabrina told me that he *is* dead."

"Lord Rainsborough is indeed dead, Lady Rainsborough," said Andrew reassuringly.

Clare stood there, and her body gradually became still. She lifted her eyes to Andrew. "Then I killed my husband, didn't I, Mr. More?"

"I am afraid so, Lady Rainsborough."

Sabrina had gone down to the library, hoping to find something to read that would keep her mind off Clare, but she had forgotten that the library was off-limits for anyone but the Runners, and so she settled herself in the morning room. That was where Andrew found her, pacing back and forth, unable to settle for a minute.

"Sabrina."

She turned, and Andrew could see from the expression on her face that she was still angry with him.

"How is she? I hope you have not upset her too much? I will go right up to her."

Andrew caught her arm just as she was about to rush past. "Lady Rainsborough needs her rest, Sabrina. And some time alone."

Sabrina tried to shrug his hand off her arm. "Let go of me, Andrew. She needs a friend near her."

"Soon, I agree, but not this moment. I believe she needs to absorb what happened to her."

"Does she remember, then?" Sabrina asked, giving in and letting Andrew lead her over to the sofa.

"Yes, I am afraid she does."

"What do you mean 'afraid,' Andrew?"

"Had she continued in a state of shock, the amnesia coupled with her rank might have given me a chance to declare her incompetent to testify. I could have brought witnesses forward who would attest to her physical condition and made the argument that she was out of her mind with terror and didn't really know what she was doing. But now . . ."

"But now?" Sabrina repeated.

"She is competent enough to take the stand. And she does remember everything."

"But surely Justin *had* terrorized her? Surely she was only defending herself."

"Oh, I believe that. The question is, can I get a coroner's jury to believe it. She killed her husband, and she did it knowingly. She could have stopped with the blow to his head. But she shot him twice with his own pistols."

"She was still terrified when I got here, Andrew. Afraid that he was still alive. Surely that shows that she was beside herself with fear? And her face and throat . . . the bruises."

"Yes, well, they will be almost gone by the time of the inquest. We will have to rely on eyewitnesses. The butler . . . her abigail."

"Myself," said Sabrina matter-of-factly.

"Surely you wouldn't want the notoriety? Sabrina."

"Surely I wouldn't want my good friend convicted of murder!"

Andrew smiled warmly at her, and Sabrina felt a stirring of pleasure at his approval. His brown eyes could change so quickly, from being intent and concentrated to softening with affection. Nonsense, she chided herself. He had no affection for her. Why should he? He hardly knew her. And he had treated her more high-handedly than anyone but Giles dared to!

"I don't think there will be any need for that. I hope there will not. Or for Giles."

"Giles?"

"Yes. He could confirm her story that she turned him away from an afternoon visit. And that the only reason he sought her out at the ball was to inquire after her health."

"Surely, no one would believe anything else?"

"Her husband did. And there are people who would sympathize with a jealous husband over a protesting wife."

"But we have hardly seen Clare these last two years."

"I know. And that will count for something. But the law is on Justin Rainsborough's side."

"The law allows a husband to murder his wife!" Sabrina said furiously.

"No, of course not. But the prosecuting counselor can make the argument that her life was not truly in danger."

Sabrina sat quietly for a moment. "Do you think you can win, Andrew?"

"I am going to do my damnedest!" he said with the quirky grin that gave him a gypsy look.

Chapter Sixteen

Giles had never felt so helpless. He wanted nothing more than to be with Clare. She needed him, now more than ever. Who else could give her the courage to face what was before her? And all because of Andrew's ridiculous precautions, he was being kept away.

Giles had been so sure these past two years that his love for Clare had changed. Recently, he had seriously been considering marrying Lucy Kirkman. She was attractive, an enjoyable companion, and would have made him an undemanding wife. She wanted him, and he knew their marriage would also have been physically satisfying. And he needed an heir.

Now the very idea seemed ridiculous. He had been lying to himself all along. Well, perhaps not lying. Perhaps he could have married Lucy and been happy, had Clare truly been in the marriage he supposed her to have. But to find out that Rainsborough had been abusing her. That she had had to bear it all alone. All the old feeling came rushing back. Clare was his love, the one and only one he had ever wanted to enfold in his arms and keep safe. And for now, the only way to keep her safe, according to Andrew, was to stay away from her. He didn't know if he could bear the frustration.

When Andrew finally called, Giles was so eager to hear his report that he quite forgot himself as a host. After they sat down in the library, and Andrew looked over at his friend and said, with a quizzical smile, "Aren't you going to offer me anything to drink, Giles? 'Tea? Sherry, Andrew?' " He mimicked Giles's even tones perfectly.

"I apologize. I have been beside myself. Tea? Sherry, Andrew?" he repeated with a smile.

"Sherry would be perfect, Giles."

Giles rang and had the footman bring them a decanter and a plate of biscuits.

Andrew sipped the sherry slowly and appreciatively. It had been a hard afternoon. He had had some grim cases in the past, but nothing that had turned his stomach like this one. He was not completely against an occasional blow. *He* wasn't the sort who would ever do it, but he could understand how a man might be driven to it by a certain kind of woman. It seemed to be human nature that the strong sometimes hurt the weak: parents beat their children, masters their servants. He didn't like it, he didn't approve of it, he wouldn't do it, but if it was kept within bounds, he was able to live with it. After all, people paid good money to watch professional pugilists go at it for hours. It wasn't *his* cup of tea, but there it was.

But Clare Dysart, Lady Rainsborough. A sweet, harmless young woman who had clearly never looked at another man. From just the little she had revealed, and he was sure he hadn't heard everything, he felt sick to his stomach. There had been madness in Justin Rainsborough, and unfortunately, society and the law gave him the right to express it.

Andrew finally looked over at Giles, his brows knitted together and Giles said quietly: "That bad?"

"Not good, Giles. Not good."

"What happened? Were you able to get a coherent story?"

"Oh, yes. It seems Lord Rainsborough has been beating his wife these past two years with increasing regularity."

Giles buried his head in his hands.

"Last night, or to be more accurate, these past few weeks, it had escalated. Evidently he had threatened to kill her several times while he choked her almost insen-

sible. Last night she believed he truly meant to do it. And
then call you out and kill you."

"Me!"

"It seems Rainsborough was beyond reason, jealous of
any attentions paid to his wife, especially yours."

"But I have hardly *seen* Clare," Giles protested.

"Yet you called on her yesterday and spoke with her
privately at the Petersham ball. That was more than
enough to set him off. He threatened to kill her if she
didn't admit you were lovers and then to challenge you to
a duel. He was a crack shot, I understand?"

"Clare denied it, of course?"

"For a while. But then he promised to stop the torture
if she admitted you had been intimate and gave her word
never to see you again. So she did."

Giles groaned.

"He put a pistol to her head, and she had enough
courage ..." Andrew looked over at Giles with an expression of wonder mixed with admiration. "I don't know
where she got it from, Giles. And of all women, Clare.
She hit him over the head with a brass candlestick. Had
she stopped there ..."

"Had she stopped there," said Giles, almost spitting the
words out, "had she stopped there he would be alive to do
it again. She might well have been dead by the end of the
Season," he added wonderingly.

"Yes, perhaps you are right. At any rate, she shot him
twice with his own dueling pistols."

Giles looked horrified. It was one thing to be glad
Clare had defended herself. It was another to imagine the
details.

"She likely would have shot him again, Giles," said
Andrew with an ironic grin, "had she known how to reload. She wasn't convinced he was dead until Sabrina
went down to see the body and reassure her."

"Oh, God. I should have been there, Andrew."

"No, you shouldn't. The worst thing in the world for

my case is for you to involve yourself. No, you must let Sabrina act the friend for both of you."

"I don't know if I can stand it. Clare needs me."

Andrew thought to himself that the last thing in the world Clare needed at this time was a man, old friend or not, but he kept his thoughts to himself.

"She is all right, Giles, I promise you."

"You will do everything you can? Spare no expense, Andrew. I will assume the costs."

"The Marquess of Howland will assume the costs, Giles," Andrew reminded him dryly.

"Yes, of course."

"I will have to question the servants. Her abigail."

"Liza is relatively new, you know," said Giles thoughtfully. "In fact, now that I think of it, I wouldn't be surprised if Rainsborough had Martha dismissed."

"Martha?"

"Her former abigail was Martha Barton."

"Hmm. Well, I will try to find this Martha. The more eyewitnesses to her husband's treatment of her, the better."

"Can you win, Andrew?"

"I will do my best, Giles."

Andrew went directly from the Whittons' to Clare's father and told him all. The marquess seemed to age five years as he listened to his daughter's ordeal.

"I know it is somehow our fault," he told Andrew. "She was a late arrival, a surprise, actually. We did not quite know how to deal with her. It was as though we had forgotten what a young child needed." He was silent for a moment or two. "It was why we sent her to the Whittons. She needed young people around her. If only she had married Giles. Had never met Rainsborough. Why did she never tell us what he was doing to her?"

"She seems to have felt hopeless that anyone on the outside could help her. And, at the same time, hopeful that the situation might change, that Rainsborough would go back to being the man she married."

"They seemed so happy together. They were notorious for being in one another's pockets."

"Yes, well evidently the doting husband turned into a violently jealous one under the influence of spirits," said Andrew. "You will not be hearing a very pretty story at the inquest, I am afraid, my lord."

"Can you help her?"

"If you wish me to take the case, I will do my best. Much will depend on Clare's ability to tell her story. And on any witnesses I can find."

"If Giles called you in, then I am sure you are the best for my daughter," said the marquess with a sad smile. "Please spare no expense or effort."

"Thank you, my lord. I know a very good solicitor who will prepare the case, but he comes high. I do need some information from you."

"Anything."

"Clare's former abigail was a woman called Martha?"

"Ah, yes. Martha. I always wondered why she was let go. Clare was very fond of her."

"I would guess that Rainsborough dismissed her because she was equally fond of Clare. But I won't know until I find her. Have you any idea how I could? Was she hired in London?"

"She was from the city, and I think she returned here shortly after she was dismissed."

Andrew frowned. "Did she stay in service?"

"I think so, but let me ask my wife's maid. She was the one who recommended Martha to us years ago and may still be in touch with her."

Andrew rose. "Don't bother to get up, my lord. I will see myself out. Please send me any information that you may obtain on Martha as soon as you can."

"Of course. And Mr. More?"

"Yes?"

"Thank you."

"Don't thank me yet, my lord," replied Andrew.

It took two days and a hired Runner to find Martha Barker, now working as a parlor maid in the Winston household. While he was waiting, Andrew had his solicitor interview both Peters and Liza about the status of the Rainsborough marriage. At first they were both reluctant to speak, and even when they did, clearly were of the opinion that however distressing Lord Rainsborough's treatment of his wife had been, it had been none of their business. Indeed, any comments or interference would have meant their jobs.

Andrew went back to the Rainsborough town house for another interview with Clare. She was beginning to look better physically: the bruises were fading, and her mouth was back to normal. She even had a little bit of color in her cheeks. But she was very subdued and unwilling to speak about her marriage. "It is all over now," she whispered, here eyes on the floor. "Surely if I tell the coroner about that last night, it will be enough."

She didn't comprehend her danger at all, thought Andrew. And he wasn't' sure he had the heart to push her so soon after her ordeal. Yet if he didn't, he wasn't sure he could get the coroner's jury to acquit her. And if the case went to trial, she had even less of a chance to get off.

On his way out, he was stopped by Sabrina, who was just coming from a morning ride. She had moved into the town house "for the duration" as she put it, not wanting Clare to be alone.

"Andrew!" she exclaimed in surprise.

"Good morning, Sabrina." Sabrina looked everything that Clare didn't: healthy, glowing, vibrant, and energetic. The severe cut of her riding habit only made her contrasting curves more noticeable, and Andrew experienced the same stirring of attraction that he always felt in her presence.

"Will you have a cup of tea with me and tell me about your progress, Andrew?"

Andrew hesitated and then agreed.

"Do you mind waiting while I change?"

"Not at all, Sabrina."

When she came back down, it was hard to keep his face blank and the appreciation out of his eyes. She was dressed in a simple round gown of deep burgundy that complemented both her complexion and her eyes.

"Come sit down, Andrew. I will pour." She suited action to words and handed him a cup of tea.

"I am afraid I have not much to tell, although we *have* found Martha and will be calling on her this afternoon."

"Oh, thank goodness," said Sabrina. "She should be very helpful in your case, shouldn't she?"

"I hope so. Peters and Liza's testimony will not do much for us. And Clare . . ."

"What about Clare," Sabrina asked protectively.

"You are like a lioness with her cub, Sabrina," Andrew commented with appreciative humor.

"She needs protection," replied Sabrina.

"Perhaps not quite so much," Andrew said thoughtfully, after a moment. "She is a grown woman after all. She made a free choice to marry Rainsborough."

"You don't understand, Andrew. Clare has always called upon my protective instincts. And Giles's. Especially Giles's."

"Well, neither you nor Giles can protect her from this, Sabrina," said Andrew finally. "She will have to tell her story to a jury of twelve men who will be convinced that her husband was completely within his rights to chastise her. And I can't get her to talk further about her marriage."

"Isn't telling them what happened the other night enough?"

"Frankly, no. It could be seen as an aberration: 'Doting husband becomes insanely jealous after wife's tête-à-tête with ex-lover.' "

"Giles and Clare were *never* lovers," protested Sabrina, incensed by the suggestion.

"You and I know that, Sabrina. But will the coroner's jury believe it? No, however painful it is, Clare must give the whole history of her marriage. And it would help me enormously if you would support her in this instead of hovering over her protectively. She killed a man, my lady. However justifiable, it was a murder."

Sabrina's face flushed with anger. "It is easy for you to speak so, Andrew. You are a man. You do not become someone's property upon marrying him."

"Is that why you have never married, Sabrina?" he asked dryly.

"I have never married . . . it is none of your business why I have never married," she replied, furious with him. "You do not know Clare as we do."

"No, I do not," he admitted in softer tones. "Nor do I know what it would be like to be in a woman's shoes. But despite the law, Sabrina, we both know women and men who live in very happy marriages. Your parents, for one. Mine. Yes, the law protected Justin Rainsborough, but surely he is an aberration."

"Perhaps. But perhaps he was an extreme example of how a man can abuse the power he has over a woman."

"I cannot single-handedly change the law, Sabrina. I can only work within it. But I tell you, I cannot defend Clare Rainsborough if she is not willing to speak of her last two years. I would advise you that the way to protect her, to be her friend, is to encourage her to speak." Andrew rose. "Thank you for the tea, my lady. I am sorry that all our conversations seem to end in disagreements about Lady Rainsborough."

Sabrina said a cool good-bye, and Andrew left, wondering why, since their disagreements kept the desired distance between them, he felt so frustrated.

After Andrew had gone, Sabrina found herself reconsidering his words. He was a most annoying man, it was true, with little or no understanding of who Clare was and what she had been through. On the other hand, he was a good friend of Giles's, and, she must presume, a good lawyer or her brother would not have recommended him. He knew the law and the courts. Perhaps he was right about Clare. Perhaps she *did* have to tell the whole story of her marriage in order to prove her innocence. And if that were true, then she, Sabrina, should be encouraging her to cooperate with Andrew.

And so, while Andrew's solicitor was interviewing Martha, Sabrina spent the afternoon with her friend, hoping that she could discern whether Clare was strong enough to do what she had to do.

The two women were bent over embroidery, when Sabrina looked over at Clare and said: "I spoke with Andrew More this morning. I find him annoyingly opinionated, but I do trust him. What do you think of him, Clare?"

Clare kept her eyes on the French knot she was working and said quietly: "Giles chose him, so I must trust him. And my very life is in his hands," she added.

"Perhaps it is also in your own, Clare," replied Sabrina, putting her hand on Clare's arm. "Andrew seems to think that unless you are willing to speak of your marriage from the early days, you will not gain enough sympathy to get off. At first I was annoyed at him, but now I am not so sure that he is wrong. Is it so painful to tell your story, Clare?"

Clare looked up at her friend. "There are some things I just . . . I can't imagine saying them in public."

"Could you tell them to me, Clare? That might be a first step." Sabrina held her breath.

Clare pushed her needle very carefully through the linen, completed her knot, and bit the thread off with her teeth. Reaching over for a small velvet pincushion, she disposed of her needle and folded up the small square of embroidery. She folded her hands just as carefully in her lap and said: "I will try, Sabrina." She sounded composed. She looked composed unless one noticed how her hands were folded over her belly, as though to protect her most vital parts.

"Tell me when all this started," Sabrina asked. "You and Justin seemed so happy together."

"We were, at first. And even afterward, as strange as that may seem." Slowly and haltingly, Clare began to tell Sabrina about the past two years. There were times during her story when Sabrina thought she would choke on her own horrified reaction, but she sensed that any response might silence Clare. At one point she felt literally nauseated and had to breathe slowly and intentionally in order not to retch. There was nothing to say at the end except, "Clare, I am so sorry." She started to put her arms around her friend, but Clare stiffened at her touch and Sabrina immediately withdrew.

"I am sorry, Sabrina. If you do that, I may just lose my nerve. It was . . . well, not good, exactly, but necessary to tell someone. Mr. More was right. It will have to be made public. I thank you for listening. I know it couldn't have been easy."

"No, no it wasn't."

"I suppose you are wondering: why didn't she tell someone? Why didn't she leave? How could she have made love to him again and again after what he did to her?" Clare asked.

"Why, no," Sabrina stammered.

"You never were a good liar, Sabrina. I find it difficult to explain myself. You see, when Justin was himself, he was the wonderful man I fell in love with. He truly was tender and loving and passionate. It was so easy to believe that the other Justin wouldn't come back. Not *this* time. Not after his promises and tears and apologies. It is almost like living in a madhouse, I suppose." Clare paused. "You are also probably thinking: "If only she'd married Giles."

"I confess I have thought that over the past few days," Sabrina admitted.

"It is only natural. I suppose I should have. But I only loved Giles as a friend. A dear friend," Clare hastened to add. "Justin wakened a part of me that I hadn't known existed. Of course," she added bitterly, "he awakened it only to torture me for it. Anyway, Giles deserves someone who loves him the way I loved my husband."

"Yes, he does," agreed Sabrina. "And I don't think it is Lucy Kirkman."

"Lucy is very good at getting what she wants, Sabrina. But I am sure Giles knows that," Clare added with a smile.

"He does," said Sabrina, throwing her hands up in mock despair.

Clare sat for a moment and then turning to Sabrina, said quietly: "I think I will have Mr. More come back tomorrow morning, Sabrina. I will tell him the whole story and agree to repeat it at the inquest. Thank you for your help. And I think I will be all right alone from now on." She laughed. "Hardly alone, I suppose, with a Runner in the house."

Sabrina protested, but Clare was adamant. "I would love to see you after Mr. More leaves, Sabrina, but you must not neglect your life just to be with me. You mustn't miss another engagement."

"All right, Clare. But I will be over tomorrow after my ride, I promise."

Chapter Seventeen

Time had never gone so slowly for Giles as the last few days. All he wanted was to be with Clare, to put his arms around her, to let her cry out all her grief and fear on his shoulder. All he got was quick visits with Sabrina and Andrew, who kept telling him that Clare was doing very well. So when Sabrina returned, obviously planning to stay, he pulled her into the morning room and insisted she sit down and give him a full report.

"You aren't abandoning Clare, are you?" he protested.

"Clare was very sure that she was ready to be alone, Giles," answered his sister, "or else I wouldn't have left. She wants me back in circulation, and she is probably right. I intend to go to the Maxwells' tonight. What about you?"

"I haven't gone out since this happened, Sabrina."

"I know, Giles. And that means that the gossips are having a fine time with Clare's story. And, no doubt, working you into it as well."

"I hadn't thought of that. Andrew's advice was to stay away from Clare. He didn't add anything else to his instructions," Giles added sarcastically.

"Andrew More can be a most annoying man, I admit, but I think we can trust him to take Clare through this safely. I finally gave in to his advice today, and found his counsel wiser than I thought."

Giles looked over at her questioningly.

"He believes that Clare must tell the whole story of her

marriage in order to convince the jury of her innocence. I didn't want him to make her dredge it all up."

"Indeed, she shouldn't have to," protested Giles. "She's gone through enough."

"He pointed out that Rainsborough's behavior could have been seen as a result of some provocation. Given the law, well, Clare needs to convince the coroner and the jury that she truly was in danger ... I listened to her whole story, Giles," said Sabrina, her voice strained.

"Tell me all, Brina."

"I can't Giles. It is Clare's story to tell, not mine. But it was horrible to listen to what she went through these past two years."

"Oh, God, if only she'd never met him. If only I hadn't waited so long to ask her to marry me."

"Oh, Giles, it had nothing to do with you. Clare loved Rainsborough in a way she didn't love you, although I know this is painful to hear."

"I still love her, you know," said Giles softly. "The more fool I."

"Oh, Giles, I know," said his sister, reaching out her hand and clasping his. "And it can never be foolish to love someone, can it? Not that I would know," she added humorously.

"You *have* kept your heart whole, haven't you, Brina. There has been no one whom you have wanted to share it with, has there?"

"No, Giles. Perhaps it is because I have had you. There is such sympathy and understanding between us that I have not really felt the lack of a man in my life. I've had my twin," she added with an appreciative smile.

Giles leaned over and gave her a quick hug. "We are lucky. But you need more than a brother, Sabrina."

"No doubt I will settle for someone one of these days," she said lightly. "Now, I am going up for a rest before I take on society for Clare. You will come with me to the ball tonight?"

"Yes, my dear," said Giles with a smile. "I will escort you into battle."

Indeed, Sabrina had a very militant look in her eye when they arrived at the Maxwell ball. She sought out her closest friends who were full of questions, but reluctant to ask them. Except, of course, Lucy Kirkman.

"Is it true, Sabrina, that Clare is under a sort of house arrest? The rumors are flying so thick and fast that it is hard to tell what is the truth."

Lady Julia Willeford exclaimed: "Lucy!" in horror at her frankness.

"Oh, Julia, don't pretend you weren't dying to ask. Come, Sabrina, tell us all you know."

"Lucy, you are incorrigible." Sabrina laughed. "Clare is, in fact, confined to her house, but as much to recover from her ordeal as anything else."

"Did she kill Lord Rainsborough, Sabrina?" asked Lucy. "I have heard so many different versions: that she mistook him for an intruder, that she brained him with a poker, and that she shot him with his own dueling pistols."

Lady Julia blanched. "Lucy, if you go on like this, I am going to become ill."

"Go right ahead, dear Julia," replied Lucy. "You have heard all the same gossip I have, my dear, and seemed to have survived it up until now. The most disturbing rumor, of course, is that Clare and Giles were lovers and provoked Rainsborough into a killing rage." Lucy said this last as lightly as she had repeated the other rumors, but Sabrina knew that this was the one she had been leading up to, the question she really wanted answered. She was surprised that she actually felt sorry for Lucy. Sabrina knew Giles would never marry her now, although Lucy would not realize that yet.

"Evidently Justin Rainsborough was an unreasonably, perhaps one could say an insanely jealous husband," Sabrina replied. "He accused Clare of many things during their marriage, none of which were true. And Giles has hardly had time to spare these last few months, Lucy. After all, he has spent much of his time with you."

"Of course," said Lucy, sounding complacent, but Sabrina could sense her relief. "And one could hardly suspect little Clare of infidelity anyway, could one?"

Sabrina spent a few more minutes convincing her friends that when the truth emerged at the inquest, Clare would be completely vindicated. They were so pleased to be the first to hear the "real" story that she knew she could count on them to start a counter-wave of gossip.

She danced several dances with her usual favorites. During her country-dance with her host, she was surprised to see Andrew More standing on the sidelines, conversing with Giles and his older brother, Lord Avery. She asked Maxwell to lead her over to them after the music stopped.

"Good evening, Lady Sabrina," said Lord Avery. He was a taller, slightly more refined-looking version of Andrew and someone Sabrina had never liked very much. She might find Andrew More annoying, but he was at least a stimulating companion. His brother was too concerned with the family name and his own importance for Sabrina's liking.

"Good evening, my lord. Good evening, Andrew. I am surprised to see you here. I thought you might be working long hours to prepare for your case."

"I have been working very closely with my solicitor, Sabrina, but you know the old saying: 'All work and no play,' " replied Andrew insouciantly.

"I was just speaking with Andrew about that," said Lord Avery. "I cannot like him being involved in such a case."

"You and the family are always after me to find a better class of client, Jonathan. I had thought you would be pleased," said Andrew with mock innocence.

"We hardly meant for you to take on a murder case, whether the murderess is a countess or not."

"I know. You'd rather I spent my time sorting out disputed family settlements."

"It is, for the son of an earl, certainly preferable to defending common criminals."

"Lady Rainsborough can hardly be called a *common* criminal, Jonathan."

"Of course not," his brother admitted. "But to be involved even peripherally with this scandal is very distressing to me."

"I assure you, Jonathan, it is far more distressing for Clare," said Andrew sarcastically.

"Of course, of course. But I still wish you weren't involved."

Andrew turned away from his brother to Sabrina, raising his eyebrows in a way that expressed all his amused frustration with his brother's attitude. She had to lift her fan to her face to hide her smile.

"Do you by any chance have a waltz free tonight, Sabrina?" he asked.

Sabrina examined her dance card carefully. Giles was her partner for the next waltz, but she was sure her brother would not mind if she danced with his friend. She glanced over at Giles with the question in her eyes, and he nodded almost imperceptibly. It was something they both took for granted now, their ability to communicate without words, and Sabrina wondered if she would ever find anyone with whom she could have as natural an intimacy as with her twin.

"I have the next waltz free, Andrew."

"And they are about to strike it up," said Andrew with a smile. "Come, let us not lose a minute of it."

Sabrina had danced with Andrew More upon many occasions over the years, and she remembered him as an average dancer. This evening, however, was different. She felt she had never been so at one with the music or the man who partnered her. They didn't speak much. It was as though they were both caught up in another dimension, one where every small movement of his hand around her waist and her fingers in his became a source of pleasure. Sabrina realized that every cell in her body was aware of Andrew in a most disturbing but also intriguing way.

When the music stopped, they both felt they had been dropped back into everyday consciousness and were suddenly embarrassed and ill at ease. Andrew escorted Sabrina back to her brother and muttering his apologies for leaving early, left almost immediately, without even an attempt at polite conversation. And when Sabrina glanced over to Giles, hoping for that instant understanding, he merely looked at her questioningly as if to say: "Yes, Sabrina, is there something that is bothering you?" She felt very empty and bereft, and for one odd moment realized it was the lovely oneness with Andrew she was missing and not the lack of communication with Giles. But that was ridiculous, she immediately told herself. Andrew More had nothing in common with her brother or herself. Except for his defense of Clare.

The morning of the inquest arrived all too quickly for those most concerned and not at all too soon for those of all classes who hoped to watch that very rare thing: the possibility of a peeress being charged with murder.

It had been unseasonably warm and humid the past two days and when Clare awoke, she felt like the weather matched her mood: heavy, oppressive, and energyless. The smells of London, which usually blew by one, hung heavy in the nostrils, but it was too hot to close her bedroom windows.

She had to wear black, of course, which made it even worse, for the only black dress she owned was of a heavy twilled silk. Andrew had insisted, though. "You must appear in mourning, if for nothing else than the happy, early days of your marriage."

She tried to eat, for Andrew had also recommended a good breakfast, but was only able to force down a half a cup of tea and one triangle of toast. She waited quietly in the drawing room until the hired chaise arrived to take her and the assigned Runner to the inquest. She had originally planned to use her own carriage, but Andrew just looked at her and said kindly: "Lady Rainsborough, the streets will be full of those who wish to catch a glimpse of you. You could even be in some danger, if the crowd becomes a mob."

Indeed, when the Runner came to greet her, he took her out the back door. "There is too much of a crowd around front, my lady," he explained. He handed her into the chaise and climbed in quickly afterward, banging on the roof to signal the driver on.

The shades of the chaise were drawn, and Clare could feel her dress begin to stick to her back. She made a nervous comment about the heat, but the Runner only nodded and then ignored her, so the long ride through the crowded streets was a silent one.

She could tell when they were close because she could hear people shouting. Some were hawking tickets to the gallery. Others were promising that they had the true, authentic story of this horrible crime for only a penny a sheet.

When the carriage finally stopped, a hush fell over the crowd. The Runner was out first, and as Clare appeared in the door of the chaise, the crowd went wild. "There she is, there's the Murdering Peeress." "Nah, it can't be 'er. She's too little to 'ave killed 'er 'usband." Clare was frozen. The Runner was in front of her but behind him was a gauntlet of Londoners, eager to see her, to touch her, perhaps even to attack her. How could she step down into that sea of humanity? How could she go through with this inquiry at all? She had killed Justin. She should just admit it and let them hang her. Then, as the door opened, she saw Andrew More. His eyes met hers, and he nodded his head as if to say: You can do it, Clare. She stepped down slowly, looking neither to the left nor right, keeping her eyes on his as though he offered her a lifeline. She hardly noticed the pawing and the grabbing, and was only half-conscious of a pulling at the hem of her gown. It was only hours later that she realized someone had actually ripped off a piece of the black silk as a souvenir.

When at last she was beside Andrew, he slammed the door behind her and took her arm solicitously. "Are you all right, Lady Rainsborough?"

Clare nodded, but her eyes were wide with fear. Andrew thought that only one time before in his life had he seen that look. He had been tramping through the woods of the family estate and came upon one of the traps set out for foxes. A half-grown fox cub was caught by his paw. Andrew knew he should have shot it, but he couldn't. He had approached the animal, whispering words of comfort and reassurance, and managed to free it. But not before he had looked deep into its eyes. There was mainly fear there, but also a desperate kind of courage. It had actually stood its ground and growled at him. He hoped he was right about Clare: that underneath was enough courage to tell her story. If there wasn't, they had both lost.

Chapter Eighteen

Giles and Sabrina had made sure to be in court early. The crowd had already begun to gather when they arrived, and they had looked at one another apprehensively. How would Clare ever survive all this? The heat became worse as the room filled, and the screaming and shouting as Clare arrived made Giles believe that he now knew what hell was like.

He watched as Andrew led her over to a side bench. She looked so pale that he could almost believe that she was cold with fear. But when he looked more closely, he could see that her curls were clinging damply to her neck, and even the black gown couldn't hide the wetness under her arms. He hit the railing in front of him in an angry gesture of helplessness and frustration, and Sabrina put a hand on his arm.

"I should be with her, Sabrina. She needs me," he said intensely.

"Andrew is right, though, Giles. Can you imagine the crowd were you to have been by her side? I know this is terrible for you, but it is best for Clare."

When the jury was seated, Giles looked each one over carefully. How on earth could this be considered a jury of her peers, he wondered. And how would they see her? As a pretty young woman who had aroused the jealousy of her husband? Or as the victim of a maniac? It was impossible to tell from their faces, which remained expressionless.

The coroner, Sir Benjamin Rooke, was a hard man,

well-known for hammering suspects into the ground. He was also not happy with the growing trend to use barristers as defense counsel. He was an older man, and more likely to be sympathetic with a husband's right to "chastise" his wife than a wife's right to defend herself.

The first witnesses called were those officials who had been summoned to the scene of the murder: the local constable and the two Runners. They all agreed on the basic details: Lord Rainsborough had been shot twice with his own dueling pistols. Upon closer examination, he was also found to have suffered a blow to the side of his head.

"Which blow might itself have killed him," asked the coroner.

"Yes, my lord."

"And Lady Rainsborough?"

"Was found standing over her husband, brandishing a poker from the fireplace."

"Was there any blood on her?"

"Yes, her dress was soaked with it."

"I have no further questions," said Rooke.

Andrew cross-examined the two Runners rather too quickly, thought Giles. When he came to the local constable, however, who had been first on the scene, he took his time.

"You say you saw Lady Rainsborough standing over her dead husband?"

"Yes."

"Holding a poker?"

"Yes."

"How?"

"How what, Mr. More?" responded the constable, who was obviously puzzled by the question.

"How was she holding the poker? By her side? In front of her?"

"Uh, lifted in front of her, Mr. More."

"As though she was trying to protect herself, isn't that true?"

"Why, yes, although there were nothing to protect herself from. Lord Rainsborough was as dead as the proverbial doornail," added the constable, looking around the court as though to get others to see the joke: the silly woman protecting herself against a man who was already dead.

"You found Lord Rainsborough's death humorous, Constable?"

The constable's face fell. "Of course not."

"The fact is, that when you entered the library, Lady Rainsborough was convinced her husband was only unconscious and was obviously in a state of terror that he was about to get up and attack her again?"

"There is no evidence to suggest that Lord Rainsborough had attacked Lady Rainsborough, Mr. More," interjected the coroner.

"My apologies, Sir Benjamin. I got a trifle ahead of myself. Constable?"

"She *did* act as though she thought he was still alive," he admitted grudgingly.

"And could you describe to us Lady Rainsborough's appearance?"

"Her dress was soaked in blood, as I said, if that's what you mean."

"Yes, and what of her face?"

"Her face?"

"Yes, Constable, her face. Did you notice anything about it?"

"Well, now that you mention it," replied the man grudgingly, "it was a little bruised."

"A little," asked Andrew softly.

"Her cheek was red, and her lip was swollen."

"And her neck?"

"I didn't notice anything about her neck."

"I see. Well, thank you very much, Constable."

Sabrina turned to Giles. "He did very well with that one, don't you think?"

"Yes, but I wish he had gotten him to testify to the bruises on her neck."

"Sh, Giles. It is Peters up next."

Peters was taken through the scenario again by the coroner, who never raised any questions about Clare's appearance. He did ask whether the servants had been aware of any quarrel between the couple that night.

"I can't say as I know of one," answered the butler, who was so full of his own importance that Giles wanted to slap him. It was clear from the man's expression that he found it extremely distasteful to be pulled into such a circus.

"What did you see on the desk and on the floor?" the coroner asked.

"The desk and the floor, my lord? Oh, the pistols, of course. Or, I should say the empty case on the desk and the two pistols on the floor."

"Did you recognize the pistols?"

"Yes, of course, my lord."

"And whose were they?"

"Lord Rainsborough's. He was very proud of them. Had them specially made. They were inlaid with rosewood and mahogany." The butler shook his head sadly.

"Yes, Peters."

"I was just thinking how ironic it is that Lady Rainsborough murdered him with his own pistols."

"Objection, my lord. We have not come to any conclusions about this killing."

The coroner bowed in Andrew's direction. "Mr. Peters, your mistress has not been proved guilty of any crime. We cannot draw any conclusions as yet. That is what this inquest is for. Your witness, Mr. More."

Andrew began his questioning with his back to the butler. "How long have you been in the Rainsborough household, Mr. Peters?" he asked casually.

"Two years, sir."

"So you are hardly an old family retainer, are you?"

"No, sir. Although I became very fond of Lord Rainsborough," he added piously.

"And where were you employed before that?"

The coroner leaned over and addressed Andrew. "I fail to see where my learned counsel is going with his questioning."

"I assure the court that I have a destination in mind," replied Andrew turning around.

The coroner waved his hand. "Continue then, Mr. More, but don't linger by the side of the road, if you please."

"I repeat, Mr. Peters, who was your employer before Lord Rainsborough?"

The butler cleared his throat. "Lord Monteith."

"And why did you leave his household?"

"I was dismissed," the butler admitted.

"Any particular reason?"

"Unsatisfactory service."

"Did you receive a reference?"

"No."

"No? And yet Lord Rainsborough hired you?"

"He was most understanding and decided to give me a chance to prove myself anew. He was a kind man, Lord Rainsborough."

"You were certainly indebted to him. An unemployed butler without a reference. You had motivation to ignore certain occurrences in Lord Rainsborough's household?"

"Mr. Peters is not the focus of this inquest, Mr. More," said the coroner.

"No, no, of course not, my lord. Tell me, Mr. Peters, what did you notice about Lady Rainsborough's face that night?"

"It was like the constable said. Red, her lip swollen."

"And her throat? Did you notice anything about her throat?"

The butler turned to the coroner as though seeking guidance.

"I am afraid Sir Benjamin wasn't there that night," Andrew commented dryly.

"There were marks on her throat."

"If you had to venture a guess at what those marks were from, what would it be, Mr. Peters?"

"I would guess . . . they looked like finger marks."

"And how would fingers leave an impression on someone's throat, do you think?"

"I suppose if someone were choking someone."

"Someone choking someone. But in this case, the only someones were Lord and Lady Rainsborough?"

The butler nodded.

"Since we will assume that Lady Rainsborough was not in the habit of choking herself, we put forward the hypothesis that Lord Rainsborough had his hands around his wife's neck and was holding her tightly enough to leave finger marks. Is that a possible explanation, Mr. Peters?"

"Yes, I suppose so."

"You suppose so. Had you ever seen Lady Rainsborough's face or neck in that condition before, Mr. Peters?"

The butler hesitated.

"You are under oath, Mr. Peters," the coroner reminded him.

"Yes."

"Once, twice, often?"

"A few times."

"A few times. And what did you do about it, Mr. Peters?"

"Do about it?" asked the butler in a puzzled tone.

"Yes. Your mistress was obviously being savagely attacked by her husband. Surely you would have wanted to protect her. Did you not feel something for Lady Rainsborough?"

"It was none of my business, Mr. More. A man has a right to beat his wife. Whatever happened in the privacy of his home was Lord Rainsborough's business, not mine."

"And you were dependent upon his goodwill, weren't you?"

"That has nothing to do with it."

"But it is true, nonetheless."

"Yes," the butler admitted reluctantly.

"Thank, you, Mr. Peters. I have no further questions," said Andrew, turning his back again on the witness. Peters sat there for a moment as though unable to believe the lawyer had dismissed him.

"You may step down, Mr. Peters," said the coroner.

"Oh, yes. Thank you, sir, thank you." The butler had to pass right by Clare, and he averted his eyes as he scurried by.

"Like a rabbit," said Giles to Sabrina. "Good for Andrew."

"I call Miss Liza Stone to the stand." The coroner's voice did not sound as confident with this witness. Now that he could see Andrew's direction, it was clear that the testimony of the abigail would be useful in the same way the butler's had been.

"Miss Stone."

"Yes, my lord." Liza looked cool and composed, thought Giles, and very different from the affectionate and impulsive Martha. How had Clare survived it, he wondered, with not even one friend to support her?

"You are in the employ of Lady Rainsborough and the late Lord Rainsborough?"

"Yes, my lord."

"Please tell the court in what capacity."

"I am Lady Rainsborough's abigail."

"What do you remember of the morning of the murder."

"I object," said Andrew.

"I beg your pardon, Mr. More," said the coroner. "The morning that Lord Rainsborough was found dead."

"I was asleep like all the other servants, my lord. I woke up sudden like."

"What woke you?"

"I couldn't say, my lord. But I heard Mr. Peters go by, and I followed him downstairs."

"Did you go into the library with him?"

"He went in first, and I stayed by the door. But then he called me in."

"And what did you see?"

Liza's voice, which had been flat and still as a pond on a windless day, became higher and an expression of fear rippled over her face, as though someone had dropped a small pebble in the pond. "The first thing I saw was Lady Rainsborough."

"And what was she doing?"

"Just what the constable said."

"We want to hear it from you, Miss Stone." The coroner prompted respectfully.

"Well, she was standing there, her dress all bloody, holding the poker in front of her."

"How did she hold the poker."

"Like he said, she had it lifted up like she was going to hit someone. Then I looked over and saw him."

"Who?"

"Lord Rainsborough. He was lying there . . . it was a terrible sight." Her voice rose a little again as she remembered what her late employer had looked like.

"Was there anyone else in the room?"

"Just Peters."

"Did it look like there had been an intruder?'

"An intruder, my lord?"

"A housebreaker."

"No, no, my lord. The windows was still closed and locked."

"So before you arrived, Lord and Lady Rainsborough would seem to have been the only ones in the library?"

"Yes, my lord."

"Why doesn't Andrew object," whispered Giles to Sabrina. "How could she know if anyone else was there?"

"I don't think Andrew wants to distract the jury with any other possibilities. After all, Clare herself is willing to admit she killed Justin."

"That is all, Miss Stone," the coroner was saying, and thinking she was finished, Liza started to get up.

"A moment of your time, Miss Stone," said Andrew, smiling his most charming smile, first at her and then at the jury, as if to say: "We all understand how much you wish this was over, but let me lead you through a few more details."

Liza sat back down and flushed with embarrassment. She knew about cross-examination, but had forgotten.

"My God, the woman is actually blushing," said Giles. "I didn't think she had any blood in her veins. Trust Andrew to throw her off balance."

Andrew moved closer to the witness stand and said, with great sympathy, "I know this has been very difficult for you, Miss Stone, but I only have a few more questions. You have already said that you saw Lady Rainsborough first and noticed that her dress was all bloodstained."

"Yes, sir."

"Did you notice anything else about her?"

Liza had been listening to the other witnesses and didn't see the sense of hemming and hawing, only to be led down the garden path, as it were.

"Yes, sir. Like the others have said, her face was red and her lip swollen."

"And her neck?"

"Had red marks on it."

"Would you call them finger marks?"

"The marks could very well have come from fingers, yes, sir."

"You are Lady Rainsborough's personal maid, Miss Stone?"

"Yes, sir."

"And a lady's maid has almost as much intimate knowledge of her mistress as her husband does, isn't that so?"

"I am not sure what you mean, Mr. More."

"Oh, nothing scandalous, I assure you. I only mean that you help your mistress dress and undress. You prepare her for her bath."

"That is what an abigail *does,* Mr. More."

"So a lady's maid must be trustworthy and loyal, Miss Stone."

"Yes, sir."

"Loyal to whom?"

Liza answered without hesitation: "Why, to her employer, Mr. More."

"And in this case, that was?"

"Lord Rainsborough."

"So your loyalties, were, in reality, with your master and not your mistress?"

Liza looked a little taken aback. "Well, now, I wouldn't exactly say that."

"Tell me, who interviewed you for your position, Miss Stone?"

"Lord Rainsborough, sir."

"And then of course, Lady Rainsborough would have met with you?"

Liza hesitated for a minute. "No, sir."

"You mean, you were hired without meeting the lady you were to serve? And she never had a chance to approve or disapprove her husband's choice?"

"No, sir."

"Didn't you think that a bit odd, Miss Stone?"

"Not really, sir. Lord Rainsborough explained that Lady Rainsborough trusted his judgment completely."

"I see. So your first loyalty was indeed to the man you worked for, not to the woman."

There is nothing she can say but yes, thought Giles. Good work, Andrew.

"Yes, Mr. More," Liza replied in a low voice.

"Could you repeat that so all the court can hear?"

"Yes, sir."

"That must have been a difficult position to be in, then, Miss Stone," said Andrew smiling sympathetically.

"I am not sure what you mean, sir."

"To work so closely with Lady Rainsborough. To come to know her well, better than you knew her husband, I suspect. To have developed sympathy for her. And yet to be completely dependent upon Lord Rainsborough's goodwill."

"It was a little difficult," said Liza, her voice softening as she responded to the attention and understanding Andrew was giving her.

"It must have been very difficult, indeed, when you had to help Lady Clare after one of her husband's beatings," continued Andrew even more sympathetically.

"There has been no evidence of beatings introduced, Mr. More," the coroner reminded him.

"Excuse me," said Andrew, turning and giving a short bow to the coroner and the jury.

"On the night in question, Miss Stone, did you take Lady Rainsborough up to her room?" Andrew's voice was harder now.

"Yes, sir."

"And you helped her bathe?"

"In the morning, Lady Sabrina came over and we both helped her, sir."

"You have already stated that you noticed a red and swollen face and finger marks on her throat. Did you notice anything else?"

Liza hesitated, and then answered slowly, "There were bruises, sir."

"Bruises? What kind of bruises? And where?"

"Rather large bruises, sir. Around her ribs. Her back . . . her belly."

"And where did you think these bruises were from, Miss Stone?"

"I don't really know, sir."

"But if you were to guess, how might they have occurred?"

"They looked as if . . . perhaps they were made by the toe of a boot, sir."

"A gentleman's boot, Miss Stone?"

The abigail nodded.

"An earl's boot?" Andrew's voice was very hard now.

"I never saw him kick her, so I couldn't say as it was Lord Rainsborough's," said Liza, relieved that she could tell the truth and yet not be giving the coroner and the jury any reason to favor Clare.

"I wonder who else would have had the opportunity," mused Andrew with pseudo-innocence. "Mr. Peters, the butler? A footman? A groom from the stable?"

Liza blanched. "No, sir, of course not."

"It would seem that a husband had the greatest opportunity, then. Would you agree with me, Miss Stone, that in all likelihood it was Lord Rainsborough's boots which had left these marks?"

"Yes, sir," Liza answered with obvious reluctance.

"And had you ever seen Lady Rainsborough in this condition before?"

"What relevance have past beatings in this case, Mr. More?"

"Every relevance in a claim of self-defense, my lord. And I am grateful for your concession that there were past beatings, my lord."

Brilliant, Andrew, brilliant. Giles wanted to shout it aloud, but he could only turn to Sabrina and smile his exaltation. "I knew he could do it."

"Hush, Giles, he hasn't done it yet," said his sister. But Sabrina was feeling the same admiration for Andrew. And something else. She had always been equally sympathetic to Andrew's and his family's views. She understood his desire to be independent of their expectations, and also their repugnance for his usual clients. Today, however, she knew that they were wrong. Andrew More had found the one thing that his intelligence and talents were meant for, and such unity of purpose and dedication had a powerful effect on Sabrina. She found herself becoming aware of little things about Andrew she had never noticed before: the way his thick brown hair sprang back into place whenever he ran his hand through it, how expressive his face was, and how he used his voice like an instrument. She had always had fleeting moments of finding him attractive, but today, it was as though something coalesced inside her, and despite her ongoing sympathy for Giles and her sense of oneness with him, something had shifted so that when she looked over at her brother, she felt more separate from him and in some strange way, connected to Andrew.

It was now after one, and the coroner informed the court that since the next witness would likely take them past dinnertime, he would adjourn the inquiry for two hours.

"Thank God," said Giles. "It is exhausting just sitting here in this heat. I can't imagine how Clare can stand it. Come, Sabrina, let us get out of here and see if we can get a hackney to take us home for dinner."

"Will we have time, Giles?"

"I think so. And we certainly will not find any eatery in this neighborhood suitable for a lady."

They were lucky that the coroner had called his recess a little bit earlier than usual, for it meant that the crowds had had no time to gather and they were able to find a cab quite easily. It was too hot, and both were too nervous to eat much, so Sabrina had a platter of cold meats and salad sent up from the kitchen for them as well as a large pitcher of lemonade.

"Unless you wish for wine, Giles?" she asked.

"No, no. I am too thirsty for anything stronger than water or lemonade."

They ate silently and quickly, and after a quick freshening up, were back at the court just a few minutes before the coroner reconvened.

Andrew had had food and drink brought in for himself and Clare, and both were feeling refreshed. They had not been able to escape the heat, however, and Sabrina could see that Andrew's hair was damp and clinging to his neck.

"Whom do you think will be called next, Giles?"

"The coroner is in charge, so I assume the only one left is Clare."

And indeed, after everyone had been reseated, the coroner called Lady Rainsborough to the stand.

Chapter Nineteen

Giles thought his heart would break when he saw Clare get up and walk slowly over to her place. She looked so small and frail that he wanted to rush down and shriek into the faces of the vulgar, curious audience, that she should be released immediately. She couldn't survive this ordeal. Wasn't it obvious? And wasn't it also obvious that such a small, weak woman could never have killed her husband. Except, of course, she had.

She had to give her oath twice for the coroner was unable to hear her the first time.

"Lady Rainsborough, I realize that this will be difficult for you, but I wish to lead you through the events of the day and evening of the sixteenth. Can you tell us exactly what transpired between you and your husband."

Clare spoke very slowly and carefully, and in a tone barely above a whisper, so that everyone in the room had to pay careful attention.

"My husband, Lord Rainsborough, went out to his club that afternoon, as he usually did. I was at home to visitors."

"Did you receive any?"

"No, my lord. Lord Whitton called on me." Clare hesitated. "But I told Peters to tell him I couldn't receive him."

"And why was that?"

"My husband is . . . was a jealous man, my lord, especially when it came to Lord Whitton."

"And did he have any reason to be?"

"Before I met Justin, my husband, there was an understanding between Lord Whitton and myself. An informal understanding. I think that Justin was never able to forget that."

"Did you see Lord Whitton often during your marriage, Lady Rainsborough?"

"No, my lord. Despite the old friendship between us, I have seen Lord Whitton and his sister Lady Sabrina very little these past two years. Only when our paths cross socially, for the most part."

"And yet Lord Whitton called on you when your husband was away."

"Yes, my lord."

"Do you know why?"

"I found out later that evening."

"I see. We will get to that later. Please continue."

"I sent Giles . . . Lord Whitton away. My husband returned just as he was leaving and was . . . upset."

"How do you mean, upset?"

"He began to accuse me of an intimacy that did not exist. When he found out that I had sent Lord Whitton away without seeing him, he calmed down and apologized for his suspicions."

"And so you were in harmony that evening."

"Yes, my lord. Absolutely."

"What happened when you got to the Petershams'? It was the Petersham ball you attended?"

"Yes. Justin and I danced. I danced with several friends and acquaintances."

"Including Lord Whitton?"

"Yes. Then my husband went into the card room, and Lord Whitton asked if he could speak with me privately. At first, I said no. I knew if my husband saw us together, he would be angry. And I would suffer for it later."

"How do you mean, Lady Rainsborough?"

"He would beat me," Clare answered in a voice so low that all strained forward to hear her.

"What did Lord Whitton have to say to you?"

"He told me that my father was concerned about my health and had asked Giles to speak with me."

"And what did you reply?"

"That all was well. That I needed to get back to the ballroom. But when we got back, there was Justin, looking for me. We left soon after."

"Did anything happen on the way home?"

"Just the usual accusations."

"Which were?"

Clare swallowed before whispering, "That I was an unfaithful wife."

"And were you, Lady Rainsborough?"

"Never, my lord," Clare responded, her voice quivering with the intensity of her emotion.

"And when you reached home?"

"He sent all the servants to bed and took me into the library. He kept at me, wanting me to admit to something I'd never done."

"Did he strike you, Lady Rainsborough?"

"He started out as usual," she answered in a matter-of-fact tone that went straight to Giles's heart. "He struck my face, my mouth. He threw me down and . . ."

"And?"

"And kicked me."

"And what did you do?"

"If I curl up," said Clare expressionlessly, "then he can't get at my belly so easily. I let him kick me until he tires of it. It ends more quickly that way. Usually, the kicking is the end of it, but lately he is pulling me up and choking me. I was hoping it wasn't one of those times."

"But it was?"

"Yes, my lord."

"Is that all that he did?"

"My God, isn't that enough for him," said Giles in a furious whisper.

"No, then he hit my head against the back of the mantel. Then he opened the gun case and took out one of his pistols. He drew it down my cheek. He put it to my temple and threatened to shoot me if I didn't admit the truth. He said he would kill me and then call Lord Whitton out if I didn't admit we were lovers."

"Did you really believe he meant to shoot you, Lady Rainsborough?" the coroner asked. His tone had subtly changed from cold and businesslike to involved and curious.

"Yes, my lord. And if he had called out Lord Whitton, he would have killed him, too, for my husband was the better shot. I . . . I didn't really care what he did to me anymore, but I couldn't let him kill Giles. Giles was innocent of everything except being my good friend."

"What happened then, Lady Rainsborough?"

"He promised that it would all end if I only admitted that Giles and I were lovers. I didn't know what else to do. The more I protested our innocence, the worse he got. So I admitted the 'truth' " said Clare with gentle irony, "and promised I would never see Giles again. Then he started to choke me again. He was going to kill me anyway and then go after Giles, despite his promise." Clare's eyes were wide, and it seemed as though she was looking at a scene far away, trying to make it out as she slowly described it. "I was bent over his desk. I reached behind me and felt the brass candlestick and brought it down on his head."

"Did that stop him from choking you?"

"Yes, my lord."

"Was your husband on the floor?"

"Yes, my lord."

"Unconscious?"

"I . . . I don't think so. He moved, he started to get up. I saw his pistol, and I picked it up and walked into his arms and shot him."

The room was mesmerized, both by Clare's quiet expressionless voice and by her story itself. When she admitted shooting her husband, a collective intake of breath was heard.

"Was that the shot in the chest, Lady Rainsborough?"

"I suppose so. I wasn't aiming or thinking about it. I just wanted to stop him."

"And he was now on the floor?"

"Yes."

"Unmoving?"

"No, no." Clare was becoming a little agitated as she relived the moment. "I saw him move. I was sure he was going to come after me again. So I took the other pistol and shot him again."

"Through the temple."

"Yes, I think so, my lord."

"And so you admit to murdering your husband, Lady Rainsborough."

"Yes, my lord."

The collective intake of breath this time was a gasp.

"I have no further questions for Lady Rainsborough, Mr. More. She is your witness," said the coroner.

"I know this is very painful for you, Lady Rainsborough, but I wish you to reenter your state of mind that night."

Clare nodded.

"When your husband was choking you, what were you feeling?"

"The first time?"

"Both times," Andrew answered gently, after a slight pause to let it sink into the jury's and the coroner's minds that the woman before them had been so used to her husband's brutality that she needed to enumerate the occasions.

"Both times I was afraid . . . terrified he would kill me. But especially the second time, after I had told him what he wanted to hear."

"And so you reached behind you?"

"It wasn't so much that I reached behind me, Mr. More, as that he was pushing me back and I was trying to keep my balance . . . my hand brushed the candlestick by chance."

"And so without thinking, you grasped it and brought it down on Lord Rainsborough's head."

"Yes."

"Why didn't you summon help, Lady Rainsborough? Your husband was, after all, almost unconscious."

Clare had a puzzled look on her face. "There was no one to help me, Mr. More. The servants were all aware of the beatings, but they would have lost their positions had they tried to help. I know that from experience," she said sadly.

"What happened then?"

"As I told his lordship, Justin started to get up. I was so scared, and then I saw the pistol on the floor where he had dropped it. I picked it up and I shot him and he fell."

"Did you think that you had killed him?"

"No," Clare said, her eyes clouded, her voice trembling, as though she were back in the library.

"Why not?"

"His arm moved. I was sure he was going to get up and come after me again."

"Surely the amount of blood would have indicated a mortal wound, Lady Rainsborough?"

Clare sat very still and then looked down at her dress. By now, she was soaking with perspiration, and the dress clung to her. She pulled at it, as though to lift it off her skin, and then looked at her hands.

"There is so much blood . . . my dress . . ." She pulled again at the black silk. "His arm . . . oh God, he is getting up, he is going to kill me and then go after Giles . . ."

The spectators were again mesmerized into silence. It was clear that Lady Rainsborough's mind had slipped gears, as it were, and she was speaking of that night as though it were the present.

"You take the other pistol . . ." Andrew was speaking very softly.

"I have to stop him, but there are no bullets left," moaned Clare. "And there, he moves again."

"And so you get the poker from the fireplace."

"It is all I have to keep him away from me."

"So you didn't think you had killed your husband, Lady Rainsborough. In fact, you hadn't intended to kill him, just to prevent him from killing you and going after Lord Whitton."

"What else could I have done," whispered Clare, coming back to the present. "There was no one to help me. There was never anyone to help me. Except for Martha," she added in a whisper.

"And who is Martha, Lady Rainsborough?"

"Martha Barton. She was my abigail when I was first married."

"And you dismissed her?"

"No. Justin dismissed her."

"Do you know why?"

"Yes."

"Could you tell the coroner and the jury?"

Clare took a deep, shuddering breath. "She had seen the results of one of his attacks on me. She stood in front of me and defended me the next morning."

"You said 'one of his attacks'? So this behavior had been going on during your marriage?"

Clare nodded.

"From the beginning?"

"Almost. We were very, very happy at first. But when Justin drank, he became jealous."

"Did he have any cause, Lady Rainsborough," Andrew asked coolly.

"If by cause, you mean, was I ever interested in anyone else? Was I ever unfaithful? No, Mr. More. Something as simple as a smile or obvious enjoyment of another man's conversation or expertise on the dance floor was enough to set him off when he was drinking."

"Why didn't you leave, then? Go back to your parents?"

"I married Justin for better or worse, Mr. More. In sickness and in health. His drinking seemed like a sickness to me. And when the illness passed, he was the same tender and loving Justin I had originally married."

"So you would say you loved your husband, Lady Rainsborough?"

"Oh, yes. Very much. And at first all he did was hit me once or twice. Cause a black eye or a swollen lip. And there would be weeks of the good Justin which would wipe out the memory of the bad. He would always cry and swear he would never hurt me again."

"And you believed him?" said Andrew, with an air of disbelief.

"It is so hard to explain, Mr. More. It was like living with two different people. Whenever I would begin to think that the drunken Justin was my true husband, that all was hopeless, the loving Justin would reappear. I thought at times I was going mad."

"Did Martha ever witness any of these early attacks?"

"No, although she saw the results of them. I always tried, had some sort of story ready, to explain my black eyes and swollen face. But I am sure she guessed."

"Then what made her finally risk her position?"

"Things were beginning to get worse. The time in between Justin's outbursts became shorter. He had started pushing me and kicking . . ." Clare's voice trailed off.

"And then?"

"I became . . . We realized we were going to become parents. I was so happy. Justin promised . . . I was sure he meant it this time . . . that he would never drink again. He was so protective of me. Almost overprotective," she added, with a laugh that was more like a sob.

"And so your marriage turned around?"

"I thought so. But then when we attended a neighbor's dinner dance, Justin had one drink. And then another. The next day he shut himself in the library with a bottle of brandy. When he came out, he was more out of control than I had ever seen him. He accused me of terrible things . . ." Clare's voice trailed off again.

"Go on," Andrew said encouragingly.

"He called me . . ." Clare stopped.

"He called you what?"

"He called me a whore and an unfaithful slut. He denied the baby was his and accused me of having an affair with one of our neighbors."

"Where were you when this was going on?"

"He had come into my bedroom."

"Did he strike you?"

"Yes. He held me up and hit me again and again. Then he threw me against the dressing table, and when I slipped and fell to the floor, he started kicking me."

"Where did he kick you, Lady Rainsborough?" Andrew's voice was gentle and sympathetic.

"In the belly. He swore he would kill my baby before he would acknowledge it for his own. And he did." Clare dropped her head in her hands and cried quietly.

"And that was what Martha saw?"

"She came in at the end of it. She was with me when I lost the baby."

"You were quite ill afterward?"

"Yes."

"And Lord Rainsborough?"

"He was distraught. He abased himself and told me he wouldn't come near me until I summoned him. He begged my forgiveness and solemnly promised on the Bible that he would never drink again."

"And so you forgave him again."

"Not right away. But eventually. It is very hard to explain, but Justin was so sincere in his repentance and his desire to change that I wouldn't turn him away."

"And yet he never changed. In fact, the man who threatened your unborn child's life, then took that life, eventually threatened yours. You had every reason to believe he would carry out his threat, didn't you, Lady Rainsborough?"

"Yes," responded Clare, her tearstained face set and strained.

"I know this has been very difficult for you, Lady Rainsborough. Thank you for telling us your story."

"I have one question for Lady Rainsborough," said the coroner.

"Of course, my lord."

"Lady Rainsborough, you have given us a vivid picture of your marriage. We have only your word for much of it, but that consideration aside, did you ever attempt to defend yourself in any way, verbally, or otherwise. Did you ever try to stop Lord Rainsborough, protest his treatment, dispute his accusations? In other words, might you not have prevented much of this, especially the awful denouement, by standing up for yourself earlier?"

Clare smiled and shook her head. "At first I tried to convince Justin he was wrong, my lord. I attempted a quarrel. I even once tried to defend myself against him by pushing him back. It only made things worse. I know I must appear a very weak person to you, my lord, but I learned very soon that if I just took the beating without protest, it ended sooner. The better part of valor, in this case, seemed discretion in every sense of the word. It did not leave me much self-respect, but it helped me survive," she added, with a show of spirit.

"Thank you, Lady Rainsborough. You may step down. I know of no other witnesses. Mr. More?"

"I would like to call two other people to the stand, my lord. The first is Martha Barton."

Chapter Twenty

Sabrina and Giles had sat very still as Clare haltingly told the story of her marriage. It was as though they, along with the other spectators, were holding their collective breath, not wanting a sound or movement to distract from any word of her testimony. By the end of it, however, tears were streaming down Sabrina's face, and Giles, handing her his handkerchief, wished he could find similar release from his strong feeling.

At first, as Clare recalled the beginning of her marriage, he had felt the old pain and jealousy. Then fury at Rainsborough. And, he was ashamed to say, at Clare. How could she have married such a man? No, not a man, a chameleon. And even if he could bring himself to understand how she had fallen in love with his looks and his charm, how could she have stayed with him, especially after it became clear that he would never change? She could have gone home to her parents. Or, if she hadn't wanted a scandal, she could have lived with him the way many a ton wife did: maintaining her independence and a separate bedroom. Instead, Clare obviously let him back into her bed again and again.

But Giles's anger at Clare and rage at her husband disappeared, leaving a curious numbness when she continued her account of Justin's attacks. How could a man treat any woman that way, especially a loving wife? Of course Giles knew of men who beat their wives. But surely it occurred mainly in the lower classes and usually involved only a black eye or a split lip. He had always ignored these signs on the shopkeeper's or farmer's wife, believing that it was a private matter. So, too, was violence between a man and his mistress. Everyone knew that Lord Carlton mistreated his bits of muslin, but that was the risk all women took when they sold their bodies.

But Justin Rainsborough, to all appearances, had been a besotted husband. Always hovering over Clare. Protecting her. Arriving late, leaving early. Why, in the first months of their marriage, men had wagered over their degrees of lateness. How could someone be so different in private? And how could any man have raised his hand to someone so small and helpless as Clare? Hold her down and punch her repeatedly? Kick her hard enough to lose a child? It was so horrible a picture, so far beyond his comprehension, that Giles couldn't respond to it at all, not with sorrow or rage.

But he reached out to take Sabrina's hand and comfort her.

"Giles, how could we not have *seen* what was happening? How could we have let her down so?"

"Hush, Sabrina," he whispered, as Martha took the stand and the court stirred around them. "How *could* we have known? She never told anyone anything. And in public at least, they appeared the most devoted of couples."

Andrew led Martha quickly through her early years as Clare's abigail.

"And so, when Lady Clare Dysart became Lady Rainsborough, she took you with her?"

"Yes, sir. We was very close by then."

"You were fond of Lady Rainsborough?"

"Very, sir. She was always kind and generous to me. I would have done anything for her."

"Including defending her from her husband?"

"Yes, sir."

"When did you become aware of Lord Rainsborough's behavior, Miss Barton?"

"Oh, from the very beginning. Me own ma were treated rough by me stepfather. I knew it wasn't no door my lady had run into. And I know all too well how brandy chases the charm away."

"Did you talk to Lord Rainsborough about it?"

"No, sir. It weren't my place."

"Did you talk to anyone else about it? Another servant?"

"Aye. To Mrs. Clarke, the housekeeper."

"And what was her response?"

"That it was none of our business."

"But you finally made it your business, Miss Barton?"

"I had to. He were kicking her and kicking her. It was not even her third month."

"So what did you do," Andrew asked quietly.

"I tried to pull him away. I screamed bloody blue murder, which is what finally stopped him," said Martha with a grim smile. "He didn't want no other servants to come running."

"After he finally stopped, what did you do?"

"I locked him out and got my lady into her bed. She started cramping something terrible." Martha's voice became lower. "She lost the babe the next morning."

"She had had no trouble with her pregnancy until then?"

"No, sir," said Martha stoutly.

"So you would conclude that it was her husband's beating that caused the miscarriage?"

Martha looked at Andrew as though he was mentally deficient. "Weren't it obvious from my story, Mr. More?"

Andrew could not help smiling. He covered his mouth with his hand and cleared his throat before his next question. "What happened a few days after?"

"I got the sack. I was told to get my things and be gone by the afternoon. I didn't even get a chance to say good-bye to my lady," added Martha, "and I always felt bad about that. I didn't want her to think I had deserted her."

"And are you employed now, Miss Barton."

Martha frowned. "Yes."

"Where?"

"As a parlor maid in the Winston household."

"That is a step down, is it not, from a lady's maid?"

"Yes, sir, but I were turned out without a reference."

"I see. Thank you very much for your testimony, Miss Barton."

"I were very happy to speak for my lady, Mr. More. And I for one says he got what was coming to him, and I hope you men," she continued, glaring at the jury, "be intelligent enough to think the same." That had not been part of her planned testimony, and Andrew tried to hide his amused consternation. "I beg the court's pardon," he said, addressing the coroner. "I have only one more witness, my lord."

"Go ahead, Mr. More," said the coroner, waving him on.

"Dr. Simkin."

Giles looked over with interest and curiosity as a plump, elderly man took the stand.

"You are Dr. Simkin?"

"Yes, sir."

"You reside in Devon."

The doctor nodded.

"Please speak up, sir."

"Yes, my family has lived there for over a hundred years. I am the youngest son of the late Baronet Simkin."

"Can you recall what you were doing on the night of January 25th?"

"I had just returned home from a call when I received a summons from Rainsborough Hall."

"Which you answered immediately?"

"Of course. I have been the Rainsborough physician for years."

"What did you find when you got to the house?"

"Lord Rainsborough was distraught. Lady Rainsborough was increasing, and he feared she was losing the child."

"How did Lord Rainsborough look?"

"As I said, he was distraught, Mr. More."

"Soberly distraught or drunkenly, Dr. Simkin," asked Andrew with some irony.

"Uh, well, it did seem as though Lord Rainsborough had been drinking. Which was understandable, given the circumstances."

"And what were the circumstances, Doctor?"

"Lady Rainsborough was indeed miscarrying."

"Could you describe Lady Rainsborough's appearance on that night?"

The doctor hesitated.

"You *did* examine her?"

"Of course. Er . . . she . . . that is, her face was bruised and swollen."

"And her belly?"

"Also was very bruised. Of course," he added eagerly, "this was understandable."

"Understandable?" asked Andrew, raising his eyebrows.

"Lord Rainsborough told me, and Lady Rainsborough confirmed it, that she had fallen from her horse."

"And did the injuries you witnessed seem consistent with that explanation?"

"Well, yes, they could have occurred that way. Certainly her face . . ."

"And her belly?"

"Lady Rainsborough herself explained that she had first been thrown against the pommel of her saddle, and I saw no reason to doubt her."

"No reason at all? Tell me, Dr. Simkin, did any other possible explanation cross your mind that night?"

"It *did* seem like extensive bruising, I admit. But Lord Rainsborough was so concerned. And, after all, it was really none of my business to ask further questions."

"Of course not," Andrew replied smoothly, and the doctor winced.

"Tell me, Dr. Simkin, you have heard Lady Rainsborough's testimony and that of her former abigail? Were the injuries to Lady Rainsborough's face such as could have been caused by the beating you have heard described?"

"Yes," replied the doctor, taking out his handkerchief and wiping the sweat from his forehead.

"And the miscarriage. Now that you have heard Lady Rainsborough's story, would you say that it was Lord Rainsborough's brutal behavior that led to the loss of their child?"

"If he kicked her like that, yes."

"If? Do you still have doubts after two eyewitnesses, Dr. Simkin?"

"Well, no, I suppose not," the doctor stammered nervously.

"Thank you, Doctor." Andrew turned away, as though he were finished, but just before the doctor began to get up, turned back again.

"Surely, Dr. Simkin, you must have suspected Lord Rainsborough of beating his wife?"

"Yes, it did cross my mind," the doctor admitted reluctantly.

"Why did you not report it?"

"I have known the family for years . . ."

"Although not Lord Rainsborough."

"That is true, but both their stories were consistent. He seemed such a devoted husband. I, uh, didn't want to intrude on what, after all, was a private matter."

"If you saw a man beating his horse on the high street, would you have protested? Taken action, Doctor?"

"I . . . really don't know. After all, a man has a right to deal with his private property as he will."

"And a wife is a man's property according to law. Well, you have made a point, Doctor," Andrew said sarcastically. "Thank you, you may step down."

The doctor opened his mouth to protest, but the coroner waved him down. "This is your last witness, Mr. More?"

"Yes, my lord."

"Then we will attempt to bring this inquest to a conclusion today. The jury will please confer in order to offer a verdict."

The twelve men who had been facing the court gathered their chairs around in a rather haphazard circle. There was no way to tell from their faces which way they were leaning, and as Giles watched them begin their consultation, he had no idea if they would take five minutes or three hours to come to a decision.

"Do you want to try for a breath of fresh air, Sabrina?" he asked his sister.

"No, I would be too afraid we might miss something, Giles."

"I thought Andrew did an excellent job, didn't you?"

Sabrina's face lit up. "Oh, yes. If anyone could convince a jury of Clare's innocence, it is Andrew." In fact, thought Sabrina, he could persuade *me* of anything. That pull toward Andrew More that had been present since she first met him, had grown stronger and stronger as she watched him expertly questioning his witnesses. He had been especially good with Clare. Something in his manner toward her subtly offered strength and support as he drew out the horrifying story of her marriage. He was sitting next to Clare now, and from Clare's occasional smile, Sabrina guessed that Andrew was trying to keep her amused and distracted. And he had made sure he was sitting in such a way as to block her view of the jury.

"What do you think they are saying, Giles," Sabrina asked, after a glance over to the conferring men.

"I do not see how they can find her anything but innocent," said Giles.

"But if they don't?"

"It is certainly not over. She would go to trial. Andrew would have more time to prepare a case. But the coroner's verdict would lend some weight, so it must end here," said Giles vehemently.

"They can't bring it to trial, Giles. The thought of her

being convicted of murder ... of the sentence ..."
Sabrina's voice trailed off.

"That particular sentence hasn't been handed down in
this century, Brina," said Giles reassuringly. "We are
more civilized in this day and age."

"Oh, yes, we are so civilized. We might very well only
hang a woman for acting in her own defense."

They were both suddenly silent, each one trying to
push out of their minds the image of Clare, eyes covered,
mounting a scaffold. Or even worse, Clare bound to a
stake, flames licking at the edge of her dress.

The images were so unthinkable for Giles that he felt
he had awakened into a nightmare, not fallen asleep into
one. How could he be sitting here in this courtroom waiting to hear if Clare, his childhood friend, the small ten-
year-old who had arrived at Whitton that summer long
ago, the woman he had grown to love, would go to trial
for murder. It was unthinkable and disorienting. Were she
released—surely she *must* be released—then he was going to get them both out of this waking dream. He was
going to offer her his name, his protection, and they
would return to Whitton and live the life they should have
had, would have had, if Justin Rainsborough had not
come along. They would walk and ride and fish and pretend that the past few years had not happened. He would
put his arms around Clare and never let her go. Never let
her be hurt again. He would stand between her and all the
world, if need be.

"Giles, they are pushing their chairs back," whispered
Sabrina.

The whole room suddenly became still, so that the only
sound was the scraping of the last juror's chair as he
moved it into place.

The coroner surveyed the court as if to say: Not a
breath, not one word, as we hear this verdict.

"Have you reached a verdict," he asked the jury.

The spokesman, a middle-aged gentleman clad in black
worsted, rose.

"We have, my lord."

"And what is your verdict?"

Giles and Sabrina's hands reached out and found each other.

"We find that Lady Rainsborough killed her husband in self-defense, my lord, and should not therefore, be charged."

"Thank God, thank God," said Giles.

The room, which had first been buzzing with whispers, now became noisier as spectators expressed their reactions to the verdict. When Giles was finally able to get Sabrina and himself downstairs and push their way toward Clare, it was only to find her gone, for as soon as Andrew heard the first syllables, he had grabbed Clare's hand and gotten her out through the side door. Giles and Sabrina stood there as people pushed their way past, out of the court. They could hear the crowd in front letting go a great cheer, and Giles looked over at his sister and smiled.

"I'll wager they would have been shouting as loud and joyfully had she been bound over for trial, but I am glad to hear it at all." He offered Sabrina his arm. "Hold on, Brina. We may as well let the crowd sweep us out."

Clare had followed where Andrew led her for the past few days: back into the awful memories of her marriage, into the courtroom, telling her story, and now, out the side door and into a waiting hackney. She felt empty and weightless, and not quite sure what the verdict had meant. She thought she had heard "will not be charged," but the spokesman hadn't even finished when Andrew grabbed her arm to rush her out before the crowd reacted.

She supposed it must have been a favorable verdict for Andrew, who had sat down opposite her, was smiling at her and telling her what a wonderful job she had done. What was it he thought she had done so well? Told her story? Survived her marriage? Killed her husband? She felt hollow and disoriented, and she leaned back against the seat and closed her eyes.

"Are you all right, Lady Rainsborough?" asked Andrew, anxiously grabbing her hands. His touch, solid and human and warm, brought her back into her body. She opened her eyes and gave him a weak smile.

"I am not sure, Mr. More. I feel . . . nothing. Not even relief," she said. "Surely I should be feeling something. I am not going to burn or hang, so it seems."

"You have been through a terrible ordeal, Lady Rainsborough, and you are likely still in shock," Andrew reassured her. "And this heat is enough to make anyone feel light-headed. Once you get home and have the time and privacy to take this all in, you will feel much more yourself."

Home? Where was that, Clare wondered. When she was small, it had been her parents' house. A place where she had never felt quite at home. Then it was Whitton. After the first year, Clare had felt that every summer she was coming home to Sabrina and especially to Giles. Why hadn't she made her home with Giles two years ago? Was it because he had become almost too familiar, too much like family? Justin and Devon had then become her home. Now, although she supposed she would inherit both the hall and the town house, she felt homeless.

But she could hardly say any of this to Andrew More, so she just nodded.

When they reached St. James Street, he handed her down. "Come, let me make sure you are made comfortable."

Peters, who had gotten home before them, opened the door, and Clare felt she was seeing him for the first time in two years. This man had been aware of her husband's brutality and had done nothing. Ah, but what could he have done, she thought. What could anyone have done?

"Please summon Lady Rainsborough's abigail, Peters," said Andrew.

"Yes, sir."

"No, Peters," Clare interjected just as the butler turned to go.

Andrew looked over at her in surprise.

"Please give Liza two months wages and dismiss her."

Peters was very proud of his ability to maintain his imperturbable expression, but this order caused him to raise his eyebrows.

"And, Peters, please send a footman over to the Winston household. If she wants to, I would like Martha Barton to return to my employ."

The butler bowed. "Yes, my lady."

"Good for you, Clare," said Andrew when the butler left. "Pardon me, I mean Lady Rainsborough."

"Please call me Clare. It seems foolish to be so formal after all we have been through today."

"Then I am Andrew."

"Will you join me in a glass of lemonade, Andrew," she asked. "You must be as exhausted as I am."

Andrew hesitated. Clare looked like she was ready to collapse, not hostess a social visit. But he was thirsty, and she probably needed refreshment as well as rest, so he nodded and said "Thank you, Lady— I mean, Clare."

The drawing room was on the side of the house, which was shaded by a large plane tree. The heat of the day was finally beginning to dissipate, and Clare had the footman who delivered their tray open the French doors.

"Even that slight breeze feels like a taste of heaven after being in hell," said Andrew, loosening his cravat without thinking. When he realized what he had done, and started to apologize, Clare said: "Please, Andrew. After what we have been through together, you may be a little informal without offending me! You are lucky that you are wearing something adjustable," she added, fingering the heavy black silk.

Andrew lifted his glass. "To the most courageous lady of my acquaintance."

Clare put up her hand as though to protest. "No, to a most persistent and articulate defender. Truly, I owe you my life, Andrew," she added with quiet fervor. "I am not sure I really understood that until now. And although I have no sense of what I will do with the rest of it, I am forever indebted to you that I have any choice at all."

"Will you stay here or go to your parents', Clare?" Andrew asked after they had both taken long swallows of their lemonade.

"I don't know, Andrew. I feel very empty of every feeling right now. And where *does* a woman go who has murdered her husband," she added, trying to sound humorous, but obviously still tormented.

"Clare, you know that if you had not killed him, he would have killed you."

"I felt that way then. When you brought me back to that night at the inquest, I felt it again. Now, however, it seems none of it happened. Or if any of it did, it was to a different person. I am outside it all, only an onlooker. It is as though there are two Clare's, one who is standing over her husband with a poker and the other who is watching her. And neither feels anything. Indeed, I don't know if I will feel anything again," she said with a sad smile.

"I have seen this before, Clare," said Andrew reassuringly. "In many cases involving violence, the victim seems to become removed. You are still in shock."

"But I am not the victim, Andrew. Justin was."

"Oh, no, my dear. You are indeed the victim in this case. Now, I think it is time you rested," said Andrew, putting his glass down and walking over to where Clare was sitting, her eyes staring out the French doors, but obviously seeing nothing.

He reached out, took her glass, and put it down on the table in front of her. She turned toward him then and really saw him for the first time that day. His hair was all elflocks and wet curls both from the heat and from running his hand through it. His cravat was pulled loose. He had dark circles under his eyes, no doubt from late-night briefings with his solicitor, preparing his defense strategies.

"Oh, Andrew, you look worse than I must," she said, with such sympathy that he wasn't insulted. "I will rest and hope that something of myself is restored. It was very painful to remember, Andrew, but thank you for making me." She hesitated. "I feel that we have become more than counsel and client. I feel we are friends. May I consider you so?"

Andrew smiled. "Of course. And as such, I fully expect to have a waltz now and again when you return to society."

Clare shook her head.

"No, you won't waltz with me?"

"I doubt I will be receiving more invitations this Season, Andrew. And even if I did, I would turn them down."

"I would wager a small fortune that you will be the most sought-after guest, my dear. At least for a few weeks, until another scandal captures the ton's attention. And I would strongly recommend you accept at least a few of those invitations. Oh, not right away. Give yourself time to recuperate. But you must show your face, Clare, to convince everyone that the jury's verdict was the right one and your counsel a most competent one," he added with a grin.

Clare shook her head again, and then swayed against him.

"Damn me for being a fool. Let's get you right to bed."

Andrew led her slowly to the door and summoned the butler. "Has Liza left yet?"

"No, sir."

"Then get her, please. She can do one last thing for her mistress before she leaves."

Andrew hated to leave Clare in Liza's hands, but there was no choice. He certainly couldn't bring her up to her bedroom himself. And by the time she awoke, Martha would certainly have returned.

He watched them both up the stairs until he was satisfied that Clare would make it.

"Tell your mistress when she awakes that I will call on her tomorrow," he said to the butler.

"Yes, sir."

"And Peters."

"Yes, Mr. More."

"If Martha arrives, please send her up to Lady Rainsborough's room and send Liza away."

Chapter Twenty-one

Clare awoke late the next morning, partly because of her exhaustion and partly because the weather had changed. The heat had finally broken during the night with the arrival of a heavy rain, and it was a dark, wet morning. She lay there, all the energy leached out of her, listening to the steady beat of the raindrops on the roof. Perhaps she would stay in bed forever, she thought. Slowly she became conscious that there was someone else in the room with her. Liza, she thought, and opened her eyes. There was Martha, sitting by the window, sewing.

"Martha?" Clare whispered.

Martha dropped the shift she was mending and hurried over to the bed.

"My lady. You are finally awake."

"What time is it, Martha? And how did you get here?"

"It is past eleven, my lady. And I left the Winstons' as soon as you sent for me."

Clare began to pull herself up, and Martha reached behind her and settled her pillows against the bedstead.

"I was hoping you would come, Martha," said Clare. "But I didn't dream it would be so soon. You have always been too good to me. I wouldn't have survived my marriage without your caring. Or your testimony," she added in a stronger voice. "Thank you. It took courage to come forward."

"Not as much courage as you, my lady."

"Do you think so? I felt I only revealed my own cowardice."

"You were as brave as any soldier when you defended yourself."

Clare gave her a wan smile. "You mean when I shot Lord Rainsborough? I was afraid for my life, Martha. And Lord Whitton's," she added.

"Which reminds me," said Martha with a smile. "Lord Whitton and his sister have been here twice already, but I had Peters send them away. They will be back again, I am sure."

Clare closed her eyes and sat back against the pillows. "I don't think I can see anyone yet, Martha. Especially not Lord Whitton. I don't know how I will ever face any of them again."

"You will do it slowly, my lady. Your father has also called, of course. And Mr. More."

Clare's expression lightened. "Did Mr. More say when he would return?"

"This afternoon, I believe."

"Perhaps you could send a message to my father, Martha. If Andrew were there to support me, I think I could see them. But not until later this afternoon," she added.

"I'll have Peters send a footman to deliver the message, my lady. And the Whittons?"

"Not yet, Martha, not yet."

Clare knew that Giles and Sabrina had been there through the whole inquest. At one point during the proceedings, she had glanced up and seen Giles leaning over the railing. He had smiled at her, a caring, encouraging smile. She had done nothing to acknowledge it. How could she? What would she have done? Smiled back and then proceeded to give her testimony. That shameful scene with Justin, where she gave in and "confessed" that she and Giles were lovers? She had tried to make it clear that she had lied only to save Giles. That she had killed Justin almost as much for Giles's safety as for her own. But in doing that, she felt she had drawn him into the horror that had been her marriage. That she had somehow contaminated him. He must despise her: for marrying

Justin, for staying with Justin, and finally, for killing Justin.

Perhaps she could receive Sabrina again. Her old friend had been faithful and so good that night of Justin's death. But she was Giles's twin. They were so close.

It was all too much. She had saved her own life, but to what purpose? What kind of life could she now look forward to? She could go back and live with her parents, she supposed. She was sure that they would ask her. Or she could return to Devon. But how could she live at Rainsborough Hall? Every room would hold a memory. Some would be good, but that would make it even worse. Of course she could stay in town, as Andrew had suggested. If she stayed in town, then at least she wouldn't lose her contact with him. He had heard her story first, and he hadn't despised her or condemned her: he had listened and comforted her and saved her life. She owed him at least the waltz he had requested.

Clare's meeting with her parents was bittersweet. At last, she thought, she was receiving their full attention. And their genuine love and concern. How could she not appreciate it and receive it. Yet letting it in at long last only made her remember how she had longed for it as a child. Perhaps if she had felt more loved then, her life would have been very different.

As she had expected, they were ready to leave London and take her with them, and were clearly disappointed when she refused. Andrew, who had arrived after her mother and father, supported her in her decision, saying that the only way to deal with scandalmongers and gossips was to brazen it out.

"But she will be expected to observe a mourning period, Andrew," protested Clare's mother.

"I think wearing black and not receiving visitors when one has oneself caused a husband's demise, might cause as much gossip, don't you think, Lady Howland?"

"I think he is right, my dear," commented the marquess. "Why on earth *should* Clare mourn the death of such a monster."

"I will come to Howland when the Season is over," Clare promised, and her parents had to accept that.

After the marquess and marchioness had gone, Sabrina was announced. Clare, who had been anxiously expecting both the Whittons was relieved and gave her a welcoming smile.

"I won't stay long," she promised. "Giles wanted to come again, but I convinced him that too many visitors today would exhaust you. He will likely call tomorrow."

"I am glad you called, Sabrina, for I wanted to thank you for your willingness to testify if you were needed."

"There is no need to thank me, Clare. It was the least I could have done. I still feel terrible that you had to suffer those two years alone."

Andrew, who had been watching Clare carefully, saw the look of anxiety that flitted across her face and broke in: "I think that Lady Rainsborough, I mean Clare, blames no one for those years and is ready to leave them behind?"

Clare nodded gratefully, and Sabrina felt shut out as her friend and Andrew shared a quick intimate glance. Andrew More had never offered her such a quick and ready sympathy. Andrew More had never done anything to demonstrate any special interest in Lady Sabrina Whitton. But it was understandable, she supposed, that his position as legal defender of Lady Clare Rainsborough might lead him to consider himself her friend. Perhaps with the potential for more?

"What are your plans for the rest of the Season, Clare? If you are not going home to Howland, Giles and I wanted you to know that we very much wish to bring you to Whitton."

"And interrupt your own Season? No, thank you, Sabrina, although I appreciate your kindness. Andrew has convinced me that staying on and doing a modest amount of socializing will make the scandal go away quicker.

And I have promised him a waltz," Clare added, trying to be humorous.

Indeed, thought Sabrina, and then was appalled by her reaction. Andrew was right. The ton was drawn to weakness the way a wolf was drawn to a lamb: try to run, and they were down on you at once. But turn and face them, and they eventually lost interest and sought out other victims. Clare did not have to resume a full social life, but staying in London and attending a few functions would, in the long run, serve her well. And why shouldn't she give a waltz to Andrew More, the man who had saved her life?

Sabrina only stayed a short while and left with Andrew, who asked if he could call her a hackney.

"No, thank you, Andrew. It is a lovely day, so I will walk home."

"Surely you should not do so unescorted. May I offer you my company?"

"It is a short walk, as you know. There is no need for you to go out of your way," Sabrina responded calmly.

"But it *is* a lovely day, and I would enjoy the walk."

Sabrina nodded, and they walked along in silence for a few minutes.

"You were truly impressive at the inquest, Andrew," said Sabrina, breaking the silence.

"Thank you, Sabrina. I was not sure that I could pull it off. And I knew if Clare's case were brought to trial, she would be more at risk. I had to be very strong at the inquest. And I, too, admire your willingness to take the stand, had I needed you."

"Oh, I think it took no courage at all compared to Clare telling her story. And she would not have done that for anyone else, Andrew, I am convinced. You were right to push her, even though I did not think so at the time."

Andrew looked over at Sabrina and lifted his eyebrows. "So I have your approval at last, Sabrina," he said teasingly. He gave her one of his quirky grins and suddenly she felt much better than she had all afternoon. He was not looking at her in that protective way he had Clare . . . but then, did she really want that from him? She enjoyed it when they spoke as equals, even if it was in disagreement. And she knew that she wanted something more from him, much more.

Giles was at his club when Sabrina reached Grosvenor Square, and she had no opportunity to talk to him. They were both to be at the Kendall ball, but had planned to arrive separately. Sabrina got there first and found herself surrounded by friends and acquaintances who wanted to know just what had occurred at the inquest.

"I heard that you were willing to testify for Clare, Sabrina," said Lucy Kirkman. "That must have been terrifying to contemplate."

"It wouldn't have been difficult for me, Lucy, since I wasn't the one in danger," Sabrina responded quietly. "It was Clare's story that convinced the jury."

"Imagine little Clare Dysart having the spirit to defend herself! Why, I remember when I dumped fish bait on her, and she only stood there, waiting for Giles to rescue her."

"Some of us change as we grow up, Lucy." Sabrina's comment, although uttered in dulcet tones, was still insulting enough to make even Lucy Kirkman shut her mouth, and when Lord Avery asked her for a dance, Lucy was quite eager to give it to him.

Sabrina was praying that Giles would arrive soon and come to her rescue when she saw Andrew approaching her. She gave him the warmest and most spontaneous welcome of their acquaintance, and he thought to himself that perhaps he was being foolish to rein in his feelings for his friend's sister. Then he took in the crowd and realized that she would probably have looked at anyone like that who could get her away from such a group.

"They are striking a waltz, Sabrina," he observed with a smile.

"Yes, they are, Andrew. And if you do not ask me for

this dance, I will never speak to you again," Sabrina said, sotto voce.

"May I have this waltz, Sabrina," Andrew asked with mock formality.

"Why, I would be delighted, Andrew."

"I am very surprised at your unladylike boldness," Andrew said with a twinkle in his eye as they moved out onto the floor.

"Had you not asked me, Andrew, I would have just grabbed you and led you out myself. *That* would have distracted them from Clare for a while."

"I thought it would be good to show my face tonight to see if I could deflect a little attention," Andrew said, expertly guiding Sabrina past an older couple with slight pressure on her waist. His hand felt warm and strong, and she was sorry when his touch became lighter again.

"I see my brother is dancing with Lucy Kirkman."

"Yes, well, I was mildly insulting to her, and she was looking for any port in a storm," smiled Sabrina. "Oh, dear, I shouldn't have suggested that your brother . . ."

"Is a rather stiff, formal fellow, full of his own consequence? Lucy is so outrageously frank that it will be good for him." Andrew was silent for a while, and Sabrina, who had been studiously focusing on his cravat, lifted her eyes to him for a moment and then lowered them quickly.

"Do you think Lucy will manage to hook Giles after all, Sabrina? I remember her as quite an angler those summers I would visit Whitton."

"I might have said yes just a week ago," Sabrina replied. "But now . . ."

"Now that Clare is free, do you mean?"

"But is she free, Andrew?" asked Sabrina as the music stopped and they began to walk off the floor. "Free to love, I mean. I suppose she is free to marry. She can hardly be expected to go into deep mourning for a husband who tried to kill her."

"I never knew Lady Rainsborough very well, Lady

Sabrina. And I never did think she was what Giles needed. But I have come to admire her very much. She has more courage and spirit than I ever gave her credit for. But she has also gone through an ordeal that would leave the strongest person in shock. I doubt she will feel ready to love or marry for a while."

Giles was announced just as Andrew and Sabrina joined a small group of friends. Andrew said: "I'll bring him over to you, Sabrina. He'll never find us in this crush." Sabrina gave him a grateful smile.

When Andrew returned with her brother in tow, Sabrina could tell that Giles was in no mood for socializing. And when Lucy Kirkman joined their group, Sabrina almost felt sorry for her. Giles was everything that was polite, but the slight current of energy that had flowed between them was no longer alive. Giles asked Lucy for the next cotillion, which was also a supper dance, but Sabrina knew, with her twin's sixth sense, that things had changed.

Giles himself was only half-present. He had spent the last few days in a state of frustration. After a year or so of convincing himself that his feelings for Clare had died back down to pure friendship, he had been taken by surprise. He desperately wanted to be by Clare's side, and it was agony to keep himself away. But he had known Andrew was right: any move on his part would have put her in jeopardy. As he had listened to her testimony, he had been torn between fury and love. Had she not killed Justin Rainsborough, he would have done it himself, cheerfully and without regret. Clare deserved to be cherished and loved, and instead she had been brutalized. She looked so small and helpless sitting there revealing the horror that was her marriage. She needed his care, and he was determined to give it to her as soon as the nightmare of the inquest had passed.

It was almost two weeks before Clare accepted an invitation. To her surprise, there had been no lack of them; indeed, she believed there might have been more than she usually received.

She chose the Duchess of Ross's ball in hopes that she would be lost in the crush. The thought of arriving alone terrified her, however. Giles had made his promised visit, but it had been a short one, and she had been terribly uncomfortable with him. All she could think of was Justin's accusation and her own false admission of guilt. She feared their friendship was hopelessly contaminated, and although she knew that Giles and Sabrina would happily have included her in their party, she couldn't ask them. She sent a short note to Andrew More asking him to call on her and very timidly asked if he would be willing to escort her to the Ross's ball.

"I did promise you a waltz, Andrew," she said, trying to make the atmosphere lighter.

"I would be delighted to support you in this, Clare," said Andrew. So when Lady Rainsborough was announced, Andrew More, Esquire was right beside her.

It seemed to Clare that the sea of faces below her turned to the door at the same time, their eyes eager and curious. For a moment she was afraid that the faces and voices had blended into a real sea, one which threatened to engulf her should she step down into it. But Andrew placed his arm under her hand and led her down, and the sea parted before them as though he were Moses.

Giles, who was hurrying over, did not miss the grateful look Clare gave his old friend and was seized by an awful jealousy. Damn it, *he* should have been the one Clare was leaning on. Yet what could be more natural than that after her ordeal, a woman would depend upon such an able defender.

Giles helped them push through the crowd and reach the corner of the room where Sabrina was waiting with Clare's parents. It felt to Clare that she walked a very long distance, though it was, in truth, not a particularly large ballroom. Her father's smile and mother's embrace welcomed her, and Sabrina squeezed her hand.

"Good for you, daughter," said the marquess.

"This is almost worse than the inquest," whispered Clare.

"Tonight will feel very hard, I am sure, Clare," said Giles reassuringly. "But the curiosity will die down soon enough. May I get you a glass of champagne?"

"I don't think I dare drink anything stronger than lemonade," said Clare in a stronger voice.

"Then I will bring you a glass," said Giles.

A few friends of Clare's parents came over and greeted Clare politely. Of course, no mention was made of her late husband then or at anytime during the evening. "It is as if Justin never existed," remarked Clare to Andrew when he came to claim his waltz.

"Society will go on the way it has begun: ignoring the brutal husband in death as well as in life. I suspect that more than a few families have the same sort of skeletons rattling in their closets, Clare. To speak of your ordeal would strike too close to home for some."

The waltz with Andrew was very comfortable. He had been the first to hear the truth of her marriage. He had received it, but had not judged her. He was very good at taking the lead, this Andrew More, while at the same time not overlooking his partner, she thought, as they danced.

Her waltz with Giles later in the evening was not so comfortable. She accepted his invitation, although she was reluctant, for how could she refuse an old friend. But she was convinced that all eyes were on them, wondering if she had really lied about their relationship. She was sure that at least some of those present had decided that Lord Justin Rainsborough had been correct in his suspicions. She had saved Giles from scandal and probable fatal injury in a duel, but she suspected that a ripple of gossip would always follow them. So how could she smile naturally or respond to the affectionate squeeze he gave her hand when he led her off the floor? It was better for him that she not encourage a return to their old easy comraderie.

Giles was very aware of Clare's attempt to keep him at a distance. His call earlier in the week had been unsatisfactory. And she had been "indisposed" the second time he had called. And she held herself stiffly in his arms as though they had only been introduced that evening.

All the feeling for her that he had thought was dead was alive again, even stronger than before. When he had danced with Lucy Kirkman earlier in the evening, he had looked down at her as though she were a stranger, not a woman whom he had seriously considered marrying. She was very attractive, Lucy, with her dark hair and sparkling dark eyes. He had wanted her once and no doubt would have enjoyed her companionship through life. But that was nothing compared to what he felt for Clare.

Surely the shock of her husband's death (Giles *could* not really imagine Clare killing Justin. She had defended herself. He had died.) would wear off soon, given the fact that the marriage had been a mistake. He and Clare had years of friendship behind them. Once it was clear that Lucy meant nothing to him, he would convince Clare that the best thing for her to do was to marry him. And soon.

Clare was shaking with fatigue and nerves when she returned home that night. Martha sat her down in front of her bedroom fire with a cup of warm milk and honey.

"Are you all right, my lady?"

Clare's teeth had begun to chatter, so she could only nod.

"No one was insulting you, was they?" asked Martha fiercely. Clare looked at her abigail's hands, which had unconsciously clenched into fists, and smiled. The warm milk, the fire, and the wool shawl Martha had laced over her shoulders was beginning to warm her.

"I am sure some things were being said behind my

back, Martha," she replied as her shivering subsided. "But for the most part, it was not as bad as I had feared."

"That nice Mr. More stayed by you, I hope?"

"Yes, Andrew was very kind."

"And Lord Whitton?" Martha asked, with studied casualness.

"Giles was, as usual, my good friend."

Her mistress's face had been clear when speaking of Andrew More, but a slight frown had creased it when she mentioned Lord Whitton. Martha, who believed her mistress needed and deserved a good man to love and take care of her, was pleased. Andrew More was very charming, there was no doubt about that. But he was not the man for Lady Rainsborough, Martha was convinced. Tension was a good sign, she decided. Lady Rainsborough was not indifferent to Lord Whitton, that was obvious. She hoped his lordship was smart enough not to let any grass grow under his feet.

She took the empty cup from her mistress's hands and said "Come, my lady, let me get you to bed."

Clare let herself be guided and fell immediately into a deep sleep.

"She sleeps like the dead," whispered Clare, the waking dreamer, looking down at the woman on the bed. The woman looked just like her. The woman *was* her, it seemed. And next to her lay the woman's husband. His hands were folded gently over his chest, but blood was seeping between his fingers, as though someone had dropped crimson rose petals on his white hands. His eyes were closed, thank God, but blood was also seeping out of a hole in his left temple. How can she sleep in the same bed with him, wondered Clare. A voice behind her in the dream, the voice of the coroner, said: "She made her bed. Now she must lie in it. But it would be a shame for such a young and beautiful woman to lie alone. So her husband will be there with her."

It seemed a fitting punishment to Clare the dreamer.

The other Clare would lie sleeping next to her murdered husband. Her sleep would be "like the dead's" forever.

When Clare awoke, she remembered the dream clearly. Indeed, when she opened her eyes, it was with the expectation of seeing Justin's body next to hers. For, in a way, she had been awake in the dream. She had seen something real, and when she awoke, she could only wonder at the everyday distinction people made between waking and sleeping. Who was to know what was a dream and what was reality? And no matter that the coroner's jury had given a verdict of self-defense. She was a woman who had killed her husband, and she suspected he would forever haunt her bed.

For the next few weeks, Clare attended a carefully chosen combination of routs, musicales, and dinner dances. Her entrances were marked less and less, and by the end of the second week, the ton was too distracted by Lady Huntly's interesting condition to pay too much attention to Clare. Cuckolding a husband was not, of course, as exciting as killing one, but when said husband had been in the service of his country for the past year, and said wife was obviously increasing . . . well, speculation as to who the father was was running wild.

Andrew continued to go out more than usual and to stay close by Lady Rainsborough's side for much of an evening. Giles Whitton was equally attentive, however, and wagers were beginning to be laid as to whether Lady Rainsborough would find a new husband this Season, and who would be the lucky man. "Although lucky may not be the right word," said one gossip with a mocking smile. "After all, the lady is deadly with a pistol."

Had he been offered a wager, Giles himself was not sure on whom he would have placed his money. Clare was, it is true, more relaxed in his company, but there was almost a palpable barrier between them. A barrier that did not seem to exist between Clare and Andrew More.

"Do you think there is anything serious between Clare and Andrew, Sabrina," asked Giles one morning at breakfast. He had been trying to read one article in the paper for the past twenty minutes, a task he had found impossible and finally had given up on.

His sister, who had been very aware of his mood, and indeed, had shared his concerns, put down her cup of tea and said: "I truly don't know, Giles. I would like to think Clare is leaning on Andrew in a way which is quite natural. After all, he saved her life. They seem to have become good friends, but I have noticed nothing romantic between them."

"But what could be more natural than for a woman to fall in love with the man who rescued her from a horrible death."

Sabrina shrugged her shoulders. "Perhaps. You have been quite noticeably neglecting Lucy Kirkman, Giles. Does this mean you are no longer thinking of marrying her?"

"I can't believe I ever did consider it. I had thought my feelings for Clare were dead. It had been two years, after all. I wanted to believe I could see Clare only as a friend, and therefore make Lucy a decent husband. But as soon as I knew Clare was free . . ." Giles looked over at his sister, and she saw in his eyes such a mixture of exultation and hopelessness, that she quickly had to lower her own.

"I almost feel sorry for Lucy," said Sabrina. "Except that her fondness for you never deepened into love, as far as I could tell. What do you plan to do, Giles?"

"I could wait," said her brother. "I *should* wait. Let Clare recover. See if this connection with Andrew is anything more than friendship. But I don't think I can wait, Brina," he added fiercely. "I intend to ask Clare to marry me before this week is out."

"Do you think that wise," Sabrina asked with gentle concern.

"Wise? I thought it wise to let her enjoy her first Season without a formal commitment and look what happened. She ended up with Justin Rainsborough!"

"Andrew More is hardly comparable, Giles," protested his sister.

"I know," Giles replied with a little of his old humor. "But Clare is vulnerable right now. And what kind of a life will she have alone? She can't want to return to Devon. And living with her parents is only a short-term solution. She needs love and security, and if I don't offer it to her, I am afraid she will settle elsewhere."

"Perhaps you are right, Giles. Although I hate to think of you rushing into anything."

"Rushing? I have loved Clare for almost half my life, Sabrina. Whatever constraints she feels with me now, I am sure I can overcome them."

"I hope so, Giles." And Sabrina did, as much for her own sake as for her brother's. For while she did not sense any romantic inclination toward Andrew on Clare's part, she knew her friend had always needed a shoulder to lean on, and Andrew's was much too available.

Chapter Twenty-two

"Lord Whitton to see you, my lady."

Clare looked up from her embroidery in surprise. Although Giles had been very attentive lately when they met socially, he had not called upon her recently.

"Send him up, Peters," she said, somewhat reluctantly. She still did not feel the old comfort in his presence, but did not want to wound him by turning him away.

"Good afternoon, Clare," said Giles, standing hesitantly at the door of the drawing room.

"Good afternoon, Giles, what a pleasant surprise. Please come in and sit down." Despite her efforts, Clare's welcome did not sound completely natural, and Giles wondered if he could ever break down the barrier she had erected between them.

"I do not intend to stay, Clare. It is such a beautiful day, I was hoping I could convince you to come for a ride in the park. We do not have to be away long," he added quickly.

Clare felt trapped. Giles and Sabrina had offered her all their comfort and support these past few weeks. They had, with Andrew, made it possible for her to return in a modified way to her place in society. And here was Giles offering to help her take another step. Yet she cringed inwardly at what the gossips might be saying about them. And the memory of what Justin had said.

She put her embroidery down and looked up at Giles. "Are you sure you wish to do this, Giles?"

"Of course, Clare. You need to appear in public a little more."

"Despite the gossip it may cause?"

Giles looked puzzled for a moment. "Clare, they will be gossiping about you for the rest of the Season. For years, most likely," he added with a quick smile. "I thought you had accepted that fact?"

"I have, Giles. I just haven't gotten used to my friends being dragged in with me."

"Surely there is nothing strange about two old friends spending time together," said Giles. And the sooner I get you to marry me, the better, he thought to himself. For after the initial uproar, things would die down, and Clare would not have to face anything alone again.

"If you think so, Giles," Clare replied after a moment's thought. "I will be with you in a moment."

When she returned, she was wearing an old chip-straw bonnet with ribbons that matched her eyes, and Giles had all he could do not to tip her chin up and drop a kiss on her lips.

When he handed her up into his curricle, he let his hand linger at her waist even after she was seated. Clare tried to ignore the sensation of warmth that remained even after he removed his hand, but she could not. Giles touch felt good and that disturbed her. Had Justin known something about her that she hadn't? Might she have been as responsive to Giles had he ever had the chance to be a potential lover as well as an old friend? Clare made sure she was on the far side of her seat so there was no chance of her leg coming into contact with Giles, and she was very glad that he had to give all his attention to his horses as they made their way through the traffic to the park.

Once there, they were of course caught up in the parade of carriages and riders that frequented the park in the afternoon. Luckily they arrived a little before the most fashionable hour, so the curricle was able to keep moving. Several friends and acquaintances of Giles greeted him and rode next to them for a few minutes, exchanging pleasantries and looking curiously at Clare when they thought she wouldn't notice.

Lucy Kirkman rode by at a canter looking very dashing in her Hussar riding habit, the jaunty cap tilted over her eye. A few minutes later she turned her chestnut mare and walked her back to Giles's curricle.

"Good afternoon, Giles. Clare, it is good to see you finally taking the air in public."

Lucy's patronizing tone made Clare feel just as she had in her childhood: small, cowardly, and helpless. And overlooked, for having politely acknowledged Clare's presence, Lucy proceeded to ignore her and chatted away to Giles. Lucy wasn't one to give up easily anything she considered her own, thought Giles, and she had certainly thought of him as someone she possessed. He had hoped that his obvious attention to Clare would have made it clear enough to Lucy that whatever course they had been on had been altered radically by the events of the past month. He was relieved when she was finally drawn away by Andrew's brother.

"That is the third time this week Lord Avery has sought Lucy out. What an odd pair they would make. I wonder if he is serious," remarked Giles.

"He would seem to be. But I think her interest still lies elsewhere." Clare was surprised by her own temerity.

Giles flushed. "At one time I had thought that Lucy and I might rub along well together. But I was never in love with her, nor she with me, Clare."

"You don't owe me **any** explanation, Giles. I shouldn't have made that comment."

"You had every right to make it, Clare, for things have changed drastically over the past weeks," responded Giles, turning and looking so seriously into her eyes that Clare had to turn away. She thought he was going to go on, but instead he touched his horses up to a trot and both of them silently enjoyed the breeze created by the curri-

cle's movement, which cooled off their faces, flushed by
intensity and embarrassment.

When Giles returned her to St. James Street, he only
walked her to the door and turned down her offer of tea
or lemonade.

"No, not this afternoon, thank you, Clare. But I will
see you tonight at the musicale? May I take you into supper or are you already spoken for?"

"No, that would be lovely, Giles. Thank you for the
lovely drive. It was indeed a . . ."

" 'Lovely' afternoon," he teased, his grin suddenly
bringing back the old friend Giles.

Clare couldn't help but laugh. "But it *was* a lovely afternoon, Giles."

"Until tonight then," he said, and was gone, leaving her
to both dread and anticipate the coming evening.

For the next few days, Clare lived with the very uncomfortable combination of excitement and fear, although
fear predominated. She felt helpless in the hands of
Fate—or Giles—she wasn't sure which. She only felt safe
when she was with Andrew More and stayed by his side
as often as she could respectably do so. There were moments when she wanted to turn to Andrew and cry: "Save
me, Mr. More," for so much of the time her life felt beyond her control. She had returned to society because she
had seen no other choice for herself. She was glad she
had, for she couldn't imagine what else she might be
doing. Yet it gave her little pleasure and exhausted her.
She spent the days in between her social engagements lying in bed, feeling tired and disoriented. There were still
mornings when Martha opened her door that she felt her
heart beat in terror, so sure was she that it was Justin
about to enter her bedroom.

She felt she was wandering in a fog, and when Andrew
More's face would emerge, he seemed a landmark to her,
the one secure thing to hold on to. She could almost wish
that he wanted to marry her. She would have said yes.

Not for the right reason, of course. But because she would have had him to support her. But despite the gossip she knew was circulating, she knew he had no romantic interest in her. It was Giles who would ask her. Of that, she was sure. He had been increasingly attentive. After the carriage ride, he had taken her into dinner at the musicale and been hovering at her side ever since, or so it felt. He had said nothing yet, but it was inevitable that he would.

One morning, while Clare was lying there agonizing over how she would answer Giles, she decided she must speak with someone about her dilemma. It could not be Sabrina. Andrew was the only other person she could trust, and she rang for Martha, feeling more energetic than she had in weeks.

"Martha, I need to visit Mr. More's office, and I need your company."

"Yes, my lady." If Martha thought the visit odd, she kept it to herself. At least her mistress had some energy and some color in her cheeks.

They took a hackney to Lincoln's Inn and found Andrew's chambers. His clerk looked at them with a curiosity he didn't even try to hide. He knew who Clare was, of course, from the inquest.

"Mr. More is busy with a client right now," he told them. "If you are willing to wait, he should be out within the quarter hour."

It was twenty minutes before an older man emerged from Andrew's office. He had obviously dressed carefully for his visit to the barrister's office, but the clothes he wore, though clean, were threadbare. If this was Andrew's usual sort of client, thought Clare, no wonder his family disapproved of him.

The clerk went into the office to announce them, and Andrew came out immediately with a look of pleased surprise upon his face.

"It is delightful to see you, Lady Rainsborough. But

what brings you here?" He gestured them both into his office, but Clare turned to Martha and asked her to wait outside.

"Please sit down, Clare," said Andrew, after he closed the door behind them.

"The man who was leaving your office, is he one of your clients, Andrew?" asked Clare as she sat down across from his desk.

"The father of one of them. His son is in Newgate for housebreaking. The old man is sure I can get him off."

"And can you?"

"I don't know. From what my solicitor has shown me, I think the boy is guilty. But I am hoping I can get him transported."

"His father did not look like he had enough money to pay you, Andrew."

Andrew pulled a chair over and sat opposite Clare. "I always ask for something, no matter how small. But you are right, Clare," said Andrew with a sheepish grin. Many of my clients are poor. I am lucky to have a small income of my own. And since I do, I always take a few poorer clients here and there."

"I am very glad that I could pay you well, then," said Clare with a smile.

"Now, what brings you here," asked Andrew.

Clare was silent for a moment. She had felt energized an hour ago, but now she could feel all that energy drain out of her.

"Andrew, I count you as my friend."

"Indeed, I hope so."

"I am not in a very good state, Andrew," she whispered.

"How can I help you, Clare," he asked, leaning forward sympathetically.

"I don't know quite who I am anymore. Or where I am, although that sounds strange, I know. It is as though there is a veil of mist between me and everything, everyone."

"Do you think the return to society has been too much for you?"

"No, no, it is not that, although even a little effort seems to exhaust me. I think it is that my old life is gone, and I am living in some limbo where the only face I feel I know and can count on is yours."

Andrew reached out and took Clare's hand. "I think that is a very natural feeling, Clare. And you know that I am here to support you in any way I can."

"I know. It is just that I am afraid. Giles has been very attentive. He is my oldest friend. Surely I should welcome his company. I *do* want his company, I think. Oh, Andrew," said Clare with a shaky laugh, "I sound like a madwoman." She took a deep breath. "Perhaps I am wrong, but I think before the Season is over, Giles is going to ask me to marry him."

"I think you are right."

"And I am afraid I will say yes."

"Why afraid, Clare?"

"Because I can't see a way out of it. I can't see any shape for my life. I feel like I have no future, Andrew. That there is only a dreamlike present that will go on and on. And I feel in some way, that I owe Giles. Had I married him in the first place, none of this would have happened."

"But you were not in love with him the way you were with Lord Rainsborough?"

"I think I could have been, had Justin not come along."

"But Rainsborough did, and you made the only choice you could have at the time. Are you in love with Giles now?"

Clare shook her head. "I don't think I am capable of feeling that for any man again. I would be cheating Giles out of something he deserves."

"You could marry me," said Andrew lightly.

"Andrew, you are surely the most supportive friend," said Clare, deeply touched.

"We could both do worse."

"I never felt you liked me very much, you know, those summers when you visited. And when I married Justin, not Giles . . ."

"I didn't. But I have come to know you much better, Clare. And to admire you sincerely."

"Will you be very insulted if I refuse you, Andrew?"

"Not at all, but I am quite serious, for all that."

"I am very grateful, more than I can say. And I care very much for you as a friend. But I have always suspected that you had special feelings for Sabrina."

Andrew looked surprised. "I have never done anything obvious, have I?"

"No, no. It is just a feeling I have had lately, since I have seen you together more. Why would you even consider tying yourself to me, when you could have Sabrina?"

"Because I can't have Sabrina, even if she wanted me. Which she doesn't. I am a younger son, Clare, and fourth in line for the succession. I am a barrister, although that in itself presents no barrier, since it is considered a gentlemanly enough calling," Andrew said ironically. "But I don't pursue it in a gentlemanly enough manner. I deal with all sorts of criminals and riffraff. I have an adequate allowance, but an earl's daughter, particularly Sabrina, deserves better."

"She doesn't seem to have been moved by any elder sons, Andrew. This is her third Season, and I see no sign of any attachment."

"She will meet someone someday." Andrew paused. "Giles, however, will not. He has always loved you, Clare. Surely that should count for something."

"But doesn't he deserve a woman who knows who she is and what she wants?"

"Be patient with yourself, Clare. I am sure these feelings will pass. Giles may be rushing things; I don't know. But I can understand. I would guess that he feels like he doesn't want to miss this chance."

"Or I will find another Justin?" asked Clare bitterly.

"Hardly. That part of your life is over, Clare. You must put it behind you."

"I hope I can, Andrew. But sometimes I am afraid Justin will always be with me."

A week after her visit with Andrew, Giles called on Clare before noon. She wanted to turn him away, but knew that she was only delaying the inevitable. If she didn't allow him to make his declaration, he would only come back again tomorrow, and tomorrow. "And tomorrow," she whispered aloud without realizing. "Creeps in this petty pace . . ."

"What is that, my lady?" asked Peters, who was waiting for her response.

"Oh, nothing, Peters. Tell Lord Whitton I will see him."

"Yes, my lady."

Macbeth had never been a favorite play of Clare's. She had preferred Shakespeare's romantic comedies over his tragedies. And of all the tragedies, a play that made a murderer the tragic hero was her least favorite. But the words had suddenly come to her from nowhere and seemed to express very well how she had been feeling. She had believed that stories had happy endings when she had married Justin. Probably that was why she had stayed: she had thought she could somehow wrest a happy ending from her marriage. She had believed and hoped anew each time he had promised to change. Even at the end, she had thought his decision to see Dr. Shipton might have turned everything around, and given her suffering some meaning.

But what meaning did that suffering have if one's husband was dead at one's own hand? Her story seemed to have become a "tale told by an idiot," going nowhere. The only meaning she could imagine finding in it, the only "happy ending" she could conceive of, would be if she gave one to Giles. Her own story signified nothing, but if she married Giles, perhaps she could give his meaning. Or at least the ending he deserved. How he could still want her, she didn't know, but if he did love her and asked her to be his wife, she would let him have her and do her best to make him not regret it.

When Giles was shown into the morning room, Clare was standing by the window, looking out at the soft, but steady rain that was falling.

"I had intended to ask you to go for a drive in the park, Clare, but the weather is against us, as you can see," he said.

"It is early for a drive, Giles," responded Clare, turning and facing him.

"I know. I was hoping we would have the park to ourselves."

Clare moved away from the window and sat down. Giles remained standing, even when she motioned to the sofa with her hand.

He cleared his throat nervously. "I know it is early for a call, Clare, but I wanted some time with you alone." He hesitated, and then continued. "I know that these past few weeks have been hell for you, no, these past two years. Perhaps I should be giving you more time . . ."

"Time for what, Giles?"

"Time to forget what you have been through, time to begin to enjoy life again. But I find I can't. I suppose it is because I did it once before and lost you. I never asked you to marry me before your first Season because I wanted you to be free to enjoy it. Of course, I never dreamed that you would really meet anyone," he added with a bitter laugh. "I still love you, Clare. I never stopped loving you, although I tried very hard to convince myself that I had."

"What about Lucy Kirkman, Giles? Would you have married her if . . . if Justin were still alive?"

"I suppose I would have," admitted Giles. "Lucy and I would have rubbed along well together, I think. But Justin's death changed everything, Clare."

"Yes, it did, Giles," Clare said softly.

"You are free of that monster. I am free. There was

never any spoken agreement between Lucy and me. And I find I don't want to wait, Clare. I want to bring you back to Whitton. I want us to spend the summer there. You need someone, Clare, someone who loves you, to help you forget the past two years."

"But do you need me, Giles? I am not sure I have much to give anyone right now."

"Of course you feel that way, Clare. I understand. I won't force you to any intimacy until you are ready. And you don't need to give me anything, my dear. Except yourself."

"That feels like a poor gift, Giles," Clare whispered.

Giles sat down on the sofa next to her and took her hands in his. "Clare, I have loved and wanted you for a long time. The fact that you are free seems like a miracle to me. We can start our story again where it left off. You will forget the last two years, I promise you. You will be safe with me."

Clare could not look up into Giles's eyes, for she was afraid of what she would see there. His love was almost too much for her, and so she looked at her hands in his. His thumb was gently and rhythmically brushing the back of her hand. It was very relaxing, and if she only focused on that sensation, she knew she could say yes, could give Giles what he wanted, what he deserved: his happy ending, his Clare.

"If you are sure, Giles?"

"I am sure."

"Then, yes, I will marry you."

Giles dropped her hands and lifted her chin with his finger. "Tell me again, Clare."

"You are my oldest and dearest friend, Giles, and I will be your wife."

Giles lowered his mouth to hers and brushed it gently with his lips. Clare felt a stirring of desire, but it so frightened her that she lowered her face. Giles reached out and smoothed her hair. "I won't rush you on this,

Clare," he said quietly. "Only on the wedding date," he added with a self-mocking smile.

"Whenever you wish, Giles. My only wish is that it be very private."

"I was assuming that you would visit with your parents at the end of the Season, Clare. Would you like to be married from your father's house?"

Clare smiled up at him, one of the first spontaneous smiles he had seen from her in a long time. "Oh, yes. I had always wanted the Reverend Stiles to marry me, but Justin wanted a London wedding."

"We can be married in the parish church with just family around us, Clare, if that is what you want."

"And Andrew More."

"Of course, Andrew. If it weren't for him . . ." Giles didn't finish, but they both sat silent for a moment. Giles put his arms around her very gently and held her to his heart before releasing her and standing up.

"I will see you tonight, Clare?"

"Yes, Giles. We do not have to make this public, do we? I don't think I could bear being the center of more scandal. It will be bad enough after we are married."

"By the fall, they will have forgotten us, Clare," said Giles with a reassuring smile. He dropped a kiss on the top of her head and was gone, leaving her to wonder whether she had just made a decision that Giles would one day come to regret.

Giles told his sister that afternoon, and she called on Clare immediately.

"I am thrilled, Clare. I have never seen Giles look so happy. He is off to speak with your father and mother."

"I hope I am doing the right thing, Sabrina."

"Because it is so soon after Justin? Don't worry about the gossip, Clare. We will all be at Whitton by then, and it will die down by the fall."

"Not just the scandal, Sabrina. I mean for Giles."

"I know Giles better than most sisters know their

brothers, Clare. He was devastated when you married, although he hid it well. And if you are at all worried about Lucy Kirkman, you shouldn't be. His heart has always been yours."

"That is exactly my concern, Sabrina. The only thing I can do for Giles to make him happy is to give him myself, but I am afraid I have not much to give."

"Clare, you have always underestimated yourself," Sabrina protested. "I think you and Giles could make each other very happy. You just have not yet taken it in that you are free from that horrible marriage. You will be safe with Giles, Clare, and will never be treated brutally again."

Or loved as passionately? wondered Clare, immediately appalled at her own question. Most of the time when she thought of Justin, it was with terror and overwhelming remorse. But occasionally she would remember the early days of their courtship and marriage, and the pleasure she had found with him. Dear God, there must be something terribly wrong with her if she could still cherish some of those glorious moments with her late husband. She had certainly paid a high enough price for that ecstasy.

Sabrina did not stay long, and shortly after she left, Andrew called. Clare received his congratulations quietly, and told him that she not only absolutely demanded his presence at the ceremony, but hoped he would come for an extended visit to Whitton that summer.

That evening, at the Bellingham rout, Andrew approached Sabrina and was lucky enough to obtain both a waltz and the opportunity to escort her in to dinner.

What Andrew thought was luck was actually Sabrina's decision to save room on her card for Andrew now that he was attending ton functions more regularly. She felt fairly secure that he would ask her but not at all sure that, were she not free, he would keep coming back on future occasions. Some men might have been that persistent, not Andrew. He was not at all full of himself, which was one reason, an acceptable one. Or possibly he did not care that much about a dance or a supper with Lady Sabrina Whitton, which was a much less acceptable explanation.

Andrew was distracted during their waltz and did not talk much. He was happy for Giles and Clare, worried about them, and envious, all at the same time. Whatever their problems, at least they were of equal rank and status. What was he doing, torturing himself by dancing with Sabrina, drinking in the sweet rosewater scent of her, when nothing could ever come of it. He was always surprised that she managed to find a dance for him, for she was very popular, and rumor had it that Lord Patrick Meade might be attempting to fix an interest. Lord Meade was exactly the sort of man she should marry: rich, titled, tall, handsome, not too staid. With him, Sabrina would have everything she was used to: wealth, a lovely country estate, and luxurious town house. With Andrew, she'd have nothing. So Andrew was very careful not to enjoy his waltz too much.

Over supper, he was quiet also, and Sabrina finally commented upon it.

"I am sorry, Sabrina. One of my cases has been preoccupying me," he lied.

"Clare told me you know of the engagement."

Andrew's face brightened. "Yes, I have wished them both happy."

"Do you think they will be, Andrew?"

He thought awhile before answering. "Perhaps not immediately. Clare needs more time to recover than Giles realizes, I am sure. But ultimately? They are very well-matched, and the affection between them runs long and deep."

Sabrina smiled. "I am glad you think so, Andrew. I can't help but worry about my twin, you know. You will come to Whitton this summer?" Sabrina asked as casually as she could.

Andrew hesitated a moment and then said: "Yes, I think I will be able to get away for a short visit."

"I will look forward to the four of us fishing and rid-ing, then," said Sabrina. "It will be just like old times."

Ah, Sabrina, thought Andrew, it can never be like old times again.

Chapter Twenty-three

By the time a small announcement appeared in the *Times*, Clare and Giles had been married a week. While it was true that society was scandalized by such a quick marriage, and between two people who had been suspected of being lovers by Lord Rainsborough, most of the ton had left London and only a few people were gossiping over tea or in the clubs. Most were on their way to the country, and by the time they heard about it, it seemed like stale news. Which was exactly what Giles had hoped would happen.

He and Clare stayed with her parents for a few days after the ceremony, and then set off for Whitton. When he handed his new wife down in front of the house, Giles remembered Clare's first visit. There was something in her eyes that reminded him of the frightened ten-year-old, and he felt the same surge of protectiveness as he led her into the house. She was still thin and tired-looking and had been very quiet these past few days.

Their things were taken to his bedroom suite, and once the bags were set down and the footman had left, Giles dismissed Martha and joined Clare in her room. She was standing there, looking lost, and he was immediately drawn to her side.

"This is all rather too much for you, isn't it, Clare?"

"I am sorry, Giles. It takes some getting used to. I have been Lady Rainsborough for two years now, and all of a sudden, I am Lady Whitton. This is not Devon, but Somerset . . . and . . ."

"And I am not Justin, only Giles."

"Thank God for that, Giles," responded Clare fervently.

"I told you on our wedding night I did not intend to rush things, Clare. The door between us will always be open, but I will wait for you to invite me into your bed."

Clare blushed. "I am sorry, Giles."

"There is no need to apologize, Clare. We will have a whole lifetime together." Giles leaned down and dropped a gentle kiss on her lips. All his kisses had been gentle and nonintrusive, and for this Clare was grateful, for they stirred only a momentary response before fear took over. She wondered if that part of her was dead. If so, it would be fitting punishment for killing her husband. But even so, eventually she would have to walk through Giles's door and pretend to a passion she might never feel again. All of a sudden, she felt an all too familiar exhaustion hit her.

"I think I would like to rest before coming down to dinner, Giles."

"Of course, my dear."

Clare spent the next week in bed. She would wake in the morning, have tea and toast in her room, summon enough energy to get up, but once at her dressing table, would be utterly overcome by the idea of leaving her bedroom and entering into her new life. She would return to bed and sleep the mornings away. She then ate a light lunch in her room, and after reading only a few pages of her book or leafing through the latest *La Belle Assemblee,* she would slide under the covers and sleep again.

She felt like something thrown up by the tide, a tide that was at its lowest ebb. A tide that might never run again, never flow back to float her, to bring her back into life. Even the thought of how she must be disappointing Giles couldn't move her.

Giles *was* disappointed, of course, but also worried. He had imagined that he and Clare would rediscover the comraderie they had enjoyed on her summer visits, and here he was, eating alone, sleeping alone, riding alone. That was not precisely true, of course, for he had Sabrina, who was there to reassure him. After the first three days, they summoned the family physician, who confirmed Sabrina's opinion that there was nothing physically wrong with Clare.

"Lady Whitton is suffering from complete exhaustion, Giles," the doctor announced. "Perhaps suffering isn't the right word," he added. "Really her body is only doing what it needs to do to restore itself. She has been through a lot these past months. You will have to be patient."

"Thank you, Doctor."

"You were right, Sabrina," Giles admitted after the doctor had gone.

"Give her time, Giles."

Giving Clare almost a fortnight seemed like giving her forever. But when at last she came downstairs, Giles had to admit that she looked much better than she had in months. The shadows were gone from under her eyes, and despite the fact that she hadn't been eating that much, she had clearly put on a little weight.

She appeared for breakfast one morning without an announcement after Giles and Sabrina had seated themselves.

"Clare!" exclaimed Sabrina, who saw her first. "Should you be up?"

Clare laughed. "After all this time, I certainly hope so, Sabrina. I feel very well. And I wasn't really sick, you know. I don't know want came over me, but I needed to rest."

"I guess so," said Giles with a teasing smile. "It is wonderful to see you up, Lady Whitton. Will you join us for breakfast?"

"I am quite ravenous," Clare admitted.

Giles gestured to a footman to fill her plate and watched happily as she ate almost everything in it.

"Do you have special plans for today, Giles," Clare asked, after setting her fork down and looking at her almost empty plate in surprise.

Giles had planned to ride over to the northwest corner of the estate to confer with one of their tenants, but immediately decided that the errand could wait for a day to two. So he said, "No, not really. Although it is a lovely day for a ride. Do you care to join me?"

Clare smiled over at him. "I was hoping I could, Giles. Sabrina," she added, turning to his sister. "Will you join us?"

Sabrina had seen the eager look in her brother's eyes and shook her head. "Unfortunately I am committed elsewhere. I promised I would help the housekeeper in the stillroom."

It was a beautiful day: sunny and warm, but with enough of a breeze to make it comfortable for riding. Giles picked one of their favorite short rides from summers past: one that led them along the cornfields and into a small wood that was the boundary between Whitton and Squire Kirkman's. They enjoyed several easy canters across the fields, and then dismounted and led their horses through the wood, enjoying a companionable silence. When they reached their destination, an old and familiar fallen tree, Clare laughed.

"I confess I had forgotten about this place, Giles," she said as she handed her reins into his outstretched hands and sat herself down on the moss-covered trunk.

Giles tied the horses and sat next to her.

"This has always been one of my favorite places on the estate," said Giles.

Clare gazed around. It was an almost perfectly circular clearing, surrounded by tall oak trees with one gap through which the sun poured in a shaft of light.

"It is almost magical."

Giles covered Clare's hand with his. "It feels like something akin to magic to be here with you, Clare. To have you as my wife."

"I hope I can be a good wife to you, Giles," she said almost in a whisper. Her hand was still under his, and she was very conscious of his thigh pressing against hers. She glanced up at him, and it was as though she saw him for the first time: the glint of green in his eyes, the pulse beating in his tanned neck, and the combination of both strength and tenderness that made up the curve of his mouth.

Giles reached out, removed her riding hat, and smiled as her blond curls sprang free. He brushed his hand through them and moved even closer. Clare's breathing quickened with a small, sharp intake of breath, and Giles leaned down and placed his lips on hers. It was a gentle kiss, like all he had given her, but longer. When she did not shrink from him, Giles pulled her into his arms and sought to deepen the kiss by teasing her mouth open. It was everything she had hoped for from him that summer years ago, and she responded eagerly. Yet almost immediately as she felt herself beginning to enjoy the embrace, she felt herself becoming scared. Her passionate feelings for Justin had only led to confusion and pain, both physical and emotional. The only experiences she had had with physical love were with a man who alternately loved her until she died again and again in his arms, and then hated her. How could she trust her body's responses again?

Giles could feel the point at which she drew back. It seemed to be at the exact moment she began to relax into him and respond to his kiss. For a few seconds, there had been a warm and willing woman in his arms, and then a passive statue.

Clare did not have to say a word, for Giles let her go instantly.

"I promised I would not rush you, Clare, and I will keep my promise."

"I did not ask you to stop, Giles," said Clare, feeling like she had failed him.

"You did not have to, my dear. I know you would allow me to kiss you, Clare. Perhaps even allow me to make love to you. But I want more than your passive acceptance."

Although Giles spoke patiently and lovingly, Clare felt terrible. She didn't know how to explain her feelings to him, for she barely understood them herself. She *was* a passionate lover, she had been with Justin. But that part of herself terrified her. Logically, she knew that Giles was not Justin; that he would *never* treat her like her late husband had. But logic and reason didn't seem to make her irrational fear go away. It was physical attraction, and her newly discovered capacity for sensual enjoyment that had led her into her disastrous marriage. Those feelings seemed dangerous and destructive, and she was not sure she could open herself up in that way to anyone again. And yet, if she could not, she was cheating Giles of everything he wanted and deserved in a wife.

"I am so sorry, Giles" was all she could think to say to him.

He patted her shoulder. "It is all right, Clare. We have all the time in the world."

Giles took every opportunity in the next few weeks to express his affection in ways that Clare could accept. He knew, almost to the second, just how long she would remain responsive to his kisses and just when she would pull back. He would think to himself that he was lucky to be a naturally patient man and one for whom passion was only a part of love. An important part, of course, but not one that would cause him to lose control with Clare. He had loved her for a long time, and he would for a long time to come. He had great faith that she would come to respond to his undemanding love. If not tomorrow, then soon.

In the meantime, he was happy to watch Clare begin to look and act like her old self. By the end of a month, she had regained all the weight she had lost the last two years. But although she wanted to begin learning the ways of the house, Giles insisted that she let Mrs. Stanton remain in charge for a little while longer. "I want you to enjoy this summer, Clare. To pretend that the last two years never happened."

She and Giles and Sabrina rode and picnicked, and when Andrew More arrived for his visit at the beginning of August, he was amazed at the transformation.

"You look wonderful, Clare," he exclaimed as he got down from his chaise. She put out both her hands to grasp his, and he marveled that the wraithlike Lady Rainsborough had been transformed into a healthy-looking young woman whose blond curls had been bleached by the sun and whose dresses were no longer hanging off her. Andrew pulled her into his arms and gave her a friendly hug.

"Now, Andrew, who gave you permission to embrace my wife," said Giles with mock anger. "And is your only greeting for her?"

Andrew released Clare and turning to his friend, pounded his shoulder. "I see you have wrought something of a miracle, Giles," he said. "Marriage to you seems to have been just what Clare needed."

Sabrina, who was beside Giles, wondered when Andrew would remember her presence. She had enjoyed the last few weeks, for summer of Whitton was always her favorite time of the year. But although Giles and Clare were not enjoying a typical honeymoon, and she was included in most of their activities, she could not help feeling a third wheel at times. Maybe her brother did not have the perfect marriage yet. But he was married to the woman he had loved for years, while she seemed likely to end up the spinster aunt to her brother's children when they began to come along. She had been looking forward to Andrew's visit, hoping that during their time together she could determine whether there was any feeling for her on his part or whether it was all her own fantasy, and here he was, ignoring her.

Andrew was very well aware of Sabrina. Indeed, although his delight at seeing Clare was genuine, his hug was as much a way to keep from embracing Sabrina as it was a spontaneous gesture of affection for Clare. It was very hard for him to keep his feelings for Giles's sister under wraps, but he had schooled himself well, and turned to her at last, giving her a quick smile and a friendly greeting.

Sabrina's heart sank. Nothing had changed. Andrew was still acting the friend of the family role he always had. Perhaps it wasn't a role. Just because she could sense what her twin was feeling did not mean she could intuit another man's reactions, Sabrina scolded herself. She wanted Andrew to want her. So much so that she had likely deceived herself and built little nothings into something. But she kept the smile on her face and welcomed him to Whitton and directed the footman to bring his bags up to the west wing where she had given him the bedroom he had always occupied.

"You know we keep country hours here, Andrew," she said, "but we have moved dinner back an hour so that you will have time to rest and freshen up before you join us."

"Thank you, Sabrina. You have always been the most thoughtful hostess."

And that is what she remained for the next few days: a most gracious hostess. Andrew should have been grateful. After all, the more polite distance there was between them, the easier it was for him to ignore his feelings for Sabrina. But in London they had become a little closer to one another, had, he thought, started to become friends, not just through their relationship to Giles. He thought Sabrina had come to appreciate him for himself and his efforts on Clare's behalf. But perhaps now that Clare was safely married to her brother, she was no longer interested in a barrister who worked so closely with criminals.

So be it: he could be as polite and distantly friendly as she.

Giles, who had watched Sabrina move from disapproval to admiration of Andrew in London, couldn't help but notice her behavior. Not that there was anything untoward about it: she was friendly and always appeared as though she was enjoying Andrew's company. But as her twin, he could tell that she was unhappy in some way, and so one afternoon when Andrew had gone off to the village and Clare was taking a nap, Giles joined his sister in the garden where she was directing the gardener.

After she finished, he put his hand on her arm and said, "Come, sit down with me, Brina."

They strolled over to the oak bench and watched the gardener and his assistant fill their basket with flowers for the house. As they moved out of earshot, Giles asked his sister if anything was bothering her.

"Why no, why do you ask, Giles?"

"Because you have been so damned *friendly* to Andrew."

"Shouldn't I be, Giles? He is our friend, after all," Sabrina responded, keeping her tone light.

"Brina, I know you too well not to sense when you are unhappy about something. I had thought in London that you and Andrew had gotten to know one another better. That perhaps . . ."

"Perhaps what, Giles?"

Giles could feel the effort it took to keep her tone even.

"That perhaps you and Andrew had discovered you would like to be more than just friends."

"Andrew certainly does not seem to want more than a polite acquaintance, Giles."

"And what do you want, Brina?"

"Oh, I'll admit it, Giles. To you, because you know me too well for me to lie. I have always been interested in Andrew, ever since his first visit here. And I have never met anyone else who was as attractive to me. Then, when

I saw him with Clare and at the inquest, my . . . feelings for him became even stronger. But it is ridiculous for me to think of him that way. He is oblivious to me, after all."

"He certainly has never shown you any more attention than would be expected from a friend of the family," mused Giles.

"No, he hasn't," agreed Sabrina with a despondent sigh.

"On the other hand, Brina, he is a younger son. He is four times removed from the title and most unlikely ever to inherit. And to the horror of his family, he spends his time among the lowlife of London. He would be unlikely to consider himself an eligible suitor for the Lady Sabrina Whitton, daughter of an earl and someone who has a substantial portion."

Sabrina sat silent for a few moments. There was a murmur of bees, humming in and out of the herb garden, and the air was redolent with the scent of mint and thyme. She felt relaxed for the first time since Andrew had arrived. Maybe Giles was right. She had never thought about it from Andrew's perspective before. *She* had never thought of his position as an obstacle. Andrew was so naturally superior to his older brother that she couldn't imagine him thinking that any woman would prefer a titled bore to him, the quirkily intelligent and committed younger son. But men had a strange sense of honor, she reminded herself. Honor seemed more important to them than love, a very odd concept for a woman to appreciate.

"I never really looked at it that way before, Giles," she finally responded.

"Mind you, Sabrina, I am not saying he *does* care. I don't know that. But I would not be at all surprised if he considered only a friendship appropriate with you. I am not sure this helps at all," said Giles, smiling sympathetically at his sister.

"Maybe I need to show a little more of my feelings,

Giles. What would you think of such a match, if it were to come about?"

"I would be very happy for you both, Sabrina. Andrew is the only man I can think of who is a match for you."

"Then wish me luck."

Chapter Twenty-four

It was easier to declare one was going to be more open than it was to do it. Andrew seemed to have created a very effective distance between himself and Sabrina. He was always polite and friendly, but also emotionally removed. But only from me, thought Sabrina, as she watched Andrew and Clare for the next few days. They had become fast friends and were obviously very comfortable with each other. All the warmth that Andrew kept from Sabrina was turned on Clare.

One afternoon, dressed in old clothes, the four of them went over to their old favorite fishing spot. It was a warm day, and Andrew and Giles gave only perfunctory apologies as they took their jackets off and rolled up their sleeves. Sabrina quickly and efficiently baited her own hook as Giles had taught her years ago, but Clare was still as repulsed by the task as ever. Before Giles had a chance to help her, Andrew stepped in and did it for her.

"There you are, Clare. Just drop your hook into the water, and you'll forget what's wriggling at the end of it."

"I am still quite hopeless at this," said Clare with a laugh. "And I wouldn't know what to do with a fish if I caught it anyway."

"Do you remember that awful trick Lucy pulled years ago?" Sabrina asked.

Clare blushed. She remembered it very well, that feeling of helplessness before outright cruelty.

"I hope I would be able to act differently now," Clare

responded quietly. "I believe I have changed a little over the years."

There were a few moments of uncomfortable silence as all busied themselves finding a place on the bank of the stream, while thinking about Clare and her late husband.

Giles broke the silence first, for Giles did not like to think about Justin Rainsborough or how he died. He understood Clare's action; a part of him applauded it. But mostly he couldn't contemplate either how she had lived with him or how she had escaped him.

"Do you suppose that old pike is still around, Brina," he asked. "Remember how we used to spend hours trying to catch him."

"I seem to remember that I was the only one ever to hook him," bragged Andrew.

"Hooked, but not landed," Giles reminded him.

"I couldn't help it if my line broke! I hope this time you have given me a strong enough line, Giles."

"Are you suggesting that I gave you an old line on purpose, Andrew," said Giles, with mock outrage.

"Oh, hush, you two, We won't catch anything if you keep making such a racket," Sabrina demanded.

They all settled down. Clare was sitting next to Andrew, and Giles and Sabrina were standing a few feet away. They were at a point in the stream where the water had collected into a deep black pool before spilling over a rocky ledge. Under the ledge on their side was a spot protected by reeds and overhung by an old willow tree. That was where the big fish was believed to spend his time, and all of them had tossed their lines in that direction.

Giles felt something first, but all he had caught was a small trout. "You would most likely have been the old pike's dinner, so you might as well be our lunch," he said as he tossed the fish into his creel.

The sun warmed their shoulders and necks, and the onyx water looked like it was hardly flowing. They were all in that semi-mesmerized state that utter relaxation can bring, when Sabrina's sudden gasp startled them.

Her pole was bent almost in half, and she had almost lost it in the sudden, powerful tug.

"My God, Sabrina, if you don't have him, you must have hooked some sort of monster," exclaimed Giles.

Andrew walked slowly to her side, speaking calmly and rhythmically, almost chanting encouragement and instruction.

"That's right, Brina, let the pole down a little. Let him feel some slack. Not too much, or he'll slip the hook. That's right, Brina, that's right." Sabrina was too intent on landing her fish to take it in, but her mind must have registered it, for later she remembered that Andrew had called her by the name only Giles used.

"Now, keep that pole up and move back a little from the bank. Yes, yes, there he is."

They could see the water churning as the great fish came closer to the surface. Clare was standing now, too, as intent as the others on the struggle, but the more the old giant attempted to escape the hook, the more sympathetic she became to him, the more she silently wished him well, not Sabrina. She knew what it was to be caught like that, and she wouldn't wish it on anyone, even a fish.

The pike turned and swam for the opposite bank, and Sabrina thought her arms might separate from their sockets. She was drawn inexorably toward the bank.

"Don't move in, Brina, move back," shouted Giles.

"I can't help it," she exclaimed, amazed at the power at the end of her line.

The pole wasn't bent, but almost level with the ground, for she didn't have the strength to lift it.

Andrew quickly stepped behind her and putting his arms around her waist, said: "I've got you, Brina. Now pull him in."

She wasn't sliding anymore, so she could put all her concentration into lifting the pole. Slowly she pulled it up, but not enough to bring the pike to the surface.

"I don't think I can do this," she gasped.

"Do you want to land him on your own, or should I

help?" Andrew asked, his face close to hers, his breath against her neck.

"Grab the pole, Andrew," Sabrina cried without even thinking, and letting go of her waist and pulling her into him, Andrew reached around and put his hands on the pole. Together they lifted and all at once, it seemed the old fish rose out of the water, dull pewter turned to silver in the sun.

As the pike rose, Andrew felt himself rise as he was pressed even closer to Sabrina, and he prayed that she was too intent on her struggle to become aware of his arousal.

The pole was bent double again, and Andrew prayed aloud that the line would not snap as he and Sabrina slowly moved backward, pulling the fish with them.

"All right, *now,*" Andrew said, and they jerked up and back. The old pike landed flopping on the bank as Sabrina and Andrew lost their balance and their grip on the pole.

The fish was right on the edge of the bank, still leaping as though air were water. He couldn't get very high, but Clare realized that he was going to be able to roll himself right over the bank and silently cheered him in his heroic effort. Then she realized that the hook was still in his mouth, still attached to the line and the pole. Without thinking, she scrambled over. She put her hand down as gently as she could on the wriggling giant, and when that made him move even more, she wrapped her skirt over him to trap him, and grabbing the side of his head, she began to work the hook out of his mouth.

"Clare, what are you doing," exclaimed Giles.

Clare worked as fast as she could, knowing that she wasn't doing it easily, only quickly and painfully. Finally it was free, leaving a jagged rip in the jaw, which she was sure would heal. She looked at the pike and whispered: "There, you are free again." And lifting her skirt, she tossed him back into the water.

Andrew and Sabrina had scrambled up by then and were standing as openmouthed as any fish. Clare turned to face them. "I am sorry," she said, in a low, choked voice. "I couldn't stand it. I couldn't stand seeing him played with and trapped like that." Tears were running down her cheeks and as Giles stepped toward her, she motioned him back. "I am sorry to spoil the fishing, Giles. I have never enjoyed it," she added, amazing herself and them. "Not the worms or the fish on the hook. Only the quiet and the trees and sun and water. I should have told you years ago." She looked down at her dress and smiled. "I am as dirty as when Lucy threw those worms at me, aren't I! I am going back to the house to change."

"You can't go alone, Clare," said Giles. "I'll come with you."

"Nonsense. You all stay here, and I will see you at tea." With that, she turned and started briskly for Whitton.

Andrew looked over at his two friends. Giles was looking after Clare and then back at the water, as though trying to take in the fact that she had actually tossed the biggest fish in Somersetshire back in the pool. Sabrina was standing there, pushing her hair back from her face with a muddy hand, leaving her cheek streaked with dirt. Her dress was torn at the hem, where Andrew must have stepped on it when they went down. Andrew looked down at himself. Thank God he was no longer aroused. But his pants were as muddy as Sabrina's hands. He let out a great shout of laughter. "Good for Clare!"

"Whatever got into her?" asked Sabrina.

"She threw him *back*," said Giles, still unable to believe that his wife had actually tossed away such a fish. "Why, that fish is a legend around here."

"You *caught* him, Sabrina," crowed Andrew.

"And *we* landed him, Andrew. I couldn't have done it without you." She suddenly remembered the sensation of Andrew pressed close against her and turned away to fuss with her dress in order to hide her flaming cheeks.

"Oh, well," said Giles, resigned to fate. "What would we have done with him but mount him on the wall. He was too old to eat. But I can't believe Clare has hated fishing all these years," he added with such naive amazement that he set Andrew and Sabrina off into gales of laughter.

"Oh, all right you two. I suppose I should have known. Or at least realized that Clare would never have said anything. At least she has enjoyed part of it, hasn't she?" he asked, wondering to himself how many things Clare had not told him, wondering how well he knew his wife after all.

"Come on, Giles, bring the trout, and we'll have him cooked for tea," said Sabrina. "I for one have done my share of fishing for the day!"

Clare walked home feeling both exhilaration and fear. For once in her life, she had said what she wanted and it left her with the sensation of having jumped off a cliff. It was exciting, this new feeling of having some power, but also frightening. Whatever would Giles say to her? She was sure he must be angry, both at her cheating them out of the most famous fish in the county and for finally admitting that she didn't like fishing and never had.

When they all gathered for tea, however, there was only a little good-natured teasing from Andrew and Sabrina, with Giles joining in the laughter. But Clare was sure he was only politely hiding his displeasure. That evening, after she retired, instead of going right to sleep, she stayed awake until she heard him come up from the library where he and Andrew had had a nightcap.

She knocked softly on the adjoining door, and Giles opened it, a look of surprise on his face. He dismissed his valet and invited Clare in.

"No, I won't stay, Giles. I just wanted to apologize for this afternoon. I am sure you must be very annoyed with me."

"Not annoyed, Clare. Just surprised. I never dreamed you felt that way about fishing all these years."

"How could you have. And I have enjoyed all but the actual fishing, Giles."

Giles smiled quizzically.

"No, I am telling the truth," protested Clare. "The walks to the stream and the fresh air. Even watching the water is very relaxing. It was just that until today, I would pretend that no fish were being caught. That wasn't too hard, since I never caught anything!" Clare was slowly becoming conscious that her husband was standing there without his cravat, his shirt half-open. She noted with pleasure that Giles had dark brown curls of hair on his chest. Justin's chest had been smooth . . . but no, she would not think of Justin.

Giles reached out and pushed Clare's hair back from her face with one finger. She lifted her mouth toward him without thinking, and he bent down and kissed her. She was open to him, and he sensed the difference immediately, so he drew her into his arms and deepened the kiss. Her mouth opened under his, and he gently probed with his tongue. When she gave a little moan of pleasure, he gave himself hungrily and completely to the kiss until he felt her pull away.

"I am sorry, Clare, I know I promised."

"No, no, I want you to, Giles. It is only that I am quite breathless," Clare said with a shy smile.

They were standing almost in the doorway between the two rooms, and Giles looked over her shoulder to her bed.

"Your bed looks very inviting, Clare. John did not have a chance to turn mine down yet. We would be much more comfortable in yours?"

Clare didn't answer, but let him lead her over to the big four-poster. Giles sat her down on the edge and slowly pulled the ribbon on her dressing gown. It was silk, as was her night rail and as soon as he opened it, it slipped off her shoulders like water.

"It is your turn, Clare," he said, nodding toward his shirt.

Clare reached out with shaking fingers and managed to undo the buttons to his waist and then froze, for his shirt was still tucked into his breeches. Giles took her hands in his and kissed her again, gently nibbling her lips and then her earlobe. His warm breath on her neck was deliciously arousing, and she could feel herself becoming slippery and wet as her center turned to liquid.

She had never felt this way with Giles before. What she was experiencing now was similar to what she had with Justin. Surely that was a good thing, she thought, as she felt Giles cup her breast in his hand. It felt wonderful to reach her own hand out and run her fingers lightly up his belly over the soft fur. And it gave her pleasure to hear him groan with pleasure. To know that at least she was giving him what he had always wanted and so deserved.

But when he whispered, "Just a minute, Clare," and stood with his back to her, pulling off his shirt and breeches, she wished he had not left her alone on the bed. For all the warmth in her belly was turning slowly into emptiness. And when he turned toward her, his manhood jutting upward, she had to lower her eyes. She hoped he would think it shyness rather than fear. She let him slip off the night rail and move her down onto the bed.

She *couldn't* stop him, she decided. He was her husband, he was her loving friend, and he had never been anything but good to her. She owed him a normal marriage. This would have occurred sooner or later, she knew, for he not only desired her, he wanted an heir. She only wished she could give him her whole self, but at the very least she could give him her body and pretend that she hadn't retreated in fear.

Giles had wanted the first time with Clare to be leisurely and more pleasurable for her than himself. But perhaps the fact that she wasn't a virgin and therefore would not experience any pain, affected his own responses, for he was unable to control his own desire as long as he wished. He was inside her soon, driven to it by her soft moans as he circled her breast with his tongue. She was ready for him, he knew, for his fingers had told him that, and so when she lifted her hips to invite him in, he thrust into her.

Clare felt she was two people: the woman on the bed making noises of simulated pleasure and a wraithlike self hovering somewhere in the corner of the ceiling gazing down. She wanted to be there for Giles, but she couldn't be, for a part of her was back in the past with Justin. Justin had made love to her, had awakened her passion, had brought her to climax again and again, when she opened her deepest self to him. And then Justin had brutalized her. She couldn't help feeling that the two things were connected: exquisitely pleasurable vulnerability that led to unimaginable terror.

When Giles reached his own climax murmuring her name over and over, she held him close. And when he lifted himself up and lowered his hand to bring her a final release, she gently pushed him away.

"I am sorry, Clare. I didn't intend this first time to be so quick. But I wish to give you your pleasure."

"It is all right, Giles," Clare whispered. "Your pleasure is mine, too." And that was partially true. A part of her *had* been there with Giles, and she *was* happy that she was at last able to give him this.

"You are sure?"

"Yes, my love." The endearment came naturally to her lips, surprising both of them. Giles turned on his side and pulled Clare against him. As he dropped kisses on the top of her head, he murmured, "All I have ever wanted was this, Clare, to hold you and to cherish you."

Chapter Twenty-five

The next morning when Giles awoke, Clare was already up, washed and dressed. She leaned over the bed and kissed his forehead. "I find I am ravenous this morning, Giles," she told him with a becoming blush. "I will see you in the breakfast room soon?" Despite their closeness the night before, he sensed again a barrier between them. Although this morning, it did not feel quite as strong. And perhaps a few nights like the last would bring it down completely.

When Giles came down a quarter of an hour later, Sabrina and Andrew were already there, discussing their plans for the day.

"I thought we had agreed to ride into Wells," Sabrina was saying.

"We had, but that was two days ago when there wasn't a cloud in the sky," Andrew replied.

"There are not that many clouds this morning, Andrew. If you are not up to the ride, just tell me."

Andrew sighed a resigned "I suppose I will have to tolerate this" sigh, which annoyed Sabrina immensely. "It is uncommonly warm and humid, Sabrina, and I wager that those few fluffy clouds we see now will be thunderheads by the afternoon. I think a shorter ride is wiser. We could go into the village."

"But I need a new pair of riding gloves, which one can only find in Wells," she protested. "Giles, tell Andrew if we start a little earlier, we will miss the weather. If there is, indeed, going to be any," she added.

"What do you think, Clare?" Giles asked, turning to his wife.

Clare looked up from her plate. "It is quite close as Andrew says, but the sky is relatively clear. I would hate to disappoint Sabrina. And, I confess, I was looking forward to the ride."

Giles looked over at Andrew, who threw up his hands. "I surrender. If the ladies are adventurous enough, who am I to stop us."

"And Mrs. Pleck has already prepared us a picnic lunch," Sabrina informed them, as though Mrs. Pleck's good food was the deciding factor to ensure good weather.

They set out a half hour earlier than they had planned, before the sun was too high in the sky. Two hours from Whitton, there was an old ruined keep where they planned to rest and eat. Wells was only a half hour beyond that.

It *was* unseasonably warm, even for early August, thought Sabrina, as she felt the back of her neck become wet with perspiration. She quickly glanced up at the sky, and was reassured. It was still blue, still only dotted here and there with clouds.

They had a few easy gallops, but for the most part did not push their horses, and by the time they reached the ruin, they were already a little behind schedule, despite the early departure.

Mrs. Pleck had provided them with a simple, light meal: cold chicken and ham, cheese, fresh bread, and some very small, early apples. There were bottles of ale and lemonade, which although not cold, were still cool enough from the cellar to be refreshing.

They tethered their horses in the shade of a large beech tree, and Andrew and Giles spread rugs on the grass inside the old keep. The crumbled stone walls reached high enough to provide some shade, and it was a very pleasant picnic indeed.

"I expect that when we reach Wells, you may feel em-

barrassed, Clare," said Andrew with unwonted serious-
ness.

"Whatever for, Andrew?" she asked, sudden concern
written all over her face. Surely word of her trial had
been heard and forgotten quickly here?

"I am sure word has spread that you are the woman
who threw back the biggest and oldest fish in the county.
I would not be surprised if there were placards greeting
us as we ride in."

Giles laughed, and Clare giggled.

"That was unfair, Andrew," said Clare. "I was worried
you meant news of the trial had proceeded me."

Andrew was immediately repentant. "I apologize,
Clare," he said, reaching out to pat her shoulder. "I never
even thought of that."

"Nor should any of us," said Giles. "It is over and
done with, Clare. You are now my wife, the Viscountess
Whitton."

Sabrina looked over at her brother. There was something different in his tone today. He sounded surer of
Clare. He sounded satisfied. She felt her cheeks grow
warm at the picture that flashed through her head. She
was all of a sudden sure that Giles and Clare were very
much husband and wife.

The shade and the coolness the stones provided were
so welcome that no one wanted to move, but finally Andrew got them going. They reached Wells very quickly
and spent a lovely hour browsing through the shops.
Sabrina found her pair of gloves, and Clare found a
length of ribbon just the perfect shade of green for trim-
ming one of her morning dresses. By the time they
reached the lending library, however, the heat had become
even more oppressive and the shop itself felt like an
oven.

Giles had been watching Clare carefully for any sign
that she was overheated or fatigued. When he saw her sit
down on a small chair against the wall, he went over to

her and after a short conversation, came up behind
Sabrina.

"Brina, Clare is feeling undone by this infernal heat. I
think we should go."

"Oh, Giles, I promised Mrs. Pleck that I would see if
the grocers had some vanilla beans. She is out, and the
grocers in Street doesn't carry them."

"Why don't you and Clare start home slowly, Giles,
and we will catch up with you," said Andrew. "I can
hurry Sabrina along to the greengrocers."

Giles looked relieved. "All right."

Sabrina, who seemed most annoyingly impervious to
the heat, spent another fifteen minutes browsing the lending library shelves, finally choosing Miss Austen's latest
and one from the Minerva Press.

Then, when they reached the grocers, she took her
time, chatting away to the proprietor and trying to decide
if she should bring the cook some cinnamon sticks as
well. "She can get these in Street, but the quality here is
so much better."

"Wrap them up, too," said Andrew, pulling some coins
out of his pocket.

Sabrina was just opening her reticule. "Andrew, don't
be silly. This all comes out of the household money. You
don't need to do this."

"Let me, Sabrina, as a gesture of gratitude for your
hospitality. I assure you, I can afford it," he added sarcastically.

"I never meant that you couldn't, Andrew," she responded coolly.

Damn the woman, and damn his response to her, thought
Andrew. She could arouse him to desire or annoyance or
anger in a moment.

By the time they mounted their horses, Giles and Clare
were a good hour ahead of them, and when they reached
the ruin, it was clear that they had not waited.

"Oh, dear, they didn't wait for us," said Sabrina.

"We did say a quarter of an hour," responded Andrew.

He glanced up at the sky. "I expect that Giles decided it wasn't wise to wait any longer," he added, pointing to the huge thunderheads that were forming directly ahead of them.

"You can say it, Andrew."

"Say what?"

"I told you so. We are riding right into them, aren't we?"

Andrew grinned. "I resigned myself to this possibility hours ago, Sabrina. Come, let us see if we can outride the storm."

When they reached the halfway point, however, it became clear that they weren't going to make it to Whitton before a cloudburst. Jagged streaks of lightning were lighting up a landscape suddenly gone dark, followed by great rumblings of thunder.

"It is moving right toward us, isn't it, Andrew?"

"Yes. I don't mind getting wet, Sabrina. In fact, it would almost feel refreshing," he added. "But the lightning worries me. Do you know of any place we could take shelter between here and home?"

Sabrina thought for a minute. "There is a deserted cottage just a few miles from here. I think we can make it before the storm breaks."

They had been sparing of their horses until now, but as they rode toward the menacing clouds, they pushed them as hard as they dared.

Sabrina was leading the way, and at one point, when her hat blew off and her hair tumbled down her back, she turned to Andrew and laughed. That was something he loved about her, that she was willing to ride into the teeth of the storm and enjoy the moment.

Sabrina pulled her horse up at the edge of a small field. "I think the cottage is over there, Andrew," she said, pointing to a small copse. A large crack of thunder startled the horses, and Andrew quickly dismounted and grabbed Sabrina's mare's bridle.

"Get down, Brina, quickly."

Sabrina slid down.

They were only halfway across the field when the heavens opened. Sabrina threw back her head as if to drink in the rain.

"Keep moving," shouted Andrew. He had never seen such a storm. There was hardly any time now between the flashes of lightning and deafening cracks of thunder, and they were very exposed in the middle of the field.

They finally reached the copse and found the small path to the cottage.

"There is a shed around the back, Andrew," Sabrina shouted. "We must get the horses out of this."

Andrew pushed her in front of him. "Get inside now, and I'll take care of the horses."

Sabrina pushed the door to the cottage open. She hadn't been here for years, but the damp, musty smell carried her back to childhood.

It looked the same inside. There was a rickety old table and two chairs in what was used as the kitchen. There was still the old cot against the other wall.

She stood dripping on the threshold until she heard Andrew running up behind her.

"For God's sake, get inside, Brina," he yelled, grabbing her arm and pushing them through the door. He pulled it closed behind them, and they both jumped as an almost simultaneous bolt of lightning and crash of thunder seemed to surround the cottage.

"It can't get any worse than that," said Sabrina, laughing shakily as they both stood in the middle of the small dwelling watching the rain come down in sheets past the window. Her hair was plastered to her head, and her light summer riding habit clung to her figure in such a way that Andrew had to turn his back to her. His own breeches were stuck to his skin, and he turned his thoughts to unpleasant thing like how many mice and rats might have taken up residence here to keep his arousal under control.

When he turned back, Sabrina was trying to do something with her hair, which hung heavy and wet on her shoulders.

"Sit down," said Andrew, pulling a chair out from the table.

She sat down gingerly, wondering whether the chairs were as worm-eaten as the shaking table.

"Now put your head back."

Sabrina leaned her head back and closed her eyes so that she did not have to gaze directly at Andrew. He lifted her hair up and twisted it together until it felt like a thick rope in his hands and then wrung it out.

"I feel like a washerwoman," he said with a laugh as rainwater fell on the floor. "But at least your hair won't be quite as wet and heavy." He looked around quickly. "There doesn't seem to be anything around that could serve as a towel, unfortunately." He let her hair down on her back and then ran his fingers gently through it to separate the strands. A few tendrils sprang back into curls by her ears and without even thinking, he reached out to play with them.

Sabrina sat there in a trancelike state aware of nothing but Andrew's hands. She would be quite happy if the storm went on forever, she realized. Suddenly, his hands were still, and she said, without thinking, "Don't stop, Andrew."

"I must, Sabrina," he replied in a low voice as he drew his hands through her hair for one last time.

Reaching back, Sabrina caught one of his hands before he could pull away, placed it on her shoulder, and leaned her head against it. Andrew turned his hand so that it cupped her cheek, and she sighed with pleasure.

"We can't do this, Sabrina."

"Do what, Andrew," she whispered.

He pulled away and walked over to the window, peering out as though he could see something beyond the rain.

Sabrina turned in her chair and gazed at this back. His shoulders were squared, and he was gripping the window-sill with both hands, as though to keep himself anchored there.

She got up and walked over to stand next to him, placing her left hand on top of his right.

"For God's sake, Sabrina . . ."

Sabrina loosened his fingers and lifted his hand to her lips.

Andrew, who had felt his control slipping from him, let it go completely and turning, grabbed her up in a fierce embrace. And then, as quickly as he had crushed her against him, he let her go.

"Sabrina, please go and sit down at the table," he said in a broken whisper.

Sabrina stood there, frozen into immobility by his rejection.

"I will not do this. I will not compromise you, Sabrina. Please."

"Damn you, Andrew More," Sabrina muttered as she walked with exaggerated dignity to the kitchen table and sat down.

"Thank you. I am sure the rain will stop soon, and we can be on our way."

"And pretend this never happened, Andrew. Do you think it is as simple as that? Or do you think I am in the habit of letting men crush the breath out of my body?"

"This never *should* have happened, Sabrina. And of course I do not think of you as wanton. It . . . it was the storm."

"What it was, Andrew, is the fact that I love you," said Sabrina whose teeth were chattering from both the terror of admitting her feelings and her cold wet clothing.

Andrew, who had not moved from the window, eagerly started toward Sabrina before catching himself halfway across the room.

"You can't," he responded bluntly.

"Well, I do. I have for some time now. And why I am so foolish as to admit it, I am sure I don't know," she added, her arms wrapped around herself to keep the deep shudders in.

Andrew finally noticed her shaking and looked around

the cottage again for something to put around her shoulders. The only thing he saw was a moth-eaten old blanket on the cot. Praying that there were no live inhabitants of either bed or blanket, he shook it out and gently draped it across Sabrina's shoulders. She clutched the blanket around her, and Andrew, who only wanted to pull her against him and warm her with his body, drew back.

"It is unfortunate that you do not feel the same way," she continued. "But don't worry, I will not embarrass you again."

Andrew's control broke at last, and he smashed his fist down on the table, causing it to shake and wobble under him.

"You think I go around embracing any woman in that way? You think I was only consumed by lust? I tell you, Sabrina, if it was desire alone I felt for you, I would never have stopped. Oh, I love you all right. More fool I."

Sabrina's face shone with sudden joy. "Do you mean that, Andrew? she asked, letting the blanket slip off her shoulders and reaching out for his hand.

"I do, God help me, I do. But don't look at me like that, Brina. It doesn't change anything."

"But why not?"

"Because I am a poor barrister whose own family despairs at my activities. Because you are an earl's daughter and I am a youngest son, very removed from the title. You could have any nobleman in London."

"I don't want any nobleman, thank you," Sabrina replied acerbically. "I want you."

"You can't have me, Brina," replied Andrew with one of his quizzical grins. "I will save you from yourself and me. What kind of friend would I be to Giles were I to take advantage of his sister's infatuation."

"Infatuation! I am no poor foolish miss blinded by infatuation, Andrew. I see you very clearly. And what I see is a man whose pride would keep us both from happiness."

"Pride? I have just told you all the reasons why I am not worthy of you. I would hardly call that pride!"

"But it *is,* Andrew. A very masculine belief in honor and duty, which places them both above love. But I am not proud, Andrew. And I will not give up."

"That is your choice, Sabrina. Perhaps when you realize that I am very serious, you will give the fever a chance to burn out."

Both were very quiet for a few minutes.

"The rain has stopped," Andrew said, getting up suddenly. "It is time we returned to Whitton. I will go get our horses, my lady." His face was shuttered, and Sabrina knew that only something like another violent storm would break through Andrew Moore's reserve.

When they finally arrived back at Whitton, Giles greeted them with great relief.

"Thank you for keeping Sabrina safe," he said to Andrew later that evening after the women had retired. "I am sure my incorrigible sister would have been ready to ride through the worst of the storm."

"Even the intrepid Sabrina was willing to seek shelter, Giles. The lightning was truly terrifying. You and Clare were lucky to be ahead of it."

"Yes, and if Sabrina hadn't taken so much time in Wells, you would have been, too," said Giles with a laugh. "But that is what I most love about Sabrina. Her reckless determination. It is, at the same time, her greatest strength and weakness."

Andrew nodded and changed the subject. After a half hour's conversation, he took one last sip of brandy and stood up. "I am more than ready for bed, Giles, after such an afternoon. And Giles, I think I will be leaving the day after tomorrow. You can inform Mrs. Stanton of that."

"I thought you were staying until Monday next?" Giles responded, surprise and disappointment in his voice.

"I remembered that I have some preparation to do with my solicitor on a troublesome case."

"I see. Well, we will certainly miss your company. Especially Sabrina," Giles added, just as Andrew closed the library door behind him.

Andrew spent the following day avoiding Sabrina as best he could without seeming impolite and left early the next morning before breakfast. His journey back to London was tedious and depressing, for he felt he was leaving behind the one chance for happiness with a woman he might ever have. Yet he had known for years that she was not for him, and had managed to resign himself to that fact. It was only that damned thunderstorm that had broken down his hard-won reserve. That, and Sabrina herself. He would have preferred making a fool of himself by confessing a one-sided passion. At least Sabrina's indifference would have added another barrier. But to know that his love was returned, no matter that for her it was likely only infatuation; well, that was very hard indeed.

Chapter Twenty-six

Giles watched his sister very closely after Andrew's departure. He could tell that she was unhappy, but since she feigned indifference and had not confided in him, he hesitated to invade her privacy. And he himself was rather preoccupied with his own dilemma of the heart.

Giles had always dreamed of a marriage like his parents, where a couple so enjoyed each other's company that they shared one bedroom. While it was true that the door between their rooms was now open, Giles felt more like a visitor to Clare's bed. A welcome visitor, he hoped. For the most part, he was sure of his welcome. Clare always seemed genuinely glad to see him in the doorway and was an active partner in their lovemaking. Yet there was something missing. Giles still had the feeling that at times, Clare retreated behind some barrier, even in their most intimate moments. And although his wife gave the appearance of a woman being satisfied, Giles was beginning to wonder if her release was, in fact, genuine. Her responses were, he realized, relatively unvaried and beginning to seem less spontaneous. Of course, he was too much a gentleman to make such an accusation. But it was beginning to bother him. If Clare was only pretending to be satisfied, what did that mean? Was she only admitting him to her bed out of a sense of duty or pity after all?

He did not consider himself as any sort of sexual expert, but he had been able to bring the other women he had been with to a much more abandoned state of pleasure. And those women included two respectable widows, not only those from the ranks of the fashionable impure.

Yet Clare so genuinely enjoyed the preliminaries of their lovemaking and cuddled against him so affectionately afterward that he decided to try to let go of his concern for a while. They were newlyweds after all, and she had been through a terrible ordeal. Time would probably take care of everything.

Clare herself felt torn. On the one hand, as Giles could tell, her welcome was genuine and her enjoyment of his kisses and caresses very real. On the other hand, as soon as she felt her own passion building, something clicked off inside her, leaving her lying there on the bed, watching Giles's attempts to bring her to her own climax as though they were two other people. She reassured him as best she could, that their coupling was as enjoyable for her as it was for him, and, in fact, made a determined effort to initiate it a few times so that he would be convinced she meant it. But he deserved better. She felt increasingly guilty that she couldn't give a most loving and gentle husband what she had given a brutal one: the gift of her innermost self.

Clare would not have said that she was miserable in her marriage. But as the summer turned to fall, it became increasingly clear that neither she nor Giles was perfectly happy in it. Perhaps "perfect happiness" was unrealistic to expect twice in one lifetime, she thought with some irony. And look at the price she had paid with Justin for those moments of ecstasy. And how real, after all, had that happiness been? Yes, there had been many times with Justin when their bodies and souls had been in so close a union that she felt as if they were one person. And then that husband, who felt like her soul's twin, had blacked an eye or broken a rib. She could not get herself beyond that. Her courtroom testimony had been the reality, and she never wanted to remember again.

* * *

Although Clare was increasingly aware of what was missing in her marriage, she was not so miserable as to be ignorant of Sabrina's unhappiness. One morning, shortly after the harvest, she invited Sabrina to come for a ride with her.

"It will be an easy one, Sabrina, and we will return before lunch," she laughingly warned her sister-in-law, knowing how Sabrina loved long and challenging rides across country.

Sabrina smiled. "That will be fine with me today, Clare. It is too warm to go too fast or far."

Indeed, the heat had been building again for the past few days, and the harvesters had constantly been looking over their shoulders as they worked, hoping to get the corn in before the weather broke.

They enjoyed a slow canter for part of their ride, but the horses were soaking wet afterward, as were their riders, and after walking their mounts to cool them, Sabrina and Clare dismounted and led them up Camden Hill.

"It feels just like the day we all rode to Wells," said Clare, sitting down on the grass. "Look at those clouds gathering in the southwest."

"Yes, you are right, Clare. We can't stay here too long. I have learned my lesson," Sabrina responded ruefully.

"Giles and I were so worried about you and Andrew that day," Clare said hesitantly, without looking at her friend. "Of course, we should have known you would find shelter. But I have wondered since then whether there was another reason to be worried?"

"Are you asking if Andrew compromised me, Clare?"

"Of course not. Andrew is a gentleman. He would have offered for you had anything happened. No, it was just that he left so suddenly, and you have not seemed yourself since then."

"I wish he *had* compromised me," Sabrina declared fiercely. "As it was, I was the one who practically made him an offer. Which he honorably refused." Sabrina added with ironic stress on the word honorably.

Clare was silent for a minute, trying to absorb what Sabrina had told her. "Then you *do* care for him. I have long thought so."

"I love him very much," whispered Sabrina. "And much good it does me."

"And Andrew? Does he return your affection?"

"I believe so. But he is too much a gentleman to want to ruin my life by proposing to me."

"Whatever do you mean?"

"He is convinced that a younger son who has no chance at the title and no great fortune is not an equal match for the daughter of an earl who has a generous portion. It is that damned sense of honor that men have. Pardon my language, Clare, but I don't know how they can put honor before everything, even love."

"Does Giles know about this?"

"I am sure he has guessed that something has happened. I doubt that Andrew would have spoken to him directly. And I haven't."

"Perhaps I could speak to Andrew when we return to London, Sabrina," said Clare thoughtfully. "We are good friends now. Maybe I could bring him to his senses. I think the two of you would be very happy together."

"As you and Giles are," Sabrina asked, not very innocently, wondering whether Clare would admit to any of the tension Sabrina could feel between her brother and his wife.

Clare merely nodded and agreed. "Yes, as Giles and I are." The horses were becoming restless, and the clouds were rolling closer. "Come, we had better go," said Clare, "or we will be caught this time."

They reached Whitton in plenty of time before the storm, but Giles was out front, pacing up and down in front of the house as they rode in.

"Sabrina, I cannot believe you would risk the weather again," he said, not bothering to check his anger.

"Giles, this is nothing like last time," his sister replied.

"It is merely a heavy rainstorm, with only a little thunder. And besides, we outrode it."

"Barely. And this time, you put Clare at risk."

Perhaps it was the injustice. Clare had always hated injustice. The ride had been *her* idea, not Sabrina's, although, to be fair, Giles was not to know that. But still, to attack his sister without any explanation was just unfair.

Perhaps it was the heat and the tension in the atmosphere that builds before such a storm. Perhaps it was the accumulated tension between her and her husband. Clare didn't know. But when Giles casually summoned a footman to help his sister dismount and turned toward Clare, grabbing the reins of her horse as though she were incapable of keeping the restless animal under control, she felt a wave of anger wash over her. She was *not* a neck or nothing rider like Sabrina, it was true, but she could handle a restive horse.

As Giles reached up to lift her down, she realized she wanted nothing more than to smack the protective, solicitous look off his face, and was immediately horrified by the violence of her thoughts. She let him help her down, but turned to face him, saying in a shaking voice: "The ride was *my* idea, Giles. And both Sabrina and I are grown women who can read the weather very well. We turned around in time. It will be a good ten minutes before the storm reaches here. Nor did we have to run the horses to get back ahead of it. I know that you and Sabrina have a free and easy relationship, but that does not warrant blaming her for everything. Nor assuming that I never have an idea of my own."

Bravo, Clare, thought Sabrina, surprised and touched by her friend's defense. She watched Clare pull away from Giles and walk into the house without looking back.

Giles stood there, completely dumbfounded. When he regained his composure, he turned to his sister and tendered her an apology. "I am sorry for accusing you without reason, Brina. If you will excuse me, I will go and make my apologies to my wife."

Clare was still shaking when she reached her bedroom. She dismissed Martha and sank into the chair by the window, lacing and unlacing her fingers as she tried to calm herself down. What had Giles done, after all, but treat Sabrina like a well-loved sister. The two had always spoken freely to one another and never shied away from a quarrel. It was just that Clare was very conscious about Sabrina's vulnerability around the aftermath of the thunderstorm. And Giles hadn't been fair. He had assumed, as always, that little Clare Dysart couldn't do anything on her own.

The breeze that had been blowing had turned into a wind, and the branches of the holly tree on the side of the house were scraping and rustling against Clare's window. The room was becoming darker as the clouds covered the sun, and Clare knew the rain could not be far behind. Her window was half-open, she realized, and she stood to close it. But the wood had swollen in the humidity of the last weeks, and although she leaned all her weight down against it, should could not get it shut.

"Here, Clare, let me help you," said Giles from behind her, and he reached around her shoulders to help her push it down.

She felt smothered by him and pulled herself away, going to stand by the fireplace. Giles turned and gave her an apologetic smile. "I am sorry if I startled you. And I am sorry for jumping on Sabrina. But it was only natural that I thought your ride her idea. And you did only make it back by a very few minutes," he added, looking at the windowpane where the first few drops were hitting. He moved over to her and lifted her hair back from her face. "I love the way your hair curls in this weather," he whispered.

He had touched her gently and with consideration, as usual. That was the problem. He was always *so careful* with her, as though she were a porcelain woman like the shepherdess on the mantel.

"Don't, Giles," she responded.

"I am sorry, Clare," he replied, immediately lowering his hand. "You are still upset with me?"

"Don't be sorry, Giles. What have you got to be sorry about?"

"Why, losing my temper at the two of you."

"No, Giles. You did not lose your temper at me. You *never* lose your temper at me. You are always the perfect, gentle knight." Clare was as surprised as Giles by her reaction. She was furious with him for being what for years she had wanted him to be: her Galahad. Oh, but Galahad would have been so difficult to live with, she thought suddenly.

Giles blanched at her tone. "I don't know what you mean, Clare. Of course I am rarely angry at you. I am hardly perfect, but I think all I need to confess to this time is wanting to keep you safe. After all, I love you."

"Do you, Giles? Do you love *me* or do you love some memory that you hold from your childhood."

Giles was stung. "How can you doubt my love, Clare? I have always loved you. I asked you to marry me as soon as it was possible. And surely, if nothing else, my behavior in our bed should convince you."

"Sometimes I think you only see Clare Dysart, Giles. The Clare Dysart you knew before she fell in love with Justin Rainsborough. Not the Clare Dysart who jilted you."

"We were never formally engaged," Giles interjected.

"Not Lady Rainsborough, Giles," Clare continued as though he had not spoken. "Lady Rainsborough gave her husband all of herself in the marriage bed, Giles. She gave him all that she cannot seem to give you. And when he beat her . . ."

"Don't talk to me of this, Clare. I don't want to hear it. And there is no need for you to torture yourself again."

"And even when he beat her and kicked her and killed

their baby, she returned to his bed," Clare continued inexorably. "You cannot tell me, Giles, that you never wondered at that even a little? For surely *I* have," she added with a bitter laugh that became a sob.

Giles looked over at the window, as though if focusing on the storm outside he could escape the inside tempest that was drawing him in. He turned back and said carefully: "I confess that there were times, particularly during the inquest when I wondered that, Clare. But I understand, truly I do." He reached out to assure her, putting his hand protectively on her shoulder.

She shook him off. "Do you, Giles? Do you? I am glad one of us does, for I most certainly do not. Do you not wonder in bed, as I do, why a woman could give herself completely to the man who treated her so horribly and cannot to the man who has loved her more than half his life?" Tears were running down Clare's cheeks almost as fast as the rain running down the windowpane. "Doesn't it ever make you *angry*, that Clare Dysart was such a foolish young woman. She could have been happy with you, Giles, and instead she chose a brute. A charming brute, I admit. And a handsome one. But a cruel man, all the same."

"I ... if I felt any anger, Clare ... I don't know, I loved you. I love you now. I tried to understand. He was deceptively charming. No one could have guessed what he would be like, let alone you."

"But didn't you nevertheless get angry, Giles?" Clare would not let him off.

"I suppose so," he admitted reluctantly.

"And do you now? Doesn't it infuriate you when I am unable to respond to you past a certain point? When I keep myself from you?"

"But I know you can't help it, Clare. If we are patient ..."

"You are too damned patient, Giles. That is the problem."

"Would you rather I raped you," Giles responded, finally moved to anger. "Would you prefer I slap you? Black your eye? Is that what arouses you, Clare?"

"No, Giles," she answered, her voice steady, but her tears still flowing. "Justin's cruelty was never what aroused me. It was his tenderness. I want so much to respond fully to you, to give you what you deserve for your faithfulness."

"I don't want your gratitude, Clare."

"I know. And I don't want your everlasting understanding, Giles. I don't want cruelty, but you have every reason in the world to be angry, to be disappointed in this marriage, and yet you have never expressed any of that."

"I have not wanted to hurt you, Clare. You have been hurt enough. We have a lifetime together to work this out."

"Life is never certain, Giles. Perhaps we have years. Perhaps not. But we will never work out our difficulties if you cannot see me as I am, not as I was. I am a grown woman now, Giles. Once I married a man who loved me in a very destructive way. Who stopped loving me and only sought to destroy me. I felt helpless with him, Giles. I had no one to protect me, no one to turn to then. I did the best I could to keep myself from being hurt. And when that wasn't enough, I killed him."

"No, Clare."

"Yes, Giles. Even though you heard it at the inquest, you don't want to believe it, do you? Sabrina saw Justin. Ask her."

"I know you killed Rainsborough, Clare, but you didn't really know what you were doing. And it was self-defense."

"I know all that, Giles. Who better. Nevertheless, I killed my husband. They found me with my dress soaked with his blood." The tears had stopped, and Clare's voice was calm. "At first, I couldn't remember it. Then, when I did, I tortured myself as much as Justin ever tortured me. Did I need to do it? How could I have done it? But do you know something, Giles? I have remembered it all, and one moment stands out for me. Just as I thought I was dying, just as my whole body was giving in to him, saying 'yes, yes, this is it, the ending I should have foreseen,' something in me, some part of me, very deep, that I hadn't even known existed, screamed *'no,'* and that *'no'* saved my life. And yours. The woman who said *'no'* is who I am, Giles. Not the timid Clare Dysart, who let Lucy Kirkman dump those worms on her years ago. Nor the innocent Clare who fell in love with a madman. For that is what Justin was, I think. Oh, I am still quiet and rather shy, Giles. But for the first time in my life, I know myself and like myself despite all my mistakes. And until you hear that woman, until you see her, Giles, our marriage will never become what we both wish it to be."

Giles stood there in silence as the room had become darker and the branches and rain beat against Clare's window. He could hardly believe it was Clare who had spoken to him so. But there she stood, the same small woman he had known for so long. Or thought he had known.

"I don't know what to say, Clare. It seems you want some sort of angry response from me that I can't give you. Perhaps I have been guilty of loving a memory rather than a real woman. I apologize for that." He hesitated. "I think, for a while at least, it is best if I do not share your bed. It is obviously becoming a burden for both of us. And if things need to change, the change will not come from there," he added.

"I agree with you, Giles," said Clare wearily.

"All I can promise is to think about what you have said. To see if I can come to understand it."

"That is all anyone can ask," said Clare with a sad smile.

"I will see you at supper, then?"

"Yes, Giles."

After he left, Clare sat by the window again watching

the storm play itself out. It was over within an hour and
when the clouds had broken, the late afternoon sunlight
revealed the whole world as clean and sparkling. The
leaves of the holly tree, which had seemed to fade in the
heat and humidity had lifted, and Clare felt a faint stirring
of hope. Perhaps her outburst would serve to disperse the
tension between her husband and herself and allow them
the same sort of new beginning.

Over the next few weeks, however, the relationship between husband and wife remained static. Giles was as
kind and considerate as ever, but now the reserve was on
his side as much as on Clare's. He never touched her unless it would have looked strange not to: dancing at a local assembly or handing her over a stile on one of their
rambles with Sabrina. He would give her a polite kiss on
the cheek at the door in the evening when they retired at
the same time, but the door between their rooms remained
closed.

It took all his self-control to restrain himself. When
they were dancing, the smell of her perfume would only
remind him of their physical intimacy. Many nights after
his cool good-night kiss, he would lie awake remembering how it felt to lose himself in her body. Aroused and
frustrated, he wondered if his wife was wanting him, if
any of the passion between them had been real.

Clare did miss his kisses and waking up curled against
him in the morning. She missed the way he had gently
but effectively aroused her and readied her for his lovemaking. She didn't miss, however, those awful moments
after his release when he would attempt to bring her to
hers. And surely, it would not have done their marriage
any good for them to have gone on pretending?

They had talked about the possibility of attending the
Little Season in the beginning of the summer, but had
come to no clear decision. Clare was relieved one morning at breakfast, when Giles raised the possibility again.

"I think it is time to think about returning to London, Clare. Sabrina? I hope you are both in agreement with me?"

Sabrina was of two minds. She wasn't sure she could stand seeing Andrew More socially. It would be painful to maintain her friendly facade now that the truth between them had been spoken. Although surely during Michaelmas Term, he would have a busy schedule? Yet as painful as it might be to return to London, at least there would be a variety of activities to distract her. And Giles and Clare. The careful politeness between them was hard to watch, and she was well aware that something had happened that was keeping Giles from his wife's bed. All in all, London seemed the better choice.

"I have enjoyed the summer, Giles," she replied. Well, she *had,* up until Andrew's visit. "But I think some time in the city would be good for all of us."

Clare smiled and nodded her agreement. Surely a change of scene could not hurt their marriage. Might even help it. And she would have a chance to speak with Andrew in London. If she couldn't bring Giles happiness, then perhaps she could help Andrew and Sabrina find it.

Chapter Twenty-seven

The first few days Andrew was back in London, his rooms seemed very cramped and dingy after the spacious elegance of Whitton, and for the first time in his life, he wished he were his brother. Well, not precisely, he thought humorously. He would never want to be as priggish, responsible, and boring as Jonathan. But had he been born the elder, he would have asked Sabrina to marry him years ago.

He would just have to put her out of his mind. Banish the memory of how soft her cheek felt, how well she fit against him when he pulled her close.

He had no reason to be in court for the next few weeks, but on his first day back, instead of going straight to his chambers, he had decided to distract himself at the Old Bailey for a few hours. Although the practice was by no means universal, it was becoming more common for victims and criminals alike to be represented by counsel, and Andrew enjoyed watching other barristers putting witnesses through their paces.

After watching two young men sentenced to the hulks for burglary, one older woman transported for stealing from her mistress, Andrew felt better. Not that he enjoyed feeding off human misery as did some court spectators. He felt sympathy for those victimized by poverty who then, in turn, victimized others. Oh, he prosecuted them, but he also sympathized. And this morning he had certainly needed to feel sorry for someone other than himself.

He spied Thomas Ruthven, one of the better-known Bow Street Runners and after the morning session, sought him out. He enjoyed socializing with Runners as much or perhaps more than with his social equals. Most of them were men of great natural intelligence, albeit uneducated, and most important of all, were not hypocrites as were so many of his own class. They knew firsthand what was important: life and death, not who was the latest cuckold. After an enjoyable dinner with Ruthven at the Garrick Head over which he caught up on the latest criminal gossip, Andrew strolled to his office, mellowed by the ale and good company, and distracted at least from his thoughts of Sabrina. All a man really needed, he decided, the ale working on him, was work, meaningful work.

When he entered his chambers, his clerk greeted him and then motioned to a young man sitting in the corner.

"He's been waiting three hours to see you, Mr. More."

Andrew glanced over. His visitor and he assumed, prospective client, was a young man, not older than twenty-four, Andrew would have guessed. He was dressed respectably and looked considerably different from many of Andrew's usual clients. He had lank, dirty-blond hair, which fell over his forehead, and a sallow complexion.

"You would like to see me, Mr. . . . ?"

The young man's face brightened. "Yes, sir. Oh, I am John Grantham."

"Come in to my office, Mr. Grantham."

The young man unfolded himself and stood up. He was at least two inches taller than Andrew, and very thin. Not a particularly healthy-looking specimen, thought Andrew, as he led him into the office and motioned him to sit down.

"Now, what is it you wanted to see me about?"

The young man cleared his throat and shifted nervously in his chair. He didn't look like a criminal, thought Andrew, but then, quite often appearances were deceiving.

"I wish you to help me prosecute someone. Er, actually, four men."

Robbery, thought Andrew. "Do you know the identity of these men, Mr. Grantham? Or will I have to call in a Runner?"

The young man smiled bleakly. "Oh, I know them very well, Mr. More. They are Richard Bennett, Frederick Oldfield, John Phillips, and Thomas Carolus. They are the proprietors of a gaming hell at 75 St. James Street."

"You wish to prosecute the proprietors of a gaming house?" Andrew was flabbergasted. No one ever brought charges against such men.

"Yes," said Grantham, his fidgeting hands still now that he had spoken. "Yes, I do. I am, or I *was*," he said bitterly, "a student at Inner Temple. I have learned something of the law. It says that 'Any person who shall at any one sitting lose the sum of ten pounds or more and pays, he is at liberty for three months to recover it.'"

Andrew lifted his eyebrows. "You are correct, Mr. Grantham. The law does say that. But I know of hardly any precedents."

"Oh, I know," said Grantham bitterly. "A gentleman pays his gaming debts. A gentleman does not complain and certainly does not attempt to get his money back. A gentleman values his honor above all things. Well, I am not a gentleman, Mr. More. Which is why I am here. Your solicitor told me you take on clients whose cases interest you. He told me to talk to you directly in the hope that mine also would."

"Tell me your story, Mr. Grantham," said Andrew, leaning back in his chair.

"I was born in India. My father is a minor official with the East India Company. His dream and also my mother's was that I would come back to England and become something a little more successful than my father. My parents scraped and saved for years, and when they finally had enough for my journey and fees, they sent me off with their lifesavings in my pockets."

"And you settled into the life of a law student?"

"Yes. But I didn't make many friends, Mr. More. Most of my fellow students are the younger sons of the nobility and had no interest in someone like me, whose family has been in trade. It has been a lonely year, but I discovered a coffeehouse in the West End, where I spent hours reading the newspaper or studying."

Andrew knew the rest of the story. An obvious "Johnny Newcome," John Grantham was the natural prey for a blackleg, one of those ruined gamesters who haunted the West End acting as "recruiting officers." But he let Grantham continue.

"I met an older man. A man called Thomas. I found out later he is called 'Coaxing Tom,' " added Grantham with a hollow laugh. "It is a good name for him. He was kind and coaxing. He told me I was too serious and too sallow. That I needed a little excitement to liven up my life, and he knew just the place. I would make friends there," he said. "And so I went."

"And played?"

"Oh, I only laid down a little the first few times. But I won back everything and more."

"Yes, they make sure of that in these houses. Everyone wins more than he loses the first few times."

"Then I started to lose. But not too much. Not enough to discourage me. And I was welcome. Oh, I've told myself I was having a hard time. I was homesick, had no friends."

"But that is the truth," said Andrew sympathetically.

"The truth is, I was naive and stupid. The truth is I *let* them fleece me out of my parents' hard-earned money. The truth is I have nothing and have had to quit my studies. And the truth is, I don't give a damn about honor and what is *done* and what isn't *done*. I want my money back. The law is on my side, and I have come to love the law, although at the end, I was giving it little enough of my time."

Andrew sat quietly through his outburst. At first, he

hadn't been drawn to this young man, partly because of his unappealing exterior, he was ashamed to say. And, also, he had to admit, because of his class. Sometimes he had an easier time with the poorest of the poor, and whether he liked it or not, he mixed with his own class confidently. He understood the middle class least. No one that he knew would ever dream of trying to get their money back. He knew men at Oxford whose fathers had lost whole estates; one whose brother had committed suicide over unpaid debts. But the code of honor demanded that a gentleman always paid what he owed, even if it meant impoverishing his family.

So at first he had only thought the young man a "whiner," unwilling to take responsibility for his actions. Then, as he listened, he began to admire him. Here he was, willing to admit he's been gulled, "fleabotomised," as the blacklegs called it, but not willing to go along with a societal code that would have meant destroying the belief his parents had in him. If he carried through with this, Grantham would be even more of an outcast than he already was. But he obviously didn't care. The principle of what was right and lawful motivated him.

And why should old Lord Marchmain have given up his estate. Or the young Viscount Blakeney shot himself? Andrew's thoughts surprised him, and he had a fleeting vision of how nice it would have been to come home to Sabrina and discuss these issues. He dismissed it as quickly as it appeared and leaned forward on his elbows.

"You realize that these men are not going to appreciate your devotion to the law, Mr. Grantham."

Grantham swallowed hard. "I do."

"They are criminals, although they appear very welcoming and genteel."

"I am not afraid," said Grantham stoutly, and then he laughed. "No, I am very afraid," he admitted. "But I must do what I believe is right."

"As long as you understand the possible consequences,

I will take you on as a client and direct my solicitor to prepare your case."

"Thank you, Mr. More, thank you," Grantham answered with great relief.

"The case cannot be brought until Michaelmas Term. I will have Mr. Lawrence contact you to prepare the brief."

Grantham got up to leave. "Mr. Grantham, there is something you have forgotten," said Andrew. "The small matter of my fee," he added dryly.

Grantham blushed. "Of course. I have a small amount of money set aside."

"Which, no doubt, you need for lodging and food?"

Grantham nodded sheepishly.

"Well, I will wait, and you can pay me when we win."

"You think we can win, then?"

"I know we will."

"Thank you for taking this case on, Mr. More," said Grantham fervently.

"You are more than welcome, Mr. Grantham," said Andrew, walking him to the door. "It will liven up my fall term considerably, I am sure." And keep my mind off Lady Sabrina Whitton, he added to himself.

The Whittons arrived in London in mid-September and spent their first few days getting settled in. By the end of their first week, however, they started to accept selected invitations. Each time Sabrina walked into a drawing room or a ballroom, she found herself trembling like a young girl about to encounter the object of her first calf-love. But Andrew More was not at Lady Edward's soiree nor the Thorndike ball, which left Sabrina both relieved and disappointed.

Giles was also on the lookout for Andrew, and when he didn't appear either evening or call on the Whittons, Giles decided it was time to call on his friend. He excused himself from the daily ride one morning, announcing over breakfast that he had some errands to do. After

Sabrina and Clare left, he took a hansom cab to Temple Bar.

Andrew's clerk greeted him and announced that Mr. More was with a client, "If you can wait, my lord."

"Of course. Mr. More had no idea I was coming."

After ten minutes, Andrew's door opened and a tall, thin young man emerged. Giles looked at him curiously. He was better dressed than Andrew's usual class of clients, and Giles wondered just what he had been accused of.

As soon as the clerk announced him, Andrew was at the door, a broad smile on his face.

"Giles! What a delightful surprise! I didn't know whether you were still in the country or had decided to do the Little Season."

"It was a quick and unanimous decision, Andrew. We only arrived at the beginning of this week. We were hoping to see you at the Thorndike's, but when we didn't, I decided to hunt you down myself."

"I have been quite busy, Giles," said Andrew, sitting on top of his desk and motioning Giles to a chair in front of him. "Michaelmas Term starts soon. And I always do the minimum socializing anyway, you know."

Giles smiled. "Yes, I know you well. Was that a new client, Andrew? He looked well-heeled compared to your usual clientele. What is he accused of?"

Andrew grinned. "He is accused of nothing, Giles. I am acting as prosecutor in this case."

Giles lifted his eyebrows questioningly.

"That young man, Mr. John Grantham, is bringing suit against Messrs. Bennett, Oldfield, Carolus, and Phillips."

"Embezzlement?"

"Of a kind, I suppose you could say," Andrew replied. "The gentlemen in question run a gaming hell at 75 St. James Street."

"You are bamming me, Andrew. That young man is trying to use the law to renege on a gaming debt?"

"Oh, no, Giles. He owes them nothing. He's paid all of

his parents' hard-earned money, which they saved to place him at the bar. He is trying to get it back. And he is quite within the law, I might add."

"Truly?"

"Absolutely. From the time of our good Queen Anne, anyone could sue to recover his losses."

"But, Andrew, no one ever would, would he? It is . . ."

"Not *done*, Giles? Not the honorable thing to do, eh, what? You are right. But it is absurd, don't you think? Do you remember Jeremy Waites?"

Giles frowned. "He was ahead of us at Oxford. Wasn't he the one whose brother killed himself?"

"Yes. Over a gambling debt. And think of Franklin. He was forced to marry a cit's daughter ten years older than he, just to get himself out of the River Tick. And she looked every day of those ten years, I might add."

"Whatever will people think of this, Andrew. Your brother will not be pleased."

"Oh, hang my brother. He has never been pleased with me, whatever I've done. He should be happy I am going after criminals instead of defending them."

"And what of Messrs. Oldfield et al.? To say they will not be pleased is surely an understatement, wouldn't you say? Is there any danger in taking on this case?"

"They have already offered the boy three times his losses to make him drop the case."

"And he didn't take it!"

"Young Mr. Grantham is a middle-class idealist, Giles. Grew up in India. Father a hardworking man dedicated to duty and the company. He believes in the law. Believes that this might help other young men who get caught up in the toils of the blacklegs. No, he didn't accept the bribe, for he is doing this as much for the principle as for the money."

"And you, Andrew?"

"Oh, they offered me a tidy sum too, Giles. Sent over their solicitor, who very tactfully suggested that this whole thing could go away for five hundred pounds."

"Now I know you are bamming me!"

Andrew shook his head. "Do you know how much these men can pull in a year, Giles?"

"Forty, fifty thousand guineas?"

"Five hundred thousand."

"No!"

"*Yes.* They don't want anyone jeopardizing that kind of profit, I can tell you." Andrew hesitated. "After I turned down the money, their solicitor hinted that the young Mr. Grantham might want to return to India, 'for health reasons.' I sent him away with an earful, I can tell you. I've had Mr. Grantham move out of his rooms into a small inn. He'll be safe."

"And what about you, Andrew," asked Giles with concern.

"Don't worry, Giles, They wouldn't dare touch a barrister. Or the younger son of an earl, for that matter," he added with a grin.

"It is nothing to joke about, Andrew."

"The only danger I am in, Giles, is social. After all, I am about to threaten everything a gentleman holds dear: the right to put his family fortune and estate at risk. I see a frown on your face, Giles. Do you disapprove?"

"What? No, I don't think so. I must confess, I have never heard anyone question my assumptions about this before. I deplore gambling, I have sincerely pitied and in some cases tried to help those caught up in it, but I never would have thought of challenging anything legally. But now that I think of it, it seems foolish not to." Giles shook his head as though to clear it. "But I do worry about you, my friend."

"Nonsense. Nothing will happen to me. I will win this case. John Grantham will go back and finish his studies at Inner Temple, where he will, no doubt, become even more of a social outcast. And gentlemen will go on ruining themselves and marrying Friday-faced cit's daughters to bring themselves about."

Giles laughed. "I suppose you are right. Now, when are we going to see you?"

"Oh, I have accepted a few invitations over the next few weeks," Andrew replied evasively.

"Will you be at the Straitons'?"

Andrew examined his fingernails. "The Straitons'? Yes, I think I did accept their invitation."

"Good, then we will see you there." Giles hesitated. "Sabrina will be pleased, I am sure," he added.

Andrew continued to look at his hand, as if there were nothing more interesting in the world than the state of his cuticles, and said nothing.

"Will you be pleased to see *her*, Andrew? Perhaps that is the more important question."

Andrew looked up at Giles and said evenly: "I am always pleased to see both of you. You know that, Giles."

"All right. I won't pry any further. You left Whitton very quickly, however. And Sabrina has been moping about ever since. I thought, but perhaps I was wrong, that something had happened between you? The afternoon of the storm?"

Andrew's eyes flashed. "Do you think I would compromise your sister and then flee, Giles!"

"Of course not, you fool. You know that as twins, Sabrina and I are closer than most brothers and sisters. I have always felt that she might have a special feeling for you, Andrew."

"And what if she did, Giles? What could come of it? Your sister is the daughter of an earl, with a substantial portion and . . ."

"And you," Giles interrupted, "are the son of . . ."

"Youngest son, Giles."

"With more brains and wit than your brother has in two fingers. Why shouldn't she be interested in you?"

"Lady Sabrina will, no doubt, meet someone more appropriate, with equal charm and more importantly, of equal rank," Andrew said finally.

"Oh, God, you sound just like your brother! Well, if

you are going to turn formal on me, I will leave. But I promise you, this is not the last conversation we will have on this topic."

As was typical of them, while Giles was worrying about the state of his sister's heart, Sabrina was very concerned about the state of his marriage. By now, everyone in the household was aware that the viscount and his wife were no longer sharing a bedroom or a bed. Sabrina watched Giles very carefully. He was everything that was kind and polite with Clare, and she with him, but instead of taking any opportunity to touch her, he was keeping himself at a distance. It was most likely not noticeable to anyone who did not know him well, but Sabrina was very aware of every missed opportunity.

She had intended to talk to her brother when the opportunity presented itself, but one afternoon, when Giles was at his club, she walked in on Clare, who was huddled on the sofa in the library. It was obvious from the crumpled handkerchief in her hand and her reddened eyes, that she had been crying.

Sabrina sat down next to her and said, "What is it, my dear? Can I help you in any way?"

Clare turned and gave her a watery smile. "I thought I was safe here."

"I'll leave if you want to be alone." Sabrina half rose, and Clare grasped her hand and pulled her down.

"No, no, I didn't mean that, Sabrina. I only meant I didn't want to bother anyone."

"Is it Giles?"

Clare nodded. "Yes. No. I don't know, Sabrina. I feel I hardly know myself these days, much less anyone else."

"This summer it seemed as though things were going well between the two of you."

"I suppose they were. We were sharing a bed, if that is what you mean."

Sabrina was surprised to find herself blushing. For all her independence of spirit, and the few years she had on

Clare, her friend had more experience in this area of life. She stammered an apology for intruding.

Clare smiled. "Don't worry, Sabrina. After having to reveal every intimate detail of my first marriage before a room full of strangers, I have little embarrassment left. I need someone's help and advice."

"Whatever I can do."

"I don't know if anyone can do anything," sighed Clare. "There is more to marriage than sharing a bed, Sabrina. The physical side is less complicated for a man than a woman. Giles and I reached a certain level of intimacy, but I found myself unable to give him more. It is distressing to both of us that my capability for a full, passionate response seems to have died with Justin. Although," Clare added in a low voice, "perhaps it is just punishment."

Sabrina had nothing to say. She was no innocent and knew what happened between a man and a woman, but the subtleties of marital intimacy were a mystery to her.

"Some of this tangle is due to my fear," Clare continued. "I was able to respond to Justin and look what happened. As soon as I feel anything like those feelings with Giles, something in me shuts down."

"But Giles is nothing like Justin, Clare. He would never hurt you."

"Of course I know that, Sabrina," Clare replied almost impatiently. "But I have changed, and he can't seem to see that. I don't think he wants to see it. He married little Clare Dysart, not Lady Clare Rainsborough, the notorious widow and murderess."

"You are *not* a murderess, Clare."

"I know it was in self-defense, Sabrina. But all the same, I killed a man. You saw him."

Sabrina shuddered.

"I wish Giles had seen him. I think as much as Giles wants to protect me, he needs to protect himself. He will not be angry with me."

"But why ever should he be?"

"Because I walked away from an understanding of many years. I walked away from his love and protection right into the arms of a charming villain. He still can't understand what it is like to live with someone like Justin. To live all the time utterly confused and helpless to change things. To tell you the truth, Sabrina, sometimes I wonder if at some level, Giles is repulsed by me. And the only way he can deal with this is to love the old Clare. But I am not that child any longer."

Sabrina looked at Clare as though seeing her friend for the first time. Because she was a woman and because she had been there the morning after, she had always had a better understanding than Giles of who Clare had become. But she, too, had been happy to split Clare into two people: the Clare she had known for years and the aberrant Clare who only existed because of her terrible marriage. Like Giles, she had seen him married to the old Clare, who somehow miraculously emerged unchanged from her ordeal.

She put her hand tentatively on Clare's. "I think you are right. I *know* you are," she continued. "It is very difficult to comprehend what these last few years have been like for you. I don't like to think about what I saw that night. I don't like to think about what you looked like. I have wanted it all to go away, so that we can return to what should have been."

"Perhaps my marrying Justin *was* what should have been, Sabrina," said Clare, covering her friend's hand with her own. "Had I married Giles two years ago, I would have been marrying my 'Galahad,' my illusion of him. I know now that no one is perfect, least of all me. I needed to learn how to protect myself. You have always known how, Sabrina. *You* would have thrown those worms right back at Lucy Kirkman," said Clare with a soft laugh. "Or pushed her into the stream!"

Sabrina smiled.

"Well, I have been through what feels like the fires of hell and have come out stronger for it. I wish protecting myself had not meant killing Justin, but I can't be the old Clare for Giles, even if it would make him more comfortable. And if he can't even see the new Clare, how can he love her?" Clare hesitated and then spoke again. "I will have to get past my fears and risk myself again. I know that, Sabrina. But I am sure that nothing will be resolved in our bed until Giles stops loving an illusion."

Clare's observations on the state of her marriage had surprised Sabrina. She thought she knew her brother very well, but she was beginning to realize that their very closeness made it difficult for her to see him whole. In some ways, Clare had the clearer picture.

Over the next few days, Sabrina observed Giles closely, trying to see him with the eye of an outside observer rather than a twin sister. He was a very good man, Giles Whitton, one who was quick to notice things that others of their class might have overlooked: a parlor maid with red eyes who had been bothered by one of the footmen, the cook's extra efforts in planning a favorite dish for him, the young lady with spots holding up the wall at a rout. And so obviously trying to be understanding with his wife.

He was much nicer than she was, Sabrina decided. *She* understood Andrew's feelings, but she was not about to wait around forever when they both cared for one another. She had always been less patient than her brother. And as she watched his chivalrous behavior with his wife, as she saw him act as though all were well between them, giving her a gentle kiss good night before they went off to separate beds, that while the value of such goodness was not to be underestimated, her brother might very well be destroying his marriage slowly, patiently, and understandingly.

Chapter Twenty-eight

The truth was that Giles was, at last, beginning to understand this. At first he had dismissed Clare's outburst. After all, what he felt for her was a genuine and lasting love. One which had *not* altered when it alteration found. How was it a fault to hold the younger Clare in his mind, to respond to that innocence and vulnerability?

But he was nothing if not honest with himself. He *did* not like to think too much of her marriage to Rainsborough. To wonder why she had not sought help. Her family's help. *His* help. And once the trial was over, he had wanted to put her husband's death completely behind them. That was the way he thought about it: her husband's death, something that had occurred, but did not have a thing to do with Clare. For how could he possibly admit to himself that his Clare, that lovely child and woman that he had loved for years had been found beaten, bruised, soaked in blood, standing over the husband she had shot with his own pistols?

He could feel Sabrina's concern, but for once did not want to talk to his sister. Somehow their very closeness stood in the way. And she was a woman, after all, with a woman's view of the matter. He needed someone to help him understand himself and his own confusion.

"Therefore, on one of the few occasions Andrew appeared in society, Giles tried to catch a few minutes with him alone, which proved impossible. Lord Avery was out to corner his brother that night, and he was successful in taking up most of Andrew's time.

Giles finally caught up with him as he was leaving.

"I see your brother has heard about your new client, Andrew," he teased.

Andrew groaned. "Wants me to drop him immediately, of course. Unheard of ungentlemanly behavior on Grantham's part. Why would I want to attempt social suicide. It is bad enough that I defended a murderess. I *am* sorry, Giles. That just slipped out."

"That is all right. In fact, I need to talk to you about that very subject, Andrew."

"I beg your pardon, Giles. You mean about Clare? I was only repeating my brother's ridiculousness. Surely you don't think I regard Clare that way?"

"No, no, I took no offense. Look, I cannot explain myself now. Will you be in your chambers tomorrow in the early evening? I thought I might stop by on my way to the Carstairs. Or we could go together?"

"I am not showing my face again until this trial is over," declared Andrew with a laugh. "But I will be there till sevenish, I imagine."

"All right then," said Giles. "I will be there."

The next day Giles excused himself from being Clare and Sabrina's escort to an early musicale, and promised to meet them at the Carstairs' rout. It had been a clear day, and he dressed for the same sort of evening. By the time he reached Andrew's chambers, however, a light shower had started, and he was happy to be admitted quickly by Andrew's clerk.

"Mr. More is just finishing up, my lord. He told me he was expecting you and asked me to offer you something to drink."

"I would love a glass of sherry," said Giles as he brushed off his evening jacket.

When Andrew opened his door a few minutes later, he dismissed his clerk and ushered Giles in.

"I see it has started raining, Giles," he observed as he peered out his window.

"Yes, damn it, and I feel a proper fool. I am to meet Clare and Sabrina later, and if this keeps up, I'll be more than a bit bedraggled."

"Don't worry, I can lend you a greatcoat if it turns into a downpour."

Andrew's clerk had placed the decanter of sherry and another glass on Andrew's desk. "More sherry, Giles?"

"Thank you."

"Now, what is it you wished to speak to me about?"

Giles hesitated. Now that he was here, it was hard to begin. How could he reveal the intimate secrets of his marriage, even to his close friend?

"From what you said last night, this is about Clare, Giles?" prompted Andrew.

"Yes. Or perhaps it is as much or more about me, Andrew."

Andrew leaned back in his chair and stretched his feet out under his desk. "I have all the time in the world, Giles, but you, I believe, are due at Lady Carstair's rout in an hour or so," he said with a smile.

"You never liked Clare very much, did you, Andrew."

"As I've told you before, when I first met her, all those years ago ... no. I worried that there was not enough, what shall I say, fire between you? The pattern of your relationship was set so early: she needed to be taken care of; you took care of her. But the contrast between Sabrina's spiritedness and Clare's milder nature always struck me."

"Sabrina is a wonderful woman, Andrew, but I have never wanted anyone exactly like my sister. One Sabrina in his life is enough for any man! Clare was everything to me, almost from that first summer. I liked the fact that she needed me, and I only ever wished for her happiness."

"Obviously," Andrew observed with a touch of sarcasm.

"And what do you mean by that?"

"Only that you were so concerned with her happiness

that you quite forgot your own. You were so *damned* understanding about Rainsborough."

"What choice did I have?"

"You might have fought for yourself. You might have reminded her of your loyalty and love."

"And have had her marry me out of guilt? That is what it would have been, Andrew. She thought of me only as a friend, and believed I loved her the same way."

"Because you let her believe that."

"You can't dictate passion, Andrew. Justin Rainsborough awakened Clare to the passionate side of her nature. It wasn't her fault."

"I don't blame her, Giles. Or you. I am only pointing out that you let her go very easily."

Giles's hand clenched around his glass almost hard enough to snap it. "I know that. Now."

"Well, you have both changed. When you asked me to defend Clare, I agreed for your sake. But after I spoke with her, I was in it for her sake, too. The woman that I had always thought of as weak and passive has more courage than I will ever claim."

"Was it courage that kept her with Rainsborough? She returned to his bed, even after his brutal treatment of her. She never asked for help, not even from her parents."

Andrew sat thoughtfully for a few minutes, sipping his sherry. "I don't think that either you or I will ever be able to comprehend what those two years were like, Giles. Justin Rainsborough did not only deceive Clare, you know. He deceived the ton. And from what Clare described, I don't even know if 'deceived' is the right word. At the beginning, at least, it seems there were two Justins, both of them real and convincing. Clare loved and responded to the loving husband, who then turned on her. And then turned again."

Giles rubbed his hand over his eyes. "I don't know which is hardest for me to accept, Andrew. That Clare loved him and stayed with him. Or . . ."

"That she killed him."

"Yes."

"It sounds like you are angry that she didn't act for herself. And appalled that she finally did."

"She killed a man, Andrew. Not just any man. Her husband."

"In self-defense. And in your defense, I might add, Giles."

Giles got up and paced the floor in front of Andrew's desk.

"I thought that if I married Clare, I could make her forget all of it. Make her happy again."

"Whom did you marry, Giles? And whom do you love? Clare Whitton, or Clare Dysart whom you loved so many years ago.

Giles turned and looked at Andrew. "Clare asked me the same thing."

"Do you have an answer?"

"I don't know. I suppose *that* is my answer. I don't know. Giles paused, and then continued in a low voice. "We are no longer sharing a bed. Or much besides the externals of our life together. Perhaps there will never be passion between us, Andrew."

Andrew was surprised to find himself embarrassed by his friend's revelations. "I am no expert on married love, Giles. Perhaps you never will. But I am an optimist. I think that when you can really see Clare and love her for who she is . . ."

"Could you love someone who killed a man, Andrew?"

"Do you love your father, Giles?"

"Of course. What has that to do with anything?"

"Your father killed many times when he served in the army."

"That was in a war. If he had not killed, he would have been killed."

"Giles," said Andrew almost harshly, "Clare only did the same thing. You wanted her to save herself. How? Divorce? She would have been ruined. Resisting? That only made him worse. In the end she had no choice. The loving husband was gone forever, and in his place was a brutal murderer. The one with blood on his hands was Justin Rainsborough, Giles. He killed their child. He almost killed his wife. Your wife."

Giles sank back into this chair. "I think I am beginning to see that you and Clare are both right. Yet there is still something in me that does not want to accept it."

"I am sorry for being so hard on you, Giles. It is much easier for me to see Clare for who she is. I haven't loved her for years the way you have. Give yourself time."

"I appreciate your honesty, Andrew. It is what I have most admired about you." Giles hesitated. "It is part of what Sabrina loves in you, too," he added.

"Ouch. A hit, Giles."

"God knows what will happen between Clare and me, Andrew. But there is nothing but your own pride keeping you from Sabrina, from what I can see."

"Sabrina deserves more, Giles. You could not want your sister to marry a disreputable fellow like myself."

"I want my sister to be happy, Andrew. To marry where she loves. And she loves you."

Andrew opened his mouth and then closed it again.

"Oh, don't try to say anything. Just think about it." Giles pulled out his watch and glanced out the window. "It *has* turned into a downpour after all. I will be soaked by the time I find a cab."

"I have my greatcoat here, Giles. Please take it."

"No, I can't. That will leave you to get just as wet."

"But I am not going to Lady Carstair's!" Andrew pulled the coat down from its hook and held it out.

Giles looked down at his evening clothes and gave in. "All right. And thank you, Andrew. For everything."

Andrew helped him into the greatcoat, and Giles pulled the collar up around his ears.

"Good luck, Giles. I wish you and Clare the happiness you both deserve."

Giles smiled and waved his hand, sinking his head as far down into the collar as he could, so that he felt like a turtle; then he stepped out into the rain. His eyes were on the wet cobblestones as he walked along, trying to avoid the deepest puddles. His evening pumps would be like wet paper in a minute, he thought, completely unaware of the two men who had emerged from the alley next to Andrew's chambers. He looked up and saw what appeared to be a hansom cab only a block away. Odd, he thought, that is not a regular cabstand, and then, before he even knew what was happening, a chloroform-soaked rag was thrust into his face, and he was being grabbed from behind in what felt like a vise. He struggled with his assailants, managing to drive an elbow back into what felt like a slack belly. He was almost free when the drug overwhelmed him and he slumped in the arms of his captors.

After Giles left him, Andrew went back to the briefs his solicitor had prepared for him, but found himself unable to concentrate. His conversation with Giles kept intruding upon his consciousness, and from time to time he would sit back in his chair and find himself wondering if there was anything he could possibly do to help with the situation. It was also impossible to dismiss Giles's comments about Sabrina. *Was* he being foolishly honorable? Was he truly protecting Sabrina from marrying beneath her or was he afraid to take the risk of marrying above himself? Had he rejected her love because he did not want to be considered a kind of fortune hunter?

After an hour of accomplishing nothing, he slammed his leather portfolio closed and decided that he *would* go to the Carstairs. At the very least, he could lighten some of the tension between Clare and Giles. And secure a waltz with Sabrina. Perhaps holding her in his arms again would clarify things?

His rooms were not above his chambers, but on Half Moon Street, and it took him awhile to get a hansom in the rain. He was therefore one of the last to arrive, and in the crush, it took him awhile to find Clare.

She was standing in a small group that included Lucy

Kirkman and his own brother, and when he lightly touched her shoulder as he came up behind her, she turned quickly with an eager smile on her face. When she saw who it was, however, her smile faded.

"Surely my face is not that unwelcome, Clare," Andrew teased.

"Oh, Andrew, I am sorry. It is only that I thought you were Giles."

Andrew looked around. "What, is he lingering on the dance floor with some pretty young thing, Clare?"

"He has not arrived at all, and I am beginning to worry," Clare answered. "He is always prompt, you know that. Sabrina and I came directly from the musicale. He was to join us here, because he had some business to take care of."

Andrew frowned. "He was with me earlier in the evening. But that was almost two hours ago. I understood him to say he was coming directly here."

Clare's face became pale and worried.

"Now, now, I am sure there is nothing to worry about, Lady Whitton," said Andrew's brother. "I am sure there is a logical explanation, isn't there, Andrew."

"He left in the middle of the worst of the downpour. He would have had a bit of a walk to a cabstand. Perhaps he got too wet and went home to change, Clare. That would explain the delay."

Clare's face brightened.

"Although I loaned him my greatcoat," Andrew continued, his voice trailing off as a sudden, horrifying idea occurred to him.

"What is it, Andrew?" Clare asked.

"Oh, nothing, nothing. I am sure Giles will be here any minute, Clare. If he is not, I will go to Grosvenor Square and inquire after him. He could just have the headache after all."

But then he would have sent a message to us, Andrew," said Sabrina, who had just joined them in time to overhear the last exchange.

"I think you should wait another half hour at least before you concern yourselves," said Lucy. "Who knows, Giles might have stopped off at his club first." The musicians were striking up a waltz, and Lord Avery said: "I believe this is our dance, Miss Kirkman?"

Clare's partner also claimed her, and Andrew and Sabrina were left alone.

"I have a feeling that all is not well with Giles," said Sabrina in a worried voice.

"Is this the famous intuition of a twin?" said Andrew lightly.

"Do not try to tease me out of it, Andrew. You know we are always very much attuned to one another's emotions. Remember the summer Giles broke his arm when you were both out riding?"

Andrew remembered. They had returned home, Giles's arm in a makeshift sling, to find Sabrina pacing at the front door, with John Coachman ready to summon the doctor. Sabrina had been driven almost distracted by experiencing Giles's suffering and being helpless to do anything.

"To tell you the truth, Sabrina, I am a little worried myself." Andrew hesitated. "Do you have a partner for this dance?"

"Yes. No. I can't even remember," said Sabrina, distractedly searching her card.

"Let me partner you then, and I promise if Giles has not arrived by the time the music stops, we will go looking for him."

Sabrina allowed herself to be led out onto the floor. She was so concerned for her brother, however, that she couldn't relax until halfway through the dance, when she finally realized that she had said nothing to Andrew, who had laced his fingers through hers as though to comfort her with the extra closeness.

When she finally looked up into his face, she was touched by the warmth and concern she saw there.

"What did Giles come to see you about, Andrew?"

"He wanted my advice on a personal matter," responded Andrew.

"You mean he is finally waking up to the fact that he
must do something about his marriage?"

"I was trying to respect his privacy, Sabrina," said Andrew with a rueful smile. "But I might have known that
you would go right to the heart of it."

"I hope you gave him good advice."

"And what would that be, Sabrina?"

"That he love his wife for who she is and not what he
thought her to be."

"Then we are of one mind, my dear," said Andrew,
smiling down at her.

The waltz ended and as he led her off the floor, Andrew said meaningfully: "Giles gave me some advice,
too."

She looked up at him quickly, wondering just what
kind of advice Andrew would have sought from her
brother. She was about to ask, hoping against hope that
Andrew's tone and the expression on his face meant that
it was advice on a matter of the heart, when she saw
Clare standing alone at the edge of the dance floor.

"Where is your partner, Clare?"

"I sent him off to get me a glass of punch. Sabrina, it
has been over two hours now and Giles has not come. I
can't stand here worrying. I must go home and see if he
is there."

Sabrina took Clare's hands in hers and turned to Andrew. "Clare is right, Andrew. If Giles were sick or even
if he lingered at his club, he would have sent us a message. Will you escort us home?"

"Of course."

The two women were silent on the ride to Grosvenor
Square, and Andrew sat there, trying to convince himself
that they would find Giles in the library of his town house
or having retired with a headache. The other possibility
that had come to mind at the rout was far too disturbing

to think about. But when they reached Grosvenor Square and inquired of the butler and Giles's valet, they were told that Lord Whitton had not returned to the house that evening.

"He told me he was going directly to the rout, and he dressed accordingly," said the valet. "He would have had no reason to come back here."

"Henley, please get us a decanter of brandy and three glasses, and bring it to the drawing room," requested Andrew.

"The fire is banked there, sir. May I suggest the library?"

Andrew led Clare and Sabrina up the stairs and sat them down upon the sofa. Now that they knew Giles was not here, he was becoming convinced that his suspicions about his friend's disappearance were on the mark, but he didn't want to say anything until the brandy arrived.

When the butler knocked on the door, Andrew called him in and had him put the tray down on Giles's desk.

"Henley, will you send a footman to Lord Whitton's club? There is still a chance that his lordship stopped there and lost all sense of time."

"I don't drink brandy," said Clare when Andrew offered her a glass.

"You might need it, Clare," he said with a sympathetic smile.

Clare took a sip and almost choked as the liquor burned its way down her throat.

"One more swallow before we talk, Clare," encouraged Andrew.

Clare had to admit, as she took a second and then a third sip, that at least the brandy was warming her and that her stomach felt unclenched for the first time in hours.

Andrew tossed back his own brandy and pulled a chair up in front of the two women.

"I think you have an idea where Giles is, Andrew,"

said Sabrina, turning her glass around and around and watching the amber liquid swirl against the crystal.

Clare glanced at Sabrina in surprise. "Why, how would Andrew know?"

Andrew cleared his throat. "I have recently been brought on to a very interesting case, Clare. I am going to act the prosecutor for a young man who is taking several very powerful criminals to court."

Both women frowned. "Whatever has that got to do with Giles, Andrew?" demanded Sabrina.

"Nothing. In fact, I think Giles's disappearance has more to do with me than himself. If I win this case, four men who are the proprietors of a gaming hell could go to prison. They have already offered my young client a bribe three times the amount of his losses."

"This young man is suing over a gambling debt," asked Sabrina, unbelievingly.

"Yes. And let us save our discussion of what is done and not done for another time, shall we?"

Clare looked over at Andrew, understanding at last dawning. "You loaned Giles your greatcoat, Andrew. That is what you told us."

He nodded. "Giles left my office with the collar pulled up around his ears. If they did not see him go in, but only got there when my clerk left, well, they would naturally have no reason to think that anyone but Andrew More would be coming out."

"And so they, whoever they are, think they have kidnapped Andrew More," said Clare slowly. "But instead they have Lord Whitton."

"I *knew* he was in danger," whispered Sabrina, reaching out to clasp Clare's hand.

"But they will let him go as soon as they discover they have the wrong man," said Clare. "Won't they?"

"When is this trial, Andrew?" Sabrina asked.

"Not for four days."

"So they kidnapped you ... Giles, so that this young

man would have to bring the case forward himself. And most likely lose."

"He is a student at Inner Temple. But you are right, Sabrina, it is likely they didn't want an experienced barrister representing him."

Andrew was happy that both women were only talking of kidnapping. He hoped Messrs. Oldfield et al. were not foolish enough to attempt anything more serious. If they were desperate men, Giles could be lying dead in some alley, a possibility he certainly would not suggest to Giles's wife or sister.

Chapter Twenty-nine

If asked, Giles would have preferred the comfort and silence of death to the pounding headache he experienced upon awakening the next morning. He had opened his eyes once and then shut them immediately, for the light made his head even worse. At first he thought he was lying in his own bed, suffering the morning-after effects of too much drink, although he was usually very abstemious. Then he became conscious of the hardness of the mattress under him and the scratchiness of the rough wool blanket under his cheek. The sounds and smells from outside were foreign, too. Although, God knows, my breath is foul enough to have drunk myself into a stupor, he thought as he propped himself up on his elbow and opened his eyes again, determined to settle once and for all if he were in the middle of a nightmare.

The vertigo that assailed him was accompanied by an attack of nausea, and he hardly had time to get his head over the bed. After he retched up bile and what felt like all his internal organs as well, he fell back, exhausted. But a few minutes later he felt a little better, and pulling himself up into a sitting position, opened his eyes again.

He was on a straw-mattressed pallet in a small filthy, dirt-floored room. From the way the light poured down through the slatted window, he guessed he was in a cellar. But whose cellar and why? It only made the pounding worse when he tried to understand what had happened, so he sat there, breathing deeply to keep the nausea at bay and letting his senses take in all the information they could.

The noise of heavy footsteps above him seemed to indicate that he was right about being in a cellar. And his ears seemed to also be telling him that the cellar was in a very poor neighborhood from the absence of friendly and familiar street cries. Instead, there seemed to be some sort of brawling going on outside. If there had been anyone to wager with, he thought, after fifteen minutes of focusing on sounds and smells, *I would wager that I am in the cellar of some rookery in Seven Dials or St. Giles. Make it St. Giles,* he thought, with an appreciation of the irony. *My patron saint. Maybe I have died and gone to hell for my sins. Although, I never thought I was that much of a sinner.*

He heard someone, two someones, coming downstairs and was instantly alert. There was a sound of metal rasping metal, and then the door opened and two men entered the room.

These are no angels but Satan's minions, he thought with an objective humor that surprised him given their threatening appearance.

One was short, squat, barrel-chested, and bald as an egg. The other was tall, with the cauliflower ears of a pugilist. Both reeked of unwashed bodies and clothes. *Although, I am certainly adding to the aroma,* admitted Giles.

"Ye're awake I see, Mr. More," said the erstwhile pugilist.

At first Giles thought he was speaking to his companion. Then it dawned on him that it was he who was being addressed. *Mr. More? Surely his name was Whitton. God's recording angel made a mistake and sent him to hell and Andrew to heaven in his place?* Andrew's name brought him out of his whimsical fog. For some strange reason these two thugs thought he was Andrew More. He closed his eyes and leaned back, willing himself to remember. *Last night he had visited Andrew . . . it was raining . . . he* had pulled Andrew's coat around him ... the hansom cab ... that awful smell.

"Awake and cast up his accounts, hi see," said the short man.

"Not feeling the thing this morning, are ye, sir."

Giles groaned and shook his head. Acting helpless would give him some time to decide what course to take. Actually, considering how awful he felt, it was hardly acting.

"May I have some water," he croaked.

"'May I?' Coo, we are being perlite now, aren't we. Don't worry, ye'll be watered and fed, gov."

"And I need a chamber pot. Soon."

"George, will ye hinfrorm the butler that Andrew More, Esquire needs a pot to piss in."

George laughed and went upstairs for a pitcher of water and the aforesaid pot.

"Why am I here?" asked Giles in a quavering voice. "'I don't even know you. What possible quarrel could you have with me?"

"Don't take this personal, gov. Hit ain't. We are just to keep ye out of court for a while."

Giles swung his legs over the side of the cot, and immediately his captor stood over him threateningly.

"Of course, hif ye give us any trouble, we 'as permission to drop you."

"At the moment," whispered Giles, not acting at all, "I am in no condition to give trouble to anyone."

"Hi can see that, gov. But by this hafternooon, ye moight be. Hi'm just warning ye for yere own good."

The door scraped open, and short and squat entered with water in a dirty-looking pitcher and a chipped and uncovered receptacle.

"No food yet, gov. Ye're stomach won't take it, and hi don't want to ask George 'ere to clean up after ye again."

George had already wiped away most of the signs of Giles's sickness, and pushed the chamber pot under the pallet.

"Settle in and make yerself comfortable, gov," said the tall man who as yet had no name. "George 'll be back this evening."

After his captors left, Giles took a drink from the pitcher, sloshing the water around in his mouth and spitting it out onto the dirt floor. The next mouthful he swallowed. He was thirsty enough to finish off the pitcher but stopped himself, realizing George the Toad would not be back before evening.

Immediately after drinking he needed to relieve himself, and he gingerly pulled out the chamber pot, which was surprisingly clean. He pushed it into the corner with his foot, not wanting to have it under his bed.

His legs were still shaky, but he decided a little exercise would do him good. He paced out the size of the room: eleven by thirteen, and while he paced he tried to work out a strategy.

Andrew More had been kidnapped to keep him out of court. Andrew's case against the gambling hell owners was before the court later this week, so Giles was certain it was they who were behind this. They could make further attempts to bribe the young client, he supposed, but if that failed, they were hoping to insure that without expert counsel, the boy would lose.

What would happen if he told his captors they had got the wrong man: Lord Giles Whitton, not Andrew More, Esq. Would they let him go, just like that? Or would they kill him and drop him somewhere. If he told them who he really was, why should they believe him? Or release him, for that matter, so he could bring the law down upon them? They could kill him and leave his body in some alley where it might not be found for days. And when it was, all would suppose he had been a victim of footpads.

As long as they thought he was Andrew, Giles did not think he himself was in immediate danger. The proprietors would have known their mistake instantly, of course. But he doubted they would be stopping by for an official visit. They would have made sure that there were no obvious connections between them and their hirelings, so they could not be prosecuted for obstructing justice.

But surely Andrew would put two and two together and realize why his friend was missing. He'd have a Runner out looking for Giles, and there was every chance he'd be rescued in a day or two. If not, then he would fight his way out.

There was no real dilemma: if he sat tight for a few days, if he put up with some discomfort, Andrew would win his case and Giles would be free. It was the least he could do for a friend, he thought ironically.

Andrew had left Sabrina and Clare to get what sleep they could and promised to return the next morning.

When he was ushered into the breakfast room the next day where Sabrina was finishing a light breakfast and Clare was merely pushing eggs around on her plate, his heart sank, and he realized he had been hoping against hope to see Giles in his usual place at the head of the table, full of apologies for causing them such worry.

"Good morning, ladies," he said as cheerfully as he could.

Sabrina gave him a grateful smile. "Thank you for coming so early, Andrew."

Clare merely put her fork down, placed her hand on Andrew's and asked anxiously: "You haven't heard anything, have you, Andrew?"

"No. And since you obviously haven't, either, I think we may assume that Giles has either fallen victim to random foul play or was mistaken for me. Either way, we need to take some action."

"We obviously need the help of a constable," said Sabrina. "Giles must be reported missing this morning."

"I have thought of that, of course," Andrew replied slowly. "But I am not sure it is the best way to go."

"Why not, Andrew," Clare asked quietly.

"Suppose it is as I suspect. If the proprietors hear they

have the wrong man ... well, perhaps they might do him harm in order to silence him."

"But they must know already that Giles is not you," protested Sabrina.

"Not necessarily. I don't think they would have kidnapped Giles personally. They would have hired someone. Giles *could* have told them who he is, of course."

"Or he is lying unconscious or dead," whispered Clare.

"Truly, I do not think they would murder a peer of the realm," Andrew reassured her.

"But you have just argued that they think he is you, Andrew," Sabrina said tartly. "If Giles may be in danger, I say we need a constable. Unless you are more afraid for the outcome of your case? It will be quite a surprise for these men when you walk into the courtroom after all."

"Sabrina, you are being unfair," Clare exclaimed.

"Perhaps she is right," said Andrew, stung by the disdain in Sabrina's voice. "I confess, that were it not a good friend, I'd be happy to know they thought I was out of the way. But Giles is my oldest friend, Sabrina. And you of all people should know me better."

Sabrina sat very still and then in a tightly controlled voice apologized. "My only excuse, Andrew, is that I am frantic with worry. I am sure Giles is still alive. I would know if he were dead, for a part of me would have died. But I am very sure that he is in pain and in danger."

"I understand, Sabrina," said Andrew gently. "Actually, I think the best course to follow is to hire a Runner to do some quick investigation. Someone near my chambers may have seen something. And if it were a random act, well, the Runners would have word of a well-dressed victim, I am sure."

"Andrew is right," agreed Clare. "Let us get a Runner here right away. And have him work quietly. We don't want to alarm anyone after all."

"We are all expected at the Bellinghams' tonight," said Sabrina. "If Giles is absent again, it will be all over town by morning that something is wrong."

"We will say that he was called back to Whitton for an emergency," said Clare matter-of-factly. "Will you go to Bow Street, Andrew?"

"Immediately."

They were lucky, for there was a Runner available and Andrew outlined the situation for him. That first afternoon's investigation yielded nothing, but the next morning, the Runner appeared at Andrew's rooms, where he was, for the most part, keeping himself.

"Have you found anything at all, Ruthven?"

"Yes, sir. There was a young woman coming out of a house across the street. One of the maids. It was raining hard so she couldn't see their faces, but she saw two men bundling a third into a hansom cab right about the time Lord Whitton would have been leaving your chambers."

"Damn them to hell," said Andrew. "Was he alive?"

"The young woman couldn't tell."

"He must have been," said Andrew, trying to reassure himself. "Why else would they take the trouble to bundle him into a hansom?"

Neither man spoke the possible answer to that question: to drop the body elsewhere, like in the river.

"There isn't very much for me to go on, Mr. More. My guess is that if Lord Whitton is alive, which we certainly hope, he is being held somewhere in one of the rookeries."

"Well, you are the professional. What do we do now?"

"I could hang around 75 St. James Street and see if either or both of these villains shows up."

"But we don't even know what they look like."

"The maid did say, sir, as they looked a bit like Jack Sprat and his wife. One tall and thin, and the other short and broad." The Runner hesitated. "The problem is, sir, that these gaming hells, well, they have a nose for a constable or a Runner. I'll never get inside, Mr. More. It could be a waste of your money to have me hanging around."

"But if there is even the slightest chance they may contact Oldfield or one of the others, you must be there. Is there anything else we can do?"

"Short of getting someone into number 75 and choking the truth out of one of them, I can't say there is, sir."

"I'd be happy to do so, but I'd never make it past the first door, either! And I don't want them to know they have the wrong man."

The first day in the cellar was not so bad, for Giles slept most of it away due to the aftereffects of the chloroform. He was shaken awake for supper by Mr. Toad, as he had come to think of him. Supper was a bowl of clear broth with a few vegetables floating around in it and one grisly piece of lamb. By that time, Giles's stomach had settled, and he was hungry enough to find it edible. He was left with a small candle and a few matches, but shortly after supper he blew out the light and went to sleep.

The next morning all traces of his headache were gone, and he was beginning to feel restless. He was pacing the room when his breakfast arrived, this time delivered by his taller jailer.

"Ere ye go, gov. A bowl of porridge and a cup of coffee."

The porridge was a gelatinous mess, burned on the bottom and with no sweetening, and the coffee had so much sugar in it that a spoon could have been stuck up in it. Giles was almost tempted to pour one upon the other, but resisted.

"How long do you intend to keep me here," he demanded.

"Why, ye know the answer to that, Mr. More."

"I suppose I do," Giles admitted. He thought Andrew had said Oldfield was the name of one of the proprietors. He fervently hoped so. "Oldfield and the rest will never get away with this, you know. Nor will you."

"Oh, hi should think they will," the ex-pugilist said,

tacitly confirming Giles's suspicions. "And hif they don't, we will. There ain't nuffink to connect them to us."

Just as the man was about to leave, Giles said: "My chamber pot needs to be emptied."

"Why, as to that, gov, we ain't got no downstairs maid," replied the tall man with a wink and left.

Giles finished his breakfast and sat down on his cot. His captors did not seem to mean him harm, but this was obviously not going to be a pleasant few days.

By the beginning of their third day of waiting for news, Sabrina and Clare were exhausted. They had decided to follow their regular schedule in order to prevent any gossip, and the effort of maintaining appearances was wearing them out. They were convinced it was worth the effort, nevertheless, since no one seemed to doubt their story about Giles's emergency trip to Whitton.

At home, Sabrina was the one in the most obvious distress, and when Andrew visited that morning to keep them up on reports from the Runner, he was amazed at how calm Clare seemed and how distraught Sabrina was.

"Has Mr. Ruthven seen anyone 'round St. James Street yet," Clare asked calmly.

"No, but I think it important to keep him there."

"Can we not do anything else, Andrew," demanded Sabrina. "I feel so helpless, sitting here in touch with Giles's distress and unable to take action."

"If you wish, I will go to St. James Street myself, Sabrina, and tell them they have got the wrong man. Maybe I should have done that immediately." He hated watching Sabrina in this state.

"No, Andrew. We still have no evidence they are behind this," said Clare.

"Oh, Clare," Sabrina exclaimed, "Of course we know they are."

"And if they are, what might they do to you and Giles if you confront them? We can't risk it, at least not yet." Clare put her arms around Sabrina. "We know through

you that Giles is still alive, Brina. We will just have to assume that they will release him as soon as they realize
their mistake." Clare turned to Andrew. "Sabrina has
been pacing the drawing room for an hour. A walk in the
park is just what she needs, and I do not have the energy.
Would you take her, Andrew?"

"Of course. Clare is right, Sabrina. You need to get
out."

Sabrina offered a token protest, and then allowed herself to be convinced.

After they had gone, Clare went up to her bedchamber
and stood by the window. The small garden below was
gray-green and brown. The crab apple tree in the corner
had dropped all its leaves but not its fruit, and was heavy
with small golden crabs. On another day, Clare might
have appreciated the picture, but despite her calm appearance, she, too, was fearful for Giles's safety.

She had spoken the truth to her sister-in-law: she did
trust Sabrina's feeling that Giles was not dead. But what
did they know of these men after all? Did they really plan
to release "Andrew More" after the trial? It would be
dangerous for them not to, it was true. Yet they seemed
to have covered themselves well. They seemed to have
hired two ruffians with no direct connection to the gaming hell or themselves. What might these ruffians do to
Giles?

Of course, if they knew they had Lord Whitton, the
kidnappers at least might be more interested in collecting
a ransom. But Clare knew Giles very well: he would
surely have guessed why he had been taken, and would
never dream of spoiling Andrew's case by identifying
himself. He was a dear, chivalrous idiot, thought Clare,
her eyes filling up with tears.

She would *not* cry. She had not cried yet, although
Sabrina had. But if any harm came to Giles, she did not
know how she would survive.

She stood there for a while, lost in thought, and then
rang for Martha. When her abigail arrived, Clare gave her

a wintry smile. "I need you to accompany me to Bruton Street, Martha."

"Bruton Street?"

"Yes. We are going to purchase a pistol."

The shop attendant was surprised to see a lady of quality at his counter. It was not the fact that she wanted to purchase a pistol; their gunsmiths had designed several lovely little guns that fit right in a lady's reticule. But ladies of the ton usually sent their husbands or brothers. It was rarely that one actually stepped into the shop.

"I have a beautiful mother-of-pearl–handled pistol that would fit comfortable in your hand, my lady."

Clare let him drop it in her palm and closed her hand around it. She shuddered as the movement brought back the evening of Justin's death.

"It is very small," she managed to whisper.

"Why, yes, just the right size for a lady's reticule."

"How effective is it?"

The clerk looked puzzled. "It will afford you protection, my lady, should anyone try to become too bold, shall we say."

"Yes, I can see that it might discourage unwanted suitors. But I am looking for something a bit more substantial. Something that would be frightening to a criminal type."

Martha and the clerk exchanged surprised glances.

"Hmmm."

"You see, I am going on a journey alone to join my husband, and although I will have outriders, I would be grateful for a pistol I can keep with me in the coach. Against highwaymen, you understand."

"Of course, of course. Well, in that case, here is something that may fit your needs. It will fit into a muff or a small basket next to you."

Clare balanced the pistol in her hand. It was smaller than Justin's pair, but looked lethal enough.

"And bullets?"

"Of course. I can show you how to load it."

"There is no need for that," Clare announced. "My ... uh ... brother can give me lessons before I leave. If you could just load it for me now, please."

"Oh, I do not recommend that you walk around with a loaded gun, my lady," the clerk said rather horrified.

"Nevertheless, I wish to purchase it loaded," Clare said insistently.

"Yes, my lady."

When they were out on the street again, Martha stepped in front of her mistress.

"Now just what is this all about, my lady. Whatever do you need a pistol for? And don't try to give me that cock-and-bull story of a long journey to meet your husband. We all in the servants' hall know that something has happened to Lord Whitton." Martha had both hands on her hips, and Clare laughed naturally for the first time since Giles had disappeared.

"Oh, thank God for you, Martha," she said.

Martha belatedly became conscious of how she sounded and how she was standing.

"I beg your pardon, my lady. But I am right, nevertheless."

"I know you only want to protect me, Martha. But I cannot think of another way to do this, truly I cannot. Believe me, I had thought never to even look at a pistol again. I cannot tell you what I am planning to do, but you must trust that I can take care of myself. And, I hope, my husband."

Chapter Thirty

By the third day of captivity, Giles would have welcomed any rescuer. The cellar room was fetid with its own ancient odors as well as the unemptied chamber pot.

His captors had not seemed personally hostile at first. Indeed, he told himself daily, they were not personally hostile now: just hostile. When he had asked to have the chamber pot removed, Mr. Toad just laughed in a particularly nasty way and said: "Do hi look loike a chambermaid? This ain't Fenton's, gov. Hif you are filling that up, we will 'ave to stop filling you up. Hit'll cost us less in the keeping of you."

And so they had, on the second day, cut him back to two meals and only one pitcher of water.

When he asked for a book, or at least a piece of paper and a pen, they laughed in his face.

This was *not*, he realized, only going to be a matter of sitting tight for a few days.

He had never been so powerless before, so at the mercy of another's whims. He spent the days trying to remember and recite every bit of poetry he had been made to learn. He paced the floor and declared Aristophanes *The Frogs* in Greek, which seemed singularly appropriate, given the physiognomy of George.

At night he tried to sleep. But he was becoming increasingly anxious about his safety. His deception had seemed so obvious and simple at first, but now he wondered why he had ever done it. Yet if he claimed his own identity now, they would likely not believe him.

Obviously he was missed. Obviously Sabrina and Clare and Andrew would have instigated a search. And what good would that do, he would think desperately, lying awake in the dark, trying to breathe through his mouth, but unable to for very long, for it dried his throat out so and they didn't give him enough water, damn their eyes.

Every night, his thoughts eventually turned to Clare. Just as he had recalled all the poetry he knew, he would lie there sleepless and go over every memory he had of his wife, from the first time he had met her. He could see her shy face as she got down from the carriage that first brought her to Whitton. The hero-worship in her eyes when he rescued her from Lucy Kirkman. The warmth and affection she had always shown him. He even remembered, though he did not want to, the way her face had lit up with love and happiness when she looked up at Justin Rainsborough after taking her vows.

And then there was the Clare who returned to London looking like a wraith. Why had he not seen the truth then? Why had he assumed, like everyone else, that she was just a long time recovering from her miscarriage? He claimed to love her, yet he had never once guessed the truth of her marriage. Then Clare at the inquest, when she told the truth and described the beating and the kicking and the choking. He had felt such a surge of protective love for her. But even then, he had not understood her. And, God forgive him, there was a small piece of him that *was* angry at her, that did think, "If she had married *me,* had ever looked at me like that, none of it would have happened."

Clare was right. He had never faced his deepest feelings about her marriage. He had held onto his image of himself as her protector, as her dear friend. A dear friend would surely want the woman he loved to be happy, even if with someone else. And he had, that was true enough. But he had also been furious with her for rejecting him, and had never been willing to admit it until now.

He would push himself further to imagine the scene in

the Rainsborough library. He would let Clare be there, let her be standing there, poker in hand, dress blood-soaked, terrified her husband was not really dead.

He had to let himself see and love that Clare: he knew that now. He just wasn't sure he could do it. And so when he couldn't be there in that library any longer, he would go back to that first summer and start all over again. Somehow he had to love her, whole and entire. If—no—when he got out of this hellhole he wanted to be able to take her face gently between his hands and look deep into her eyes, seeing everything and loving everything she was.

Clare had given up on the Bow Street Runner early in the game. It was clear that the proprietors of St. James Street would have wanted no connection made between them and the kidnappers, and therefore it was highly unlikely that they would be contacted at the gaming hell.

She would never get into St. James Street herself, of course, or else she would have been there by the second day. No, she would have to get one of them to come to her. If they were all correct, Giles would not have given them his name, and Whitton would mean nothing to them.

Accordingly, the day after she had purchased the pistol, the day before the trial, she sat down and carefully penned a note, which she handed to James Footman.

"I want you to take this to Mr. Oldfield at 75 St. James Street. I have asked him to wait on me this afternoon, so wait for a reply."

James bowed and left. All the servants were of course aware of what had happened, what with Lord Whitton gone, Andrew More around all the time, and that trial to start on the morrow. He probably should not be letting his mistress do this, he thought, as he lingered on the steps and watched Andrew More coming up the street. He should give this note to Mr. More and let him deal with it. But his first loyalty was to Lady Whitton. Hiring a

Runner had seemingly done no good. Maybe a lady's tears would do more. And no harm could come to her in the house, after all. And so he merely bowed to Andrew as he passed him and hurried down the street.

"Do you have any news, Andrew?" Clare asked when he was shown into the drawing room. She and Sabrina asked the same questions every day and received the same answer: "No, not yet."

"Is Sabrina in, Clare?"

"She is, and I am worried about her."

Andrew looked immediately concerned as she had known he would.

"I think she needs an outing this afternoon, but I could not persuade her to accompany me to the park. Perhaps you could, Andrew."

"I can try."

Clare rang for Henley. "Henley, can you send upstairs to Lady Sabrina and tell her Mr. More is here."

"Yes, my lady."

"Tomorrow is the trial, Andrew. Do you really think they will release Giles?"

"As soon as he tells them who he is. Which he will do tomorrow, I am sure."

Are you really, Andrew? wondered Clare. Why would the kidnappers want to place themselves in any danger? Once they found out they had seized a peer of the realm, wouldn't they want to silence him, rather than have him go to the authorities?

Andrew's eyes went to the door when Sabrina entered. She *did* look wretched, thought Clare, as of course, they all were.

"Sabrina, Andrew was just asking if we would like to go for a stroll in the park. I have some correspondence to catch up on, but perhaps you could keep him company?"

"It is a lovely day, Sabrina. We would both be the better for a little exercise," Andrew said encouragingly.

"Oh, I am sure you have cooked up something between

you, but yes, all right. I will go. Just let me get my pe-lisse."

"Thank you, Andrew," said Clare.

"No need, my dear. You know that it is my pleasure."

"And a bit painful, too, I think, my friend."

"A bit painful, yes," he admitted.

"Yet only because of your own stubborn sense of honor, I think?"

"So she has told you?"

"Not until I had guessed already."

"You must understand my reasons, Clare."

Clare smiled. "Oh, I do, Andrew. But honor has so little to do with love."

They heard Sabrina's step in the hall, and Andrew bowed his good-bye.

As they walked toward the park, Andrew stole a glance at his companion's face. Sabrina, who had never in his memory looked anything but vibrant and alive was like a washed-out watercolor. Even Clare had more life in her face. "Have you been eating and sleeping, Brina?" he asked her gently.

"Do I look that hagged, then, Andrew," she answered attempting a light, teasing tone.

"Don't try to evade me, my dear. I think this ordeal has been as hard on you as on Clare. Perhaps harder, because of your special bond with Giles."

"Please don't be too kind, Andrew," Sabrina responded in a voice choked with tears, "or I will be completely undone. And I must hold myself together for Clare's sake."

"I think Clare is holding up very well, considering. In fact, this morning, she looked more energetic than she has in days. Almost as though she had something to accomplish."

"Perhaps it was only getting us out of the house together," said Sabrina with a smile.

They were crossing the thoroughfare at the entrance to the park, and Andrew had to concentrate on getting

Sabrina safely through the traffic. It wasn't until they were in the park and down one of the side paths that he responded to her.

"This is the first time we have been alone since this summer," he admitted.

"Yes, you have kept yourself quite scarce," she said with a tinge of bitterness in her voice. "Please don't remind me of my foolishness."

"Do you know what Giles came to see me about that evening? He came to talk about Clare. It seems they have been having their problems."

"I know. It all seemed to start out very well, but something happened, and they are no longer . . . there has been some sort of estrangement."

"Giles told me that Clare accused him of not being able to love the woman she has become. That he can't let himself admit to the reality of the past two years. What do you think of that, Sabrina?"

"I believe she may be right," Sabrina answered thoughtfully. "We all had a certain picture of Clare in our minds, didn't we? But you and I seem to have been able to adjust to the changes. You would think it would not be so. That Giles, who has loved her for years, would find it easier to appreciate the way she has changed," Sabrina added wonderingly.

"I think love blinds people in different ways," said Andrew quietly.

Sabrina hesitated. "Yes, it does," she answered, wondering where their conversation was going.

"For instance," Andrew continued matter-of-factly, "I have always seen you as impetuous and headstrong."

"A madcap, hoydenish girl? Is that all you saw, Andrew?"

"I think it was all I wanted to see. I loved you for it, of course."

Sabrina's breath caught in her throat.

"You were such a lovely counterpoint to Giles's quiet kindness. But my love for that lively mischievous girl blinded me to the vulnerability of the woman you grew into."

They had come to a side path, and Andrew, linking his arm through Sabrina's, led her down a few hundred yards.

"Ah, yes, here it is," he said as they came upon a small wrought-iron bench, and sat them down on it.

He turned to Sabrina and continued: "Even when you asked me to marry you . . ."

"I *never* asked you to marry me, Andrew."

"Everything but, my dear," he said, his eyes crinkling up as he gave her one of his most charming smiles. "I still saw myself as the only one in a vulnerable position. After all, I am a . . ."

"Younger son. I know," she answered with mock exasperation.

"Youngest. I'd loved you for years, you know, but had schooled myself very well to see the situation from one side only."

"I see." Sabrina sat very still. "And have things changed, Andrew?" she asked, clasping her hands together to keep them from trembling.

"I am not sure that anything has changed, Sabrina."

She thought she had never felt so empty.

"But I see what there is very differently now. For instance, now I can see that you need me. I never saw that before."

Sabrina felt that she had been to hell and come back in one instant.

"Perhaps I was never very good at showing you, Andrew." Her whole frame was trembling now, a reaction to the strain of the past week and her sense that her whole life was about to change.

"Giles and I talked about more than his marriage, Sabrina. He said he would welcome me as a brother-in-law. He said I was as stupid and proud as you had accused me of being." As he was speaking, Andrew felt her shivering and without thinking, put his arm around her and drew her under his cloak.

It took a few minutes, but slowly the warmth of his body penetrated to hers, and she relaxed against him.

"I am hoping that your proposal is still open, Sabrina," said Andrew softly, lifting her chin with his finger.

"I did *not* propose to you, Andrew."

"Then I suppose I will have to propose to you," he said with a grin. "Sabrina, will you be my wife?"

"Do you love me, Andrew?"

"Haven't I been telling you that?"

"Not in the last few minutes, Andrew."

"I love you, Sabrina Whitton."

"And I love you, Andrew More," she whispered, lifting her face up to his and closing her eyes.

He leaned down and kissed her gently. "I like the way you fit right into my body, my love. And it is good to know that I can offer you comfort."

"And I need your comfort so, Andrew." Tears started to stream down her cheeks, and she brushed them away quickly, but not before he realized she was crying.

"I am sure Giles is all right, Brina. He will be released as soon as the trial begins and they see they have the wrong man."

"Oh, Andrew, I am sorry to spoil this moment. It isn't that I don't want you to continue kissing me."

"There will be plenty of time for kisses and more, I promise you that, my dear. Now isn't the time to celebrate anyway. But we could go back and tell Clare the news? If you are sure you can be satisfied with a disreputable barrister. You could have had anyone, even the viscount himself!"

"I have always only wanted you, Andrew." They started slowly back down the path, this time with Andrew's arm around her waist. "And I suspect Miss Lucy Kirkman has her claws in your brother, whether he knows it or not."

Chapter Thirty-one

Clare's note had invited Mr. Oldfield to call upon Lady Whitton immediately to discuss a way of settling her brother's gambling debts. The name Whitton could mean nothing to him, and she hoped that Lady Whitton's forgetfulness about mentioning her "brother's" name would be overlooked in the interest of obtaining money.

She was lucky. Mr. Oldfield had been in. Mr. Oldfield was available to Lady Whitton. Mr. Oldfield showed up on the doorstep twenty minutes after she had sent her note, eager to discover just who Lady Whitton's brother was: young Payne, who owed three hundred pounds, or Lieutenant Britton, who had dropped even more two nights ago.

Mr. Oldfield's appearance surprised Clare. She had expected the proprietor of a gaming hell to be vulgar and common. But Mr. Oldfield was a well-built, quietly dressed man of medium height who bowed politely to her and waited for her to speak.

"Thank you so much for responding so quickly to my note, Mr. Oldfield."

"It is my pleasure, Lady Whitton."

Clare had her embroidery basket next to her on the sofa, and she ran her fingers over the silks as she spoke. "You see, I only found out about my brother's troubles last night," she added. "I have asked my husband to help my brother in the past, but a few weeks ago he declared it was the last time. My brother is young and foolish, though, and told me he went back one last time to the tables so he could repay my lord. Of course, he lost everything."

Mr. Oldfield looked appropriately sympathetic and clucked his tongue. "Young men are often like that, my lady. It is sad, but we can do little about it when they insist upon playing until they bleed themselves dry."

"Yet gaming is illegal, is it not?" Clare asked with assumed innocence.

Oldfield cleared his throat. "There are laws on the books, yes. But the habit of play is too ingrained in so many, my lady." He paused, and then said tactfully: "Now about the small matter of your brother's debts. Just what is the young man's name, and I can tell you exactly what he owes."

"My husband must never hear about this, Mr. Oldfield." Clare pulled the basket on her lap and gripped it tightly in both hands. "That is why I asked you to come immediately, for he is away this afternoon."

"There would be no reason for me to tell Lord Whitton, my lady," Oldfield reassured her. "Indeed, I do not believe I have ever even met Lord Whitton. I would guess, if he disapproves of your brother, he is not a gaming man himself."

"Yet I think some acquaintances of yours *have* met him." Clare got up and carried her basket over to the small table directly behind him. "I do not think so, my lady," said Oldfield, turning to address her and finding himself staring into the barrel of a cocked pistol.

"Lady Whitton, I am sure I don't know why you wish to threaten me?" he said after a moment of shocked silence.

"Threaten you, Mr. Oldfield?"

"Uh, yes, threaten me into releasing your brother from his debts. As a gentleman, your brother himself would not approve. Here. Let me take that," he said, starting to reach out slowly, "before you harm yourself. An inexperienced hand should never be holding a cocked firearm, my lady."

Clare took a step back. "Oh, but my hands are quite experienced." Her hands were also shaking, and she drew them into her body to steady them. It was very hard to have them curled around a pistol again. In front of her was Mr. Oldfield, but he also seemed to be Justin. She took a deep breath and shook her head a little. "Do you know what my name was before I married Lord Whitton?"

"No, my lady. But if you told me, I would know who your brother is and could arrange to settle his debts very easily. Or even cancel them altogether."

The man was very cool, thought Clare, and everything depended upon him believing her capable of killing him. Please God, she had been notorious enough.

"I was married to Lord Justin Rainsborough. Until I killed him."

Oldfield's eyes widened, and his face paled very satisfactorily.

"You have heard of me, I see."

"Yes, my lady. Everyone in London heard of that, uh, incident, I believe."

"Then you know that I am not fond of bullies, Mr. Oldfield. And that having killed once, I am quite capable of doing so again."

Oldfield put his hands out, palms up, and said plaintively: "But how am I bullying you, Lady Rainsborough, I mean, Lady Whitton. You asked me here. I came. I have offered to release your brother from his debts. What more can I do for you?"

Clare moved in quickly and had the pistol against his temple before he knew it.

"You can take me to where you are holding Mr. Andrew More, Esquire."

Oldfield stared, and then became very still as he felt the pistol barrel brush his temple.

"You are confusing me, my lady. I do not know a Mr. More."

"Oh, I think you do. Mr. More is to meet you in court

tomorrow, and if he wins his case, you and your partners may very well spend some time in prison. And so you had him kidnapped."

"Even if that were true, my lady, which of course, it is not, what has this Andrew More to do with you? Unless *he* is your brother?"

"I have no younger brother, Mr. Oldfield. And you have no Andrew More. Mr. More is in the park right now with my sister-in-law. Your knaves grabbed the wrong man. They took my husband, Lord Giles Whitton, and you are going to lead me to him."

Oldfield seemed to realize that further denial was foolish, for he only said quietly: "And what if I refuse, Lady Whitton?"

"I will shoot you through the temple."

"But then you will not see your husband again."

"Oh, I believe I will. You see, then I will summon Mr. Carolus or Mr. Phillips or Mr. Bennett. I am sure one of you will be willing to take me there, especially if he sees what happened to his partners." Clare could feel hysterical laughter rising at the thought of the bodies piling up in her drawing room, but willed it down. He *must* believe she was capable of this for her plan to work.

Apparently, he did. "All right, Lady Whitton. I have no idea how this mistake happened, but I can take you to your husband. He is being held in a rookery in St. Giles, however, not a pleasant place for a lady."

"Don't worry about my sensibilities, Mr. Oldfield. I assure you, I have become rather hardened over the past two years, due to my experiences." Clare took a deep breath. "You are going to stand up, and I am going to hold my pistol close by your side. We will walk down to the street, where my butler will have summoned my chaise."

"Yes, my lady."

They proceeded down the stairs just as she had said. "Is the chaise outside, Henley," Clare asked when they reached the door.

"Yes, my lady. Let me get your pelisse."

"No, thank you, Henley. I am in rather a hurry."

The butler wanted to protest, but it was hardly his place. The sun had disappeared behind clouds, and it had become a chilly afternoon. But he could not insist. He opened the door and watched his mistress and her visitor down the steps, and frowned as he saw the man climb into the chaise ahead of her and not even reach back to help her in. He would have to find out just where Lady Whitton summoned this Mr. Oldfield from.

Clare sat facing Oldfield, the pistol pointing straight at his stomach. "I do not claim to be anything of a marksman, so I will not threaten to shoot you straight through the heart should you move," she said with an ironic smile. "But I do not believe being gut shot is a pleasant fate."

"No, my lady, I would agree," Oldfield responded dryly.

They were silent for a while, and then he spoke again.

"If I may ask, Lady Whitton, how did you figure out why your husband had disappeared?"

"There was no other reason for him to have disappeared. When Andrew More remembered he had loaned Giles his greatcoat to keep off the rain and when a Runner found witnesses who had seen Giles bundled into a cab, we decided it had been you and your partners trying to insure the success of their case."

"But your husband could have just identified himself, and he would have been released."

"No doubt Giles realized whom you thought you had. He is very chivalrous, my husband, and a good friend of Andrew More's."

"I see." Oldfield was sitting there silently cursing his hired thugs. It was one thing to hold Andrew More, Esquire for a few days, quite another to hold the Viscount Whitton. He hoped they had treated their prisoner decently.

The chaise was going slowly now as the coachman

picked his way through the narrow streets of St. Giles. Oldfield had given him the address, but several times the driver had to stop and ask directions from some street urchin or beggar.

"I haven't been here in years myself," said Oldfield, holding his handkerchief to his nose distastefully.

"So these men do not know you?"

"Oh, we didn't hire them sight unseen, Lady Whitton. One of our blacklegs, Boniface, knows them and brought them to 75 St. James Street for instructions."

"And what *were* their instructions?" asked Clare, dreading the answer.

"Only to hold Mr. More until the trial had begun and then release him that evening."

"So my husband would have been released by tomorrow night, then?"

"Yes, you see all this effort is for no good reason, Lady Whitton."

"I don't think so, Mr. Oldfield," Clare answered thoughtfully. "Once you and your partners saw Andrew More in court, you may well have decided to dispose of your mysterious prisoner. You were very good at hiding your associations with these men. We have had a Runner watching you for these last few days, and he could pick up nothing out of the ordinary."

"Of course not. We were very careful. Only two of us have even met these men, Lady Whitton. You are very lucky that I happen to be one of them." Oldfield paused. "As for your husband, I will not lie to you: we may well have ordered him disposed of, especially since we didn't know who he was. And it might have happened even without our orders, once the men found out they had the wrong man."

Clare shuddered.

"So perhaps, Lord Whitton should be grateful after all that he wed a murderess."

"Indeed, Mr. Oldfield, I think he should!" Clare replied boldly, hoping that her brave words would convince herself as well as him that she was able to go through with this.

The chaise finally stopped at the corner of what looked like an alley but was actually a narrow street. The coachman came to the door and announced that he could not get the chaise any farther if this was indeed the place.

"You said number three?" Clare asked.

"Yes, Lady Whitton."

"Robert, I am going to remain in the chaise with Mr. Oldfield. You will go to the door of number three and inform—?" she glanced over to Oldfield.

"George and Henry."

". . . That Mr. Oldfield is here to see them regarding their prisoner. Bring them here to us."

"Yes, my lady." Robert knew that his mistress had embarked on something dangerous but important to Lord Whitton's release, and so he overcame his own fear and distaste, and stepped down the street.

Chapter Thirty-two

Giles had stopped eating after his second day in the cellar. He had tried, but the smells from the building, the street, and his own waste had made it impossible for him to keep food down. He had developed a great thirst, however, and asked for more water, but Toad only laughed and said, "We don't want yer chamber pot overflowing, do we, gov," and so he still received only a pitcher a day. He arranged his days around what he thought were mealtimes, and made drinking his cup of water as much of a ritual as eating a full meal, forcing himself to sit and sip slowly rather than gulp it down as he had the first day.

He kept to his regimen of exercise also, pacing to the rhythm of Greek and Urdu poetry. Occasionally, to keep up his spirits, he declaimed the verses loudly and dramatically, trying to imagine himself in an amphitheater.

The evenings were the worst of all, and after his "supper" it had been dark already for hours. He would fall asleep and then awaken in what he imagined was the middle of the night. He would lie there for hours, or so it seemed, unable to summon poetry or anything else to comfort him. He would reassure himself that this ordeal was almost over. He wasn't a prisoner of war, after all, condemned to years of this, nor was he a criminal condemned to a lifetime of more subtle torture. Andrew will be made to pay for this, he would say to himself, trying for humor.

They were not very pleasant, his midnight thoughts, and by the fourth day, he was not able to confine them to the dead of night. By the fourth day, he was nearly out of his mind with hunger, thirst, and the stench. He walked a little in the morning, but was too weak to get off his pallet in the afternoon. He was lying there, drifting in and out of consciousness when he felt someone shake his shoulder.

" 'E's not dead, is 'e?"

"Don't be a fool, George. Of course not. Get up, Mr. More."

Giles sat up slowly. Sitting up made him dizzy and nauseous, and he sank his head into his hands to keep the room from spinning around him.

" 'E don't look well, 'Enry."

" 'E don't 'ave to. 'E ain't going to see the queen, just Oldfield."

Giles felt himself being dragged to his feet, and the sudden vertigo made him uncontrollably nauseous. There was nothing in his stomach, so all his retching brought up was bile. His captor let go, and Giles fell to his knees on the dirt floor.

"Get 'im up," grumbled Tall Man.

Toad yanked Giles to his feet again, and this time his head was clearer.

He stumbled up the stairs, and when the door to the street was opened, he was blinded by the light and groaned as he covered his eyes with his hands. He didn't see the chaise or recognize his own coachman. He was only conscious that Toad was handing him over to someone else, and a shiver of fear went through him. Did they know who he was? No, they had called him Mr. More. Were they letting him go or was this new captor going to dump him in the river? After they had walked a few steps, he pretended to stumble again and pulled away in the half second that the grip on his arm relaxed. He couldn't see well enough to do more than a stumbling run, and in a minute someone was next to him. "It is all right, my lord," the someone said as he tried to get away. "The chaise is only a few yards now."

"My lord?" Then they did know who he was. Giles felt himself being pushed into the chaise, and the last thing he thought before losing consciousness was: "She is going to kill me, too," as he saw Clare, or a phantom that looked like Clare, pointing a pistol in his direction.

"You may get out, Mr. Oldfield," said Clare, gesturing with the pistol. "I am sure you will be able to find your way home somehow?" she added sarcastically.

"Indeed, my lady." Oldfield climbed down and let his breath out in a sigh of relief. Clare may have tried hard to keep her hands steady, but he had seen the trembling, which had scared him even more, for he knew how easy it was for a cocked pistol to go off.

"Ye're a day early, ain't ye, gov?"

"And you're five days with the wrong man, you fools," Oldfield replied. "That wasn't Andrew More. That was Viscount Whitton. Andrew More will be in court bright and early tomorrow, and will no doubt win his client's case."

Clare had kept the pistol pointed at Oldfield as he stepped out and even as they drove off, just in case he and his henchmen tried to rush her. When they finally were out of sight, she lowered her arms and dropped the pistol on the floor. Except, when she looked down, the pistol was still in her hands, which just wouldn't, couldn't open, they had been clenched so tight so long. And so she sat there with the pistol on her lap, gazing over at Giles, who was slumped on the seat opposite her.

He smelled so awful that Clare had to breathe out of her mouth. He had no obvious bruises on him, although she knew better than anyone that didn't mean there weren't any. But she hoped his fainting spell was from shock and lack of food or water, not from injury.

When they pulled up in front of the house, she had to wait for Henley to open the door, for her hands were still wrapped around the pistol. She climbed down awkwardly.

"Get the coachman to help you," she said. "Lord Whitton is still unconscious."

The door opened before she was even up the steps, and Andrew was by her side in a second.

"My God, Clare, where have you been? We have been out of our minds with worry since Martha told us of your visitor. And your 'shopping trip,' " he added, glancing down at the pistol.

"I can't seem to let it go, Andrew," she said, giving him an ironic smile as he reached down and gently released the hammer. "But otherwise, I am fine. Help Henley with Giles."

Sabrina, who had been right behind Andrew, put her arms around Clare and led her into the hall, where Clare's hands finally relaxed and the pistol dropped to the floor with a clatter. Clare looked down at it and then her hands, and finally giving in to the pent-up emotions of the day, shook uncontrollably from head to foot. Her teeth were chattering so, she could hardly give coherent directions as Giles was carried in.

"Take him upstairs, Henley, and strip those clothes off before you put him to bed. Sabrina, we will need the doctor."

"Yes, I will send for him immediately."

Andrew watched as they carried Giles upstairs and then led Clare up to the library where a fire was roaring. He sat her down in the wing chair next to the fireplace, and poured a glass of brandy.

"Drink this, my dear."

Her teeth where chattering so hard that he thought she would bite through the glass, but he managed to get some down her throat. As the warmth of the liquor hit her stomach, her shivering slowly subsided and some color returned to her face.

"Here, have a little more, Clare, and then we will find out what you have been up to."

"Don't push her, Andrew," said Sabrina, who had come in after them.

"No, I am all right now," said Clare, starting to get up. "It is Giles I am worried about."

"Sit down, my dear. There is nothing you can do right this minute."

Clare sank back down. "I couldn't wait any longer, Andrew. I was afraid once they found out they had the wrong man, they might harm Giles."

"I have been afraid of that, too, I must confess, but couldn't think of anything to do."

"There wasn't much you could do, Andrew. To show yourself would have endangered Giles. But I realized that none of them would recognize my name immediately, so I sent for Oldfield, telling him I wanted to settle my younger brother's debts."

"But you don't have a younger brother, Clare," said Sabrina.

"You and I know that, Sabrina, but he didn't. And it got him here where I wanted him. Then, when he found out I was the notorious Lady Rainsborough, I had no trouble convincing him I was willing to kill again."

"My God, Clare, were you mad?" Andrew exclaimed.

"A little, I think, Andrew," she admitted, looking down at her lap. She still could not open her hands completely. "I kept seeing Justin's face flashing before me, threatening Giles . . ." They were all still a moment. "I think that helped me convince Mr. Oldfield, however," she said with a shaky laugh.

"Could you have killed him, Clare?" Sabrina asked in a low voice.

"I don't know," Clare admitted. "But I told him I would summon one after another of them until one took me to my husband."

"Where is Oldfield now, Clare?"

"Back in some filthy alley of St. Giles," she said. "And I hope he has to walk all the way back to St. James Street."

* * *

When the doctor arrived, Clare insisted on being present when he examined Giles, who was still unconscious.

"Aside from being dehydrated and exhausted, I believe Lord Whitton is all right, my lady." He gave Clare an inquiring look. "I don't suppose you can tell me just how a peer of the realm came to be in this condition, Lady Whitton?"

"He was in the hands of two ruffians for a few days, Doctor. But I would rather not say why."

"He has no bruises or injuries, so I believe he will be conscious by morning."

"Then I will sit with him," said Clare.

"You are looking very worn yourself, Lady Whitton, if I may say so."

"One more night with little sleep won't make any difference, now that Giles is safe," said Clare with a grateful smile as she showed the doctor out, and then pulled a chair close to her husband's bed.

Giles's hair was lank and greasy, and there was a faint trace of the smells of the cellar hanging about him, for his valet had only stripped off his clothes and put him in a clean nightshirt. There were dark circles under his eyes, and Clare guessed that he had lost half a stone as she had watched the doctor examine him. But he was safe at home, thank God. She looked down at her hands and made herself open and close them repeatedly, until she was able to straighten out her fingers. She glanced at Giles and then back down at her hands. Whatever would Giles think of her now? If he could not allow himself to see the Clare who had killed her husband, how on earth would he be able to tolerate a Clare who had been willing to kill again, even if it had been for his sake? *Especially* since it had been for his sake.

Clare sat very still as tears began to slip down her cheeks, releasing all the tension of the past few days. She could cry for weeks, she thought, and never run dry, for here she was, so in love with a husband who could only care for the girl she had been, not the woman she had be-

come. Her own exhaustion caught up with her, however,
and she finally slept.

Giles had been dreaming. In his dream, Tall Man and
Squat Toad had pulled him up the stairs into the light, and
in that light floated Clare's face, set and grim. "Does he
know me yet," she asked his jailers and they shook their
heads. "Then take him back to the cellar." Giles opened
his mouth to protest, but no words would come out. It
was clear his captivity would never end until he could tell
his wife he loved her for herself. And he had lost his
voice.

He awoke to the semi-darkness of early morning. But
the cellar wasn't usually this light when he woke, he
thought. He was even more disoriented when he became
aware that he was in a comfortable bed, his own bed, in
fact. He turned his head, and by the light of a guttering
candle on the bedside table, saw his sleeping wife.
Slowly, very slowly, to keep the room from spinning, he
pulled himself up into a sitting position.

Clare was still in her walking dress, and as he watched
her, he began to remember. Clare *had* been there when
they brought him up from the cellar. But to bring him
safely home, not to keep him her prisoner. He had a
vague memory of being thrust into the chaise and looking
up into her set white face. But it had been a face set with
fear and determination, not hostility. Somehow, his Clare
had set out and rescued him. The lady had accepted a
quest and rescued her knight, not the other way around.

Her hands had held a pistol, that much he also remembered. She had looked quite capable of killing someone.
She *was* capable of killing someone. She *had* killed
someone, his brave wife. To save herself from certain
death, and him from the possibility of it.

He lay back, head resting on the pillows, turned toward
her, learning every curve and line of her, his courageous
wife. He had been so blind for so long. And afraid.
Afraid if he admitted to himself that Clare Dysart had

hurt him terribly and then gone on to a horrendous marriage that she couldn't be the Clare he loved anymore. And since he did love her, she *had* to be the old Clare. For how could he love a woman who had hurt him so, suffered so, and bought their present marriage with such a bloody deed.

But he saw now that his Clare was this Clare. Circumstances and her own inner strength had combined to transform her. But not beyond recognition. And please God, not beyond the possibility of redeeming their marriage.

The door opened slowly, and Giles lifted his hand in greeting as Sabrina tiptoed in.

"You are awake, Giles," she whispered. She sat down on the edge of the bed and put her hand on his. "It has been a horrible five days. If I didn't love Andrew so much, I would have hated him for getting you into this."

Giles shook his head. "It wasn't his fault, Brina. I was just too stubborn to tell them who I was."

"Thank God for that," she answered. "I suspect your life would have meant very little to those men."

Sabrina had spoken aloud, and Clare started and opened her eyes. Her face lit up when she saw that Giles was awake, then shut down as she remembered what she had done.

"Giles," she said evenly, "I am glad you are awake." She stood up stiffly. "I will get Henley and have him bring you some barley water."

Giles made a face, and Sabrina said: "It is what the doctor ordered for the first day. So bear with it, Giles."

"Plain water. Plain, cold water," he requested. "And some porridge, Clare?"

"All right, Giles," she said with a quick smile, and was gone.

"And some hot water for a bath as soon as you get your strength back," teased Sabrina, wrinkling her nose.

Giles ran his hand through his hair. "Maybe even a fine-tooth comb," he said, and laughed as Sabrina jumped back. "Now *I* am teasing, Brina. There are no small residents, as far as I know."

"I will order lye soap, just in case, Giles," said his sister.

Chapter Thirty-three

A few hours later as Giles lay in his bath, he thought that he had taken far too much for granted in his life. Water, gruel, and a hot bath . . . simple things, really, but he'd take them over any luxury offered him.

Sabrina had sent up lye soap and a fine-tooth comb. Which was lucky, said his valet, for he was sure he had seen a louse or two in his master's hair.

Giles only laughed. "Comb them out, then, John."

He slept away the rest of the day and only awoke again in the late afternoon when the doctor came by again.

"You are feeling better, my lord?"

"Much, thank you, Doctor."

"And drinking a lot of water?"

"Cool, clean water, which tastes like champagne to me," said Giles with a smile.

"I am not surprised. You were dehydrated when I saw you last night. You may start eating solid food tomorrow."

Sabrina came in after the doctor left and uttered a protest as Giles climbed out of bed.

"I am not ill, Sabrina."

"No, and we wish you not to be."

"Hand me my dressing gown, Brina."

Sabrina helped him slip his arms into the burgundy silk and gave him her arm as he walked slowly back and forth around the room. He was muttering something under his breath.

"I beg your pardon, Giles?"

He looked down and smiled at her and said something rhythmically in Greek. "Now you, I suppose, would have been repeating mathematical formulas, but I kept sane with Aristophanes."

"Oh, Giles," his sister cried, and threw herself into his arms.

"No, now, Brina, I was not made a galley slave. Five days in a cellar isn't really all that bad."

"They might have killed you."

"So they might have. But they didn't. Thanks, I believe, to my wife?"

Sabrina pulled herself out of his arms.

"Clare was magnificent, Giles."

"So I guessed. And where is she? She hasn't been in to see me since morning."

"She has been sleeping, too, Giles. To make up for the last four nights."

Giles let go of his sister's arms and walked slowly over to the wing chair.

"I am still a bit shaky, or I would go in to her. Will you have her come in when she awakes, Sabrina?"

"Of course."

"Now tell me the whole story."

Sabrina perched on the bed and told him what she knew.

"I will have to get Clare to fill me in on the details," Giles said with a smile.

"Indeed. You have a valiant wife, Giles," said Sabrina as she was leaving.

"I know that," he said softly as she closed the door behind her.

Clare approached Giles's bedroom apprehensively. She found him in his dressing gown, seated in the wing chair with a book in his hands. His head was back and his eyes were closed, and for a moment she thought he was asleep. But as she walked slowly toward him, he opened his eyes and smiled directly into hers, which made her legs feel as shaky as they had yesterday.

"It is my lioness wife come to visit," he said in an affectionate, teasing voice.

Clare blushed. "Hardly a lioness, Giles," she replied. "I am pleased to see you up."

"Yes, I am feeling much more myself. Except for my eyes," he added. "They are more tired than I am now. I suppose it was the lack of light in the cellar."

Clare shuddered. "It must have been awful, Giles."

"Well, it was," he admitted. "But not unbearable."

"Why did you not tell them who you were?"

"And ruin Andrew's case? Four or five days in that hole seemed like it would be easy." Giles paused and gave her a crooked grin. "At first."

"We were frantic."

"I know. But I think I made the right decision," he continued in a more serious tone. "I suspect it would have been very inconvenient for Tall Man and Toad to have a viscount on their hands."

Clare nodded. "Andrew didn't seem to think you were in danger, but they could have killed you and dropped the body anywhere. That is why I did what I did, Giles," said Clare in a tight voice. She was still standing, and Giles motioned her to the bed.

"Come, sit down, and tell me your story, Clare."

Clare sat on the edge of the bed and kept her eyes on the floor as she began.

"I was so afraid that once they saw Andrew in court and knew they had been tricked, they would get rid of you to save themselves. Andrew couldn't go to them, of course."

"So you went to 75 St. James Street?"

"Well, no. Actually, I summoned Mr. Oldfield here on the pretext that I wanted to settle a younger brother's debts. He had never heard of Lord or Lady Whitton, you see."

"And once he was here, you told him what?"

"I held a pistol to his head. And he knew I was capable of using it because . . ." Clare paused.

"Why, Clare?" Giles asked softly.

"I told him I had been the notorious Lady Rainsborough before my marriage, and if he didn't lead me to you, I was quite happy to shoot him and summon one of his partners." Clare looked up and gave a shaky laugh. "I said I would happily pile the bodies up until one of them broke. He believed me."

"I should think he would."

"Once I had convinced him, it was not difficult. The chaise was at the door, and I kept the pistol pointed at him the whole time."

"Yes, I remember seeing it in your hands as I was pushed inside."

Clare looked down at her hands. "I truly couldn't think of any other way, Giles. I hated having a pistol in my hands again. But I would have killed Oldfield and the others, too, to get you back," she added defiantly.

"I believe you, Clare. And thank God he did, too."

Giles got up and sat down beside her on the bed. He took her hands in his. "You have small hands, Clare, but I am grateful that you held my life in them, for they are stronger than they look. As you are."

"They were shaking so I had to clutch the pistol with both of them," she murmured. "And I was holding on to it so tightly that I couldn't let it go. . . . Oh, Giles, I wish . . ."

"You wish what, my dear?"

"I wish I were . . ." Clare paused and took a deep breath. "No, I don't. I don't wish I could be the Clare you fell in love with. I just wish you could love who I am now."

Giles wanted to catch her up in his arms and prove both his love and passion physically, but he forced himself to sit very still. "I have thought a lot about what you said to me, Clare. Indeed, I have had nothing but time to think these past few days. And maybe the darkness of that hellhole made some things clearer. You were right. I have not wanted to face the truth of what lies between us."

"And what is that, Giles?" she asked quietly.

"My anger, for one thing. I *was* furious, Clare. And I couldn't allow myself to be. I thought it would make things more difficult for you and for all of us, and so I ignored it. As I ignored my heartbreak." Giles let go of her hands and said lightly: "My heart *did* break, you know. But I blithely ignored that and went on being your selfless friend Giles. You hurt me so very much when you chose Rainsborough, Clare."

"I knew I must have," she whispered.

"I am ashamed to confess that a part of me was almost glad that you eventually suffered from that decision, too. When you lost your baby—I didn't know the reason then, of course—I thought to myself: had she married me, this wouldn't have happened. And in the courtroom, when you told your story, there was again that dark side of me that smiled to himself and thought: "Maybe she deserved this, for being so foolish as to let her passion blind her." Giles put his head in his hands and groaned. "Oh, God, I am so ashamed to admit this. And when we made love, do not think it was all you, Clare. Sometimes I would hear that dark voice saying: 'You didn't really wish for a passionate response, did you? Look what it led to last time.'"

Even though she knew Giles needed to say these things, it hurt to hear them, and Clare could not stop the tears or check her sobs. Oh, please, Giles, please, she thought, do not leave me alone in this now. If he couldn't somehow love her despite all this, she knew they would stay cold and separate the rest of their married lives. She sat crying for what seemed a long time, but it was only a minute or so before Giles, so afraid of touching her, touched her anyway.

He put his arm around her shoulders and pulled her close to him.

"I didn't want to hurt you, Clare. Or maybe I did," he wondered aloud. "But we had to have the truth between us at last." Her shoulders finally stopped shaking, and Giles let her go. Her blond curls were all tousled, her eyes swollen and red, but she had never looked so beautiful to him. He leaned over and gently licked the tears off her cheeks, his tongue reaching into the corner of her mouth, where they had gathered. As he started to kiss her, he felt her shiver and pulled back immediately.

"If you don't want me, Clare, I understand." She answered by pulling him down to her again and opening her mouth to his.

Their kiss was long and deep, and Clare wanted it to go on forever. She moaned with disappointment when Giles finally released her.

He looked down at her and said tenderly and humorously: "I am not sure what I can promise you tonight, Clare, for I am still a little tired from my ordeal. But I would like it if you stayed with me tonight."

As an answer, Clare merely busied her hands with the belt of his dressing gown, and Giles laughed softly. After she released the knot, he turned her around so that he could open her dress.

They both stood up at the same time, so that their clothes fell from them, and Giles caught her to him.

"I think you have recovered, Giles," said Clare with a low laugh as she felt his manhood pressing against her thigh.

"We shall see just how much endurance I have, though," he teased as he pulled her down on the bed.

The beginnings of their lovemaking had always been good, and this was no exception. But at first, both of them were wondering what would happen at the end. Soon, however, they were lost in sensation: Clare melting away as Giles lazily circled her breast with his tongue, and Giles, realizing that his tiredness had certain benefits, for he was in no rush to experience his own release, but content to move slowly.

They were lying side by side, and Giles was languorously running his fingers up her thigh and slowly seeking out her center of pleasure. Clare was lying still, wondering if she would experience the same block as before. And for one moment of fear she did. She knew Giles felt her stiffen as his fingers found her and started their slow, gentle caressing. It was as though a wall dropped between them. And then something in Clare, life, love, whatever it was that had enabled her to say "no" to Justin at last, rose up from the depths of her being. She was only conscious that her voice was saying: "Yes, yes." Perhaps I needed to learn "no" before I could say a "yes," she thought wonderingly as Giles moved on top of her and entered her. His movements were at first as excruciatingly and pleasurably slow as before, but as she closed her legs around him and drew him in deeper, all his languor fell away, as did her hesitation, and they let their passion drive them to a shattering climax. Clare's ecstasy had been almost silent, but Giles sobbed out his wife's name as he found his release. When he lifted himself off her, she touched his wet cheek as he smoothed her hair back from her face.

"I never dreamed . . . but, no, I have dreamed for years," Giles whispered. "But it was never like this."

"I am not sure where you begin and I end, Giles. I think I felt your pleasure more than my own. Yet that might not be possible," she whispered shyly.

Giles gathered her in his arms, and they fell asleep in moments, like children.

Chapter Thirty-four

The entire household was, of course, aware that Lord and Lady Whitton had shared a bed the night before, and there was a pleasant energy permeating the house when Andrew More arrived the next morning.

"Is Lady Sabrina available, Henley? And how is Lord Whitton?"

"Lady Sabrina is in the breakfast room. And Lord Whitton is recovering well, I would say," announced Henley, seeming very pleased with himself, as though he were personally responsible for Giles's recovery, thought Andrew as he walked upstairs.

Sabrina jumped up as soon as she saw him at the door. "Andrew! I thought you would have been here yesterday evening. Whatever happened in court?"

"Sit down my lady jack-in-the-box," teased Andrew, "and I will tell you." He walked over to the sideboard and started filling his plate. "I am ravenous," he declared as he spooned eggs and kippers and sausage.

"Andrew!"

"Messers. Oldfield et al. each received two years' hard labor. And young Mr. Grantham got his money back. He will continue at Inner Temple, and, no doubt, make a fine solicitor."

Sabrina jumped up again and threw her arms around Andrew.

"It is very lucky for my waistcoat that I know your fits and starts, Sabrina," he said affectionately, holding his plate high as she hugged him fiercely.

"Oh, damn your breakfast, Andrew."

Andrew sighed, put the plate on the sideboard, and kissed Sabrina soundly.

"Now, that is quite enough," he said as the kiss began to arouse him. "Henley will throw me out of here if I am not careful."

Sabrina released him reluctantly. "Oh, go back to your sausages and eggs, Andrew. I am sure I don't care."

Andrew gave her one more kiss for good measure before rescuing his plate and sitting down next to her.

"How is Giles this morning?"

"Since it is all over the household that Lord and Lady Whitton spent the night together, I assume he is quite recovered."

"Clare sat by him the night before, didn't she?"

"Sitting up in a chair while he slept. I do not think she spent last night in the wing chair, Andrew."

"You are incorrigible and shameless, Sabrina." Andrew laughed. "But I am very glad to see you back to your old self."

"And I am very glad to have those villains out of commission. Do you intend to charge them with kidnapping also?"

"I think I will leave that up to Giles."

"What will you leave up to me, Andrew," said a voice from the doorway.

"Giles! Shouldn't you be in bed?" exclaimed Sabrina.

"Excuse my dressing gown, Andrew, Sabrina. And no, Sabrina, I have spent enough hours lying around this past week. I don't think I could stand being confined to my bedchamber." Giles spoke lightly, but Andrew could tell that he was quite serious.

"I *am* sorry that you had to go through all this, Giles. I, we all felt so helpless."

"Except for my valiant wife!"

"Dear God, when I think of how she got us out of the house so she could confront Oldfield," exclaimed Andrew.

"Do you know how she convinced him? She held a pistol to his head and revealed herself as the infamous Lady Rainsborough. When he asked her what she would do if he refused to lead her to me, she calmly declared she would kill him and summon one of his partners!"

"Imagine Clare Dysart bullying such a man."

"Not Clare Dysart or Clare Rainsborough any longer, Andrew," said Giles seriously. "Clare Whitton. At long last." Giles sat down next to his sister and looked over at his friend. "I am ravenous, Andrew. Would you fill me a plate?"

"My dear Giles, for your chivalrous foolishness, for which I will be forever grateful, I would come over and serve you breakfast every day for the rest of my life."

"Where is Clare, Giles?" Sabrina asked quietly.

"Upstairs. Still sleeping. I think this took as much out of her as it did me."

"Out of all of us, Giles."

Giles patted her hand.

"I knew you were not dead," added his sister. "But I could still feel that you were suffering."

"It was not too bad, the first day or two. It was only toward the end. Lord, that stench! I don't know if I will ever get it out of my nostrils. But it is over. Or is it, Andrew? How did the trial go?"

"I won, Giles, and those villains will be locked away for two years. Unless you want to prosecute them further? We could get them for kidnapping, you know, with Clare's testimony."

"Absolutely not," said Giles quietly but firmly. "I would never subject her to that again. But they need not know that, of course. You might try and get word to them that they have that hanging over their heads, lest they are tempted to send Tall Man and Toad for revenge."

"Tall Man and Toad?" asked Sabrina.

"My name for my jailers, Brina."

"All right, Giles, we will leave it for now."

* * *

Clare slept until mid-morning, when the sun pouring through the window onto her pillow woke her. She turned sleepily to Giles, only to discover he wasn't next to her. She lay there, lonely and desolate, wondering whether last night was only a dream. Or an isolated occurrence. Perhaps it was only that Giles's guard had been down. Perhaps this morning he would be seeing things differently.

She was empty beyond tears as she lay there, imagining the worst. She could not go back to their marriage as it had been. She could not. There was a soft knock at the door, and Martha came in.

"I hope I didn't wake you, my lady."

"No, Martha. The sun woke me." Clare started to sit up and then blushed, remembering that she was naked under the sheets. She was also stiff and sticky from lovemaking.

"I would love a bath, Martha. Could you have the hot water brought up. And some fresh towels."

"Of course, my lady. Do you want some chocolate?"

"Later, thank you, Martha. And Lord Whitton? Is he up and about this morning?"

"Yes, my lady. He joined Lady Sabrina and Mr. More for breakfast a few hours ago and is in the library now, I believe."

Clare's heart sank. Giles was clearly on his way to recovery and had left her there to wake alone. She closed her eyes and dozed while the maids filled her bath, and dismissed them and Martha as soon as the water was ready.

It felt good to slip down into the scented water. She could feel all her protesting muscles relax, and she rested her head against the bath and closed her eyes.

She dozed off again for a few minutes, but wakened when she heard the door open quietly. Without opening her eyes, she murmured: "Do you have more hot water, Martha? The bath is cooling down."

There was a murmur of assent, and Clare sank down

farther as the hot water slid over her shoulders and breasts.

"Let me relax you more, Clare," said a deep voice, and Clare's eyes flew open as Giles's hands began to knead her neck and shoulder muscles. She pushed herself up, but Giles held her there gently.

"I thought you might sleep the day away," he said.

"Is that why you left me?" Clare blurted out.

"I was afraid if I stayed, I would not have been able to keep myself from awakening you," he replied.

"Oh," whispered Clare.

"Did you miss me, Clare?"

She nodded and then took a deep breath as his hands, now lathered, began to soap her back, and then her breast and belly. When he reached between her legs, she protested. "Giles, it is broad daylight. And I am in my bath!"

"And delightfully wet and pink, my dear. And slippery," he added as his fingers parted her. "I can feel your own wetness, even with all this water."

And so could Clare. At that moment, she would have pulled Giles in, had there been room.

"Have you ever been to Bath, Giles," she murmured.

"Clare!" exclaimed Giles in a mock-injured tone. "At such a moment you are only interested in my travels?"

Clare caught his wrist and turned to face him. "I was only thinking, Giles, that we had something to learn from the Romans if we'd only paid attention. At least there was room for more than one in their baths."

Giles chuckled. "You are a little sensualist, Clare."

"I am sorry," she said, embarrassed.

"Sorry? I am delighted. If I could only coax you out of your bath, I can assure you there is room on the bed, wife."

Clare stood up, and Giles held her hand as she stepped out. He reached out to hold one shimmering breast in his hand. "You are like Venus, rising from the sea," he whispered. "No, don't put a towel around you," he said as she started to cover herself up. He stood and let his dressing gown fall open.

"I think you need a bath, too," she said with a glint in her eye.

"Perhaps I do, I can still smell that stench hanging around me."

He stepped in and lowered himself into the warm water. Clare knelt beside the tub and ran her hand around the water, searching for the bar of soap Giles had dropped.

"Here it is," she said.

"Oh, no it is not."

"But it is hard and slippery, like soap, and keeps slipping out of my fingers," she teased.

Giles groaned. "Oh, God, Clare, stop. I am not as tired as I was last night."

"Then you are clean enough," she laughed, pulling at his hand. "Now we are both wet and slippery."

"Are you sure a British bath won't hold two, Clare?" he asked, pulling her in on top of him.

"Giles! The water is splashing all over the floor!"

"It is good, clean water, Clare. And it will dry."

Clare gave in to the delightful sensation as Giles's manhood slipped and slid between her legs and against her belly. It was something like bobbing for apples, she thought, as she would try to position herself over him and he would slip away.

"You are torturing me, woman."

Finally, Clare reached down and placed Giles just where she needed him to be and lowered herself gently onto him. He slid in, and she fit him like a glove. For a moment she sat still, enjoying the feeling of him filling and stretching her. Then he placed his hands on her hips and moved her gently.

Her mouth opened into a sweet "Oh," and he pulled her down farther and thrust his tongue in as she lifted herself up and down on him.

"Yes, Clare, yes. It is your turn to ride," he murmured when the kiss was done.

Giles didn't notice the hardness of the tub against his back, nor Clare the splashing of the water over the sides as they rocked together. Just as Giles was about to climax, he slipped his hand between her thighs and lifting her just a little, filled her, and caressed her at the same time, so that they came together.

She sank down on him, gasping and sobbing into his shoulder while he stroked her hair.

After a moment he whispered into her ear: "Clare, I must get up, or I will turn into a corkscrew."

She nodded against his shoulder but didn't move.

"Clare, really, I am cramping up."

"Where, Giles?" she asked, moving her hand down. He caught her wrist. "Oh, no, you are not going to start again."

"I find the tub a perfect fit, Giles," she teased.

"That is fine for you to say, my little pocket Venus. I am a good foot taller than you, and my leg *is* cramping, really, Clare."

She climbed out as he stood up with a grimace on his face.

"It is not funny, woman," he protested, hearing her giggle as he tried to flex his toes.

Clare picked up one of the towels and wrapped it around her. "Here, Giles, you will get chilled," she said, and handed one to him.

Giles wrapped it around his waist, and walked up and down a few paces to work the cramp out of his leg.

Most of the water was out of the bath and on the floor, and Clare started mopping it up with the last towel.

"Leave it for the maids, Clare," said Giles, smiling down at her.

"Oh, Giles, whatever will they think of us?"

"They will think that Lord and Lady Whitton have a true marriage at last," declared Giles, pulling his wife up and over to the bed. They were still partly wet when they crawled under the covers, and Giles pulled his wife to him.

"Despite all that has happened, we are at last truly married."

"Perhaps it is *because* of all that happened, Giles," Clare replied, cuddling against him.

They lay back to front, and Giles's chin rested on the top of her head and his arms were around her waist. They fell asleep that way and never heard Martha's knock or saw her grin as she took in the puddled floor, before closing the door behind her, leaving them to their next sweet awakening.

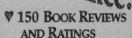